MIXING BUSINESS WITH PLEASURE

"I heard you talking to Tracy today," she slipped in. "Anything going on?"

He shook his head. "Nothing more than the usual craziness."

"Are you and Tracy . . . a thing?" She couldn't help asking. Besides it not being her business, why should she care? Other than the kiss, of course.

"Why? You jealous?"

"No . . . don't be silly. Of course not."

Brows up, he said, "I don't fool around with employees."

Ha, Sam laughed to herself. Not unless he was kissing the breath out of them. "But if she weren't your employee—?"

"Not my type."

"What is your type?"

"Physically, you. But everything else about you is wrong."

She flinched. "That was an awfully mean thing to say."

"I bet Royce doesn't think so."

She got to her feet, but before she could walk out on him, he pulled her into an embrace, crushed her against his chest and kissed her until the world seemed to turn on its axis. Ravenous, his mouth moved over hers, plundering. He tasted like wine and man and she could feel his heat and hardness pressing against her.

"I don't want to do this," he whispered against her mouth.

"Then stop." He made her so crazy with desire she could barely find her equilibrium.

"I can't . . ."

Books by Stacy Finz

GOING HOME

FINDING HOPE

SECOND CHANCES

STARTING OVER

Published by Kensington Publishing Corporation

STARTING
OVER

A
NUGGET
ROMANCE

STACY FINZ

LYRICAL PRESS
Kensington Publishing Corp.
www.kensingtonbooks.com

LYRICAL PRESS BOOKS are published by

Kensington Publishing Corp.
119 West 40th Street
New York, NY 10018

All Kensington titles, imprints, and distributed lines are available at special quantity discounts for bulk purchases for sales promotion, premiums, fund-raising, educational, or institutional use.

Special book excerpts or customized printings can also be created to fit specific needs. For details, write or phone the office of the Kensington Sales Manager: Kensington Publishing Corp., 119 West 40th Street, New York, NY 10018. Attn. Sales Department. Phone: 1-800-221-2647.

Lyrical and the L logo are trademarks of Kensington Publishing Corp.

First Electronic Edition: August 2015
eISBN-13: 978-1-61650-919-4
eISBN-10: 1-61650-919-8

First Print Edition: August 2015
ISBN-13: 978-1-61650-920-0
ISBN-10: 1-61650-920-1

Printed in the United States of America

To my aunt, Janet Finz, for giving me the inspiration.

ACKNOWLEDGMENTS

A special thanks to my beta readers: Jaxon Van Derbeken, Wendy Miller, and, as always, my family.

To everyone who made this book happen: Agent Melissa Jeglinski of the Knight Agency; my editor, John Scognamiglio; production editor, Rebecca Cremonese; and all the other folks at Kensington Publishing who worked tirelessly on the entire series. Thank you.

Chapter 1

Nate shielded his eyes against the flashing red lights and followed the ambulance into the Lumber Baron parking lot and up to the front door. At least the driver had the good sense to kill the siren. No need waking the entire inn. Not at this hour, when they had a houseful of paying guests.

He wondered if Samantha had already arrived and kind of hoped she hadn't. His sister Maddy, while still on maternity leave, had been the one to hire the inept socialite to handle the everyday running of the Lumber Baron. Why, he had no idea. Samantha Dunsbury had more money than brain cells and wasn't exactly reliable. Just four months ago she'd left her fiancé at the altar without so much as a goodbye text, got in her car and drove west from New York City. Given that the Dunsburys were Old Greenwich, Connecticut, money and there had been bogus reports that Samantha had been kidnapped for ransom, the fiasco wedding made national headlines. Folks in Nugget couldn't stop talking about it. Of course, it didn't take a whole lot to get the residents running their mouths. Pretty much anything remotely titillating got broadcast through the California town's expansive grapevine like political fodder on the cable news networks.

Here, Samantha Dunsbury may as well have been Paris Hilton. And the mystery of why she'd dumped her groom-to-be, a Wall Street tycoon, in the eleventh hour only added to the woman's mystique.

Nate didn't care what reason she had for leaving her intended standing in a Manhattan church looking like the world's biggest chump. His only concern was making sure she didn't treat the Lumber Baron with the same indifference. He suspected that the spoiled heiress would have no qualms about leaving him in the lurch when she got bored with playing innkeeper.

Nate glanced at his watch, let out a frustrated breath, and hopped out of his car. By the time he got inside the inn, the paramedics were rushing up the staircase to room 206. He trailed behind them, not wanting to get in the way, only to find that Samantha had indeed beaten him to the scene.

"Take deep breaths, Mrs. Abernathy." Sam held the guest's hand. Nate didn't know why Sam wanted the woman to focus on her breathing. According to Maddy, Mrs. Abernathy was having stomach problems, not a baby. "Maybe it's just one of those twenty-four-hour flus."

"Sam, dear, I'm an emergency-room nurse," Mrs. Abernathy said, her face mottled in pain. "It's appendicitis and I want the damn thing out."

Sam looked up from Mrs. Abernathy and made eye contact with Nate. "What are you doing here?"

The woman clearly thought she was the lady of the manor, and Nate wanted very much to set her straight. Not the time, nor the place, he told himself. "Maddy called me."

"Oh," was all she said as one of the medics jostled her aside.

"You need help, Mr. Abernathy?" Samantha called to a man Nate presumed was Mrs. Abernathy's husband. He'd been hurrying around the room, gathering up assorted personal items and stuffing them into a suitcase.

"I think I got everything," he said, his brows knitted as he watched the paramedics check Mrs. Abernathy's vital signs and move her onto a gurney. "How you doing, Alice?"

"I've been better," she responded, and Mr. Abernathy stopped packing to gently squeeze her foot, the only part of her he could get to while the medics worked.

"If you leave anything, don't worry," Samantha assured him. "I'll mail it to you. Let me take you to the hospital, Mr. Abernathy. I hate for you to drive when you're stressed out like this. I could drive your car and Nate could follow. Or maybe you would prefer to go in the ambulance?"

"You've gone to enough trouble," Mr. Abernathy said, patting Sam on the back. "We appreciate everything you've done and hope we didn't wake the entire inn."

"Don't be silly. I'm just sorry Mrs. Abernathy is sick and that you'll miss your bird-watching tour. I know how much the both of you were looking forward to it."

Nate had to keep from rolling his eyes. Sam poured it on a little thick. He moved out of the doorway so the paramedics could get through with the stretcher. As they lifted Mrs. Abernathy out of the room and down the staircase, her husband reached for the suitcase. Before Sam could help him with it, Nate grabbed the handle out of her hand and joined the procession to the main floor.

"You sure you don't want me to take you?" Sam asked the husband again.

"I'm fine, dear." Mr. Abernathy pulled a set of keys from his pocket. "Alice is one tough cookie. Aren't you, Alice?" He winked at his wife, who responded with a faint nod.

"I'll live," she said, and reached for her husband's hand.

Mr. Abernathy turned to Sam. "You have my credit card number, so we're square, right?"

"No charge, Mr. Abernathy," Samantha said, and Nate stiffened. "You just come back and see us when Mrs. Abernathy is better."

"We will certainly do that. And thank you, Sam. For everything." Mr. Abernathy quickly headed to the back of the ambulance, told his wife he'd be right behind her, and kissed her on the forehead before the paramedics closed the door.

Afterward, Nate helped him load the luggage into the couple's Honda Accord and went back inside to find Samantha behind the check-in desk at the computer. She was probably voiding the couple's credit card transaction.

"Hey, little Miss Sunshine, next time you decide to give away three nights in one of our best rooms, check with me first," he told her. "We have a forty-eight-hour cancelation policy."

"I'm sure Mrs. Abernathy didn't know two days ago that she'd be coming down with appendicitis or she would have canceled," Samantha said, her blue eyes narrowing.

Nate didn't appreciate the attitude. "Those are the rules," he said. "I'm sorry she got sick. I really am. But while this may be a hobby to you, it's a for-profit business for the rest of us."

"Why do you always talk to me like that?" She raised her chin above the computer and stared him straight in the face. Still, he detected a slight tremble in her voice.

Here come the tears. It was nearly two in the morning and he didn't have the patience for any more drama. He wanted to go home and back to bed.

"You ever think that doing the right thing is good for business?" she asked. No tears. Just a bucketload of indignation.

Great, now she wanted to tell him how to run a hotel. Well, he had news for her: He'd been working in the hospitality industry before she was old enough to teethe on her silver spoon. His parents ran one of the most successful boutique hotel operations in the Midwest and he'd learned how to take a reservation before he could ride a bicycle without training wheels.

"Samantha, just check with me before you start comping the guests. Where's Andy?"

She looked down at her shoes, designer ones if Nate had to guess. "I told him he could go in the break room. There was no reason for the both of us to—"

"He's in there working on his music, isn't he?" Nate wanted to put finger quotes around music, because the emo crap Andy wrote sounded more like the caterwauling of a feline in heat. Nate shook his head and wondered when he'd begun running a charity for slackers and dilettantes. At least the members of his staff in San Francisco were professionals. Every last one of them. "Well, get him back in here. Come on, I'll follow you home. At least you can catch a few hours of sleep before opening."

"I don't need you to follow me home," she said, and headed to the break room in the back. The staff lounge was isolated from the guest rooms so that employees could take breaks without fear of disturbing sleeping residents. Sam returned with a repentant-looking Andy and seemed to be stalling. But Nate would be damned if he'd let her walk to her car alone. Nugget was a safe country town—his brother-in-law, the police chief, kept it that way. But bad things could happen anywhere.

When Nate and Maddy had first bought the Lumber Baron, they'd had their own brush with crime. A meth head had set up shop in the then-decrepit Victorian and attacked Maddy when she'd been there alone. Then Rhys Shepard had saved the day. He'd shot the bad guy, married Maddy, and the town had been relatively crime-free ever since.

Nate glowered at Andy and turned to Samantha, who was gathering up her purse and jacket. "You ready to go?"

Between clenched teeth, she said, "You go ahead. I'm fine on my own." She clearly disliked him as much as he did her, which was fine as long as she did her job.

"Oh, for Christ's sake, Samantha, we live next door to each other." Not by Nate's choice. He'd bought his house before Sam and her Mercedes convertible had slammed into Nugget. That had been right after Christmas, back when half the town thought the woman had escaped from a loony bin. But because Sierra Heights had the fanciest homes in town, Miss Richie Rich had to lease the place next to his. Right on the golf course.

"Whatever," she huffed, and turned for the door, giving him a spectacular view of her heart-shaped ass, not that he wanted to look. He knew all about beautiful spoiled princesses. Been there, done that, and had the returned engagement ring to prove it.

He followed her to the gated community where they both lived, watched her taillights disappear behind her garage door, and waited until he saw her silhouette through the living room window before pulling into his own driveway.

He walked into his empty house. Other than the log bed he'd bought from Colin Burke, Nugget's resident furniture builder, he hadn't had time to purchase couches or even a kitchen table. Anyway, he usually ate all his meals at the Ponderosa, Nugget's only sit-down restaurant, which seconded as a bowling alley. His best friends owned the joint and were the reason he and Maddy had chosen Nugget as the location for their hotel in the first place.

Hoping that if they built it, tourists would come, he and Maddy had bought the Lumber Baron eighteen months ago. At the time, the Victorian mansion was the most dilapidated building on the town's square. They'd sunk a ton of money into renovating, fought the city for a lodging permit, and opened their doors on a wing and a prayer.

Ever since, business had fluctuated. Sometimes, like now, it was better than Nate could've imagined. But during the months of December, January, and February, when Nugget got socked in with snow, the place had been emptier than a bar after last call. Ordinarily, spring would've been the perfect time to go full bore on promoting the fledgling bed-and-breakfast with extra ad campaigns and more Internet visibility, but Maddy had to go and get herself knocked up. Nate tried to do his best, but he had nine other hotels to operate in San Francisco, four hours away.

That's why he constantly traveled back and forth. But living out of a suitcase had started to wear on him, so he'd bought the Sierra Heights house, thinking it would be a good investment. Mostly, though, he liked having his own space, especially since lately he spent more time here than in the city. The house—a sprawling two-story log cabin with mammoth picture windows—also had plenty of space for Lilly, his daughter. He went to bed thinking how much he missed seeing her every day and experiencing parenthood the way a normal father would.

Just about the time he drifted off to sleep, the incessant beeping of his clock roused him awake. Nate shut off the alarm and lay there for a few minutes with his arm covering his eyes, then got up and took a shower. The huge tiled stall had multiple spray nozzles and a rain showerhead. The house had a lot of great features: tall ceilings, radiant floor heating, a state-of-the-art kitchen, and views that wouldn't quit. But he hadn't exactly made it a home. Between the birth of his daughter and running Breyer Hotels, there hadn't been time.

In San Francisco he lived in one of his hotel's penthouses. Small but fully furnished, the suite came with round-the-clock room service. As the boss, he never had to wait long for anything. Despite the ease of living there, he found it impersonal, and all the pampering and sucking up made him feel soft.

No pampering here. He didn't even have a coffeemaker. He knew Samantha had one; a stainless-steel job that looked like it would also rotate your tires. The one and only time he'd been inside her place, he'd seen the machine, along with enough paintings and sculptures to fill the de Young. If you asked him, she'd decorated the place a little over the top for a town like Nugget, where chainsaw bears and mud-flap girls amounted to high art.

He put on a pair of boxer shorts, went to his bedroom window, and separated a few of the blind slats with his fingers to peek at her window. She had her drapes drawn so he couldn't see anything. For all he knew, she'd already left for work.

One thing he'd say for Sam was that she was always on time. He presumed she'd read somewhere that being prompt was a big part of keeping a job. According to Maddy, other than volunteering, Sam had never actually worked a day in her adult life. Nate couldn't imagine being that idle, not to mention that his parents wouldn't have tolerated it. The Breyers might be relatively well-off, but they'd earned their fortune, not inherited it. And they'd worked damned hard and had raised their kids to do the same.

He finished getting dressed, made half a dozen phone calls to check on his San Francisco hotels, and jetted over to the Ponderosa. He'd barely been there long enough to get comfortable when Owen slid into his booth. The barber was the unofficial leader of the "Nugget Mafia," a group of the town's power brokers who also happened to be the biggest busybodies around.

"What's up, Owen?" Nate had helped himself to a cup of coffee and was waiting for a waitress to take his order. There was no sign of Sophie or Mariah, the Ponderosa's proprietors. But Nate seemed to remember something about them doing errands in Reno.

"How's the redhead?"

"Who? Samantha?"

"No. Howdy Doody. Who else would I be talking about?" Owen waved over a server. "Who does a guy have to sleep with around here to get some service?" He pointed to Nate. "This fellow wants to order."

Nate got his usual: two fried eggs, hash browns, bacon, and toast. When the waitress left, Nate said, "She's doing fine, Owen."

True to form, Owen actually expected Nate to share personnel information with him. Not a lot of professional decorum—or boundaries of any kind—in this town.

"Why do you ask?" Nate asked, curious. Sometimes Owen's nosiness paid off. The man usually had the best intel in Nugget.

"Just curious. You gotta admit she's a hottie."

She was that. She was also a fickle, spoiled, trust-fund baby. Something Nate didn't plan to lose sight of.

"Why do ya think she left that fiancé of hers?" Owen continued.

"How would I know?"

Nate's food came and he prayed Owen would let him eat in peace. No such luck. Owen was a man born to loiter. "Don't you have hair to cut?"

"It's Darla's day," Owen said.

Darla was Owen's daughter, who'd taken over the barbershop so the old man could retire. Nate, however, doubted that would ever happen. Owen liked being at the center of it all, and the barbershop was practically town hall. That's why the old geezer held on to a few longtime customers, mostly members of the Nugget Mafia.

"You think he might've been one of those Bernie Madoff characters?"

"Who?" Nate asked, flagging over the waitress for more coffee.

"Sam's ex."

"I don't know, Owen. I don't know anything about the guy." Just that Nate felt an affinity for the dupe.

"Well, why else would she have left him? Unless he beat her. You think he beat her?"

Nate blew out a breath. "You watch too much daytime television, Owen. But if you're so curious, ask Darla. She probably knows."

"Beautician-client privilege," Owen said.

But Nate doubted that even Darla knew the truth. From what he'd heard, the runaway bride had kept the secret of her failed nuptials pretty close to her Versace vest.

All anyone knew about Samantha Dunsbury was that she'd shown up in Nugget with a head of hacked hair and 2,700 miles of road stuck to her tires. According to her story, she'd gone scissor happy on her hair the morning of her wedding, got in her car, and kept driving until she landed here, the middle of nowhere. Then she holed up at the Lumber Baron until Darla fixed her hair and Maddy gave her a job.

None of her story sounded very credible to Nate. But then again, how could he know the mind of an airhead? He figured she'd eventually get bored living in a small town, working at a country inn, and would hightail it home to Wall Street Boy and her rich family.

Vaya con Dios.

Except for when she walked into the Ponderosa five minutes later in a stretchy nude dress that clung to her body like a second skin, he wasn't thinking about God.

Chapter 2

"Thank goodness you're here." Sam rushed to Nate's table. "Your cell's not working."

"Yes, it is." Annoyed, he pulled it from his pocket, played with it for a second or two, then pulled a face. "I must've inadvertently shut it off. What's the crisis?" he asked, intimating that if she had her hand in it, it must be a catastrophe.

Why the man had to be so boorish, Sam didn't know. For some reason he'd taken an instant dislike to her.

"No crisis," she said, and noticed the barber sitting on the other side of Nate's banquette. "Hi, Owen."

"How you doing there, missy?" He flashed his dentures and started to squeeze out of the booth. "I best be getting over to the bowling alley. Me and the fellows have a standing game."

Once Owen was out of earshot, Sam said, "A businessman from San Francisco may want to book the entire inn for a family reunion in July, but two of the rooms have already been spoken for on the dates he wants."

"Get him to take another date," Nate said, and drained his coffee before calling the waitress over to pay his bill.

"That's the problem. He only wants that one week and made a big deal that I should Google him. Can you imagine the audacity? I had half a mind to tell him to go elsewhere."

"Who is he?"

"Some guy named Landon Lowery. Owns a company called Zergy. I never heard of it."

Nate's eyes grew wide. "It's only the largest video gaming company in the world. Tell me you didn't tell him to go elsewhere."

"Of course I didn't. I've been around high-handed rich and famous people my whole life. I know how to handle them."

"Yet you didn't know who Landon Lowery was." Nate, obviously tired of waiting for the server to return with his credit card, stomped over to the cash register to complete his transaction, grabbed his sports coat off the rack, and shrugged it on.

"I'll take care of it," he told Sam, dismissing her like she had a feather duster for a brain. It reminded her of all those years of living with her dictatorial father. Well, she didn't plan to put up with it anymore.

"What do you mean, you'll take care of it?" She practically chased him across the square. But with those long legs of his, she didn't stand a chance of catching up. "It's my account."

He stopped at the stairs of the Lumber Baron, turned and squinted his chocolaty-brown eyes at her. "It's my hotel."

"Mr. Lowery and I already have a rapport."

"You all but said he was an asshole. What kind of rapport is that?"

"Enough of a rapport that he's coming to check the place out next week and wants me to show him around."

"Great." He rolled his eyes. "You've been here all of four months. What do you know about the Sierra Nevada?"

"Nate, Maddy put me in charge of event planning," she said, intending to hold her ground. This was her first job and she desperately wanted to show that she could do it. "Mr. Lowery wants his family reunion to have activities—organized tours, a meal program, shopping excursions. Basically, he wants a week-long party. I may not have hotel experience, but I know how to throw a party." It was the only skillset she had, and Sam wanted to put it to use—as a vocation, not a hobby.

Nate turned his back on her, went inside the inn, and disappeared into his office, shutting the door behind him. Conversation over. The man was truly insufferable—a complete jackass. Why couldn't he at least be ugly? A troll with a hunchback. But no, even that was too much to ask. Physically speaking, Nathaniel Breyer was a Roman god sent down from the heavens. A full head of thick, brown hair that made you want to run your fingers through it. An angular face, too sharp to be pretty but breathtaking just the same. And a lean, hard body that would make a weaker woman quiver.

The only thing lacking in Nate's road to perfection was a personality.

Sam stood at his door, wondering whether she should burst in and demand that he let her do her job, or give him a little time to come to his senses. Settling on the latter, she went into Maddy's office, which she had commandeered as her own, and returned three calls—brides inquiring about using the inn for their weddings. Her own had been an unmitigated disaster. Or at least it would've been if she'd bothered to show up. The marriage, however, would've been even worse. The four months she'd lived in Nugget, Royce had only called twice—once to scream at her for "making me look like a goddamned fool," and the second time to demand his ring back. He'd insisted that one of his ancestors had brought it with her on the *Mayflower*, when Sam knew for a fact that he'd purchased it on West Forty-Seventh Street, Manhattan's Diamond District.

Well, she was here now, away from Royce, and never before had each day seemed so filled with possibility. Like yesterday afternoon. It had been her day off, before Mrs. Abernathy had gotten sick, and she'd driven across state lines to Nevada's Washoe Lake to see the wildflowers. She'd been told that April was still a little early, but even so, the land was awash in color—greens and purples and yellows. No stranger to travel—Sam had been all over the world, but mostly to plush resorts and big cities—she'd never seen anything like the desert, where a person could see forever. It was solitary, but not lonely; silent, but so alive. It seemed freer than any place on earth. Not just the land, but the people. They didn't seem to care who you were or what you did or where you came from, only that you were a decent person.

People here even talked differently than they did on the East Coast. Not just the accent, a barely detectable twang, but they used odd expressions, like "airin' the lungs" for cursing or someone with a "leaky mouth" gossiped too much. Just the other day she'd heard Owen describe Portia Cane, the lady who owned Nugget's tour-guide company, as a "Montgomery Ward woman." Sam had thought he'd meant that Portia shopped at the department store, but Owen corrected her. *It means she's U-G-L-Y.*

She supposed Westerners were all around more colorful people. Here, the fact that she'd run out on her wedding made her a minor celebrity. Not a day went by when Donna Thurston, proprietor of the Bun Boy burger shack, didn't shout across the square, "You go, girl."

Back in Connecticut it had made her a laughing stock. But leaving that day had been the best thing she'd ever done, even if Daddy was threatening to cut her off. The truth was he could shut down her Dunsbury bank accounts and she'd still be wealthier than anyone had a right to be. Her mother, an Astor, had left her a fortune when she died, and Daddy couldn't touch that money. Oddly enough, she did miss him, though. George Dunsbury IV might be domineering, demanding, and detached, but she loved him. And she knew that he loved her too, even if he'd tried to "wrangle" (local rancher Clay McCreedy's word for forcing cattle to do things they didn't want to do) her into a loveless marriage.

Unlike Royce, he called every day, pleading for her to come home. And when that didn't work, he threw out harsh ultimatums. But she wasn't going anywhere until she figured out her future, which included carving out a real profession for herself. Life as the hostess with the mostest had become terminally dull—and meaningless. Samantha would never find a cure for cancer or balance the economy or stop global warming, but at least she could make a difference in people's lives, even if it was only to plan them the perfect weekend getaway.

A tapping at the door shook Samantha from her reverie. "Come in."

Nate pushed open the door and stuck his head in. "I'm having Tracy Cohen from corporate take over with Landon Lowery. Send me his contact info and the dates he wants."

"You're kidding me." Sam stood up and folded her arms over her chest. "Tracy has never even been here. When we talk on the phone she acts like Nugget's in a foreign country."

"Sam, this is too important to let you play at being an event planner. Lowery could mean big business for Breyer Hotels—not only this reunion, but corporate events. The man's a legend in the tech world."

Sam glared at him and Nate said, "Let me boil it down for you: It would be like having a Kennedy show up at one of your fund-raisers."

"Kennedys regularly show up at my fund-raisers." She pointed her chin at him in challenge. "That's why I'm perfect for this job."

He looked up at the ceiling, his patience clearly wearing thin. "Look, if this were an old blueblood looking to book a family reunion at the inn, I'd probably give you a crack at it. But this is Silicon Valley. It's a different breed than New England old money. They're like rock stars, and Tracy knows how to handle these people. Hell, she and Marissa Mayer went to Stanford together."

"So that automatically makes her more capable than me?" Sam had gone to Vassar with lots of successful people. At least she didn't go around bragging about it. Not like Nate. *I'm so great, I went to Harvard.* Whoop-de-do.

"She's more capable because unlike you"—he jabbed his finger at her—"she actually does this for a living." And with that he started to walk away.

"What do I do about the other guests, the ones who already booked for that week?"

"If we get the Lowery gig, we cancel them and hopefully get them to book for another time slot."

"We can't do that," Sam said in disgust. "Some of them may have already bought plane tickets or at the very least gotten the time off of work."

"Yes, we can. Read the fine print. Any reservation can be canceled for a conference, event, or large group."

Sam was aghast. "That's an awful way of doing business."

"That's the only way to do business." Nate propped his shoulder against the doorjamb. He looked so arrogant that Sam wanted to smack him. "Again, let me remind you, we're a for-profit company. Emphasis on profit. If you don't believe me, ask your father. Doesn't he manage one of the largest hedge funds in the country?"

It was clearly a rhetorical question, since they both knew that George Dunsbury's financial prowess was legendary. Her father had once been short-listed to be chairman of the Federal Reserve Board, but he'd declined and Ben Bernanke got the position.

Nate walked away before she could answer and shut his door a little louder than usual.

She had half a mind to barge into his office and quit. But if she wanted to launch this new life of hers, she needed the job. The only reason she'd gotten it in the first place was that Maddy believed in her. That, and Maddy had been desperate to find a replacement during her maternity leave. Otherwise, Sam wasn't the least bit employable. Not unless you counted her bulging résumé of lunching with the ladies and throwing charity galas as a prerequisite for a job. But in a way, it was the perfect experience for planning events at a small inn. She had the fortitude to deal with difficult people—nothing was more challenging than planning a charity auction or cotillion with a group of insanely rich, narcissistic women. Hello, Judith Forsyth, the biggest bitch in Connecticut, who wanted to take credit just for breathing. And there was Muffy Vandertilten, whose husband would threaten to sue the committee if the Muffmeister didn't get her way. But the biggest takeaway was that Samantha knew how to make every detail, from the color of the napkins to the party favors, blend seamlessly with the theme of every event.

And no one knew better how to fix a last-minute catastrophe than Samantha. And believe it or not, large-scale society events were rife with catastrophes. When Tony Bennett came down with pharyngitis six hours before performing a charity concert in New Canaan, Sam had managed to rope Billy Joel into doing the show. She went over to Long Island and drove him back to Connecticut herself. She had a contact list filled with florists, caterers, and celebrities who would come to her rescue at a moment's notice. Sure, having the Dunsbury name helped, but even without it, Sam had an aptitude for creating memorable parties.

People were still talking about her Snow Ball. She'd put the entire affair under a glass dome, used nothing but diamond white as her theme color, and created a winter wonderland complete with a machine that dropped fake flurries from the sky to make the event look like a giant snow globe.

She might not be a cutthroat business person like Nate or her father, but she knew that if given the chance she could increase sales tenfold at the Lumber Baron. For that reason, she gritted her teeth and got back to work. She'd just gotten off the phone with a linen vendor when she heard a fuss coming from the lobby and went out to investigate. Maddy had come in to show off baby Emma to the housekeeping staff.

"Look who's here." Sam gave Maddy a hug and kissed Emma on the forehead, getting a sweet whiff of baby smell. "You look fantastic, by the way." Sam had only known Maddy since the tail end of her second trimester, but now she looked slender and glowing.

"Thanks. You too. Love that dress."

"You here to put in a few hours, or just visiting?" Sam asked.

"Just visiting. I'm meeting Emily and Pam at the Ponderosa in a bit, but is there anything I can do?"

Yeah, tell your bother he's a colossal jerk. "I think we have everything under control."

"Nate told me about the Abernathys," Maddy said. "I've never had a guest with appendicitis before. But it sounds like you handled it perfectly."

"Thank you." Now why couldn't Nate throw a little praise around every once in a while? "I called the hospital earlier and she's doing much better."

"Good," Maddy said. "Poor thing. Anything else going on?"

"Landon Lowery's interested in the inn for a family reunion."

"The gaming guy? He wants to stay here?"

Why was it that everyone knew who Landon Lowery was except Sam? "He's thinking of booking the entire inn for a week in July."

They were still standing in the lobby, near the reservation desk, where Andy pretended not to be eavesdropping. Maddy motioned that they should move the conversation to someplace more private, parked the stroller in a corner, and carried Emma into her old office. "You're kidding. That would be huge, not just because it's a guaranteed full house for a week, but it's . . . uh . . . Landon Lowery. Wow!"

"He's coming next week to tour the grounds."

"Be sure to show him the millpond in Graeagle. And don't forget about the rodeo. You have that box, remember? Call Grace over at the Nugget Farm Supply to get the schedule. It might be something he'd be interested in." Maddy waved her hand in the air. "But you already know all this stuff."

"Nate's having Tracy from corporate handle it," Sam said, and tried not to sound peeved.

"What? She's never been to the inn. As far as I know she's never been to Plumas County."

Sam wondered if Nate was still next door and could hear every word they said. It wouldn't help their already tenuous relationship if he thought she was going around him. Although she got the sense that while Maddy was in charge of the Lumber Baron, Nate held ultimate veto power. Breyer Hotels was his, after all. The inn was the only property the siblings held together.

"She has a lot of experience and I'm pretty new at this," Sam said.

"Is that what Nate said? Because that's just bull." Sam tried to shush her, but Maddy wouldn't have it. "No. He's wrong. You love this place and that's what we want our guests to see. Tracy is an excellent event planner—for big luxury hotels, not small country inns. I'll talk to Nate."

"Don't get me in trouble, Maddy. He already doesn't like me." "Detest" was closer to the mark.

"Of course he likes you. Nate's just very brusque—and driven. When we were kids, my sister and I had to book appointments with his secretary, i.e., our housekeeper, when we wanted to talk to him." Maddy laughed. "But he's mostly bluster."

Sam must've looked doubtful, because Maddy said, "I don't know if you know this, but he bought this place to get me back on my feet after I went through a nasty divorce. And Sophie and Mariah . . . Well, look what he did for them. He's a good guy, Sam."

Everyone knew that Nate had fathered Lilly, Sophie and Mariah's child. Which even Sam had to admit was going above and beyond, even for a best friend. Truthfully, she never would've expected Nate to be so progressive. The man seemed more conservative than any person she'd met in California so far. And he was wound tighter than a spool of thread. Although, to be honest, he seemed fairly loose when he was around anyone besides her. For the life of her she didn't know what she had done to make him dislike her so much.

She was punctual, positive, and professional. But from day one he'd given her the cold shoulder.

The man's ears must've been burning, because he pushed the door open—he didn't even bother to knock—and stepped in.

"I heard a rumor you were here," he said to Maddy, and lifted Emma out of her arms and muttered something about her getting big.

"She's in the ninetieth percentile for length," Maddy said. "She must get it from her daddy."

Maddy's husband, Rhys, the police chief, was tall, even taller than Nate. In Sam's opinion, though, not as handsome.

"What brings you in?" Nate asked his sister. "I thought that husband of yours wanted you home, barefoot and pregnant."

Maddy took back Emma and punched him in the arm. "I'm meeting Emily and Pam, but wanted to drop in for a visit. I miss the place."

"Come back, then." Nate said.

"I don't miss it that much. Plus, you've got Sam. I heard she bagged you Landon Lowery."

Oh boy, here we go. "We haven't bagged him yet," he said. "But I'm confident Tracy'll reel him in." Clearly the comment had been for Sam's benefit.

"I don't think that's such a hot idea, Nate." Maddy swayed and bounced a fussing Emma.

"You want to come back to handle Lowery?" he asked.

"I think Sam should do it."

"Maddy"—Nate's voice dripped with annoyance—"you really want to do this now?" He looked at Sam pointedly.

"I was just leaving," Sam said, grabbing her pashmina off the chair and making a beeline for the porch.

She sat on one of Colin Burke's rocking chairs. The man had made half the furniture in her house. Before coming to Nugget, his rustic pine pieces never would've appealed to her. But now she wouldn't part with them for anything. She gazed out over the square and pondered the wisdom of getting a cup of coffee at the Bun Boy— her third one today and it wasn't even noon. She could see Donna's new employee, a local kid trying to earn college money, manning the window at the takeout stand, and waved. Carl Rudd had redone the windows of his sporting goods store with Tour de Manure bicycle jerseys. The race, a sixty-two-mile loop through the Sierra Valley's ranchlands and historic townships, brought cyclists from all over. The inn was already booked solid for the ride.

Yes, she thought, it was a nice town. No one here seemed to care about a person's net worth, portfolio, or bloodline. And while the townsfolk had been leery of her, as they seemed to be of any new-comer—she knew they called her the runaway bride behind her back—they'd accepted her into their fold. Especially Maddy.

She continued to survey her new home, thinking about how she'd chosen her own course for the first time in her life. And while she sat there reveling in that decision, her father sent her a text with his lat-est ultimatum.

And this time it was a doozy.

Chapter 3

"Maddy, what is it with you and this woman? You hardly freakin' know her." Nate got up, tired of sitting. He was tired of the whole damn conversation.

"She thinks you don't like her," Maddy replied. The baby had finally settled down and was asleep in her arms.

"Because I don't."

"Why not? What is there to possibly dislike about Samantha Dunsbury?"

Nate shrugged. "She's a flake."

"What are you talking about? She's the least flaky employee we've ever had."

"She's self-entitled," he said.

"Everyone else in town likes her. You think you might be crazy?"

"Must be," he said, looking at the clock on the wall and leaning down to kiss Maddy on the top of her head. "I've gotta go. Take care of my niece."

"Where? We're not done talking about this, Nate."

"To play basketball and yes, we are. Tracy'll do a good job, you'll see."

"Nate, are you sleeping with Tracy?"

He jerked in disbelief. "What the hell kind of question is that? She's a vice president in my company. I don't sleep with employees. You know that."

"I just don't get why you're so hot and heavy for Tracy. In all the time she's worked for you, she's never shown an interest in this property. Whereas Sam loves the inn—loves Nugget."

"Maddy, this is all a big game to her—the socialite playing innkeeper, or whatever she's doing here." He looked at the clock again. "Look, as much as I love having you second-guess my decisions, if I don't get going they'll start without me."

She got to her feet. "I'll walk you out. Tell Rhys to take it easy. He just got over a cold."

As if he'd tell his badass competitive brother-in-law to take it easy. The man carried a gun. "Will do," he said.

"Wanna come to dinner tonight?"

"I'm watching Lilly so Sophie and Mariah can go to a concert in Reno," Nate said. "Maybe I'll bring her over."

"What concert?" Maddy asked, surprised. Since having Lilly, Sophie and Mariah were mostly homebodies.

"Melissa Etheridge," he said, and smirked.

"You made that up." Maddy swatted at him.

"Yep." He laughed. "I have no idea. But they bought the tickets a while ago and could use a night out."

"That's nice of you to babysit," Maddy said, gathering up her purse. "Just bring the porta-crib and we'll set it up in Emma's nursery."

"All right, I'll see you tonight, then." He grabbed his gym bag and jogged across the square.

At lunchtime there was always a game of pickup behind the police station where Rhys had installed two in-ground basketball hoops. Anyone who wanted to play could.

Nate changed in the police station's locker room, a spare bathroom with a shower, and headed to the court. Eight people, including Rhys, his officer Wyatt, and dispatcher Connie, leaned up against the stucco wall, waiting. Usually, Jake, another member of Nugget's finest, also played. Nate figured he must be holding down the fort today.

Clay McCreedy, a local cattle rancher who'd grown up with Rhys, arrived a few minutes later and they broke into teams.

"Hey," Clay said to Nate. "You've been around a lot lately. I thought you had the redhead picking up the slack for Maddy."

"She's not quite up to speed. And I'm trying to help out with Lilly."

"She's a pretty little thing and getting big." Clay had two boys of his own. "Things slow in San Francisco?"

Nate sighed. "Things are never slow in San Francisco, but I have a good staff there." Unlike here, where he had Daisy Buchanan running the show.

"Good," Clay said. "Then you'll be coming to the wedding."

Clay and Emily Mathews, a local cookbook author, were getting married in June. The rest of the women in Nugget were in mourning, as Clay was the local heartthrob. His first wife, who from what Nate had heard was a serious hobag, had died in a car accident while having an affair with the developer of Sierra Heights. Sometimes life in Nugget imitated a soap opera.

"I'll be there," Nate said.

"Bring the redhead too."

"Uh, are we ready to get this party started?" Connie said, dribbling the ball. "Or do you ladies want to continue your conversation about babies and weddings?"

Nate laughed. The dispatcher liked to play hard-ass and was legendary for busting balls in the police department. But Nate got a kick out of her.

Sometimes he'd go into the police station and bum a cup of coffee off her. The inn made great coffee, but Connie's was better. She was a certified coffee snob, ordering beans from a specialty roaster in Oakland.

For about an hour they played basketball, running up and down the court until they were sweaty and out of breath. As much as he missed the city, he liked it here. There were a number of guys his age and they had a nice camaraderie, especially between him and his brother-in-law. Rhys Shepard was about the most stand-up guy Nate knew. If not for Maddy, Nate probably never would've gotten close with Rhys. The two men trucked with different people. Nate had more in common with Maddy's first husband, also a hotelier. But when Dave cheated on Maddy, Nate had cut all ties with his sister's ex. As a matter of fact, he'd like to hurt the guy.

But now his sister had a good man, a baby, and two teenagers, who Nate loved like his own family. The teenagers were Rhys's much younger half siblings, who'd been left in his care when Rhys's father died. Lina had recently gone off to college, but Samuel (there were too many Sams in this town) was still in middle school. They lived in a big white Victorian near McCreedy Ranch.

Attending one of their big rambunctious dinners reminded Nate of growing up in Madison, Wisconsin, where his parents and other sister, Claire, and her family lived. Nate was the only one in the family who wasn't hitched, with kids. Although he had Lilly, it wasn't the same. The deal he'd made with Sophie and Mariah was that he would always play a minor role in Lilly's life, but they were her parents. The terms had seemed easy at the time, when all he'd wanted to do was help his two best friends make a baby. Now, not so much. Especially when he held her in his arms and gazed into those saucer-sized brown eyes that so much mirrored his own.

Nate showered and changed into his work clothes. When he got back to the inn, Sam was giving a young couple a tour of the grounds. It sounded to Nate like they wanted to hold their wedding at the Lumber Baron and Samantha was showing them their options. He leaned against the porch railing to eavesdrop.

"If you decide on August we could hold the ceremony on this side of the property where you'll have a magnificent view of the sun setting over the mountains," she told them. "Then we can move the party to a big tent on the other side of the inn."

The bride seemed to like that idea.

"What if the weather's bad?" This from the groom.

"We'll get a tent with sides that we can close," Sam said. "As for the ceremony, we can move that inside. Given the size of your guest list it'll be pretty tight, but we can make it work. Obviously, I can't guarantee weather, but that time of year is a pretty safe bet."

"I'm not worried about the weather," the bride said. "My biggest concern is orchestrating everything—flowers, food, photos, music—from Sacramento."

It was roughly three hours away, so not a bad question as far as Nate was concerned.

"That's what I'm for," Sam said. "I will help you find everything you need. We'll pick a weekend when the both of you can come up—maybe you want to bring your parents—and I'll set up back-to-back appointments for you with vendors that the inn has used and we are eager to recommend."

Nate had to give it to her, she sounded polished, not at all pushy but assertive and knowledgeable. He suspected it was the old money upbringing. It bred confidence. His ex, Kayla, had been the same way. They'd go to parties in Cambridge and she would hijack the conversation, pontificating about the latest exhibit at the MFA or how Kayla's bankruptcy law professor should be the next president—because she was that brilliant. That had been nearly a decade ago. But even today, Nate remembered Kayla working a room like a royal. Confident. Gracious. Charming.

And poisonous as a snake.

It looked like the wedding kids were ready to sign a contract. Nate watched as Sam ushered them into her office. She must've sensed his spying because she shut the door practically in his face. Impertinent woman.

"Excuse me."

Nate turned around to find a beefy man with a florid face, wearing a baseball cap that advertised a brand of pro-rodeo gear Nate had never heard of. Not that Nate knew a lot about rodeo gear. "Can I help you?"

The man examined the lobby, stuck his head inside the guest parlor with its grand fireplace, and seemed pleased with what he saw. "I was wondering if you have a vacancy for the night."

Nate looked around for Andy, who had the uncanny knack of never being around when you needed him. He was supposed to be working the reservation desk when Sam had clients. Nate planned to give the kid a good talking-to.

"Let me see," Nate said, clicking through the computer. It had been a while since he'd checked in a guest. "How many nights would you like to stay, sir?"

"Just tonight. I have an appointment in the morning with Lucky Rodriguez." He said it like Nate would automatically know who Lucky Rodriguez was. He didn't.

"Is that so? Looks like we can accommodate you, Mr. . . . ."

"Danvers. Rick Danvers." He pulled a credit card from his wallet and slid it across the counter.

Nate asked for an ID and noticed that Mr. Danvers had a Florida license. Didn't get too many Floridians up in the mountains.

"Is there a place to eat around here?"

Nate started to tell Danvers about the Ponderosa, but Sam and the wedding couple came out of her office.

Sam saw Nate fumbling with the computer and said, "I'll take care of that." She flashed Danvers a kilowatt smile. "I'll be right with you, sir."

The guy did a visual lap over that clingy dress of hers, lingering on her breasts, and seemed more than happy to wait. He pretended to thumb through a tour guide—Maddy kept a stack of them on the counter—while he checked out Sam's ass.

Samantha said goodbye to the wedding couple, giving the girl a hug like they'd known each other for years, and told them that she'd be sending them a packet of literature in the mail. When she returned to the reservation desk, Nate thought Danvers's tongue might fall out of his mouth.

"I gave Mr. Danvers room 208," Nate told her.

"You're in luck, Mr. Danvers, that's my favorite room."

"Is it?" Danvers raised his brows and gave Sam another once-over, zooming in on her chest again.

Nate stood in front of her, hoping to send a subtle message to the man, but Sam maneuvered him out of the way. "I heard you ask about restaurants."

Nate listened to Sam describe Nugget's two dining options—the Ponderosa and the Bun Boy. Danvers seemed more interested in Sam's lips than the words coming out of them. Done watching the buffoon disgrace himself, Nate headed back to his office.

A few minutes later, he realized he'd left his gym bag behind the reservation desk and went back to retrieve it. Danvers and Samantha were gone. And the door to her office was wide open with the room empty.

Shit!

Had the idiotic woman actually taken Danvers up to his room alone? Nate took the stairs two at a time. Now he was going to kill Andy.

"Mr. Danvers, stop that," he could hear Sam saying.

"Call me Rick."

"I'm going to call the police if you don't get your hands off me."

"Sam, you up here?" Nate called.

"Right here." It came out as a squeak.

When he rounded the corner, she was straightening her dress, her face red as a fire engine. Danvers jammed his hands in his pockets, trying to look like he hadn't just been mauling Nate's employee.

Before Nate killed Andy, he planned to kill Rick Danvers. He'd heave his dead, bloated body out the window until the gardener came tomorrow with a wood chipper.

"You've got a call," he told Sam.

"Okay," she said, and he could tell she wasn't sure how much he'd seen or heard, but tried to compose herself. "You coming?"

"I'll be right down," he said.

When he was sure she'd made it out of earshot, he grabbed Danvers by the collar. "I want you out of here in five seconds."

"Okay, man. Take it easy. I don't know what you think you saw, but nothing happened."

Nate took his hands away from the guy's neck and shoved them in his pockets so he wouldn't strangle him.

Danvers straightened his collar. "Where am I supposed to stay?"

"Not my problem." Nate looked at his watch. "That was two seconds."

"Don't you think you're overreacting? We were just flirting."

Nate glared at him and Danvers must have realized that he was a hair's breadth away from getting the crap knocked out of him, because he yanked up his duffel and briefcase and beat it down the stairs and out the door. Nate followed just to make sure Danvers didn't harass Sam on the way out.

"What happened?" Sam stood behind the reservation desk, looking rattled.

"Mr. Danvers is no longer a guest here. Get Andy in here, now! We're having a mandatory staff meeting in five minutes."

Until then, Nate needed to cool off. He went outside and sat on the porch steps. A few seconds later, he heard the squeak of the screen door. Sam and her dress sat down beside him. The dress was really quite modest and completely professional, so he didn't know why he found it so provocative. Must've been the way she filled it out.

Nate let out a breath, fisted his hands in his lap, and said, "First rule in hotels—for women and men—a guest comes on to you or ogles you the way Danvers did, you never, ever put yourself in a position of being alone with him."

"I didn't know that," she said, her voice low. "I'm sorry."

He stared out over the square. "Sorry for what? That the guy was a prick?"

"For not knowing the rule."

"Well, you know it now," he said, then asked, "Sam, why are you doing this?"

"What?" she asked, confused.

"Living in Nugget, working at the Lumber Baron. It's not like you need the money."

"I like it here, I like the job, and I think I can be good at it. That couple from before reserved the Lumber Baron for their wedding."

"I noticed," he said.

He could tell she wanted praise for getting the booking and when he didn't give it, she said, "Why don't you like me, Nate?"

"Because you're playing, Sam. And this little game of make-believe of yours will ultimately wind up screwing my bottom line."

"If that's the way you feel about it, then you should fire me," Sam said, throwing down the gauntlet. "Because I won't quit." She got up, went inside the inn, and slammed the screen door behind her.

Sam planned to give Nate until five o'clock to fire her. Regardless of whether he did or not, she was going to the Ponderosa for happy hour and ordering a large platter of nachos with everything on it and a glass of Chardonnay.

She reached for the cell phone on her desk and looked at her father's text for the sixth or seventh time since he'd sent it, and shook her head.

"Well, Daddy, you may just wind up getting your way after all." At least part of it, anyway.

No threat would get her to marry Royce. Not in this or any other lifetime. But she'd be lying to herself if she didn't admit that her father's latest proviso had scared her.

He'd threatened to sell the summerhouse if she didn't come home. The Nantucket property had been in her mother's family since the nineteenth century when one of her ancestors, a wealthy sea captain, had built it on a Sconset bluff, overlooking the Atlantic. Over the years, relatives had added onto the mansion and modernized it. But despite the remodels, the place maintained its quirky originality—crooked ceilings and slanted floors and endless hallways that led nowhere. To Samantha, the summerhouse represented the happiest times of her life.

Every July until she turned eighteen, her mother, aunts, and cousins would open the old house and take up residence for two blissful months of nothing but swimming, playing, and lounging. It's where she'd read *Rebecca* and *Gone with the Wind* and *The Sun Also Rises*. On the hottest days, she and her cousins would ride their bikes in their bathing suits to Main Street, deliberate over what flavor of ice cream to get, and walk from shop window to shop window, licking their cones.

It was at the summerhouse where she'd met her first love. The boy, the gardener's son, had been seventeen, two years her senior. They used to steal away to the boathouse and make out for hours. On her seventeenth birthday, she lost her virginity to him, slow and sweet. To this day, they still kept in touch through Facebook and Christmas cards. He was a cop in Worcester, married with two children.

As for the summerhouse, her father bought her aunts' shares when Sam's mother died. The women had gotten too old to use it and Sam's cousins had chosen to vacation with their families in more exotic locales. The bottom line was, no one wanted to pay exorbitant property taxes for an empty house. No one but Sam. So her father had rescued the house and planned to give it to Sam. She in turn intended to set up a trust to keep the property in the Astor family forever.

But George Dunsbury IV never had a problem manipulating situations when he couldn't get his way. Sam feared that if she didn't go home, he'd do it. He'd sell the summerhouse to the highest bidder. For some unfathomable reason George believed that Sam and Royce could still pick up where they left off. Tie the knot and merge two great families. It didn't matter to George that Sam didn't want to marry Royce. Family came first. And in his mind, the only thing that could improve the Dunsbury family bloodline was melding it with Royce Whitley's. It was as if she were a racehorse, not a human being with feelings. Then again, Sam's mother and father had shared a loveless marriage in order to unite two "great" families. Poor Mimi Astor Dunsbury had been miserable. But she'd always been faithful, despite George dangling his paramours right under her nose. Sam suspected that Mimi had gotten her revenge by only giving George one child. And a girl, no less.

The whole thing was crazy to Sam. Who married that way in the twenty-first century—or in the case of her parents, the twentieth century? Even the Kennedys did whatever they wanted and married whomever they pleased. Of course, George had always called the Kennedys bootlegging trash. Sam thought it awfully ironic that she'd had to travel to a little backwater town in the California mountains to escape the Stone Age. Here, she could be whoever she wanted and no longer had to adhere to the dictates of her "station." Here she didn't have Daddy controlling her every move. And here she could actually have an ordinary life.

But she couldn't let her father sell the summerhouse. Mimi, who'd loved the place as much as Sam, would turn over in her grave. Somehow she'd hold her father off. Sam, after all, could be as stubborn as George when she put her mind to it.

She sighed and looked at the clock on the wall. Five fifteen and apparently still gainfully employed. Time for nachos. Sam gathered up her purse and jacket and headed out. Maybe she'd come back after dinner and do a little paperwork.

She passed through the hallway without seeing Nate and wondered if he too had called it a day. Andy stood at the front desk, looking put out, as usual.

"You missed the meeting," he said.

"I had a phone appointment that couldn't be changed," Sam lied.

"He wrote me up, said I'm never around and that if I don't start pulling my weight around here, he's going to fire me. Can you believe it?"

Sam couldn't say she blamed Nate. Andy wasn't the most conscientious worker, but he was a sweet young man. "I'm sorry, Andy."

"Hey, it's not your fault. The guy's a jack-off. It'll be better when Maddy comes back; then he'll stay in San Francisco."

Sam silently agreed. "Is Denny working the night shift?"

"Yep. You want to come see my band play tonight? We've got a gig at Rounders in Sierraville. I could put you on the list."

"Andy, I'd love to see your band, just not tonight. Could I have a rain check?"

"Hell yeah. We like packing the place with hot chicks. It's good for business."

Sam smiled, having never thought of herself as a "hot chick." "Great. Then count me in for the next show."

She strolled across the square, enjoying the cool breeze. Even though spring had arrived, the temperatures dropped in the evenings. Some mornings, before the sun fully came out, a thin layer of frost covered the ground. The afternoons, though, were mild, clear, and ridiculously gorgeous. Everything smelled so green and fresh.

A small crowd had already assembled at the Ponderosa. Across the room two women waved at her to join them. Harlee, owner of the *Nugget Tribune*, and Darla, Owen's daughter, who'd taken over her father's barbershop, came for happy hour most weeknights. Sometimes Colin, Harlee's fiancé, would join them. And when Darla's police officer boyfriend, Wyatt Lambert, wasn't on duty, he'd come too.

"Hi," she said, and plopped into the women's booth like she was deadweight. Both drank frothy-looking cocktails. "Ooh, maybe I'll have one of those."

"You look like you could use one," Harlee said. "Long day?"

"You don't know the half of it," she said. "Nate Breyer loathes me and I have no idea why." Harlee and Darla exchanged glances.

"What?" Sam wanted to know.

"We did notice that he's always harshing on you," Darla said. "Maybe he has a crush on you."

"Uh, we're in our thirties. I'm sure if he had a crush, he'd just tell me instead of treating me like an incompetent who's been foisted on him."

"Maddy thinks you're doing a great job," Harlee said, sipping her cocktail. "I know this for a fact, because Colin was over at her house, making some repairs to the guest cottage, and she went on and on about you. How you're booking weddings and all sorts of parties and that it's boosting profits. I just think Nate's overwhelmed with the extra work of running the inn as well as his San Francisco hotels and he's taking it out on you."

"Maybe," Sam said, but thought it doubtful. "But it is true. I've gotten a lot of events in the short time I've worked there. Just today, I may have landed a big tech guy for a family reunion."

"Who's the tech guy?" Harlee asked, obviously trying to sniff out a scoop for her website.

Sam wondered if she should've kept her big mouth shut. "Consider that information off the record."

"Uh-uh." Harlee laughed. "You have to say it's off the record before you tell me, otherwise it's fair game."

"Great, you want to make Nate hate me even more?"

"Don't worry," Harlee said. "I won't use it—at least not until it's a done deal. And I'll find another source to cover your butt. So who's the guy? Mark Zuckerberg? Sergey Brin? Biz Stone?"

She ticked off the names like they were celebrities, and Sam supposed they were, especially here, where they were only a half day's drive from Silicon Valley. But still, Sam wouldn't be able to pick famous computer nerds out of photo lineup. Nate had been right, these tech gurus, probably listed on the Forbes wealthiest-people list, were not part of her old-money world.

Sam pretended to zip her lips. "Not telling."

"Ah," Harlee grumbled. "You suck."

"Leave her alone, Lois Lane." Darla came to Sam's rescue, then reached out and finger combed Sam's hair. "Time for a trim, unless you're trying to grow it out?"

"No, I just haven't found the time to come in." Sam used to have nothing but time for haircuts, manicures, massages, shopping, and lunch with her friends. But being too busy for frivolity felt good. Honestly, it felt euphoric. Sam had never realized until now just how bored she'd been. "Could I come in on Saturday?"

Darla pulled her phone out of a big, plastic, neon-green handbag that matched her nails. Never one to shy away from bold colors and even bolder accessories, Darla sported a jet-black wig and giant hoop earrings. "I've got an opening at three," she said, scrolling through a calendar. "Does that work for you?"

"That's great," Sam said as a server approached their table. "I'm getting nachos. Will you help me eat them?"

"Uh, yeah," Darla said. "They're so good here, right?"

"I've been craving them all day," Sam said. The nachos—and smacking Nate in the face. Why, oh why, did the man have to be so extraordinarily good-looking and so odious at the same time? "One of our guests tried to molest me today."

"What?" Harlee put her drink down, waiting to hear the story.

Sam attempted to make light of the creep putting his hands all over her. "It was kind of comical. Nate kicked him out of the inn."

"Really?" Harlee turned up her lips in a sly smile. "So he rescued you."

"Not quite." Sam hated to crush Harlee's romantic illusion that Nate had rushed in like an avenging hero. "He berated me for being alone with the guy."

Harlee rolled her eyes. "I don't know what Nate's deal is. Usually, he's such a nice guy. Don't you think, Darla?"

"Yeah," she said. "He's always seemed pretty easygoing for a tight-ass hotel executive."

"Speaking of Mr. Tight Ass." Harlee nudged her chin at the door where Nate had just walked into the restaurant and up to the bar.

He'd changed into faded jeans and a long-sleeved San Francisco Giants jersey that accentuated those broad shoulders of his. The man looked good enough to eat, and if he wasn't so hateful she might be tempted to fall for all that luscious handsomeness.

Luckily she wasn't. And even if she was, part of Samantha's new life included resisting bad men. Nate definitely fell into that category.

But when Sophie handed him a bulging diaper bag and laid tiny Lilly into his big, strong arms, Sam warmed just a little toward her archenemy. And when she saw Nate kiss the baby on her plump red cheek, she lost the war and melted into a big puddle right there on the floor.

Chapter 4

"We're screwed," Sam told Nate as he walked into the Lumber Baron kitchen the next morning to find it in complete disarray.

His so-called event planner stood at the center island, covered in flour, the phone cradled against her ear. "Carmela didn't show up this morning."

Nate started to say something, but Sam held up a finger, listened to someone on the other end of the line, and hung up.

"That was Clay," she said. "He was trying to track down Emily for us. But she's on her way to Reno with Donna and your sister to get her wedding dress fitted. I was hoping she or Donna could pinch hit. Breakfast is in less than an hour."

"Can't you just throw something together, like a big omelet or French toast?" Nate asked. He'd do it, but didn't think instant oatmeal, the only dish besides grilled cheese sandwiches in his vast cooking repertoire, would cut it.

"Nate, the extent of my cooking experience is watching my family's French chef throw things at his staff." She looked down at the mess now covering her knit suit and at the opened cookbook on the countertop. "I tried to make biscuits. They're in the garbage if you're interested. And by the way, I've got a birthday party consultation in forty minutes."

"Hand me the phone." He wagged his hand at her.

Ten minutes later and a hundred bucks lighter, he'd bribed Tater, head chef at the Ponderosa, to whip up a couple of breakfast soufflés, home fried potatoes, and a batch of fresh muffins.

"Can you at least make coffee?" Nate handed her a bag of beans.

"That I can do," she said. "And I'm very good at setting a table."

She opened cabinets and began assembling serving platters, dishes, and silverware.

He supposed she'd learned that particular skill at finishing school or in the Junior League or wherever the hell she got her education, and tried to keep his voice from dripping with disdain when he said, "Great."

At least she'd admitted to that bit about having a French chef. A French chef. Jesus Christ.

"I think we have to prepare for the possibility that Carmela isn't coming back." Sam found the cloth napkins in a drawer and piled them next to the rest of the tableware. "She didn't even bother to call out today, and looking back on it she seemed distracted this last week."

"Yep," he said. "I think that's a pretty good assessment."

"Maybe I can talk Emily into doing it until we find a replacement."

Nate had to give Sam kudos for being a team player. And if she could actually persuade Emily to stand in until they found someone else, that would be a real coup for the inn. A few times the well-known cookbook author had held special tasting events and afternoon teas at the Lumber Baron, and they'd been big financial successes.

"See what you can do," he said, knowing that between Emily's wedding, her cookbook deadlines, and helping to raise her soon-to-be stepsons, she had her hands full. But if Sam could somehow convince Emily, that would be great by him.

He started to go to the Ponderosa to pick up the breakfast fare and grab a cup of coffee when Sam asked him, "Did you have a nice time with Lilly last night?"

Lilly was only four months old, incapable of doing much more than eating, sleeping, crying, and dirtying her diaper. And not necessarily in that order. Yet, he couldn't remember when he'd had a better time.

"It was babysitting," he said, and walked away.

As he cut through the green to get to the other side of the square, Nate wondered if Sam had asked about Lilly to kiss up after the argument they'd had yesterday. *Why don't you just fire me?* she'd said. *Because I won't quit.*

Yeah, right. He'd give her two more months, max.

At the Ponderosa, Nate's brother-in-law sat on a bar stool, eating a slice of pie.

"Nice breakfast." Nate lifted his brows as he eyed the streusel topping and took the stool next to Rhys.

"Maddy and Emma went to Reno with Emily for some wedding stuff... Sammy had to be at school early." Rhys shook his head. "I don't need an excuse to eat pie." He shoveled a heaping forkful into his mouth. "I can have all the pie I want."

"Yes, you can," Nate said, and lowered his gaze until it rested on Rhys's gut.

"Screw you. I'm in the best shape of my life."

Nate had to admit that his sister's husband was pretty damned fit. "What's going on?"

"I've got nothing," Rhys said. "You?"

"It looks like we may have lost our cook. She didn't show today. No call, no email, no nothing."

"That sucks. But Maddy's not coming back, Nate. She's got five more months of maternity leave."

It was closer to four, but Nate wouldn't quibble. "Maddy can't cook, anyway." His sister knew how to microwave and make cookies from store-bought dough.

"What about Samantha?"

"Are you kidding?" Nate laughed. "I doubt the woman makes her own bed."

Rhys lifted his shoulders. "I hear she's doing well with the event planning. At least that's what Maddy tells me."

"So far, she's only booked events. We'll see if she lasts long enough to actually coordinate them."

"I got the impression she was happy here."

"For now," Nate said.

"Look"—Rhys pinned Nate with his famous cop stare—"if you know something, come clean, because that woman is Maddy's safety net. She'd be a nervous wreck taking this time off if not for Sam. I'll personally chain the woman to the inn if she's planning on quitting."

"I'm taking care of the inn," Nate said, a little offended.

"Who are you kidding, Nate? You're spread so thin it's a wonder that you haven't dropped from exhaustion."

Before Maddy's maternity leave, Nate had spent the bulk of his time in the city, tending to the Lumber Baron a few weekends a month. His big hotels needed him more. But now, with Lilly, he couldn't seem to tear himself away from Nugget, afraid he'd miss her first smile, first step, first words, and any other milestone.

With Maddy out, the inn had become a handy excuse to stick around. Because if Sophie and Mariah knew the truth, they'd worry that he was backing out of their deal. When Nate had donated his sperm thirteen months ago to help his friends make a baby, he'd never considered becoming this attached to Lilly. He'd promised that Sophie and Mariah would be Lilly's sole parents. The problem was, he didn't know exactly where he fit in or how lightly he needed to tread. So every time Nate wanted to see Lilly, he felt like he had to make up an excuse. Bring dinner, volunteer to babysit, anything to help out the new parents. When all he really wanted to do was hold his daughter.

"Sam hasn't said she's quitting," Nate told Rhys. "But I'm predicting it won't be long until she decides to go home to Connecticut and resume her former life as an idle heiress instead of slumming it in Nugget."

"Well, while she's here, why don't you relinquish some of the reins to her and give yourself a break? You can't do it all, Nate. And from what I'm hearing from Maddy, Sam has a natural instinct for this hospitality stuff."

"Maybe for throwing charity galas, but the woman has zero experience in the business world. If I left her to her own devices, she'd bankrupt us. The other day, she comped a couple a three-night stay. Three freaking nights. We have a chance to book a family reunion for . . . let's just say a prestigious name in the tech world, and she's got her panties in a bunch because it'll require us to bump a few prior reservations. It's hard to believe her father's George Dunsbury. The man manages one of the largest hedge funds in the world and she wants to give away the store."

"Why don't you coach her?" Rhys said. "I'm sure you could teach her to be a shark in no time."

Nate didn't want to mentor her; he just wanted the woman to go home before she booked them solid with parties and left them high and dry to coordinate them. He could find a new cook easily enough, but an experienced event planner in Nugget would be impossible.

Tater whistled from the kitchen. The chef was a man of few words, but could cook. Nate clapped Rhys on the back and Tater helped him carry the Lumber Baron's breakfast across the square. True to her word, Sam had set the buffet table and it looked like something out of one of those fancy home magazines. She helped Rhys unload the food and put it in chafing dishes.

"Don't you have a consult?" he asked.

She looked at her watch. "In five minutes. It's for a January party. They've really got a jump on things."

Fantastic, Nate thought. Sam would be gone by winter. "Thanks for your help dealing with the breakfast debacle."

Sam did a double take, clearly surprised. So what if he wasn't that forthcoming with compliments? This was the real world; bosses didn't stop every few minutes to tell their employees what a good job they were doing.

"You're welcome," she said.

"If you could talk to Emily, that would be helpful. If not Emily, we could try Donna. In the meantime, I'll put out feelers for someone permanent. And who knows, maybe Carmela will show up tomorrow with a good excuse."

Nate went into his office and spent most of the day managing his other hotels long distance. Soon he'd have to spend quality time in San Francisco. The first weekend in June, the Belvedere, the second largest of his properties, was hosting a bridal expo. It was the largest wedding fair on the West Coast and the hotel was booked solid. Breyer Hotels had a booth to exhibit its various venues. He'd been thinking about sending Sam to pimp the Lumber Baron. Perhaps a little stay in San Francisco would make her homesick for expensive shopping, good restaurants, and luxury accommodations—and get her the hell out of Nugget.

The woman reminded him so much of Kayla it was scary. Not so much her looks. Kayla was a blonde with pale blue eyes and a willowy body. She looked great in clothes. Out of them, she'd been too thin for Nate's taste. Frankly, Sam leaned more toward his flavor in the figure department. Curvy in all the right places, with nice breasts. And the red hair was sexy as hell.

But that's where the differences between Sam and Kayla stopped. Both came from extremely wealthy families, both were spoiled rotten, and both liked to dabble in whatever interests suddenly caught their attention. He'd watched Kayla quit law school to become an archaeologist, and when that became too tedious for her, she'd gone to culinary school. Last he heard she was an interior decorator.

And what do you know? Both women were equally indecisive in love. In Nate's case, Kayla had at least given him a full twenty hours before calling off their wedding. Just enough time for her family to cancel the caterers and call back the guests. But ten years hadn't been time enough to salve the humiliation. Or the hole she'd left in his heart.

Later that evening, Sam drove to McCreedy Ranch, hoping to talk Emily into being the Lumber Baron's temporary cook. Carmela had finally called to say she'd gotten a better job in a Reno casino restaurant, working the line, and wouldn't be coming back.

Sam had made do for the inn's afternoon wine and cheese service by using an assortment of frozen finger foods found at the Nugget Market. It was pretty low-rent, and they couldn't keep improvising. Part of Nate's strategy to make the Lumber Baron a destination inn included bringing up the quality of the food. The man might be a complete bear, but Samantha couldn't deny he had excellent business sense, although he was a bit rigid and tight if you asked her.

As she cruised up McCreedy Road, Sam marveled at the scenery. Although she'd been here a couple of times since moving to Nugget, the view never failed to impress her. Lots of gorgeous green rolling hills, compliments of the wet winter. The mighty Sierra mountains, which loomed in the background, looked as if they'd been dipped in whipped cream. Even in spring, the snowy caps had yet to melt. During the cooler summers they stayed that way year round, she'd learned from the locals.

The land, a working cattle ranch, had been in the McCreedy family since the gold rush. According to the town gossips, Clay's first wife had begged him to sell the place. Then she'd died in a drunken-driving accident while having an affair with the developer of Sierra Heights. Nugget might be smaller and less affluent than Greenwich, but both were Peyton Places as far as drama was concerned.

She pulled up to the big white farmhouse and sucked in a breath, thinking that maybe she should've called first. But people here were forever popping in on each other. No formality whatsoever. So when in Rome . . . Plus, she hadn't wanted to give Emily too much of a heads-up to think about it and say no.

Three big dogs circled her car, barking and jumping up on her door. Sam stayed put. She wasn't afraid of dogs, but these seemed more territorial than most. One was baring its teeth.

"Down, boys," a teenager who looked a lot like Clay yelled at the beasts, then came up to the driver's side to shoo them away.

"Is it safe to come out?" She laughed.

"Yes, ma'am."

"I'm Samantha Dunsbury."

The boy wiped his palm on the leg of his jeans before shaking her hand. "Justin McCreedy," he said.

"Nice to meet you, Justin. Is Emily home?"

"She's in the house." He didn't move, just stood in place gawking at her. "Are you new around here?"

"Pretty new," Sam said. "I've been here about four months. I work at the Lumber Baron."

"With Aunt Maddy and Uncle Nate." He nodded, still gaping. Sam wondered if she had something stuck between her teeth.

"Should I just go up myself?" She pointed at the wide porch that wrapped around the house.

"Oh yeah, I'll take you." He led her inside the front door and yelled, "Emily, we've got company," then resumed staring at her. Seriously, the kid was giving her a complex.

A few minutes later, Emily appeared, untying her apron. "Sam! How nice to see you." She kissed her on the cheek and turned to Justin. "Did you introduce yourself to Samantha?"

"Of course I did." And a smile lit his face, giving Sam a glimpse of the lady-killer he'd someday be. Right now, he probably held the hearts of every teenage girl in Nugget. "I've got to finish getting the horses in. Catch you later."

"Hey, buddy," Emily called to him. "You forgetting something?"

He circled back around. "It was nice to meet you, Sam."

"Likewise," she said.

Emily took her into the kitchen, a warm and inviting room that seemed to embrace Sam in a big hug, and asked if she was hungry.

"This is spectacular," Sam said, looking around.

"This is Colin Burke," Emily said. "He redid the space from top to bottom. Clay grew up in this kitchen and was having palpitations at the idea of changing it. But even he loves what Colin did."

"I can see why." She spied the old-fashioned Wedgewood stove and the gleaming marble countertops.

"So what brings you to the ranch?" Emily motioned to a giant farm table that sat next to two picture windows with views of the range and the mountains. "Sit. We'll have tea."

She put a pot on to boil, removed a pair of cups and saucers from the cupboard, piled a platter with cookies—homemade if Sam was to guess—and set one end of the table. Papers, notes, magazine cutouts, and a fat binder cluttered the other end.

Sam nudged her head at the stack. "Wedding stuff?"

"Yep." Emily eyed the pile and winced. "Barely two months to go and I feel as disorganized as when I first started. I don't know how we went from a midsize gathering for family and friends to five hundred guests. But I'm blaming Clay, who's decided to invite everyone in Plumas County."

"Oh my," Sam said. "You're doing this yourself?"

"Yep." Emily nodded her head. "And did I mention that I have a cookbook deadline? Crazy, right?"

"Just a little." Sam made an inch with her thumb and forefinger. *And now I'm going to ask you to cook for the inn.*

"And guess what happened today?" Before Sam could ask what, Emily blurted, "The florist canceled—just called and said, 'I know your wedding is in June, but something has come up and I can't do it.' Can you believe that?"

"What are you going to do?"

"Beats the hell out of me. Have any ideas?"

"I might have someone for you," Sam said. "Let me sleep on it."

"Sure. But enough about me, what's going on with you? How's life at the Lumber Baron?" The water started to boil and Emily got up to make the tea.

"Life at the Lumber Baron is . . ." She had no intention of telling Maddy's best friend her troubles with Nate, but, boy, would it be nice to have a shoulder to cry on. "We lost our cook today."

"Uh-oh," Emily said. "What are you planning to do?"

Sam looked at her and started to laugh. "I was going to ask you to do it . . . just temporarily . . . until we can hire someone. Bad idea, right?"

"Ah jeez, Sam. Any other time I'd be happy to pitch in. But I'm drowning. What about Donna?"

"She's next on my list. It's just that we really wanted... Don't worry about it. We'll find someone. Hopefully Donna will do it."

"You're sure?"

"Of course," Sam said, though she wanted to beg and plead.

Everyone loved Donna, even if she had a broken filter and said the first outrageous thing that popped into her head. Yesterday she'd told Sam that her blouse made her look pregnant with twins. Otherwise she was a fabulous person and a wonderful cook. It's just that her food, more down-home fare, wasn't as sophisticated as Emily's. Sam knew Nate preferred sophisticated, and for some unfathomable reason she wanted his approval. Pathetic, especially as he'd made it perfectly clear that he wanted her gone from the inn. But Sam intended to show him that she was no quitter and that she was born to the job of event planning.

Ditto for her dad, who needed to understand that his daughter was more than an ornament. In the meantime, she had a plan to keep him from selling the summerhouse. The scheme still needed finessing, but she had an appointment with a lawyer next week.

"You liking the work at the Lumber Baron?" Emily asked, pushing a plate of cookies closer to Sam.

"I am." She took one and nibbled. "It's challenging, but in a good way."

"Nate's a great boss, isn't he?" Sam must have looked at her funny, because she said, "I did a cookbook for Breyer Hotels. He commissioned it."

"Really? I didn't know that."

"Yeah. He pretty much gave me full rein on it and loved the finished product. Are you two not working well together?"

"Yes... well kind of... no," Sam said. "Not so good. Although today we had sort of a breakthrough. He thanked me for helping with breakfast after Carmela was a no-show. But the bottom line is he wishes Maddy would've chosen someone with more experience, because this is my first job—ever."

"Maddy says you're killing it," Emily said, and Sam didn't detect any judgment on her part, even though most thirty-one-year-olds had had multiple jobs by now.

"I'm trying. And I'm really enjoying it."

"Nate will come around, you'll see. He's a terrific guy."

"I hope so." Sam grabbed her purse and got up to go. "I know you've got lots to do, so I'll get out of your hair."

"And if you think of a florist, you'll let me know?"

"Of course," Sam said. She was nearly out the door when an idea struck. "Emily, what if I did your wedding planning for you? I know I just told you that I've never had a job before, but I've been planning parties and big charity events since my twenties. I could do this for you."

"I don't know, Sam. It's a lot of work and you already have a full-time job."

"But if you took over the cooking duties at the Lumber Baron until we can find someone to do it permanently, I know Nate would free me up to work on your wedding." Sam didn't really know that, but it was worth a shot. Besides, she wanted to do it, never having planned anything on a cattle ranch before. Country weddings were extremely popular right now, and this would look great in her portfolio, not to mention that poor Emily could use the help.

"There's a lot to do. I have the food covered and Clay's hired the band, but we haven't chosen our linens, haven't hired a photographer or videographer, and haven't . . . well, you know about the flowers."

"You just give me those magazine pictures you snipped and I can take care of all of that—with your input, of course."

"And all I'd have to do is make breakfast for the inn?"

"As well as hors d'oeuvres for our afternoon wine and cheese service. But you wouldn't have to be there for that. You could just make them ahead of time, and I could pop them in the oven right before serving them."

"In exchange, you would do all this wedding stuff—help me with the seating arrangements, sending out the invitations, the whole caboodle?"

"All of it," Sam said. "And Emily, I'll make it beautiful. I could show you pictures of some of the parties I've planned." The elegant black-and-white ball at the Waldorf. And the Greenwich debutante cotillion, a stodgy old affair that Sam had revamped and turned into the "it" event of the season.

"I have no doubt about your abilities, Sam. But keep in mind that I don't have a bottomless budget."

"You just tell me what it is and I'll stick to it," Sam said, beaming with excitement. She loved the idea that she would have a part in making their big day.

"Okay, you've got yourself a deal," Emily said. "You have time now to sit down and we could go over a few details?"

"Absolutely."

For the next hour, Emily highlighted some of her ideas, and by the time Sam left she had a long to-do list and a binder full of inspiration. She just hoped that Nate would be on board. Otherwise, she might have bitten off more than she could chew. After all, there were only so many hours in a day.

The next morning she decided to break the news to Nate about the deal she'd brokered with Emily gently, starting with the good news first. Unlike most days, when he wore suits or a sports jacket with a tie, today he'd gone casual—Levi's and an oxford shirt. As loath as she was to admit it, he looked extremely good in jeans. They rode low on his hips and hugged about the best butt she'd ever seen. But staring at her boss's ass was probably a "don't" in the employee handbook, so she quickly looked away as he bent over the kitchen coffeemaker to pour himself a second cup.

"You have a minute?" Sam asked.

He grunted something unintelligible, but gave her his attention.

"Today's the last time we'll have to scramble for breakfast." Nate had paid Tater again to prepare a French toast bread pudding, fruit salad, and potatoes.

"How's that?" He looked interested.

"I got Emily to do it—just temporarily, until we find someone else."

"No kidding," he said. "That's great."

"I'm glad you think so, because I had to promise to help plan her wedding in exchange. It's a lot of work and I'll have to use some of my time here to do it."

"Ah," he said. "Bored already and moving on to the next thing, huh?"

She straightened to her full five feet, seven inches. *How dare he?* "No, I did this to help the Lumber Baron, because unless I took over the planning of her wedding, Emily wasn't going to cook for us."

"Mm-hmm," Nate said, and Sam contemplated wiping the dubious expression off his face. With her fist.

"What is your problem?"

"My problem is that running this inn and planning events here is a full-time job, Samantha. It's not something you fit in between helping your girlfriends. I'm thrilled you got Emily to sign on, but we could've just paid her. Fiscally it makes more sense than lending her one of my employees to help her pick out bridal lace."

"Do you realize how demeaning you sound?"

"What, the heiress doesn't like it when people are frank with her?"

"You want frank, I'll give you frank. You're an asshole, Nate. I am putting everything I have and then some into this job. I won't apologize for being born into wealth, which you seem to resent so much. Why, I have no idea, since you don't exactly seem to be hurting for money. Is that the Jag you drove to work this morning or the Range Rover?"

"I earned every cent of my money."

"Good for you. And how much of it have you used to help others? This may be my first job, but I've raised and given away millions of dollars to people in need, the arts, and a dozen other important causes. How much have you raised?"

Before he could answer, she added, "And by the way, Emily wouldn't have saved our butts for a paycheck. She only did it for my services." Sam started to walk away. "Don't worry, I'll have my stuff packed and be out of here in the next hour. Thank you for at least having given me the opportunity."

Nate leaned against the counter, sipping his coffee, and raised his eyes over the mug to stare at her. "Quitting so soon?"

"I'm not quitting. I just figure you'll fire me for insubordination."

"I wasn't planning on it." He turned to leave the kitchen but stopped to say, "I've gotta go to San Francisco for a few days. Hold down the fort while I'm gone, would ya?"

"What about Emily's wedding?" she asked, unsure of what game he was playing.

"I guess we don't have much of a choice. Just try to organize your time wisely."

He left her standing there, stunned. *The man must have a brain tumor,* she thought. What else could explain his complete capriciousness?

Nate returned from San Francisco four days later, just in time to meet with Landon Lowery. Tracy rode up with him and planned to catch a commercial flight back to the city from Reno-Tahoe International as soon as they concluded the conference.

The woman had talked his ear off during the long drive. She was good-looking, though, with a tight little body. If Nate hadn't had a policy about dating employees, he might've asked her out. She'd come on to him plenty, making it known that she'd be amenable to dating, sex, and pretty much anything Nate wanted. For that reason, he questioned how smart it was for them to be sharing a car together. But having her fly both ways when he was driving anyway, seemed stupid.

Tracy took a quick tour of the Lumber Baron, then commandeered Maddy's office, forcing Sam to conduct her business at the front desk. Tracy had also asked Sam for a cup of coffee. Sam got it for her willingly enough, but Nate figured she had to be bristling at being treated like the help. He also figured it was good for her.

They stood around in the lobby, watching the clock and waiting. When Landon finally pulled up, Sam seemed surprised that he drove a Prius. "That's his car?" she said, as if she expected a limousine.

Tracy snorted. "Boy, you really are new." She trotted down the porch steps and gave Landon a big hello.

"Nice place," he said, staring up at the Lumber Baron.

"We like it," Tracy said, and Nate laughed to himself. Not until thirty minutes ago had she ever stepped foot on the property.

Tracy escorted Landon onto the veranda and introduced him to Nate, skipping over Sam. Undaunted, Sam stepped up and shook Landon's hand. "Samantha Dunsbury. We talked on the phone."

"Hey, Samantha. You were right about the drive. It was insanely awesome."

Tracy wedged her way between the two. "Landon, can Sam get you something to drink or eat?"

"I'll take a Red Bull, if you've got one."

"Hon"—Tracy called to Sam as she led Landon away—"why don't you bring that to the conference room. And mineral waters for Nate and me."

The conference room had been the innkeeper's quarters before Maddy had married Rhys and moved into his farmhouse at the end of McCreedy Road. They decided that turning the suite into a luxurious meeting room, done up in Victorian furnishings and gumwood wainscoting, might snag them extra business, including companies looking to hold small retreats.

In the room, Tracy had set up a PowerPoint presentation, showcasing the inn's amenities as well as various local attractions. The three of them made small talk for a while—what's the weather like in July, you get a lot of bears in summer, blah, blah, blah. As Tracy readied to boot up her laptop, Sam came in with the drinks. Where she'd dug up the Red Bull Nate would never know.

"These are some nibbles Emily made." Sam set a platter of cheese puffs, palmiers, and mini quiches on the table. For Landon's benefit she said, "Emily Mathews is our chef."

"Thanks, Samantha," Tracy said, waiting for her to leave.

Sam took the hint and backed out of the room. For the next hour Tracy did her shtick. Afterward, she took Landon on a tour of the property and a drive through town to show him the hot spots. Nate had excused himself from that part of the program, confident that Tracy could close the deal on her own. Unfortunately, the pile of work on his desk needed attention.

On the way to his office, Nate couldn't find Sam. She'd probably gone to a late lunch or out, doing wedding errands for Emily. Lost in his work, he didn't hear Tracy and Landon return until Tracy's high heels clicked past his office on the hardwood floors. From what he could tell, they'd gone into Maddy's office—probably to sign a contract.

But ten minutes later, a panicked Tracy popped her head in. "I need help."

Nate came around his big pine desk and followed her to the lobby, where Landon peered at the Donner Party picture exhibit Maddy had hung on the wall. Sam was back to sitting behind the front desk.

Sam pointed to the pictures. "It happened just down the road. Did Tracy show you the memorial?"

"Dude, there's a memorial?"

"There's a whole Donner state park with a museum, a marked trail where the pioneers got stranded, even one of their cabins. It's eerie."

"Does it have stuff about them eating each other?" Landon asked.

"It's all there." Sam laughed. "Even historical accounts of the cannibalism."

"Seriously? I might have to hit that on my way home."

"The guests find it fascinating," she said and went back to something on her smartphone.

"So what do you think?" Nate asked Landon. "This a good spot for your reunion?"

Landon bent down to tie his high-top tennis shoe. "The inn's great. I'm just not sure there's enough to keep everyone occupied for a week. I guess I was hoping for more points of interest." He looked over at Sam, who was still messing with her phone. "What are you doing?"

Sam let out a frustrated noise. "I just got this app that's supposed to organize all my events for the inn, but I can't get it to work right."

Landon held out his hand for her to give him the phone and became immersed in tapping the display keys. He played with it for a few minutes before handing it back to Sam. "Here you go."

Nate wanted to strangle her for sidetracking Landon and getting them off topic.

"Landon, I think we could put together a nice itinerary for you." Nate tried to maneuver the conversation back to business. "One of the days we could bus you all to Reno—"

"Oh my God, how did you do that?" Sam squealed. "You added icons."

"Dude?" Landon looked at Sam like *Seriously? Don't you know I'm a tech genius?*

Nate still wanted to kill her for running them off course.

"Thank you, Landon." Sam smiled so sweetly at him that Nate got an instant toothache. "Did Tracy show you the Western Pacific Railroad Museum? I read in your bio that you're a train enthusiast. You know it has the largest collection of Western Pacific memorabilia in the country?"

"Yeah, that's why I picked Nugget in the first place," he said. "I wanted one day for us to take that train-tour deal through gold country. Tracy and I went over to the station and they said they're booked the whole month of July."

"But Tracy told them you're with the Lumber Baron, right?" Sam said, and all eyes fell on Tracy. "They reserve space for our guests."

Nate wondered if she was making this shit up, because it was news to him.

Sam picked up the phone and dialed. "Hey, Lloyd, it's Samantha

Dunsbury . . . I'm well, how are you? . . . Good, I'm so glad to hear that. And the family? . . . Excellent. I'm calling because we have a guest who is interested in holding a family reunion at the Lumber Baron in July and would like to take the train . . . Hang on a sec." She turned to Landon. "How many seats?"

"Maybe twenty."

"Did you hear that, Lloyd? . . . So is that doable?" She nodded at Landon. "Great. We really appreciate you doing that for us . . . Oh, that's so nice . . . No, he hasn't quite decided yet, but you'll hold them for a few days, right? . . . Terrific. Thanks, Lloyd. Talk to you soon."

Sam hung up the phone and turned to Landon. "We can also get you into the Plumas County rodeo. The events sell out every year, but the Lumber Baron has a box." This too was news to Nate. "And you cannot miss cowboy poetry at the grange hall—so Americana. One of the days during your visit we can set up a picnic hike, nothing too strenuous for the older folks, but the wildflowers that time of year—amazing."

Landon nodded his head, seemingly into it.

"And the millpond in Graeagle, did anyone talk to you about that?" She didn't wait for an answer. "It's this lovely swimming beach where you can rent paddle boards and pedal boats. Kids love it. The shops there are also adorable. For the more adventurous among you, there's horseback riding and mountain biking. Honestly, Landon, you could stay for a year and not run out of things to do."

"What's that rodeo like?" Landon wanted to know.

"I just went for the first time a few weeks ago," Sam said. "And I loved it." Nate highly doubted that.

"Although a lot of the participants are local ranchers and not professional, it's still very exciting," she continued, describing to Landon the various events. Nate noticed that Lowery appeared much more interested.

"You can really make that train ride happen?" Landon asked Sam, and Nate knew she'd hooked him.

"Of course. And the horseback riding, bird watching, river rafting. We'll keep you busy from day to night."

Landon peered into the main parlor and took in every little detail. "My folks would really love the inn," he said, stuffing his hands into the pockets of his jeans. "You'll personally handle it, right?" This was directed at Sam, and Nate noticed Tracy stiffen.

"I'll take charge of the entire itinerary and set up everything," Sam said. "I can even make up an activity list and put it in each guest's room."

"All right, I'm sold," Landon said.

"I'm so glad." Sam beamed. "I promise we'll make your reunion truly memorable. What about the Donner Memorial, you want me to include that too?"

"Hell to the yes!" he said, and Sam looked at Nate as if to say *Ha, you should've given me the project in the first place.*

Tracy took over the contract end of the deal. Once everything was signed and sealed, Landon left in his Prius and Andy took Tracy to the airport. Nate had to hand it to Sam for saving the day. A guy like Landon Lowery could generate lots of business for the Lumber Baron and they'd been this close to losing him. Then Sam had jumped in, spouting off activities that Nate hadn't even known the Lumber Baron had special access to. She'd surprised the hell out of him. If Sam could make Landon's family reunion a success, the inn would attract other VIPs for retreats, conferences, even parties.

Nate found Sam in the kitchen plating Emily's hors d'oeuvres for the guests.

"Do you need something?" she asked.

He walked straight up to her and planted a kiss on her cheek. Just a congratulatory peck, nothing that could get him into hot water. "You did good."

"Really?" Her face positively lit up, and Nate's gut squeezed. She really was an extraordinarily pretty woman.

"Hell to the yes," he said. "Just tell me there really is a Lloyd and that we have a box for the rodeo."

"Of course there's a Lloyd and we absolutely have a box for the rodeo."

"Since when?" He popped one of the cheese puffs in his mouth and she slapped his hand.

"Those are for the guests. When I first started, Maddy told me to go out, meet people, make contacts, and learn about the area. Grace's husband, over at Farm Supply, practically runs the rodeo. It's every weekend during the summer, so Maddy and I decided to buy a box for guests to use. In the scheme of things it's a pretty small expense and I think the guests will adore it. As far as the train, you would not believe how popular it is. So popular that it sells out the entire summer. So I introduced myself to Lloyd, who's a sweet old volunteer, and worked out a deal so that they reserve seats for our guests and in exchange we make a small donation to the museum." She blinked up at him, like maybe he'd be angry. "Maddy said it was okay."

"It certainly paid for itself today. But what's small?" he asked.

"Five thousand."

He lifted his shoulders in resignation. Five thousand wasn't too bad. "You won't quit before the Lowery reunion, right?"

"No. Why are you so convinced that I'm such a short-timer, Nate?"

Because I knew someone just like you once. "How can this town possibly hold the interest of someone in your position for long?"

"You mean someone who's rich? You're rich, you like it."

"I'm not the same kind of rich as you, Sam. So don't compare us. What I'm saying is that you're young, you're single, you're sophisticated, and this town can be kind of a freak show."

She laughed. "And you don't think Greenwich can be a freak show?"

He looked at her. "A freak show with access to some of the best culture on earth. Here you have to travel nearly five hours for that."

"Here, I can just be me."

"Yeah, and who's that?"

"The Lumber Baron's event planner. I have to get these out there." She lifted the tray of appetizers and started to leave.

For some odd reason, he wanted to stop her and ask her why she'd ditched her fiancé. Had she just tired of him the same way Kayla had of Nate?

The next time he saw Sam, she was leaving for the evening. "Hey," he called to her. "You want to go to the Ponderosa and have a celebratory drink?" Nate at least owed her that for what she'd pulled off.

She looked taken aback. "Uh . . . could we do it tomorrow?"

"Why not tonight?" Maybe she had a date. Not his business.

"I have to meet with my lawyer."

Again, not his business, but the words left his mouth before he could stop them. "Your lawyer? What do you need a lawyer for?"

"I'm suing my father. See you tomorrow."

Chapter 5

"Can you break away for about an hour after breakfast?" Emily asked, putting the last touches on the best eggs Florentine Sam had ever eaten. It was only her first week on the job, but Emily seemed like she'd been working here forever. "Get those out while they're still hot, okay?"

Sam scooped them onto individual plates and carried them out to the Dolbys from room 210. The couple, school teachers, were visiting from Seattle.

"Thanks, Sam," Mrs. Dolby said. "Everything is delicious."

"Just let me know if there's anything else I can get you," Sam said, and dashed back into the kitchen. "Where are we going?"

"To get wedding boots." Emily said it while her head was in the oven, so Sam thought she might've heard wrong.

"Wedding boots?"

"Yep." Emily straightened. "They're a surprise for Clay."

"That's nice. You know his size?"

"They're for me. To wear with my wedding gown. Clay has a thing for me in cowboy boots."

Sam giggled. "Seriously?"

"What do you want? He's a cowboy." And Emily giggled too. "There is a woman across town who custom designs them, and she said if I come in today she can have them done in time."

"So you want me to come with you?"

"I want to make sure the style works with my dress. And you're my bridal consultant."

"Yes, I am," Sam said with pride.

"Donna's coming too. Maddy had to take Emma to a doctor's appointment."

"Is everything all right?"

"Everything is fine," Emily said. "Just a routine checkup."

Sam served the stragglers, cleared the tables, and loaded the dishwasher. Until she'd worked at the Lumber Baron, she hadn't done too many domestic chores, but now she did a little bit of everything. Emily had already wiped down the stainless-steel countertops. The kitchen in the inn was as efficient as it was beautiful. Sam especially loved the copper pots and pans that hung over the center island.

"You ready to go?"

"Yep, let me call Donna and tell her to meet us there," Emily said.

On their way out, Sam left a sticky note on Nate's door, letting him know she'd stepped out for a while. He'd been deep in the weeds all morning and she didn't want to disturb him—or disrupt what seemed to be a silent truce between them.

Emily drove them in her van to a part of Nugget Sam had never seen before. It looked pretty shabby, with small, crowded homes, broken-down porches, and dirt yards. The streets didn't even have sidewalks.

They pulled up in front of one of the nicer homes. A tiny Craftsman with a fresh coat of paint and a wreath of dried flowers on the door.

Emily stuck her head out of her window and read the address on the mailbox. "This is it," she said.

"Should we wait for Donna?"

"Nah. Let's go in."

Sam grabbed her purse and followed Emily onto the front porch. Before they even knocked, a young girl about nine or ten answered the door.

"Hi, is your mother home? I'm here to get boots made."

The girl didn't say a word, just disappeared inside the house. Emily and Sam looked at each other like *What do we do now?* But a few minutes later a woman appeared.

"Hi, I'm Tawny."

"Emily Mathews. I called about boots."

"Yeah, come on in." Tawny opened the screen door for them.

Like the outside, the inside was tidy but extremely modest, with only a worn couch and a set of mismatched recliners in the living room. Tawny led them through the closet-sized kitchen, out the back door to a stand-alone workroom. The space, probably an old garage, housed bolts of every kind of leather imaginable. Along one wall sat a line of worktables and several industrial-looking sewing machines. Rows and rows of boots cluttered the other walls.

Sam didn't know where to look first. There were cowboy boots made from exotic skins, ones with fancy stitching, others with elaborate inlaid designs, and ones that were monogrammed. Every one a work of art.

"Wow," Sam said. "You made all these?"

"Yes," Tawny said, and Sam noticed that she was quite pretty. Long brown hair and green eyes that tilted up like a cat's. But there was also something hard about her, like maybe life hadn't treated her too well.

"I've never had boots made for me. How do we do this?" Emily asked.

"First I'll trace your feet, then you'll pick heel and toe styles, shaft height, and the leather you want. After that, we can start working on a design."

"Okay," Emily said, examining the rows of boots and looking a little lost. "The only thing I'm absolutely set on is that they're white to match my dress. And I'd like the McCreedy Ranch brand on them. The rest I'm open to."

"Have you done wedding boots before?" Sam asked.

"Yep." Tawny went over to a shelf, pulled out a fat binder, plopped it down on the table, and opened the book, which was filled with pictures of wedding boots. Some were tacky with cut-out hearts and appliqués with the words "Just Hitched."

"We wouldn't want anything like that," Sam said, pointing to the ones with a cartoon bride and groom, and noticed a barely perceptible smile on Tawny's lips.

"It's entirely up to you," she said.

"We probably just want simple. Right, Emily?"

"Yeah, but with a little flair."

Tawny motioned for Emily to sit in the chair in the back of her studio. "Let's get the measuring and tracing out of the way."

Emily sat and kicked off her flats. Tawny went to work drawing, while Sam and Emily continued to eye the shelves.

"I like those," Emily said, pointing to a brown pair with bright floral embroidery.

Tawny finished tracing and got them down off the shelf so Emily could take a closer look.

"I guess all these colors would be too much," Emily said, and Sam could tell she really loved the boots.

"What if we did a tone on tone thing, making the background one shade of white and the flowers a slightly different shade of the same color?" Sam asked.

"We could do that." Tawny leafed through her white leather samples and threw a couple of choices on the table. In a plastic tub, she sorted through a dozen spools of white thread and just like that put together a palette of varying shades of white.

"What about the McCreedy brand? Where would we put it?" Emily asked, getting out of the chair. "I've got pictures of it in the van."

"I have it." Tawny walked over to a bank of file cabinets and pulled out sketches of the brand. When Emily looked a little surprised, Tawny said, "I used to make Tip's boots."

Emily told Sam, "Tip was Clay's father. He died two years ago from a heart attack."

"That's awful. I'm sorry."

"Where on the boot do you want the brand?" Tawny seemed anxious to move this along.

"Hey, ladies." Donna glided into the workshop in her usual exuberant fashion. "You pick something yet?"

"These." Emily held up the embroidered boots. "We're talking about doing a white-on-white thing."

"Ooh, I like." Donna walked around the room, gazing at all the boots. "Tawny, where's the ones you made for Merle Haggard?"

"At his house," she said, and Sam presumed Tawny and Donna were friends. In a town like this, Donna had probably watched Tawny grow up.

"Show the girls what they look like," Donna said.

Tawny got out another fat binder, turned the pages and pointed to a pair of snakeskin boots.

"Do you make boots for a lot of country music stars?" Sam asked.

"Not just country-western singers," Donna boasted. "She made a pair for Tom Hanks. And the one who sings like a girl . . . you know . . . the one with the hair."

"Chris Isaak," Tawny said.

"Really?" Emily got excited. "I love him. Was he nice?"

"Very nice." Tawny nodded.

"Who else have you made boots for?" Emily wanted to know. "What about the Dixie Chicks?"

"No. Some of the players for the San Francisco Giants. A couple of winemakers and lots of rodeo cowboys."

Sam wondered why then did Tawny seem so down on her luck. Boots like these must cost a pretty penny.

"So where do you think we should put the brand?" Emily held up her inspiration boots.

"Is your wedding gown full length ?" Tawny asked, and Sam dug into her purse for a picture of the tea-length dress to show her. "If you want people to see it, you'll have to put it on the vamp. It might look funny with all these flowers."

"Hmm, what about here?" Emily pointed to a low spot on the boot next to the heel.

"That could work." Tawny seemed to be thinking about it. "Do you have any accent colors? I don't think we should do the brand in white. It'll get lost."

"It could be your something blue," Sam said.

"I love that idea," Donna agreed, and Tawny went back to her samples to pull a few swatches of blue leather.

"I thought we would just burn it in, like they do to the cows," Emily said.

"We could do that. But I thought this would be dressier." Tawny grabbed a pair of black boots off the rack and showed her a brown leather brand that had been inlaid onto the shaft.

"I like that," Emily said. "Can we go with the same kind of heel and toe on the embroidered boots?"

"Yep. We'll keep this whole shape—same shaft height and everything. Does that work?"

"Perfect," Emily said, and Tawny asked to measure her calves one last time.

There would still be a few fittings, but Tawny assured Emily that the boots would be done on time. Sam, who had never owned a pair of cowboy boots, was seriously considering coming back for a custom pair. She'd have to think about a design, something that would depict her new life here.

* * *

When Sam got back to the inn, Maddy's husband, the police chief, was there.

"Is everything okay?" she asked, fearing that there'd been an emergency.

"Yep. Just dropped by to see Nate. We're holding a little shindig at the house this Sunday." His radio went off with Connie, Nugget's 911 dispatcher, on the other end. "I've got to respond to this," he told Sam. "Get the details about the party from Nate." Seconds later he ran out the door.

Andy sat at the front desk, looking glum. Sam leaned over the counter to see if she'd gotten any messages. Most people called her direct line and left a voice mail, but occasionally they would call the inn's main number.

"Your father called." Andy handed her a pink slip with a message. "He says you don't answer your cell or office phone."

She'd actually blocked his calls. Why couldn't he be a normal father and let her live her own life? The man had to be the most controlling person in the entire universe.

"How was your gig, Andy?"

"It was great. You missed a hell of a show."

"Next time for sure," she said. "Is Nate in his office?"

"Yeah. The jack-off's been here all day."

"You shouldn't call him that."

"Why not?"

"Because it's disrespectful, and one day he might hear you."

Andy didn't look too concerned. "I might get a job at the Gas and Go, working for Griffin Parks. Now he's a decent guy."

The last thing Griffin needed was an employee like Andy. But she kept that to herself. Griffin had recently bought Nugget's one and only gas station and had completely modernized it. He also ran a custom motorcycle shop in the same garage. And as the owner of Sierra Heights, Griffin also happened to be Sam's landlord. Small town.

"What are you doing this weekend?" Andy asked.

"I'm getting my hair cut on Saturday." And apparently going to a party on Sunday, which ordinarily she would've totally enjoyed. But having her boss there would make it weird. Especially given that her boss was Nate.

"You wanna hang out?"

Oh boy. Andy had to be at least eight years younger than her. "Uh, I don't think this weekend will work, Andy."

"Okay. Maybe next weekend."

"Mm-hmm." She turned around and smacked directly into Nate's hard chest. He gently grasped her shoulders to right her and Sam felt an electrical charge go through her. She chalked the sensation up to being a red-blooded woman who appreciated a nice-looking man. Nothing more.

"Where have you been?" he asked.

"I had to do a wedding errand with Emily."

She wanted to avoid this conversation like the Ebola virus. Still riding high from yesterday's Landon victory, Sam didn't want to upset their ceasefire.

"Come into my office for a second?"

Uh-oh. Sam wanted to make up an excuse why she couldn't, but followed him anyway. Either he planned to scold her for taking too long at Tawny's, or he'd found some other infraction to hang on her.

"Shut the door," he said, and Sam thought *not good.* "Have a seat."

Sam dragged the wing chair from the corner so she'd be facing him.

"I just wanted to thank you again for landing the Lowery reunion," he said. "It's huge for us and if not for you, we would've lost him. I also wanted to see if you'd be up for working a bridal expo the first weekend in June. A couple of Breyer Hotel representatives, including Tracy, will be there. It'll be a good opportunity for networking and selling."

Okay, not what she had expected. "It's in San Francisco?"

"Yep. It's actually at the Belvedere, a Breyer property. We'll fly you down, put you up, and take care of your meals."

"Will you be there?" She didn't know why she'd asked that. Nerves, she supposed.

"In San Francisco, but not at the expo. Is that a problem?"

"Of course not," she said. "I'd be happy to do it."

"Good." He flashed a smile that made her insides do somersaults. The man could be charming when he wanted to.

She figured the sudden turnaround was due to the Landon deal, but she didn't plan to question it too hard. Nope, just go with it, she told herself.

"Is that it?" she asked.

"That's it."

She got up to leave, and he said, "I still owe you a drink."

"Okay"—she threw up her arms—"why are you being so nice to me?"

He leaned his chair back on two legs and chuckled. "The truth: I'm trying to apologize. Tracy was about to blow the Lowery deal big-time, and that was on me for taking it away from you and giving it to her in the first place. I still think you'll get bored and leave us high and dry. But you at least deserve credit for Lowery."

She shook her head in exasperation. "Well, thank you for that. I'm going to my office now."

"Why are you suing your dad?"

"Uh . . . nosy much?" Only four months in Nugget and she already talked like Harlee and Darla.

He shot her another one of his big, fat smiles. "You brought it up last night."

She plopped back down into the chair. "He's trying to extort me to come home."

"Oh yeah? What does he have on you?"

Her beloved summerhouse. "Property that has been in my mother's family for centuries. He's threatening to sell it."

"But if you return to Connecticut he won't?"

And marry Royce too. Her father hadn't made it one of the conditions, but knowing him, it was all part of his grand scheme to manipulate her into being his Stepford daughter. "Right."

"Did your mother leave you the property?" Nate asked.

"She left me her share—a third. The other shares belonged to my two aunts."

"Belonged?" He was still leaning back in the chair, his head resting against the wall.

"My father bought them after my mother died," she said. "And he promised to leave them to me in his will." Unfortunately, George Dunsbury's promises weren't worth penny stocks.

Nate looked doubtful. "It seems like he would be pretty well within his rights to change his mind. What did your lawyer say?"

"That I don't have a case. He can leave the property or sell his shares to whomever he wants."

"So what do you plan to do?"

"Sue him anyway. It could stop a sale, since I own a third of the house and don't want to put it on the market. But more important, my father hates when our family business is aired publically and a lawsuit would be very public."

"The old man must've had a coronary over the headlines generated by your . . . uh . . . failed wedding."

The "Runaway Bride" headlines had put him over the edge. "To say he was unhappy about it would be an understatement."

"Samantha"—he sat upright—"are you just trying to assert your independence or do you really not want to go home?"

She didn't hesitate. "Both."

He studied her for a few minutes, obviously trying to determine her true motives for the lawsuit. The man had it stuck in his head that her new life in Nugget was a charade; no matter how hard she tried to convince him otherwise. She didn't get it. But it was his problem, not hers.

"Then I wish you luck," he said. "I have a good real estate lawyer, if you want a second opinion."

"Thank you. But I'm okay for now." She hoped that the mere threat of a lawsuit would be enough to stop her father from meddling in her life. What she really wished is that George would come out here and see Nugget for himself. Maybe then he would understand how she'd fallen in love with the place.

She got to her feet and remembered the party. "Rhys invited me to the house on Sunday, but he got a call before he could give me the details. He said I should get them from you."

"I'll email it to you," he said, already lost in something on his computer.

Chapter 6

"Get away from the grill, you're destroying supper." Rhys pulled the spatula out of Nate's hand, shoved him away from the Weber, and flipped a row of burgers away from the flame just in the nick of time. "What? You fall asleep?"

The truth was Nate had been focusing all his attention on Samantha, who stood with a klatch of women on Rhys and Maddy's porch, drinking wine. She had on a pair of jeans, a crisp white button-down blouse, and some kind of jaunty scarf tied around her neck. The whole outfit should've been overkill for a backyard barbecue, but it wasn't.

She looked like a freaking goddess.

"Who you looking at?" Rhys smirked and let his eyes wander over to Samantha. The man never missed a thing.

Nate ignored his brother-in-law. "When are Sophie and Mariah getting here?" He wanted to see his daughter. Every day Lilly seemed to change in some subtle but miraculous way. Her eyes got browner and her hands moved more. Last time he'd seen her she'd grabbed for his necktie. Nate hated the thought of missing any of the big moments.

Rhys shrugged. "When they get here. Why don't you make yourself useful and replenish the beer."

Nate started for the house and got waylaid by Donna. "You hear about the Addisons putting in a swimming pool?"

"At the Beary Quaint?" The motel was the only other lodging option in Nugget and there was nothing quaint about it. The owners had gone bonkers with bears. Every kind of bear imaginable—stuffed, wooden, plastic, ceramic, even bear toilet-seat covers—littered the property like a creepy theme park. Seriously, the place could be the setting for a horror movie . . . the bears coming alive, doing freaky things to the guests.

Besides despising the Beary Quaint, Nate didn't like the motor lodge's owners. When he and Maddy had first bought the Lumber Baron, the Addisons had tried to put them out of business. They'd pulled all kinds of stunts to turn the city against him and Maddy. In the end, of course, the Addisons lost. But Nate was known to hold a grudge or two.

"Yep," Donna said. "From what I hear, they're putting the pool right in front, so motorists can see it from the highway. And are you ready for this? The main attraction is a water slide that goes through the belly of a bear."

Nate nearly choked. "Those people are on crack."

"Who's on crack?" Maddy handed Emma to Sam and came off the porch.

"The Addisons are putting in a swimming pool, complete with a bear slide," Nate told her.

"No!"

"Yes," Donna said. "Apparently the Lumber Baron has them running scared."

"They're not even in our league," Nate said.

"Maybe we should get a pool." Maddy bit her bottom lip, like maybe the Addisons were on to something. "Of course ours would be tasteful."

"With one of those swim-up tiki bars," Donna added. "And cabana boys. Lots of cabana boys."

"We're not getting a pool." Nate needed to ditch the crazy ladies. Like now.

He scanned the party for Soph or Mariah and when he didn't see them, excused himself from Fantasy Island to get the beer. On his way into the house, he passed Sam. She smiled at him and an image of her wearing nothing but that smile surfaced. Not good. *Back away from the redhead.*

He didn't know when it had happened, but she'd become a distraction. Not just her looks, which, yeah, totally did it for him, but she didn't take his shit. With the exception of his parents and Maddy, everyone took his shit. But Sam stood up to him. And he liked that. A lot.

The truth: He was starting to like everything about her. Her expressive blue eyes, her perfectly pressed outfits, even her cockamamie scheme to sue her father. And he needed his head examined, because being attracted to Samantha Dunsbury was a disaster waiting to happen. Hell, hadn't he learned his lesson from the last rich, flighty, schizophrenic woman he'd fallen for?

So he smiled back and ducked into Maddy's living room. A bunch of kids were in there playing video games, and Nate considered joining them. But then he remembered that Rhys was waiting on the beer.

When he came back outside, Sam had relinquished Emma to Maddy and asked Nate if he wanted help. She followed him to a big metal trough filled with ice and drinks and together they made room for the beer. He struggled to find something to say, which was weird, because he'd never had trouble making conversation with women before.

Finally, he settled on, "You got a haircut."

"Yes." She let out a nervous laugh. Apparently he wasn't the only one feeling tongue-tied. "Just a trim."

"It looks nice."

"Thanks." She self-consciously ran her fingers through the back of her hair. "Would it be a terrible faux pas to talk shop?"

"No. I don't mind." And he really didn't, unless Sam was pulling a Kayla, who'd always become manic about her latest obsession. For a time, her obsession had been him. But like with everything else, when Kayla got bored, she'd tossed him away like an old toy. Nate suspected that Sam's latest obsession was the inn.

"After you told me about the bridal expo, I did a little research," she said, growing animated. "There is another one in Sacramento in mid-May. I was thinking that I should go to that one too. A lot of our guests come from Sacramento. It seems like a wonderful opportunity for the inn."

"Sure," he said, and grinned. The problem with manic people was that their enthusiasm was infectious—at least in the beginning, before they jumped to the next fixation . . . and the next one . . . and the next one after that.

"So you don't mind if I go? It'll just be one day. I could go the night before—"

"Sam, I said yes. You can go. However you want to do it. It's fine with me."

"Does this mean you're starting to trust me?"

Nate shook his head. "Nope. I think this is a game to you. But you're making us money, so I'll play."

"You're a cynic, Nate Breyer."

He certainly was that. And she was a temptress. "Okay," he said. "No more shoptalk."

She looked around the yard at the paper lanterns Maddy had strung through the trees. "It's a lovely party."

"Yep. Pretty low-key." She smelled good, like expensive perfume. But she hadn't doused herself in it, the way some women did. "My parents used to throw something similar in Madison every spring."

"Is that where you're from?"

"Can't you hear the Wisconsin accent?" He said it like *Wuh-skaaaahn-sin.*

She laughed again. "You sound like you're from California to me. How long have you lived here?"

"I came out right after graduate school, about ten years ago. A guy I knew was opening a hotel. He wanted me to be his general manager. But the place turned out to be a giant headache. Investors pulled out at the last minute and the place was swimming in debt. You name it, and it went wrong. So I eventually quit and started my own hotel management company."

"Is this what you always wanted to do?"

"Actually, I wanted to play first base for the Brewers, but I got cut in the minors."

"Really?"

"No." He smiled. "I always wanted to run hotels, like my parents. How 'bout you?"

Her face lost that happy glow. "Nothing. It never occurred to me that I could be anything other than a Dunsbury. My whole life I thought that should be enough, and then suddenly I realized that it never was and it never could be."

It's not what Nate had expected to hear. He'd been prepared for her to tick off all the interests she'd pursued and then dropped to chase the next shiny dime. Unfortunately, he didn't know which life was sadder—the one where you were satisfied with nothing, or the one where nothing satisfied you.

"So"—she lit up again—"here I am, starting over. And every day I feel more fulfilled than I did the day before. It's wonderful."

Then she did this happy little twirl thing and he felt something tighten in his gut—and groin. He chalked it up to the fact that like everything else about her he was turned on by her passion. Nothing wrong with feeling a little lust, he told himself. Not as long as he didn't act on it. He could look his fill, just not touch. Because Nate knew from experience that touching would be an instant death knell.

"Oh"—she peered over his shoulder—"there's Emily. I need to talk to her about something."

And as he watched her walk away, those jeans hugging that sweet ass, a realization struck him like a ten-ton truck.

I'm a dead man.

The next night, Nate went to Sophie and Mariah's house for dinner. While the women worked in the kitchen, he got to feed Lilly and put her down for the night in her crib. For a while, he just stood there watching her sleep, her tiny chest moving up and down as she softly snored. His beautiful little girl.

Correction: Sophie and Mariah's beautiful little girl. He needed to keep reminding himself of that important fact.

So to distract himself, Nate stared up at the open-beamed ceiling. The house was fairly new, built to Sophie and Mariah's specifications. And he had to say, the one-level contemporary had exceeded all of their expectations. It was frigging magnificent, with sweeping views of the Sierra, big, open interior spaces, and a stone fireplace large enough to spit-roast a pig.

He left Lilly's bedroom, careful to shut the door quietly, and made his way into the great room. Colin's furniture pieces were sprinkled throughout the house, including bookcases, which lined the massive foyer wall and were filled with Sophie and Mariah's books. A lot of personality here.

He made himself comfortable in one of their leather club chairs, reflecting on how Sophie and Mariah had made a nice life for themselves. Up until almost three years ago, the women had lived in the Bay Area. Sophie had been a high-powered marketing executive and Mariah had founded a tech start-up. Both had made a shitload of money and wanted out of the rat race. So they'd bought the Ponderosa, moved to Nugget, and completely revamped the restaurant-bowling alley. The only thing missing in their life had been a baby. They'd gone to a sperm bank, but Sophie had been conflicted about using a stranger's DNA to father their child.

That's when Nate had offered to be their baby's daddy. He and Sophie had been best friends for years. They'd met while Nate had been dating her younger sister; the two of them hadn't stuck, but Sophie had. Nate wound up hiring Sophie to do the marketing for all of his hotels and the two of them became pals. When Sophie married Mariah, Nate was the best man at their wedding. And when they wanted a baby, he knew he was the best man for that, too.

Now he was second-guessing that choice, even though he knew that no one could ask for better parents than Sophie and Mariah. They loved Lilly with all their hearts. And that baby had a piece of both of them, since it had been Mariah's eggs and Sophie's uterus that had made her.

But Nate was just as much a part of Lilly and was having trouble figuring out where he fit into their family. That was the thing; this was *their* family. If he wanted one, he needed to get his own. The experts had told them that this might happen, and Mariah had all but predicted it. But Nate had promised that Lilly would be Sophie and Mariah's and he had to stick to his word.

"Hey"—Mariah leaned over the counter and called to him—"dinner is ready."

Nate made his way into the kitchen and opened the bottle of wine he'd brought. "I guess I should've let it breathe."

Sophie hitched her shoulders. "A little late now, because I'm not waiting." She poured herself a glass and filled one for him and Mariah. "Mmm. Nice." She looked at the label. "You didn't get this at the Nugget Market."

"Nope. It's from my own private stash."

"Meaning, you stole it from one of your hotels," Mariah said.

"You know it." He helped himself to salad, chicken, and rice. "Looks good."

They sat down at Colin's big farm table, which Sophie had set with her usual elegance. Mariah put on some music. Lyle Lovett.

"This is nice," he said.

"I feel like with the construction of the house, and Lilly, we haven't done this in a while." Sophie topped off his wineglass.

"Nope," he said.

"I've missed it." She topped Mariah's glass too.

Mariah laughed. "Are you trying to get us drunk?"

"*Moi?* Never." And then, because Sophie pulled no punches, she said, "What's the deal with you and Samantha Dunsbury? It seems to me that you've been holding out on us."

"What are you talking about?" He got up to get a glass of water from the kitchen.

"We saw you two looking pretty cozy at the barbecue yesterday," Mariah called to him over the counter.

"You guys are high. We were talking about work."

"What about work?" Sophie wanted to know.

"She wants to pimp the Lumber Baron at a wedding fair in Sacramento."

"That's a great idea," Sophie said as Nate took his seat again at the table.

"Not exactly original. We're having one at the Belvedere. That's how she got the idea. But, yeah, it can't hurt."

"From what Maddy says she's signed quite a few events, including Landon Lowery's." Sophie leaned over to high-five him. "Fantastic news."

"Mariah, do you know him?" He figured all the tech people knew each other. It was the same in the hospitality industry.

"Nah. He's way after my time. What is he, twelve?"

Nate laughed. "Yeah. Something like that. Says 'dude' a lot. But he likes Sam, that's for sure."

"Well, what's not to like?" Sophie said. "She's lovely."

Nate knew where this was going. She and Mariah were always on his ass to get serious with a woman and settle down.

"You like her?" Mariah, like her partner in crime, never beat around the bush.

He'd like to do her. There was a difference. "She's my employee. She just broke up with her fiancé and she's not my type."

"Ooh," Mariah said. "Do you know why she dumped the guy? If so, do tell. I have a bet with Owen."

Nate looked at her and shook his head. "With Owen?"

"Whatever the reason," Sophie interrupted, "Sam's no longer with him, which makes her available. As far as the employee thing . . ." She waved her hand in the air as if there weren't workplace rules about having sex with a subordinate. "And she is too your type."

"Really? What's my type, Soph?"

"Beautiful women with big boobs and brains. And Sam's a sweetheart to boot."

"When did you two become bosom buddies?"

"I wouldn't say we're bosom buddies. But I like her. You like her too, right, Mariah?"

"I do," Mariah said. "I give her a lot of credit for starting over the way she has. Especially in a town like this—not your typical milieu for a woman like her. But she seems to fit right in."

"Well, I'm not in the market for a spoiled rich girl, even if she's slumming it with the rest of us."

Sophie reached for his hand. "It's time to let what happened between you and Kayla go, Nate. It's been ten years. If you're not into Sam, you're not into her. But don't compare her to Kayla just because both women come from similar backgrounds." Then she looked at him like she could see right inside his head. "I've seen you with a lot of women, Nate. But yesterday, with Sam, it was different. The current between the two of you was so strong, I could feel the charge clear across the yard. That kind of chemistry is hard to find. Don't ignore it because you hold a decade-old grudge against someone who bears a few likenesses to Sam."

Sophie tended to be overly romantic. He didn't know what she'd seen at Maddy and Rhys's barbecue, but whatever it was, Sophie had read too much into it. Sam was hot. Any single guy would've spent his time talking to her, hoping to get lucky.

That wasn't electricity Sophie felt clear across the yard, that was hormones.

In May, Nate went to San Francisco and left Sam in charge of the Lumber Baron. He said he would be back in time to relieve her for the bridal fair in Sacramento. But oddly, the place felt lonely without him breathing down her neck.

One afternoon, Harlee and Darla came over and the three of them ate Emily's breakfast leftovers in the kitchen.

"How are the McCreedy wedding plans coming along?" Harlee asked, pouring herself a second cup of coffee.

"Good," Sam said. "We picked out the table linens yesterday. I talked her into these beautiful flouncy floral tablecloths—very British countryside. I think it might be the most gorgeous wedding ever."

"Hey," Harlee called out. "What about mine and Colin's?" Their wedding would be in August.

Sam smiled mischievously. "I'll have to up my game for yours, since I didn't realize it was a competition. Please tell me you ordered the dress."

"Done. And I picked out the bridesmaids' dresses for Darla, my brother's wife, and Colin's sister, Fiona. Darla loves them, don't you, Darla?"

"I do, even though they're a little subdued for my taste." One of those crazy fascinator hats with a bird bath on it would be too subdued for Darla's taste.

"Good," Sam said. "We've got to get going on your invitations."

"My mom is coming next weekend. Maybe we can do it then."

"Uh-uh," Sam said. "I'm in Sacramento for a wedding fair. Oh my gosh, you guys should come. It'll be a great way for you to look at all the vendors, everything from party favors to DJs. You can stay in the hotel with me."

Harlee's eyes danced with excitement. "I'll cancel my mom and tell her to come the following weekend."

A wedding fair to a bride-to-be was like Christmas to a child. Sam hadn't gone to any while engaged to Royce. Not all that strange, given their situation.

"You in, Darla?" Harlee asked.

"I'm booked all Saturday with hair appointments and I promised to spend Sunday with Wyatt. He'll be upset if I cancel."

Harlee looked momentarily disappointed, but said, "I'll send you pictures from the fair. You can text me yea or nay."

"Sounds good." Darla cut her muffin down the middle and gave half of it to Sam. "I'm trying to diet. Did you guys hear Lucky Rodriguez is coming back?"

"Who's Lucky Rodriguez?" Harlee asked.

"Uh, world champion bull rider and the most famous person to ever hail from Nugget. Not to mention a hunk of burning love."

"World champion bull rider, huh? Sounds like a good feature story." Harlee pulled a reporter's notebook from her purse. "Do you know how to reach him?"

"No, but he's buying the old Roland summer camp on the other side of town. You can drive by and see if he's around."

Harlee whipped out her phone, searched Lucky Rodriguez on Google and showed the picture that came up to Darla. "Is this him?"

"Yep." Darla waggled her brows and handed the phone to Sam for a look-see.

"Oh my," she uttered, because the man was quite nice-looking.

"Why's he coming back? And where's he been?" Harlee, the consummate reporter, asked.

"I guess he's been traveling with the PBR. I don't know why he's coming back; maybe he's retiring. He's getting kind of old for that stuff."

"What's the PBR?" Sam asked.

"Professional Bull Riders," Darla and Harlee said in unison.

"It's dangerous, isn't it?" It had certainly looked death-defying at the one and only rodeo Sam had attended.

"Uh, yeah." Darla finished her own muffin half, grabbed back the piece she'd put on Sam's plate, and took a big bite. "They're so good."

"He's actually buying the property?" Harlee asked.

With her mouth full, Darla said, "That's what I was told. My dad heard that he's opening a dude ranch."

"Really?" Sam said. She didn't know much about dude ranches, but she did know that they entailed lodging, which could be competition for the Lumber Baron. Jeez, she'd only been here four months and already she felt proprietary. When had that happened?

Darla nodded. "But you know how gossip works in this town. Half of it is usually wrong."

"But it makes sense," Harlee chimed in. "Why else would he buy such a big place? I saw it once when I went out on a story. It has a big lodge and a bunch of outbuildings."

The phone rang. Andy had gone out to lunch, leaving Sam to mind the store. "I need to get that. Don't say anything important until I get off the phone."

She grabbed the phone in the kitchen. "Lumber Baron Inn."

"What took you so long?" Nate barked.

The man was so moody, but stupidly she liked hearing his voice. "Give me a break. I'm here alone." Unless she counted Harlee and Darla. "What's up?"

"Just checking on things. Everything okay?"

"Yes. Hold on a second." She took the phone to her office. "Do you know a Lucky Rodriguez?"

Nate went quiet on the other end. "No. But the name sounds familiar. What about him?"

"He rides bulls for something called the PBJ."

"PBR." Nate laughed. "So?"

"Apparently he's buying the Roland property. Do you know the place?"

"Yes. Why's he buying it?" Nate suddenly sounded very interested.

"Darla says that Owen heard that he's opening a dude ranch."

Silence. Then finally, "Hmm. Do me a favor—the next time you talk to Emily, ask her about it. Clay would know about that kind of news."

"Why? Are you worried?"

"Not worried, just curious. How we doing today?"

"Good, especially for a Tuesday. Only four vacancies."

"Nice. Where the hell is Andy?"

"He's at lunch, Nate." Sam felt protective of Andy, even though he was a loafer.

"All right. I'll be back in time for your Sacramento deal. If you have any emergencies you can always call Maddy."

"I'm fine, Nate. See you when you get back." She hoped it would be soon. Only because having a little eye candy in the office broke up the workday.

"Thanks for taking care of the place and for the intel."

"You're welcome. See, I'm reliable." Sam missed dueling with him. At first, he'd intimidated her. But she'd learned that as long as she worked hard, Nate didn't have a problem with her speaking her mind. In fact, she got the impression he enjoyed clashing swords with her.

She went back into the kitchen to dish some more with the girls, but Harlee and Darla needed to get back to work. Darla had a cut and color at one thirty and Harlee wanted to hunt down Lucky. Reporter on the prowl.

"You'll tell us if you find out anything?" Sam said.

"If I find anything, I'm getting the story out as fast as my fingers can type it." Harlee updated the *Nugget Tribune*, once a weekly rag, now a daily website, constantly. The residents loved it because they could read up-to-the-minute Nugget news—like when Maddy and Rhys gave birth to Emma—on their phones. "Last thing I need is ESPN scooping me in my own backyard."

Sam planned to watch the website like a hawk today. Four months ago, the goings-on of a hometown rodeo star wouldn't have rated high on her scale of interests. But being up on Nugget gossip was a town requirement, and Sam had to admit that it made her feel like part of the community. She also didn't want this Lucky Rodriguez character horning in on her business.

In her office, she plugged "dude ranch" into her computer search engine and checked out various sites. A lot of rustic ones, where the guests stayed in bunkhouses and worked for their supper. She didn't see how those would attract the same kind of clientele as the Lumber Baron. It was the ones that were like resorts with swimming pools, game rooms, and four-star chefs that had her worried. A lot of those specialized in large events like weddings, family reunions, and corporate retreats. Not good if that's what this Lucky Rodriguez fellow had in mind. Not good at all.

"Hey, Sam?" Back from lunch, Andy, who hadn't learned the fine art of knocking, barged into her office. "Your dad's on the phone."

Oh no! "Did you tell him I was here?"

"Yeah," Andy said. "You want me to tell him you're in the bathroom?"

"No, no. I'll take it." She looked at the blinking line on her telephone and wondered why she hadn't heard it ring. Andy, of course, just stood there. "Thanks, Andy."

She sat there, waiting for him to leave, and when he finally got the clue, Sam shut the door behind him. Blowing out a long breath, she answered the phone.

"Hi, Daddy."

"What the hell do you think you're doing?"

"So I guess you got a call from my attorney." She held the phone receiver against her chest and counted to five. He was still yelling when she came back on. "Daddy, Daddy . . . Daddy . . . Oh, for goodness' sake, will you just let me get a word in?"

"Do you know what kind of negative press a stunt like this could cost our family? Really, Samantha, why are you doing this? Why would you intentionally try to embarrass us this way?"

"I haven't filed anything yet, Daddy. But I will if you leave me no choice."

"All I want is for you to come home and stop this nonsense. Is that too much for a father to ask?"

"Yes, it is," she said. "Can't you understand that I want my own life?"

"You can have your own life, here, at Dunsbury Hall, where you belong."

She cringed. Dunsbury Hall. Now that she'd left, it sounded so pretentious. "I like it here, Daddy."

"What about Royce?"

He didn't know about Royce, and even if he did, he wouldn't understand. "There is no Royce," she said. "There is zero chance of reconciliation."

Her father started to say more on the Royce topic when Andy rushed into her office again. "We've got trouble."

"Daddy . . . Daddy, I have to go. I'll call you tonight. Love you." She hung up and got to her feet. "What's wrong?"

"The couple in room 207 say the bathroom above them is leaking. All their stuff's ruined."

Great! Why did this have to happen on her watch? She went out into the lobby to find two livid people. Neither of them said a word, just folded their arms over their chests and stared daggers at her.

Finally the woman said, "We want our money back and we want to be reimbursed for the damage."

Nate would surely kill her, but what else could Sam do in a situation like this. "Of course," she said. Her ready acquiescence seemed to surprise the woman. "We are so sorry for the inconvenience this caused. Let me just run upstairs and assess the damage and then I'll get you settled."

She grabbed the master key and jogged up the stairs, praying that the room wasn't a swimming pool. It turned out it was only a slow drip coming through the ceiling. Not the end of the world. Sam wiped the dresser where the water had started to puddle, grabbed a bucket from the utility closet, and placed it under the leak. Crisis averted. At least until she could get Colin out to fix the problem.

When she returned to the registration desk, the husband put his open valise on the top of the counter and shoved it at her. "All these clothes, ruined."

They merely looked soggy to Sam. She glanced at the front desk cheat sheet for a name and said, "Mr. Cole, we're terribly sorry. The Lumber Baron would be happy to launder your clothing or else pay for your cleaning bill, whichever you prefer. We'll also get you moved to a dry room."

"We don't want another room, we want our money back," he said. "As for the clothes, these will all need to be replaced—not laundered."

Sam felt the mother of all headaches coming on and tried to guess what Nate would do in a situation like this. The leak was hardly the deluge these people were making it out to be, but wasn't there a rule that the customer was always right?

"We will absolutely reimburse you for the room, Mr. Cole. You and your wife are welcome to stay in another room as our guests. As for the garments, I really think a good laundering ought to do it."

"That's unsatisfactory," he said.

"Could we at least try?" She looked inside the suitcase again. "It looks like it's mostly jeans and sweatshirts."

The man continued to argue with her, when Mrs. Cole stepped in. "How long would it take?"

"I could have it taken care of right now." Sam hoped that would appease them because she really didn't think the Lumber Baron should have to buy the Coles a new wardrobe. Compensating them for the room seemed above and beyond. God, now she was sounding like Nate.

"All right," Mrs. Cole said. "We'll have lunch at that place across the square in the meantime."

"Thank you, Mrs. Cole. Would you like me to get another room ready for you? Or, if you prefer, I could give you directions to the Beary Quaint just down the road." That would be her revenge. Although she'd never been inside the motor lodge, Sam had driven by enough times to know the place was of a much lower caliber than the Lumber Baron. Shabby, really. Besides, Nate and Maddy didn't like the Beary Quaint owners. So let them deal with difficult guests.

Mrs. Cole looked at her husband, who gave a slight nod. Apparently, he'd had time to cool off and wanted to stay.

"Great," Sam said. "We'll get that ready for you and have your fresh laundry delivered to your new room."

As soon as they were out the door, Sam called Colin. Besides making stunning furniture, the man could fix anything. He'd been intimately involved in the Lumber Baron's rehab, so he'd know exactly how to trace the leak. Afterward, she found Loretta, the inn's head of housekeeping, and gave her the bundle of laundry with instructions to make the Coles' clothes as shiny and new as if they'd come straight from the factory.

Sam sighed with relief, thinking her troubles were over. Then she found two hundred pounds of cowboy in her lobby.

Chapter 7

"Lucky Rodriguez." He clutched his cowboy hat in one hand and held out the other to shake Sam's hand.

"How do you do? I'm Samantha Dunsbury."

He eyed her up and down, not in a suggestive way but in a way that said *How did a girl like you wind up in a town like this?*

Admittedly, she had on a Chanel suit. She wore it in Nugget because no one here would know it was from last spring's collection. Then those big brown eyes swept the lobby, taking in everything from the stained glass to the mahogany staircase.

"Well, I'll be damned. This place never looked like this when I lived here." He continued to gape, then let out a low whistle. "How much this set you back?"

She blinked, because where she came from people weren't so blunt—especially when it came to money.

"I wouldn't know, Mr. Rodriguez. But it is lovely, isn't it?"

"Yeah," he said, and poked his head inside the front parlor. "Wow. You able to fill this joint?"

"You seem surprised." Sam didn't want to divulge too much information, but Lucky appeared so genuinely impressed with the restoration that she let it slip that they had very few vacancies.

"Nice," he said, and wandered into the dining room, checking out the fireplace and the built-ins that Colin had painstakingly stripped of layers of paint and brought back to the original wood grain. Sam knew because she'd seen the before and after pictures.

"Would you like a tour?"

"I would," he said. "But I was actually hoping to meet with the owner. I take it you're not the owner."

"No, Mr. Rodriguez. I'm the Lumber Baron's event planner. Nate and Maddy Breyer own the inn. Nate's in San Francisco and Maddy's on maternity leave. Perhaps I could help you?"

Okay, she was probably overstepping, but curiosity was killing her. Plus, Nate wanted her to do reconnaissance. Hadn't he asked her to feel out Emily?

"Call me Lucky."

She nodded, noticing that he wasn't as tall as he'd seemed in the pictures Harlee had found on the Internet. Maybe five-eleven at the most—and ripped. He was certainly handsome in a rugged kind of way, but not nearly as good-looking as Nate. And why was she comparing them?

"A tour would be great," he said. "I'm buying some property on the other side of town and was hoping to pick your brains."

"Oh?" Sam tried to sound nonchalant as she took him through the main floor of the inn.

"You know the old Roland summer camp?" He explored the kitchen with her but seemed more interested in the common rooms.

"I've never been there, but I'm familiar with the place."

"I'm planning to raise rodeo stock." When she looked at him quizzically, he said, "You aren't from around here, are you?"

"Connecticut."

"Connecticut, huh?" He lifted his brows and rubbed the scruff on his chin. "Then let me break it down for you. I'm raising bucking bulls, broncs, and roping steers for rodeos and PBR events."

"But you ride bulls, right?"

He looked a little taken aback, then flashed a cocky grin. "So you know who I am?"

Busted. "People talk. They also say you're opening a dude ranch."

"I don't know where they came up with that. Owen, right? The guy never could get a story right."

"So you're not opening a dude ranch?"

"Nope. A cowboy camp. For corporate team building and anyone who wants to experience ranch life."

"How's a cowboy camp different from a dude ranch?" Because it sounded a lot like a dude ranch to her.

"For one thing we won't be doing any lame nose-to-tail trail rides. The guests will get to ride bulls, broncs, and wrestle steers."

She wondered what insurance agency would be crazy enough to give him a policy. "What do you want to know from us? It sounds like you have a good idea of what you want to do, and bull riding is your bailiwick, not ours." She laughed at the notion.

They climbed the stairs so she could show him one of the vacant rooms—not the one with the leak, of course. He seemed to want to see everything and couldn't be more complimentary.

"I want to talk to you guys about the lodging end of it. I don't know fu . . . fudge about running a hotel. I'm even thinking that some of our more finicky participants may prefer better digs than a bunkhouse, and we could work out some kind of a crossover deal."

"You're not planning to have private rooms?" Her head was already spinning with ideas—like maybe some of the Lumber Baron guests, especially the event guests, might like to do a day at cowboy camp. This could actually be a boon.

"Nah, not the kind of place I have in mind. I'm looking at something real authentic. At the end of the day, the place will still be a working ranch."

"You'd have to talk to Nate," Sam said. "But I think we could probably work something out."

"I was hoping you'd say that." He glanced around room 200 at the antique four-poster bed, crocheted canopy, and thick Aubusson rugs. "They all look like this?"

She showed him the bathroom, which had a vanity with a double sink, spa tub, and a walk-in shower. "Some are even better appointed. And we have a couple of suites on the third floor to accommodate families."

"How many rooms total?" he asked.

"Twenty. Some of the suites can sleep up to five."

"Yep," he said, almost like he was talking to himself. "This will work real fine."

Lucky turned to look at her like he was taking her measure. "You're the event planner, huh? Maybe you want to moonlight and do a little work for me? I could use help getting this thing off the ground."

"I don't think my current employer would appreciate that." Not to mention that she knew nothing of cowboy camps or bull riding. Then again, she'd known nothing about the hospitality industry until four months ago. "But if Nate likes the idea of us doing business together, I'm sure we could work something out."

"When will this Nate fellow be around?" He was clearly anxious to get going on the project.

"Later this week. How soon until you open your dude . . . uh, cowboy camp?"

"The property needs work, the bunkhouses are a disaster, and the lodge could use some cleaning. But I have a crew coming in tomorrow. Shouldn't take too long. My stock'll be here in a month. I'm hoping to open by summer."

It seemed rather ambitious to Sam, but clearly he envisioned the camp as a working ranch, not a resort. In that case, maybe he could set up quickly.

"Will you do meals?" If so, they'd be in competition for a chef. Emily wasn't going to stay on forever at the Lumber Baron and they were having enough trouble finding someone to replace her.

"Three squares a day for the folks who stay. I've already got a cookie." When she looked confused, he said, "That's a ranch cook—an old buddy of mine. This'll be the real deal. No fancy California cuisine, no spa treatments, no Sleep Number beds. If our guests want that, then we'll send them to you."

"This is just a hypothetical," Sam said. "But what if our guests wanted to participate in your cowboy camp, but only for a day or a few hours?"

"We could work something out," he said, and seemed to be examining her shoes. Jimmy Choos. "How long have you lived in Nugget?"

"Less than a year. How come you chose Nugget for your camp?"

"I'm from here, born and raised." He said it with pride, even got a gleam in his eyes.

Well, why not? Despite the town's somewhat run-down appearance, Sam thought the Sierra was one of the most beautiful places she'd ever seen. Here a person could breathe.

And just be.

"What brought you here?" he asked.

Apparently he hadn't read the news clips—didn't know she was the "runaway bride." "I was looking for a change and fell in love with the place." Lucky didn't probe, which was fine with her.

"I need to get going." He handed her a business card. "But we'll be in touch?"

"Absolutely. I'll call you as soon as Nate gets back."

Two days later, Nate pulled into his garage at Sierra Heights. He'd left the city after six to avoid the evening traffic and stopped near Roseville to get a bite. Five hours on the road, plus a nine-hour work day. He was bone tired.

Once inside the house, Nate switched on a few lights, went into his bedroom, and automatically glanced out his window at Sam's room. It had become a bad habit.

Her house was dark, which meant she'd turned in for the night. What did he expect? It was after eleven. More important, why did he care? A question he wasn't prepared to dwell on.

He'd already talked to her on the phone today and gotten caught up on the daily sales numbers, the continuing saga of the leak in room 207, and more about Lucky Rodriguez, who, according to Sam, was the greatest thing since sliced bread. Nate hadn't even met the guy and already knew he didn't like him. Although Nate agreed with Sam that Lucky's dude ranch—cowboy camp—whatever he wanted to call it—could be a license to mint money for the Lumber Baron, he'd have to meet the guy. See if he was on the level.

Nate continued to stare out his window at hers. At one point he could've sworn he saw a flicker from a television. He deliberated for few minutes and then said, "Ah, screw it" and opened his bedroom slider to the back deck, hopped over the railing, walked to Sam's house, and rang her doorbell.

When she didn't answer, he started to walk away. Epically dumb idea to go there in the first place. Not just because it was late, but he was her freaking boss.

"Nate?"

He turned around to find Sam standing in her doorway in a silky robe that gaped open at the top, showing something lacy as well as a fair amount of cleavage. Her hair was mussed and her face flushed . . . and under the category of dumb ideas this one went into the Hall of Fame.

"Is everything okay?" she asked.

"Yeah. I just got in and thought I'd check in with you." At nearly midnight with a hard-on.

God, he needed to start dating someone.

"You want to come in?" She tied the sash tighter around her waist—a waist he could span with his hands—and motioned for Nate to come inside. To temptation.

"I woke you," he said, looking at his watch. "Damn, I didn't realize the time. Tomorrow. We'll talk tomorrow."

"It's fine. I was just reading." She continued to hold the door open and he went in, hoping that his shirt covered the evidence of his arousal.

"I'll make some tea," she said, and wandered toward the kitchen, signaling that he should follow.

And if he thought the robe had given him a nice peek at her breasts, the way it molded to her ass should've been outlawed in all fifty states.

"You like chamomile?" She reached into the cupboard to get a box of tea and he watched the silk ride up on her. The woman was killing him.

"Yeah. Sure," he managed to say, even though he didn't like tea, and took a seat at the center island.

He watched her hands prepare two cups, hoping that it would keep his mind off the rest of her. But even her long, slender fingers turned him on.

"How was the drive?" she said.

"Fine." Small talk was good. "What's going on with the leak?"

"Colin's pretty sure he fixed it, but we'll want to watch it for the next couple of days."

Nate nodded. "You ready for Sacramento?"

"I think so. I picked up the pamphlets from the printer. They're fabulous." He'd given her a budget to have event brochures made. "I used a lot of pictures from the wedding and anniversary parties you held at the Lumber Baron last summer."

"Mmm. That's good," Nate said. "What's going on with the dispute between you and your dad?" Maybe she'd tell him that she'd decided to go back to Connecticut. Then they could have hot sex and not worry about it.

"We're at a stalemate," she said, and seemed reluctant to discuss it further. Weird, because she'd been an open book about it the last time.

"You still suing him?"

"I don't know. It seemed like a good idea at the time. But on further reflection, do I need to further embarrass myself?"

You mean like when you left your fiancé and twelve hundred wedding guests stranded? But he didn't go there. "So you'll let him sell the property?"

"He's agreed to hold off until we can come to a mutually satisfactory resolution, which means Daddy getting his way." She obviously felt bad talking about him, because she was quick to add, "He really does love me."

Nate's heart broke a little for her, because she seemed so divided on whether to be loyal to her family or to herself.

"Ever since my mother died, he's been overly needy," she continued. "It's not like they had a stellar relationship, but she was the Dunsbury anchor. And now he expects me to be that."

"What's your plan?"

"To stay here and keep working at the Lumber Baron."

Nate highly doubted it. Right now she was going through a rebellious stage. But when the dust cleared, she'd take her rightful place in the family. Families like the Dunsburys, the Kennedys, the Vanderbilts, and of course Kayla's family, the Cumberlands, weren't like the rest of Americans, Nate knew. They operated like royals. Princesses didn't live in the dusty back roads of Nugget, California.

"Just don't leave us in the lurch, Samantha." He sipped the repulsive tea she'd made for him.

"Do you ever notice that you call me Samantha when you want to assert your power?"

"You ever notice that your eyes get really blue when you try to challenge me?" he threw back. "Seriously. They go all cobalt and make you look possessed." Like a sex witch.

She laughed. "Have you been drinking?"

He smiled and held up his teacup. "You put anything in this besides that chamomile crap?"

She reached into the cabinet again, brought down a bottle of brandy, and arched one cinnamon brow.

Nate wagged his fingers at her. "Give it here," he said, taking the bottle from her and pouring them both a generous portion. "Ah." He took a sip. "Much better."

Sam held up her teacup. "*Cin-cin*," she said, and took a healthy slug.

"So, you're an alcoholic, huh?"

This time she giggled. "I am not. And since when are you fun?"

"I'm always fun." He downed the rest of the spiked tea and this time poured himself a brandy. "You want more?" Maybe he'd get her liquored up and have his way with her.

"No. But let me get you a snifter for that." She quickly opened another cabinet and of course had a whole shelf full of crystal snifters. Probably Baccarat.

He held the dainty china cup to his lips and shook his head. "Nah, no use dirtying another glass."

"No, you're not," she said, and Nate remembered they were talking about fun. "You're always scowling."

"At least I don't have crazy eyes."

"I don't have crazy eyes . . . do I?"

No. She had eyes that balladeers wrote songs about. Blue like the Aegean Sea. Precious like sapphire. "A little bit." And then he smiled to let her know he was teasing. And shamelessly flirting.

"You want something to eat?"

"What do you got?" He could eat . . . her.

She opened the refrigerator and bent over to scope out the offerings. And again he watched the silk of her robe do nice things. "Duck liver pâté. And I have some lovely crackers."

"Duck pâté? Where the hell did you find that in Nugget?"

"A man in Sierraville makes it. He brought it over for Emily to taste and wants us to serve it at the Lumber Baron. It's quite good."

"It's quite illegal."

"What are you talking about?"

"The state of California banned foie gras—cruelty to ducks. Here, let me try it." He spread it on one of the crackers she'd plated and put on the counter. "Damn, this is good. But don't serve it at the inn, unless you want to wind up in lockup with a cellmate named Bubba. You want one?" Nate made another cracker and passed it to her, then made several more for himself.

She watched him eat. "Didn't you have dinner?"

"Yeah, but that was hours ago."

"If I ate like that, I'd be big as a house."

He couldn't keep his eyes from drifting down her body, lingering in the place where the robe had started to gape again. "Yep, you better watch it."

She shook her head, but smiled. "What do you think of Lucky Rodriguez's cowboy camp?"

"It could be good for business. But if it's some jerry-rigged operation without the proper permits and insurance, I don't want us associated with it."

"I agree," she said.

"Oh, do you now?" He winked at her and got up to put his dishes in the sink.

"I'll do that," she said, and brushed up against him to take over loading the dishwasher.

He could smell her perfume, feel her heat, and wanted to touch her so badly his body ached with it. That's when he knew he was in trouble.

"It's late," he said. "You have a big day tomorrow, driving to Sacramento. I should get going."

"Okay."

But he thought she might've sounded disappointed. Maybe he just wanted her to sound that way. "Thanks for the company and the contraband pâté."

Sam walked him to the door and when he stepped out onto the porch she said, "Anytime you feel like coming over . . ."

He stood there for a beat too long. *Don't kiss her . . . Don't kiss her.* And then he kissed her.

Chapter 8

By the time Sam trudged into the Lumber Baron Monday morning, she was two hours late. Nate was going to kill her.

She'd overslept, hadn't had any clean clothes, and craved a Bun Boy breakfast sandwich. The fast-food restaurant—everyone called it the frosty—made them with bacon and cheese and they were greasy and phenomenal.

Thinking that it would only take a few minutes to hit the burger stand, she'd stopped off before crossing the square to the Lumber Baron. Unfortunately, half the town had had the same idea and wanted to chitchat.

"You meet Lucky Rodriguez yet?" . . . "Isn't he gorgeous?" . . . "We're running a special on fishing rentals, be sure to send your guests over."

Once safely cloistered in her office, Sam hoped she'd dodged Nate's notice. She had other reasons to avoid him too. Like that amazing heart-stopping kiss Thursday night. Either the man was an extraordinary kisser or she'd had some really lousy lovers.

In any event, she'd had three Nate-free days driving to Sacramento and back to think about that kiss. Dissect it. Analyze its meaning. Crave an instant replay. And figure out how it affected her and Nate's relationship. Do they go back to just being employer and employee, forgetting it ever happened? Did it mean they were officially friends, even though the kiss felt way more than friendly? Maybe friends with benefits?

It turned out she didn't have long to wait for clarification.

Nate knocked, let himself in, closed the door, and took a seat. "Why are you here today?"

Sam supposed she could now classify the kiss as a firing offense.

Weren't there laws against that? "Why wouldn't I be here today?" she said, jutting her chin at him.

"Because you worked over the weekend, doing the bridal fair. I don't know about Connecticut, but here in California we have strict rules about seven-day workweeks. Like the fact that I have to pay you shitloads of money for the overtime."

That had never occurred to her. "Do you want me to leave?"

"No. You're already here. But take two days off sometime this week."

"I don't think I can," she said. "I'm swamped."

He let out a long breath, which seemed like resignation to Sam. "All right. Then I'll pay you overtime. But don't make a habit of it, please. How did it go?"

"Good . . . I think. A couple of people made appointments for consultations and I expect there will be more, since almost all the brochures are gone."

"Nice. You make good contacts?"

"I pretty much exchanged cards with every vendor in the place. Lots of people sounded excited about the prospect of working with us."

"Well done," he said, and started to get up to leave, but plopped back down in the chair again. "Sam, we've gotta talk about Thursday night."

"Okay."

"That shouldn't have happened."

"You coming over to my house, eating illegal foie gras, or kissing me?"

"All of the above," he said. "But mostly because the other two led to the kiss. And kisses with employees, like seven-day workweeks, are deeply frowned upon by the California labor board. You're not planning to sue, are you? Because one thing I've noticed about you is that you're a little sue happy."

She laughed. "It was just a kiss, Nate."

He looked affronted, because Lord knew it hadn't been *just* a kiss. It was the best kiss she'd ever had. Royce hadn't even liked to kiss. He just wanted to get straight to the main course, and then he only lasted about five minutes. She suspected Nate would last longer— much longer.

"Okay. So we're good?" he said.

"We're fine, Nate." But the truth was, she was hoping for more of his kisses. She'd even take them in lieu of her hourly wage, which honestly was a bit on the meager side. The kisses, though, were a whole lot more.

"Good," he said. "I have a meeting set up this afternoon with Rodriguez. You want to sit in?"

"Sure." But she wondered if Nate was throwing her a bone because he thought he'd sexually harassed her.

"Okay," he said.

Then they said a lot more awkward okays until he finally left. For the next few hours she buried herself in work, following up with some of the brides she'd met at the fair. She stepped out for about thirty minutes to meet Emily at the Ponderosa and go over a few final details for the wedding. They only had one month to go and Emily wanted to make sure they'd covered everything, which of course Sam had. But Sam realized that Emily needed to go through the motions of marking it off her checklist. She'd be less jittery that way.

Sam had learned that being an event planner also entailed being a therapist. But so far she hadn't encountered too many bridezillas, mainly just women who made themselves crazy over getting their big day perfect.

Sam had been blasé about her own wedding, leaving the big decisions up to her wedding consultant. When Dana had suggested red anthuriums—"They're perfect for a Christmas wedding."—Sam had acquiesced, even though she thought the little yellow things sticking out of the flowers looked like penises. Sam had approved a shellfish bar, even though oysters and crabs sent her into anaphylactic shock. And she'd agreed to wear her mother's bridal gown, despite that the dress represented forty-five years of bad marriage.

In hindsight, all those things should've been big flashing neon signs to call off the marriage. But not until she'd overheard Royce's insulting and hateful words did she realize just how big a mistake she'd made. By then, though, it had been too late to save face. So she'd taken the cowardly route of running.

When she got back to the inn, Lucky had already arrived. She met them in the conference room. The two men sat in stark contrast to one another. Nate with his dark good looks in a Brooks Brothers suit and Lucky, the all-American rodeo star, in a pair of faded Levi's and Western shirt. His cowboy hat rested on the table at his side.

Lucky got up to pull a chair out for Sam, and Nate scowled.

"Sorry I'm late. I had a wedding consultation."

"No problem," Lucky said, and proceeded to pull out a fat file of paperwork.

For the next hour they discussed various ways the Lumber Baron could partner with Lucky's cowboy camp. A few times during the meeting, Sam caught Nate staring at her and wondered if he was trying to convey a secret message. New to business conferences and negotiations, she wished that if he had something to tell her, he'd just slip her a note. Or text her. But each time she tried to read his gaze, he turned away. It got to the point where she thought she'd imagined the whole thing.

After the meeting, she pulled him aside. "What was that about?"

"What?"

"You kept staring at me. I thought you were trying to tell me something."

"No. Maybe you had lipstick on your teeth."

Sam dove for her purse, pulled out a compact, and checked herself in the mirror. "I do not."

"I don't know what to tell you." He shrugged.

The man could be such a beast. "Well? What did you think of Lucky? It sounds like he has permits and insurance—all the things you wanted."

"Yep. We'll see," he said, and sat again, leaning his chair back on two legs. One day he was going to fall and hurt himself like that. "Did the guy sort of bug the crap out of you? Because he did me."

"Why?" she asked in exasperation. "He's a perfectly nice man. And he seems smart."

"Smart? He rides two-thousand-pound bucking bulls for a living."

Nate had a point there. "What about him bugged you?"

"Cocky. Too high on himself."

Sort of like you, Sam wanted to say, but refrained. "He's a professional athlete. They're all like that. Who cares, if he brings us business?"

"Whoa!" Nate stared at her. "When did you become such a barracuda? Just a few weeks ago you were giving away my rooms. 'Oh, Mr. Abernathy, I love you so much.'"

She swatted his arm. "Don't be ridiculous. This could help me increase events at the inn. Nate, I know you think I'm just a piece of society fluff, but I think I can be good at this. It's important to me . . . to succeed at something." Sam looked away, afraid that she'd divulged too much. Furthermore, she'd sounded pathetic.

He gently turned her to face him. "You are good at this, Samantha. Your skills are no longer in question. If you're truly committed to making a go at this, you'll succeed."

"But you don't think I'm committed?"

"It doesn't matter what I think."

But it did to her. For some indefinable reason it mattered very much.

Lucky took the long way back to the Roland property. Even though he owned it now, in his mind it was still the old summer camp where he used to work weekends and vacations to earn a few extra bucks. In those days, he and his mother desperately needed the money.

But that was a decade ago, just before he'd left Nugget to seek fame and fortune on the rodeo circuit. Now that he was back, he figured it was high time to get reacquainted with his hometown. That's why he drove the back roads instead of cutting across town and taking the highway. Or at least that's what he told himself. The fact that he'd be passing the Rock and River Ranch was just a coincidence. *Yeah, right.*

He'd heard Raylene had come back to live with her parents. According to well-placed sources, her husband had dumped her for her best friend. He wanted to feel good about that, take pleasure in her failure, but he couldn't bring himself to be that mean. Maybe it meant that he'd gotten over her.

But if he had, he probably wouldn't be going out of his way to pass by her place, would he? When he'd decided on Nugget for his cowboy camp, he'd known it was a possibility that they'd run into each other. Actually, more than a possibility, since even with the weekender population, the town had fewer than six thousand people. With only one grocery store, one gas station, and one sit-down restaurant, they were bound to bump. This time, though, it would be different. He was no longer the housekeeper's ragamuffin son.

Nope, Lucky Rodriguez had more money and silver buckles than any cowboy in the PBR. This time it would be Raylene who was down on her luck. Again, he tried, but still couldn't drudge up any satisfaction at her misfortune.

He drove along an irrigation ditch until the road zigzagged under the highway and along the Feather River. When the Rock and River's big wrought-iron gate came into view, Lucky pulled over in a turnout on the other side of the road and turned off the ignition. He didn't know what he hoped to see. The ranch house was too far back to catch a glimpse of Raylene, unless she happened to be riding along the fence line or getting the mail.

Lucky felt like a stalker sitting there, yet he couldn't seem to make himself pull away. Ten years was a long time to hold a torch for a woman. Especially a woman who hadn't wanted what he'd had to offer. Since then, there had been plenty of others—buckle bunnies, even a few non-rodeo types. But Raylene had never been far from his mind.

He started his truck and nosed out onto the road. Work at the camp wasn't going to get done by itself. To open by summer, he needed to bust a move. The meeting with Nate Breyer and Sam Dunsbury had gone well, he thought. Now, there were two people who had the hots for each other. For all Lucky knew they were an official couple. But that wasn't the vibe he got at the meeting. He detected something his mama would've called "a lot of pussyfooting around." One thing he knew, every time he looked at Sam, he got a death glare from Nate. Lucky laughed. Poor, lovesick fools.

When he got back to the old Roland property, Clay McCreedy was waiting, leaning against his truck. Clay had been six years ahead of him in school, but everyone in Nugget knew and liked the McCreedys. Tip McCreedy used to hire Lucky to wrangle during branding season. Best boss Lucky ever had. Tough as nails, but generous to a fault.

"Howdy, stranger." Clay shielded his eyes from the sun.

Lucky joined him at his Ford and both men sat on the tailgate. "Long time, no see."

"Too long," Clay said. "So what's this I hear about you opening a dude ranch?"

Lucky let out a puff of air. The dude ranch rumor had gotten way out of control. "It's a cowboy camp."

Clay tried to stifle a grin. "Yeah, that's what I said, a dude ranch."

"Nah, man, it's totally different."

"Oh?" Clay's brows hitched. "How's that?"

Lucky launched into his rigmarole and damned if Clay didn't laugh.

"You can call it whatever you want," Clay said. "But it sounds like a good idea to me."

"Yeah?" He was sort of surprised at Clay's endorsement. The cattleman was the real deal and one of the largest beef producers in the state, not to mention a decorated navy pilot who'd fought in Afghanistan and Iraq.

"The town could use the business," Clay said. "The Lumber Baron and the Ponderosa have certainly helped, but the Roland camp was going to waste sitting empty like that. It's nice what you're doing—teaching people about our way of life and preserving the cowboy traditions."

Lucky hadn't thought about the cowboy camp that way. At twentynine, his bull riding days were nearly past him and he'd needed to come up with a new game plan. He might've been able to become an announcer, like Ty Murray. But the plan had always been to come home. Back to Nugget. At first, he'd just wanted to raise rodeo stock. But he'd always loved the camp, which had been used by churches, schools, and other large groups for retreats, and it seemed a shame not to take advantage of the infrastructure, including the big lodge.

"I'm talking with the folks from the Lumber Baron about working a crossover deal," Lucky said. "If you've got any pull with them, I'd appreciate a good word. That Nate fellow seems a mite cautious."

"That Nate fellow owns nine other big hotels in San Francisco." Clay smiled. "I suspect his being a mite cautious made him successful. But, yeah, I'll put in a good word for you. The co-owner, Maddy, is married to Rhys Shepard."

"No kiddin'." Lucky had a faint memory of Rhys, but like Clay, he was older. And a troublemaker, if Lucky recalled right. "He's the police chief, huh?"

"Yep. Best one we've ever had. Very protective of that wife of his, so don't rub him the wrong way." How Lucky had earned the reputation as a womanizer, he'd never know. "When's your stock coming?"

"As soon as I get corrals built and fences mended. Hopefully next month."

"How's your ma doing?"

Lucky grinned. Maybe he was a cowboy cliché, but he loved his mama. The woman had raised him right—and on her own. "She's real good. Thanks for asking."

"She sure is proud of that big house you bought her."

Lucky would've bought her a castle if she'd wanted one, but Cecilia had been content with a rambling one-story in a nice part of town. She'd never have to work another day in her life. "She wants to help out with the cowboy camp. Nothing too rigorous, but it will be a hoot to have her around."

"I'll tell you what, if you need two extra ranch hands, I'll send my boys over. They're not doing summer camp this year and I don't like them sitting on the couch playing video games."

"Hey, I'll take 'em whenever you don't need them."

"Good catching up with you." Clay slapped him on the back. "But I better get back."

The two of them hopped off the tailgate and Clay slammed it shut. Lucky's crew looked like they were packing up for the day. Maybe he'd head into town later and try out the new Ponderosa. Well, new to him. Before he'd left Nugget, the place had been a dive. Bad food and bowling lanes that never worked. From what he'd heard, the latest owners had fixed it up real good.

Clay climbed into his truck and rolled down his window. "I forgot the reason why I came. I wanted to invite you to my wedding." He grinned, and Lucky saw a man in love. "Your ma's coming, get the details from her."

"I'll do that. Thanks for the invite."

Lucky watched Clay motor down the driveway, kicking up dust with his big tires. A wedding, huh? He scratched his chin and wondered if Raylene would be there.

Nate spent an hour at Sophie and Mariah's getting face time with Lilly. Now she could roll over, and Nate liked watching her tirelessly kick her chubby legs. She also seemed to know him; perhaps she recognized his smell or could decipher the shape of his face or maybe she just innately felt the paternal connection.

Nate felt so filled with the bond that it often clogged his throat and expanded his chest so wide that he thought his heart would burst.

"She's amazing, isn't she?" Sophie watched her daughter swat at the figures on the mobile that hung above her crib. He'd never seen Sophie's face so filled with awe and love.

"She is," Nate said.

"Thank you, Nate. Thank you for enabling Mariah and me to have this precious gift."

He nodded, not knowing what to say. *You're welcome* seemed feeble. "I've got to go."

"You just got here," Sophie said.

"Maddy invited me for dinner. You want to come?" Mariah had Ponderosa duty. "We'll pack up the kid and head out."

"Thanks, but I'm looking forward to a quiet evening in. Maybe this one"—she nudged her head at Lilly—"will sleep."

"Good luck with that." He chuckled.

"I heard you met with our resident celebrity bull rider. How did that go?"

"All right. I don't know the guy, but if he pulls off this cowboy camp operation, it could be good for business. All our businesses."

"That's what I'm thinking too. He's got a big name, and I suppose that will attract people."

"Could be. I just don't know what kind of businessman he is. Time will tell."

"I suppose it will," she said. "Anything going on in the Sam department?"

"Like what?" Nate wondered if she'd heard about the kiss. All it would've taken is for Sam to tell one person for it to be telegraphed throughout the entire town.

"I don't know, like maybe you asked her out on a date."

"Good night, Soph." He kissed her on the cheek, grabbed his jacket off Lilly's rocking chair, and headed for the door.

When Nate pulled up in front of Maddy and Rhys's white Victorian, a mini replica of the Lumber Baron, Samuel and Clay's youngest were playing basketball in the yard. A dog Nate didn't recognize chased the two up and down the court, nipping at their Warriors jerseys. Nate had given the shirts to the boys for Christmas.

The whole scene reminded him of a portrait of the American family and it gave him a sudden pang of longing. Since Kayla, he'd given up on the notion of the house, the station wagon, and the two-point-five kids. Being a bachelor, having lots of women to choose from and the freedom to do whatever he wanted, suited him fine. Perhaps Lilly had changed Nate's perspective. But hopefully it was temporary. Just a phase. Because there was no nuclear family in his future.

"Hey." Rhys waved to him from the porch. "Want a beer?"

His brother-in-law still had on his sidearm, which meant he'd just gotten home from work. He disappeared behind the front door. By the time Nate made it to the porch, Rhys tossed him a cold one.

"Give me a couple of minutes to change," Rhys said, and flipped his chin at the porch. "It's a nice evening. I'll meet you out here. Maddy's trying to put Emma down."

He returned a short time later, and the two of them sat in the rockers, watching the boys play. The sun set, painting reds and blues and purples over the Sierra. The smell of fresh-cut hay from McCreedy Ranch filled the air.

"What's going on at the inn?" Rhys moved his chair closer to the porch railing so that he could use it as a footrest.

"I met with the bull rider today about his cowboy camp. Looks like we might work out a co–business venture."

"Sounds good," Rhys said. "I haven't seen him for years, but Lucky was a good kid. Hard worker. His mom was the housekeeper at the Rock and River Ranch. He used to pick up work there and at a few of the other ranches in the area to help provide for his family. Cecilia was a single mom. Good person, always nice to me and Shep."

Shep, Rhys's late father, had been the town's resident asshole. Rhys had never gotten along with him, but they'd somewhat reconciled before he died of complications from Alzheimer's disease last summer.

"You still think Sam Dunsbury is leaving?" Rhys wanted to know.

"Not yet." Not while she tried to assert her independence from her father. But when that pissing match was over, who knew? "She may well double our revenue this summer from last, with all the events she's booking. That's where the money is for a small inn like the Lumber Baron."

"I know you don't want to hear this, but Maddy thinks the woman is on fire. She says the guests love her."

Of course they did. She was poised, conscientious, and looked like a million bucks. "She's got an aptitude for the job. I'm not saying she doesn't. But, Rhys, she makes more in stock dividends in a day than we pay her in three months."

"Nate, not everyone chooses a career based on money. If that were the case, I'd be back at Houston P.D., making six figures. It's about the passion. Look at Griffin Parks. He's rich and I've never seen a person work harder."

Griffin had recently come into his money. He was part Wigluk Indian and was entitled to proceeds from the tribe's various ventures, including the largest gaming casino in California. He'd immediately reinvested some of that money into Sierra Heights and the Nugget Gas and Go.

"Maybe," Nate said. Still, he thought Sam would get bored. That was the thing about independently wealthy people; they could afford to get bored. "When's Lina coming home?" He wanted to change the subject.

"She's got an internship this summer in San Francisco." Rhys's sister went to USF. "So we won't be seeing much of her, unfortunately. I was hoping you'd look out for her."

"As much as I'm back there, you know I will. She renting an apartment or staying on campus?"

Rhys, who in Nate's opinion was overly protective of Lina, let out a sigh. "She's subletting with five other kids in some nasty neighborhood."

"She'll be fine." Nate remembered with fondness his undergrad days when he and his buddies had rented a small home and turned it into party central.

Maddy came out the door, holding the phone, her brows creased in worry. "It's Connie. Sam just reported a break-in at her house. Her alarm is going off and she's afraid to go inside."

Rhys tugged the phone out of Maddy's hand. "Connie, you have Sam on the other line? . . . Good. Tell her to wait in her locked car. I'm on my way."

Nate didn't wait for an invitation, just headed straight for Rhys's police SUV. "Come on! Let's go."

Rhys ignored him, went inside the house, and returned with his belt half off so he could strap on his gun holster. "It's against department policy for you to ride with me."

"Give me a break," Nate said.

Rhys shook his head and unlocked the passenger side of the vehicle. "When we get there, stay in the truck. You hear?"

Nate didn't answer. Rhys got behind the wheel and turned on the siren. It was probably just kids, Nate told himself. Before Griff bought the development, bored teenagers, including Clay's oldest son, had vandalized one of the houses. Nate's biggest fear was that Sam hadn't listened to Connie and had gone in, alone. Even teenagers could turn mean to keep from getting caught. The thought of her getting hurt . . .

But when they arrived in her driveway, Sam was sitting safe in her car. *Good girl.* Jake Stryker, Rhys's most experienced officer, was already there. Rhys reiterated his original order, adding a commanding glare for good measure, as he got out of the SUV. Nate waited just until Rhys had rounded the back of the house, gun drawn, before jumping out.

Sam's house alarm screamed like an air-raid siren. All the houses in Sierra Heights had them. Nate never turned his on.

Sam opened the door of her car and got out. "Were you with Rhys when the call came in?"

"Yeah. You okay?" He looked her over. She still wore her work clothes and he wondered where she'd been, since it was well after Lumber Baron hours.

"I'm fine. You think whoever broke in is still in there?"

"Probably not." Nate figured the alarm would've sent them running. The question was, how much did the intruders make off with before they'd left? Sam had expensive things. "How long has the alarm been going off?"

"The company called me just as I pulled up. We both called the police."

"You didn't see anyone run out?" Obviously she hadn't or she would've said.

"No. But they could've gone out the back way." It wasn't quite dark yet, but someone could've gone undetected by running through the trees and across the golf course.

"I'll go see what's going on," Nate said, but Sam grabbed his arm.

"Let the police take care of it, Nate." She continued to grip him firmly, digging her nails into his biceps. "Stay with me, please."

He couldn't very well leave her after she'd said that. It would be ungentlemanlike. Eventually, Rhys and Jake came out, Jake grabbing something from the back of his truck.

Rhys approached Nate and Sam, shaking his head. "I told y'all to wait in the car."

"Did I have a break-in?" Sam asked.

"Yup," Rhys answered. "They're still in there, cut through your screen door."

"Oh my God." Sam leaned back against Nate's chest and he instinctively wrapped his arms around her. Rhys pretended not to notice, but Nate knew he had.

"How many are there? And why are you leaving them in there?" Just as Nate thought, it had to be teenagers. Knowing his brother-in-law, Rhys had tied the kids up to scare the hell out of them. At least they hadn't gotten away with any of Sam's valuables.

"That's what the trap is for." Jake held up the contraption he'd retrieved from his truck.

Sam and Nate looked at Rhys.

Rhys laughed. "It's raccoons. Two of 'em. And I won't lie to you. They've made a big mess. As soon as we came in, they took cover in your pantry. We thought we'd try to catch them before calling animal control. Those folks have got their hands full with bears getting into people's garbage."

"Raccoons?" Sam said, and made a face like humans might've been more preferable. Nate, though, was relieved.

"Sam, you can't leave windows open, especially ones that wildlife can get through," Rhys admonished. "Luckily, these two critters were big enough to trigger your alarm, because they're mean cusses." Rhys left them to join Jake back inside the house.

"I better give them a hand," Nate said, but Sam continued to hold on to his arm. "Hey, they're just raccoons."

"I know. I'll come with you."

"You don't have to, if you don't want to. You can go over to my place and hang out on my . . . nonexistent couch." He'd almost said bed.

Given that they'd shared that mind-blowing kiss, bed might've sounded suggestive. What the hell was he thinking? Of course it would've sounded suggestive. But when he got around her, he started thinking of beds. And the backseats of cars, her kitchen countertop, and the front desk at the inn. *Show a little freaking willpower, would ya? And some maturity, while you're at it.* It wasn't like Nate was a teenager.

"I want to assess the damage," Sam said, and walked past him to get to the door.

"Hang on a sec. Let me go first."

She tossed him a look like he was a moron. "You said it yourself, they're raccoons, Nate. Not gun-wielding robbers."

"Suit yourself," he said. "Hopefully they're not rabid."

She waved him off and went inside with Nate on her heels. She stood in the front room, peering into the open kitchen. "Is the coast clear?" she called to Rhys and Jake.

"We got one," Jake said. "Just need to get the other." Somewhere along the line, Rhys had brought in another trap.

Nate went into the kitchen, where Rhys held the pantry door open a crack and watched to see if the second coon would take the bait. Food was strewn everywhere. Torn bags of rice and pasta covered the floor. Red sauce was smeared across the cabinets. Shards of glass and dishware littered the countertops. They'd had themselves a real party.

"Got it!" Rhys yelled, and opened the pantry door to grab the trap.

"What will you do with them?" Sam came closer, but didn't step foot inside the kitchen.

"Take them out to the state park and turn them loose," Rhys said, holding the trap away from his side, gauging the mess. "Told you it wasn't pretty. But at least they didn't get the silver." He laughed, and Nate supposed it was country cop humor.

Yeah, not really that funny.

"You ready to go, Nate?" Rhys said, and looked at his watch. Maddy was surely keeping dinner warm.

"Nah, I'll stay here and help Sam clean up."

"You don't have to do that," she protested. "Really, it's no problem. I'll have it cleaned up in no time."

"Then we'll get it done even faster with the two of us. Then you can drive me to Rhys and Maddy's to pick up my car."

"Sounds like a solid plan," Rhys said, and looked down at the cage he was holding. "I want to get rid of this guy. See y'all later."

When they heard Rhys's truck drive away, Sam got out the cleaning supplies. Nate wondered if she had maids, because he couldn't see her doing housework. But she dug in like a pro. Nate found her stash of heavy-duty trash bags and began tossing away the broken glass.

"Was any of this good stuff?" He looked at the pieces of china he threw into the bag.

"Nothing that can't be replaced." She stopped from wiping the tomato sauce off the wall and turned to face him. "Thanks, Nate."

He hitched his shoulders. "Just being a good neighbor."

"To tell you the truth, I was glad you stayed. I know they were just raccoons, but it still feels like a violation."

"Don't have a lot of wildlife in Connecticut, do you?"

"Are you kidding? In back-country Greenwich? But I also lived in a house full of people. Part of the reason I chose this house was because it is next to you. Sierra Heights is kind of a ghost town."

He nodded in understanding. There were still a lot of empty houses in the subdivision. Even though Sam had probably lived on a fairly large spread, it wasn't as remote as this. Hell, at the Cumberland estate, Kayla's family had so many servants you couldn't be alone if you tried.

"You go out after work?" Nate eyed her work clothes again. A tailored pantsuit that looked like it was custom-made to hug her smoking body.

"I stopped in at the Ponderosa to have a drink with Harlee and Darla, and Lucky was there. He and I wound up having dinner and talking about his cowboy camp. He's really excited about it."

Nate wanted to tell her that if she liked Lucky so much, she should call him to help her clean up this mess. Petty, he knew, but it bothered him that she was palling around with the bull rider. What bothered him more, though, was that he was bothered. Nate had never been the jealous type, not even with Kayla. Being possessive about Sam was crazy. They were barely friends.

"What were you and Rhys doing?" she asked.

"I was over at their house, about to have dinner."

"Ah, Nate. You must be starved. After we finish this, I could pop a frozen pizza into the oven." She glanced around the room and cringed. "Better yet, I could take you out."

"Nah, Maddy will warm something up for me. I just need to get my car."

"You sure?" She stood up and stretched her back, giving him a nice view of breasts straining against silk.

"Positive."

"Is this about the kiss?"

"Yep," he said. "That absolutely can't happen again."

"Nate, we can eat and not kiss, you know."

"You already ate." With Lucky.

"I could eat again. In fact, I'm craving salad."

Nate knew that was bullshit, since no one craved salad. "I'm good, Sam."

"Don't sell yourself short, Nate. You're better than good." She said it with a big flirtatious smile on her face. She was teasing him and he liked it. "That kiss was one of the best—ever."

He decided to play along, even though he knew he'd entered the danger zone. Flirting had a nasty way of leading to more kisses. "Oh yeah, whose was better? Your ex's?"

"Not hardly," she said, and turned her face away.

"Is that why you left him at the altar? He was a bad kisser?" Okay, he was flirting—and fishing. But suddenly it seemed important that he know why she dumped her fiancé.

Her back went straight as a soldier's. "Maybe I was bored and thought I could do better."

Nate flinched, feeling as if he'd been kicked in the stomach. Her words echoed Kayla's almost to a tee. And the memory washed over him like an ice-cold shower. A wake-up call, because Samantha Dunsbury sure the hell wouldn't do better with him. No way was he getting played a second time.

Chapter 9

What Sam really thought was that she deserved better than a man who just wanted to use her for her pedigree. But telling Nate about Royce would've been beyond degrading. Her ex-fiancé's words still echoed in her ear. Still made her shudder with humiliation.

The dumb cow is nothing more than a for-show wife. After the wedding we can live in separate houses for all I care.

Sam met Royce at the Black and White Ball. It was Sam's event and everything from the black-and-white striped chairs to the Fortuny-inspired lamp shades had been her idea. The ballroom had never looked more glamorous. As the band played "Wonderful Tonight," Sam felt wonderful in a strapless, bodice-hugging Oscar de la Renta. It had taken her five weeks of dieting to fit into the dress. Unlike the other women of her social stratum, who starved themselves year round to fit into the latest couture designs, Sam was considered more curvaceous than what was fashionable. She could deny herself until the cows came home (another one of Clay McCreedy's sayings), but Sam would never be X-ray thin. Not her body type. No matter how much she tried to cover them up, Sam had hips, breasts, and a butt. And her so-called friends never missed an opportunity to remind her of them.

"Samantha is the Marilyn Monroe of our bunch," they'd say. On its face, it sounded like a compliment. But Sam knew a subtle dig when she heard one.

The subtext was that Sam was fat. In her circle, being fat was worse than being addicted to OxyContin or beating a child. And having a slow metabolism was a far bigger medical emergency than having anorexia.

But on the night of the Black and White Ball she felt svelte and gorgeous. And men noticed, a few blatantly giving her that slow up-and-down. Crude when a construction worker did it, but somehow perfectly acceptable from a man in a tuxedo with a seven-figure bank account. Sam's world was full of ridiculous double standards like that.

Of all the men to pay attention to her, Royce was by far the most handsome. Tall, blond, and all-American, like he'd just walked out of a Tommy Hilfiger ad to dock his sailboat then join the boys on the lawn for a quick game of touch football. Everyone knew Royce Whitley was the most eligible male in New England.

Because, yes, he was one of *those* Whitleys.

And her father, a blue-blooded opportunist, seduced by the prospect of adding a new string of regal DNA to the family lineage, pounced. He invited Royce to sit at the Dunsbury table. Royce, who should've won an Academy Award for his command performance, pretended to be enchanted to spend the evening with George Dunsbury's only daughter. He spun her around the dance floor, made sure her glass was always full, and entertained her with story upon story of his favorite person—himself. He talked about his polo ponies, his pied-à-terre in Paris, and how he had the strongest strain of genetically modified weed known to mankind back at his penthouse, and asked her if she wanted to get stoned later.

Despite his many farcical traits, which quite frankly were common in most of the men of his ilk, he seemed genuinely nice. He complimented her repeatedly. Offered to take her on a tour of the "Big Board," otherwise known as the New York Stock Exchange. And after the party, walked her home to her family's apartment on the Upper East Side. They bought a knish from one of the food carts and shared it as they strolled Eighty-Sixth Street, peering into the shop windows.

Ordinarily, she would've thought Royce Whitley to be a stuffed shirt. But it turned out he was rather personable. Charming, really. They stopped inside the Barnes & Noble and browsed through the books. No one gave them a second look in their black-tie attire. The beauty of Manhattan.

Once they got to Sam's building, Royce left her at the front door with a chaste kiss and a promise to call the next day. And much to her surprise—and delight—he did. For the next three months they were inseparable. Royce took her to his annual fraternity reunion at Yale. Afterward, they and a bunch of his frat brothers wound up at a bar near campus and got smashed on Jägermeister. They went to Yankees games, to parties in the Hamptons, and to his family's home in Newport, Rhode Island.

For an entire week they stayed at the summerhouse, where he took her in his arms each and every night and told her, "You own my heart, Red."

In early fall, she found a three-carat diamond engagement ring at the bottom of her champagne flute. Royce got down on bended knee in the middle of Per Se and proposed. She said yes, making George Dunsbury and the Whitleys ecstatic. The next day, *Page Six* declared them the match of the millennium.

Then little by little Royce began to change. Imperceptibly at first, like forgetting to meet her for lunch at the Plaza. Or coming late to an engagement party in their honor. "Sorry, Red, I got caught up at work and couldn't find a cab."

As the big day got closer, Royce got more distant. Sometimes he didn't call her for days. And when he did, he seemed primed for a fight. "Sam, can't you just handle it? I don't give a shit what flowers we go with."

Apparently, neither did she because she started handing off more and more of the wedding decisions to her bridal consultant. At the time, she marked it up to Royce's erratic behavior. How could she focus on a wedding when her fiancé seemed to be falling apart?

One day, Royce showed up to dinner—drunk—with his shirt on inside out.

"Are you seeing someone?" she asked, thinking it was the only explanation for his conduct.

"Why is that the first conclusion you jump to?" he asked, his tone antagonistic, like it was for most of their conversations those days. "Does it ever occur to you that I'm scared out of my skull of messing this up? That you're the best thing that ever happened to me?"

A tear ran down her cheek and he leaned across the table to wipe it away with his thumb. "I'm sorry, Red. Let's spend tomorrow together. I'll come to Connecticut. We'll take a long drive and look at the fall colors—just you and me."

"Okay," she said, hoping that they could go back to the way it was before they'd become engaged.

But the next day he never showed. Never called. Didn't even text. When Sam called his work, Royce's secretary said he was gone for the day. Fearing that he had been in a car accident, Sam was just about to phone the police, when Royce emailed.

A client has an emergency. Won't be able to make it today. Love you, babe.

That night, Sam called an emergency dinner with her best friend, Wendy. They'd gone to boarding school and Vassar together. But unlike Samantha, Wendy had shunned her upper-crust background to become a social worker, riding herd over nine female teenagers in a group home in one of Norwalk's toughest neighborhoods. They met at a small café in Stamford and Sam poured her heart out.

Wendy, always the voice of reason, said, "He could be having an affair or he could be having major pre-wedding jitters. He wouldn't be the first guy to have them and he certainly won't be the last. The question is, what do you want to do about it?"

"I want to call the wedding off until he and I hash it out."

"Then tomorrow, before he leaves for work, you go to his apartment in the city and tell him."

"My dad's going to have a conniption," Sam said. And the Whitleys would be devastated.

"Don't say you're calling it off. Tell George you're postponing, which is true, right?"

"I don't know," Sam said as the server brought them their glasses of wine and salads. "The truth is, I don't know how I feel. Maybe I'm not ready to get married either." Or perhaps she wasn't prepared to marry someone who had turned her life upside down with his volatile mood swings. One day he loved her, the next day he left her twisting in the wind.

At the crack of dawn, Sam took the train into Manhattan and caught a cab to Royce's penthouse. He lived in a brick and limestone building off Park Avenue. She came ready to do battle in a two-tone Marc Jacobs sheath dress and a pair of nude sledge pumps.

Royce's doorman, who by now had become an old friend, seemed startled to see her. "Ms. Dunsbury, you're here early. Let me ring Mr. Whitley for you."

"No need," she said, pushing past him to the elevator. "I have a key, Jacob."

Sam figured she wouldn't make it to the fifteenth floor without

Jacob diming her out to Royce. But she knew that catching her fiancé off guard, before he could come up with a million and one excuses, was her best strategy. And if he had something to hide . . .

But when the doors slid open into his large, open apartment, there was no sign of him. She checked the kitchen, thinking he'd be guzzling coffee before he headed to work. It was too late for him to still be sleeping, which made her suspicious. Where had he stayed the night? And with whom? The emergency client?

Before she jumped to conclusions, she checked his bedroom. There he lay in the center of the bed, sprawled across the blankets. Alone. She felt part relief and part guilt for thinking the worst, then she shook him awake.

"Get up, Royce. What are you, in a coma?"

He squinted up at her, sleep still in his eyes. "Hey, Red, you here for a bootie call?" Royce pulled her down onto the bed and rolled her under him. Leaning up on both elbows, he looked down at her and smiled.

"Why are you still in bed?"

"Had a hell of a night. One of my clients lost everything in a bunk investment and I had to talk him off the ledge."

"That's terrible." Particularly terrible because she hadn't believed him. "Is he okay?"

"Better." He rolled to his side so he wouldn't squash her. "What brings you to Manhattan this early in the morning? Wedding appointments?"

"It's not that early anymore. But we have to talk, Royce."

"Shit," he said. "I haven't exactly been a peach, have I?"

"The truth: You've been awful." Except now he was back to his old self—jokey and affectionate. "I'm thinking we should hold off on the wedding until we work this out. If you're having second—"

"No," he said, and she detected a glimmer of panic in his eyes. "We're good, Sam. Work's been a bitch and all this wedding insanity demanding. Come on, baby, we love each other. Don't you want to be Mrs. Whitley?"

She hadn't even thought about last names, which struck her as strange. There was always the hyphenated thing. Samantha Dunsbury-Whitley. Eww. Then again, maybe not.

"I'm not saying we call it off indefinitely, but temporarily postpone it. Just until we know this is what we want."

"Come on, Sam, what's this really about? I know what I want. You call off the wedding . . . Hell, you may as well stick a stake in my mother's heart. She loves you like a daughter."

Samantha knew that for the fib that it was. Helen Whitley wasn't exactly what you would call maternal. "You have to admit, Royce, you've been more than distracted. Half the time you act like you don't like me, let alone want to marry me."

"Ah, now you're just being silly. I love you, Sam. And this insecurity shit you're pulling—well, it doesn't look good on you."

He reached up her sheath dress and played with the elastic band on her panties.

"What are you doing?"

"Shhh," he whispered, and started undressing her.

They made love, and by the time Sam left the apartment her confidence in Royce and their relationship had shifted back to solid ground. She just needed to get through Thanksgiving at the Whitleys', then she could put all her focus on their Christmas-day wedding.

Every Thanksgiving, Royce's family threw a dinner party for a hundred guests. Helen hired the best caterers in Newport, used the Whitley china, which only came out when dignitaries visited, and brought in a *sinfonietta* for after-dinner dancing.

In comparison, the Dunsburys' Thanksgivings had been much more understated. But Sam had always enjoyed her family's holiday. Everyone in the house, servants included, ate together. After dinner, she and her father would retire to the den, sit by the fire with snifters of brandy, and play Scrabble.

There would be no Scrabble at the Whitleys'.

"Be sure to wear something special," Royce told her. As if she would somehow dress inappropriately.

As Royce's fiancée, she had been invited with her father to stay at the Whitley estate. They got there a couple of hours early, were shown to their rooms, and dressed for the evening. Before dinner started, Sam went looking for Royce, surprised that he hadn't been there to greet them when they'd arrived. His bedroom was in the south wing of the house and she wandered through the hallways until she found it. She knocked a few times and when no one answered, she let herself in. The only sign that Royce had been there was that the room reeked of pot.

Jeez, a person could get a contact high just from the stink.

Sam quickly shut the door and found her way to the dining room, where finishing touches were being made to the centerpieces. Helen stood in the center of the activity, directing traffic.

"Do you need any help?" Sam asked, and Helen looked at her like she spoke a foreign language.

"I'm fine, Samantha."

"You wouldn't happen to know where Royce is?"

Helen coughed. "I thought he was with you."

"No, I haven't seen him all evening. I checked his room, but he wasn't there."

Perhaps it was Sam's imagination, but Helen looked uncomfortable. She failed to make eye contact, studying the table settings instead. Could just be hostess nerves, Sam supposed.

"I'm sure he's somewhere around here," Helen said, and darted off in search of a missing fork.

But Sam didn't see him until dinner was served. In typical society fashion, she wasn't even seated next to him. When he threw her a kiss from the other end of the table, her stomach seemed to settle. And during the dancing he was quite attentive.

"You look fantastic," he said as he waltzed her around the dance floor, trying to peek down the front of her dress.

"Where've you been?" she asked, trying to modulate her voice so it sounded like a casual inquiry. Not accusatory. Even though she had a funny feeling about his earlier absence, a tiny tickle that something wasn't right. Yet, she couldn't identify why and told herself she was crazy.

"At dinner with you," he said.

"Before dinner?"

"Showering, getting dressed, you want a full accounting?"

"No," she said. "I just missed you."

"Don't worry." He playfully dipped her in the center of the dance floor and waggled his brows. "We'll make up for it later tonight."

Royce pretended to like sex, but from what Sam could tell he wasn't that into it. Often it was a quick affair, just long enough for him to climax. Still, it never stopped him from acting like they had amazing chemistry in bed. Perhaps he honestly thought they did. Sam convinced herself that they could work out a more satisfying love life with time.

"I just wanted to make sure you're okay," she said, but he didn't respond, distracted by something across the room. "What's wrong?"

"Uh, nothing. Just someone I haven't seen for a while. You mind if I go say hello?"

"No, of course not." But she wondered why he hadn't suggested introducing her. She was his fiancée, after all.

He escorted her off the dance floor, deposited her with a group of women she knew, and disappeared into another room. After what seemed like forever, her curiosity got the best of her and she went looking for him again. But he wasn't in any of the public rooms. She felt awkward pushing through private doors, chasing after him like an insecure girlfriend, so she went back to the ballroom. An hour later, he reappeared, his eyes bloodshot with a hint of eau de cannabis clinging to him.

Mystery solved. "Were you getting high all this time?" she asked, trying to sound calm.

He smiled at her sheepishly. "Yeah. So?"

"What are you, eighteen?"

"What are you, a fucking nag?"

She flinched. He'd never used obscenities like that in her presence.

Realizing his mistake instantly, Royce wrapped his arms around her and nuzzled her neck, whispering, "Come on, this party is stuffy. Come with me, we'll smoke a bowl and . . ." Again with the eyebrow waggle.

The party really was excruciating and for a few seconds she was tempted. Not to get stoned, but to steal away and spend some quality time with him. It seemed like they never did that anymore.

"We can't, Royce. Look, your mother is glancing our way. She'd notice if we suddenly ducked out."

"Yeah." He sighed. "You're probably right."

And for the rest of the night, Royce lavished her with attention. A cynical person might've thought it too much. Sam just felt relief.

In December, two weeks before the wedding, Royce announced that he had business in New Orleans—some kind of brokers' conference. "I'd take you," he told Sam, "but you have your hands full with the wedding. Besides, it would be boring, just a bunch of guys talking shop."

The conference lasted five days, but Royce decided to stay an extra two to catch up with a few friends. As much as Sam tried, she could never reach him. No answer in his hotel room, and his cell seemed to have gone dead.

So, distracted by her MIA fiancé, she left the last details of the wedding to her bridal consultant. By this point, even her father seemed annoyed.

"After the wedding, you'll whip that boy into shape," George told Sam over coffee. "But this is a good match and Royce has lots of potential. All he needs is a good woman to set him right."

She wanted to tell him that she was plagued with second thoughts and that she didn't want to set anyone right. That by thirty-seven, Royce Whitley should've had his shit together. But George patted her on the back like she was an Irish setter and said, "You're a good daughter, Samantha," and walked out of the dining room.

Royce barely had time to unpack when he returned from New Orleans before he boarded a plane to Jamaica for his bachelor party. He and twenty of his best friends planned to enjoy white-sand beaches, reggae music, and something stronger than Blue Mountain coffee. Sam just hoped her future husband didn't wind up in a Caribbean prison.

"You and your girlfriends should do something," Royce told her. "Hire a stripper. I don't care. I trust you completely."

Too bad she couldn't say the same for him.

The closer the big day came, the more melancholy Samantha got. At her last fitting, Sam's mother's gown practically swam on her. She'd lost that much weight, an unprecedented feat given that Sam liked to eat.

On Christmas Eve, the Whitleys hosted a combination holiday and rehearsal dinner for three hundred guests at the Four Seasons. Royce was on his best behavior, but Sam could barely choke down her Sweet Gems salad. Nothing about this felt right.

One of the Greenwich matrons accosted her in the bathroom. "Samantha, I heard you're wearing your mother's gown. What a traditional and lovely tribute. You've always been such a good girl."

"You and Royce Whitley," one of her father's cronies bellowed in the hallway. "Fantastic match, my dear girl."

Back in the ballroom, her co-chair on the debutante committee air-kissed her on both cheeks. "Oh my God, Sam, you look almost thin. Royce is such a good influence."

Sure. He was probably in one of the men's stalls right now, burning a fatty.

Twice she had to pop outside for air, because inside she felt suffocated. On one such trip, she found Royce cloistered in a ring of women. He snaked his arm out, wrapped it around her waist, and pulled her inside the circle.

"Where have you been?"

"Mingling," she said, and he tugged her over to the bar for a drink.

"You need to loosen up," he gently reprimanded.

She couldn't help herself and blurted, "Are you really ready for this, Royce? Because you don't seem ready."

"I'm ready, Sam, and you're just nervous, which is perfectly normal. I went through it last month, but I'm primed now, baby. This marriage is going to be so good. You and me, a team."

"We've never even talked about family, Royce. I have no idea how you feel about children."

Royce looked around the room, clearly afraid of being overheard. "Let's take this some place private."

He got them each a martini and found a quiet corner. "Of course we'll have kids. It's all my parents have been hounding me about since I turned thirty."

"Don't you want to know how I feel about having children?"

"What's there to know, Sam? Of course you want kids. All women want kids. Stop working yourself up. All you need to know is that I love you and that I plan to make you the happiest woman alive."

"I want to make you happy too, Royce. I'm glad we're talking. I wish we would've talked more. We haven't even discussed where we'll live."

"Relax," he said, and kissed her. "Where do you want to live? New York? Connecticut? We could keep my place in the city and buy a house in Greenwich or live at your dad's place. Whatever you want. After the honeymoon, we'll figure it out."

Shouldn't they have already made these pertinent decisions, like children and living arrangements? It seemed to Sam that they'd been engaged nearly four months and hadn't talked about anything important. Having these conversations the night before their wedding seemed absurd. Or could it be that she was just psyching herself out?

"Sam, honey, take deep breaths," Royce said. "We're all good. Everything is going to be fine. I love you."

"Okay," she said, somewhat mollified, sure that it was just pre-wedding nerves.

"Did I mention that you look absolutely gorgeous tonight?" Royce kissed her again and then glanced at his watch. "Look, a couple of the guys and me have a tradition. Before one of us gets married we each do a shot of tequila and make a toast. It gets a little ribald, so we're going to take it up to my room. You okay with that?"

"Of course," she said. "But I'll see you later, right?"

"Save the last dance for me." He dashed off, looking virile and handsome and happy. And Samantha's tensions started to melt away.

For the rest of the night she enjoyed herself, reveling in her father's pride and the myriad praise and compliments being tossed at her by the guests, like bridal bouquets.

She went to get a second martini and the bartender asked, "You the bride?"

"I will be tomorrow."

"That guy who got you the drink earlier, he the groom?"

"He is." She scraped the olive off the skewer with her teeth.

"Congratulations," he said, and smiled, but the smile never quite reached his eyes. Maybe he had a thing against marriage.

She gazed around the room, saw that the party had thinned considerably and wondered why Royce hadn't returned. From the looks of the band members, who appeared ready to wilt, the last dance wasn't too far off. Besides, she had to get up early for hair and makeup. The ceremony was at eleven o'clock at Trinity Church with a reception to follow at the Carlyle. The Dunsburys' and Whitleys' inner circle had been invited to return to Greenwich for Christmas dinner.

Sam decided to go up to Royce's room and bring him down for their last dance. Knowing him, he and the boys were enjoying more than tequila. Earlier, she'd gotten an extra key card to Royce's room so her bridal consultant could deliver the groomsmen's gifts. She took the elevator to the eleventh floor, found the suite without any difficulty, and knocked on the door. No one answered. But voices and loud laughter came from inside. Someone was having a good time, Sam thought and let herself in. The suite was larger than most people's Manhattan apartments. Royce's rumpled tux jacket lay over a chair in the front area, a spacious living room with plump couches and a flat-screen TV.

She followed the noise through a hallway and quickly stopped when someone said, "Here's to the man who's marrying the woman with the best tits in the tri-state area." Sam rolled her eyes and pressed her back to the wall.

"Here's to a shitty life of fidelity," another one roared, and Sam considered whether to announce herself.

"Fidelity? Ha! Not in this lifetime." It was Royce's voice. Sam stayed pinned to the wall, out of sight. "I just hope being married is as much of an aphrodisiac to women as being engaged. Man, I've never gotten more tail."

"I saw you with that little tattooed chick at your parents' house, Thanksgiving. Who was that?"

"One of the caterers," Royce said, and Sam felt ready to hyperventilate.

She wanted to leave before anyone saw her, before they could witness her mortification, but her feet couldn't seem to move.

"You missed out on Jamaica, Ryan." This from a voice Sam didn't recognize. "Royce here did us proud."

"You've been screwing around on her the whole time?" It sounded like Ryan, but Sam couldn't be sure.

"I had to finally break it off with Lindsey."

"Lindsey from bookkeeping?" someone asked.

"Yeah. She went ballistic about the engagement and threatened to blow the whistle on us to Sam. Apparently she was under the false impression that screwing me twenty ways to the moon ensured her place as the future Mrs. Whitley. Can you imagine? The woman's father is a friggin' plumber from New Jersey."

"What about Sam? She suspect you of catting around? Because in my experience they always find out." That was Reynolds Howl, who was on wife number two.

"Nah, the woman's delusional enough to think that I'm madly in love with her," Royce said. "I'm doing this to get my parents off my back. They think I need to settle down. Fine, I'll fucking settle down. All I have to do is clinch the deal tomorrow. But the dumb cow is nothing more than a for-show wife. After the wedding we can live in separate houses for all I care."

Sam shoved a fist into her mouth to keep from crying out, ran out of the suite and down the staircase, eleven flights, and hailed a cab to the Upper East Side, where she locked herself in her bedroom and sobbed her eyes out. All the doubts she'd had about Royce came to the surface. He was a lying, cheating, smarmy scumbag. But she was worse. She was gullible and pathetic. Everything about her life was a cliché—right down to the people with whom she kept company. Rich, neurotic, superficial, selfish bastards.

Like Royce.

Deep down inside she knew he'd done her a gigantic favor by exposing himself as the degenerate that he was. But how would she fix this? Make it right? Make her life right?

A glimpse of her mother's bridal gown, hanging on a dress form, pressed and perfect, caught her eye. The sudden urge to rip it to shreds became so overwhelming that Sam searched high and low for a pair of scissors. When she finally found one, she used it on her hair instead, going at her long red locks like a maniac. Hacking and chopping. It should have felt destructive or masochistic, but it felt cathartic, as if Sam was shedding her old skin, like a caterpillar.

But when she caught her reflection in the mirror, she looked demented, which would only make it more embarrassing when she had to show up at the church in the morning, get up before twelve hundred guests and cancel the wedding. That's when the idea of running began to take hold. The spectacle of Royce standing at the altar, waiting and waiting and waiting for her to walk down the aisle, his face flushed with embarrassment, seemed like poetic justice.

Her humiliation for his.

But thinking of her father made her reconsider. George would also be humiliated and that was the last thing she wanted to do to Daddy. She waited for him to finally stumble in the door and met him in the den, where she knew he'd have a nightcap before turning in for the night.

"Good God, girl, what have you done to your hair?" He inspected her with a sniff as he poured himself two fingers of scotch.

"Daddy, I need to talk to you."

"Nice party," he said, talking over her. "Helen doesn't have the same flair as your mother did, but she puts on a good affair. Excellent turnout."

"Daddy, I need to talk to you about the wedding."

"Samantha, it's late. Can't we do this in the morning?"

"I'm not going through with it," she said, and threw herself down onto the couch, watching him down his drink.

He let out a long breath, sat next to her, and patted her knee. "Pre-wedding jitters, my dear girl. Get a good night's sleep and you'll be raring to go in the morning."

"No, I won't, Daddy. Royce isn't the man you thought he was." She wouldn't tell him everything. It was too demeaning. But she would tell him enough to make him understand.

"You mean that he's a spoiled, narcissistic brat?"

"That and he's not loyal, Daddy."

"Oh, Samantha, tell me something I don't know."

"Daddy, how can you want me to marry a person like that?"

"You'll make him a better man." It was George's mantra. Like all she had to do was sprinkle fairy dust on Royce and he would no longer be an asshole. She knew better. "Sam, I expect you to do the right thing, here. You made a commitment, and Dunsburys keep their word."

"But Royce hasn't kept his word." She locked looks with her father, silently begging him to understand.

"After tomorrow, it's your job to make sure he does." He stood up, his way of saying he was finished with the discussion, and kissed Samantha on the top of her head. "Good night, sweet girl, and merry Christmas." On his way out, she heard him humming the tune "Get Me to the Church on Time."

For the rest of the night Samantha tossed and turned. By morning she was a mess. And by the time her hair and makeup people arrived, she was in Pennsylvania. Ohio flew by. But when she pulled into Illinois, the FBI had put out an all-points bulletin. Royce had told them that she'd been kidnapped for ransom. Of course, Honest George told the feds that news of Sam's kidnapping had been greatly exaggerated.

So on the day she arrived in Nugget, California, "Pride of the West," as the sign decreed, she was free. Truly free to do or be whatever she wanted.

Chapter 10

Nate didn't say much on the ride back to Maddy and Rhys's. They'd gotten Sam's kitchen clean and he'd found some extra screening in his garage to replace her torn one. By June, she'd definitely want to open her windows at night. As cold as it got in Nugget, it could be very hot in the summer.

"You sure you don't want to stop somewhere and eat?" Sam asked.

"Nope." He knew he sounded terse, but didn't care.

"Maybe I was bored and thought I could do better." The words proved everything he ever thought about her. Why he should feel disappointed was beyond his comprehension.

"You have got to be starved," she continued.

Nate wanted to tell her to slow down. She was doing sixty on a country road on a night with no moonlight. "Maddy will have food," he said, watching as she overshot the turnoff to his sister's house. "Didn't you see the road back there? You missed it."

She pulled to the side and started to flip a U-turn, when they both heard a popping noise and felt her car drag to the right. Good thing she'd finally slowed down, because she was having trouble keeping control of the car.

"What's happening?" she said, braking.

"I think you blew your front tire. Stop braking. Steer toward that embankment." The ridge stopped the car and they sat there for a few seconds in silence—just the sound of Sam breathing. "You okay?"

"Yes."

"Let me have a look." He got out of the car, Sam on his heels, and assessed the situation. "Looks like you ran over barbed wire. The tire's trashed."

"Great!" she said. No question she was having a bad day.

"You have a spare? I'll change it for you."

"You know how?"

"Of course I know how." What did she think? He popped her trunk and found the spare, but it was one of those temporary tires. "This isn't safe to go too far on. We should head straight to the Gas and Go and get you a new tire."

"I doubt they have one for this model of Mercedes," she said, and was probably right. Just plenty of Ford, Chevy, and Ram truck tires.

It had gotten dark. He used his phone as a flashlight and searched for her jack and wrench. In no time he had the car up, the old tire off and the new tire on.

"What?" he asked Sam as she stood over his shoulder, watching him tighten the lug nuts.

"I don't know. Most of the guys I know would've called Triple A."

"Really? Why? It could take a tow truck an hour to get here. Why would I wait?"

"I guess you're right." She sat on the ground in her pretty pants suit while he finished. "What else do you know how to do?"

"No more flirting, Sam. I'm not kidding. Knock it off."

"I didn't mean it as a flirt. You're just sort of an enigma to me."

"Because I can change a tire? Next time I'll teach you how to do it. Seriously, a slow child could pull it off."

"Gee, thanks," she said, and made a face at him. "I was talking in terms of how flexible you are. One minute you're a high-powered hotel executive and the next you're shoveling raccoon poop out of my kitchen sink."

"You do what you gotta do." He got off the ground, put the tools away, and wiped his hands on his jeans. "Let me drive."

That got her back up. "Why?"

"Because I like this car and I've never driven one before." That took the air out of her sails.

"Okay." She tossed him the keys. "Let's get your car at Rhys and Maddy's, though. That way you can eat and I can go to the Gas and Go on my own."

"I don't want to take this doughnut tire over their rutted road. Don't worry about my car. I'll get it later."

When they got to the Gas and Go, Griffin was still there. Since buying the gas station, he'd kept it open twenty-four hours, seven days a week, which had divided the town. Half loved having the convenience, while the other half argued that it would bring too much interstate traffic downtown.

"Hey, neighbors. What up?"

Nate popped the trunk again and got out of the car. "You have a tire for this thing?" He showed Griff the old one.

Griffin examined the damage and lifted his brows. "This one's hopeless." He motioned for them to follow him into the garage, where he thumbed through a catalog. "Mercedes SLK-Class roadster... hmm... It'll take a week to get it in."

Sam looked at Nate like *I told you so.* "All right. Just let me know when it's in."

"You shouldn't drive around on that one." Griff pointed at the spare. "It's safe to get you home and back to here, but I wouldn't push it more than that."

Sam sighed. "How am I supposed to get back and forth to work?"

Before Nate knew it, he'd volunteered to be her taxi driver for the next several days. It was because he needed her at the inn. At least that's what he told himself. "I'll ask Rhys and Maddy to bring my car to Sierra Heights," he told her.

"Where is it?" Griffin asked.

"It's at my sister's house. Sam was giving me a ride there when she got the flat."

"I could take you on the bike." Griffin had a Ducati and a handful of custom bikes he'd made himself. Nate was tempted to take him up on his offer. Especially because of Emma, he didn't want to inconvenience his sister and brother-in-law, but he also didn't want Sam driving alone on the worthless spare.

"Thanks, but I should be okay. If not, I'll hit you up tomorrow." Griffin lived on the other side of Sierra Heights from them.

"Sounds good," Griff said. "So how's Lina doing? She coming home for the summer?"

Nate knew the man had it bad for his brother-in-law's sister. But rumor had it that they'd had a falling out and were seeing other people. Probably for the best, since Lina wasn't even legal yet and Griff was in his mid- to late-twenties as far as Nate could guess.

Nate shook his head. "Nah, she's doing some kind of internship in San Francisco."

"Yeah?" Griffin said, trying to sound casual. "That's good."

Griffin finished the order for Sam's tire and the two of them left.

"I insist we stop at the Ponderosa to get you some dinner," Sam said, glancing at her watch. "It's nine o'clock and you haven't eaten."

"All right." He acquiesced because he was starving.

When they got there, the juke box was playing country-western music and competitive bull-riding was on the flat-screen above the bar. Not exactly what he was used to in San Francisco. He looked for Mariah, but she must've left for the night. Tater came out of the kitchen and waved before a hostess took them to a table.

The place was pretty dead, mostly just a few truckers at the bar. Nugget was a ranching and railroad town. Things shut up pretty early. Nate ordered a beer and Sam got a pinot grigio. When the server came back with their drinks, she took their orders. True to her word, Sam got a salad. Nate went full bore with a steak, potato, and grilled vegetables.

"Sounds good," Sam said.

"Then why didn't you get it?"

"I can't eat like that this late at night. As it is, I just look at food and it makes me fat."

"Yeah, you're tremendous. Do you just say that to get compliments? Because you've gotta know you have a perfect body—" He stopped himself. "I'm not flirting with you. This is not sexual harassment."

"Perfect body? My whole life I've been told that I'm one croissant shy of a plus size."

"Who's been telling you that? Blind people?"

"Friends. People in my social group in Greenwich."

"Women?" he asked, and laughed when she nodded. "Yeah, that's what I thought. Women are warped."

"I don't know what's with you these days. All of a sudden, you're so nice. Like genuinely nice. I trusted you more when you were mean."

"Do not mistake this for nice." He took a drag on his beer. "I don't do nice. This is just us having an honest conversation and me making a factual observation. You're not fat. Not even close to fat."

She smiled so happily that his chest expanded. He liked her smile, especially when she fired it up over something he did or said.

"Then what would you call helping me clean up after the raccoons?" she asked. "Or going with me to get a new tire?"

"Being a decent human, which by the way does not include giving away free rooms at the Lumber Baron."

"Despite what you would have me believe, you're nice."

"Just don't sue me," he said.

Their food came. He cut a piece of his steak and put it on top of her salad. "Protein."

She shook her head in exasperation. "Why are you still single?"

"I was engaged once." It came out before he had time to stop it. "It turned out she wasn't for me."

"I'm sorry."

"It was a long time ago."

"And you never met anyone since?"

"I've met lots of women since." He dug into his potato. "Want some?"

"No, thanks. But no one serious?"

"I'm not looking for serious. I have ten hotels to run, including the Lumber Baron, which as you know is a challenge." And a daughter.

"Don't you think the inn is doing better, though? It seems like reservations are up from when I first got here."

"That's because when you first got here it was winter. We'll always have problems booking the place when Nugget is snowed in."

"How do we get around that?" she asked.

He waited until he finished chewing to answer. "Do more events in winter. That way we're guaranteed the room bookings. But people know it's risky because of the weather. Ideally, we should book local events with people who don't have far to come and are used to driving in the snow."

"I could try to do that."

Nate could already see her head traveling in a dozen different directions.

"Could we offer specials? You know, like an incentive to get people to throw parties?"

He chuckled. "Yes. But we still have to profit from the event, which means before offering any kind of deal we have to crunch the numbers."

"Okay. I'll work up a few ideas. Maybe we could advertise in some of the local papers."

He nodded. "What's Lucky planning to do in the winter as far as his cowboy camp?"

"I don't know," she said. "I'll talk to him. Perhaps we could plan a few events together."

"Especially if his bunks aren't winterized. His guests will need a warm place to stay."

He didn't particularly care for the notion of her working closely with Lucky. But he had no claims on her. Didn't *want* any claims on her.

They finished dinner and talked about a number of ideas Sam had for the inn. He liked her enthusiasm. He really did. But he wondered how long before she flamed out and went back to Connecticut. The best advice he could give himself was not to get too dependent on her.

When they got back to Sierra Heights he walked her to the door. Sam stood on her porch a beat longer than necessary and Nate knew she wanted him to kiss her. Truth be told, he wanted to do much more than kiss. Instead, he stuck his hands in his pockets and waited for her to go inside and lock the door.

He walked home, proud of himself for showing such restraint, then made arrangements to get his car back and climbed into a cold shower.

Other than giving Sam rides to and from the inn, Nate managed to avoid her as much as possible. They were getting a little too chummy for his taste. He didn't need any more women friends. He had plenty. Just ask Sophie and Mariah.

Tracy called from San Francisco. The committee for the annual opera gala wanted to book the Theodore for the event. The Theodore was Nate's largest hotel and the opera gala was one of the most exclusive events in San Francisco. A windfall for Breyer Hotels.

"I want you to usher the event all the way through," Nate told Tracy. "Anything they want, you do."

"When are you coming back to San Francisco?" Tracy asked in her affected, whiny voice. Apparently she thought it was sexy. "We miss you."

"I was just there," he said, but no doubt about it, Nugget had become his home base, which didn't exactly inspire confidence in his San Francisco troops. "I'll be back in a few days."

It was time he started splitting his time more evenly, but he hated to leave Lilly. And if he wanted to be honest with himself, he liked working with the redhead.

"Nate—"

Speak of the devil. Sam came floating into his office in a blue dress that matched her eyes. He motioned that he was on the phone, but she waited anyway.

When he clicked off, she said, "There's a couple here who want to talk to you."

"Guests?"

"I don't think so, but they wouldn't say who they are." She bent over, giving him a nice view of her cleavage, and whispered, "They're wearing teddy bear T-shirts. Like something you would dress an infant in, except they're adult sized."

Nate tipped his chair back. "That would be the Addisons."

She made an O with her lips. "The Beary Quaint people? They seem really upset about something."

"They're always upset about something. Let's let 'em wait."

"Nate!" she admonished, and he laughed.

"I just need to check the Giants' score." He played around on his computer for a few minutes while she stood there tapping her toe. "All right." He got to his feet and motioned for her to follow. "We're up two, by the way."

When she looked at him quizzically, he said, "The Giants against the Dodgers."

The Addisons waited for him in the lobby, doing their best to look like they weren't snooping, which they were.

"Sandy, Cal, good to see you. I hear you're putting in a pool." Nate slapped Cal on the back good-naturedly and Nate could've sworn the guy's nut sack shriveled. Not that he was looking down there.

Cal, as usual, let his wife do the talking.

"We'd like to meet with you in your office," Sandy said.

"Have you met Samantha Dunsbury? She's our event planner," Nate said.

Sam stuck out her hand. "Delighted to meet you."

Sandy ignored the hand and pressed by her. "Where's your office?"

"Let's take this into the conference room." Nate didn't want them stepping foot in his office.

He signaled for them to take seats at the big table and Sam offered them soft drinks from the mini bar.

"Let's cut to the chase here," Sandy said. "It's our understanding that you've gotten that Matthews woman to turn the place into a restaurant."

"Yeah, well, you understood wrong," Nate said, and Sam looked at him like she thought he was being rude, which he was, because the Addisons bugged the crap out of him.

"Well, we have it on excellent authority," Sandy said, and Nate could've sworn the 3-D bear on her shirt nodded. "It's all over town that you're running a restaurant on the side. You don't have permits for that and we'll shut you down."

"Go for it," Nate dared, and started to get up to walk away.

Sam cleared her throat and beckoned him with her eyes to stay put. For whatever reason he followed her lead. The woman sure was bossy.

"You've gotten bad information, Sandy," Sam said. "We've hired Emily to prepare breakfasts and late afternoon snacks for our guests. It's included in their room rate. We are not serving meals to anyone who is not staying here, unless you include members of the staff, who eat for free."

"That's not at all what we've heard," Sandy insisted. "We heard you're running a restaurant."

"We can't help what you heard," Nate said. "What Sam said is the truth. As for permits, we're perfectly within our rights to serve food to our guests, since we are a bed and breakfast." He emphasized "breakfast."

Sandy started to say something, but Nate cut her off. "We're done. Good luck with your bear pool." And with that he walked out, not wanting to give the Addisons any more of his time.

A little while later, Sam found him in his office catching up on a pile of paperwork. "*Good luck with your bear pool*? You really had to throw that in?"

"Just keeping it classy," he said, and turned his focus back to the work he'd been doing. When Sam didn't leave, he asked, "You need something?"

"No. Just checking in. Checking in . . . get it? Hotel humor."

He lifted his head slightly. "You're weird. Now go away."

On her way out, Nate got a nice view of her awesome ass . . . and he really needed to stop doing that. What he needed was to spend more time in San Francisco and date women he didn't work with, didn't live next door to, and who didn't make bad hotel jokes.

Checking in. He rolled his eyes and laughed.

Chapter 11

"So this it, huh?" Sam walked around Lucky's property, watching a crew of men erect a row of pipe corrals. They were closing in on mid-May and he still planned to open by summer.

"What do you think?" Lucky asked.

To Sam it looked like there was still a lot of work to be done, but she didn't want to hurt his feelings. "It's . . . it's getting there."

"You didn't see it before," Lucky said. "But I'm making progress. Come check out the lodge."

When Sam had first driven up, she'd seen the large stack-stone and log structure. What made it particularly impressive was the roofline—a series of staggered peaks that rose to the sky like majestic wooden tepees.

"This is it," Lucky said, taking her inside the lodge's massive double doors. "You ever see *Dirty Dancing*?"

"Of course," she said, trailing behind him, stopping to take in the interesting architecture—Native American meets Frank Lloyd Wright's prairie style. "Patrick Swayze. Jennifer Grey. They spend the summer at a resort in the Catskills. I'm surprised you've seen it. Isn't it considered a chick film?"

Lucky grinned. "I've been known to see chick flicks every now and again. This place sort of reminds me of that."

Not so much to Sam. But it was something all right. Sam took in the knotty-pine pitched ceilings, the mammoth picture windows and the tongue-and-groove plank floors. She walked in little circles until her gaze fell on the stone fireplace in the corner. "This place is beyond spectacular."

"Ain't it though?" Lucky stared up at the ceiling as if he was seeing it for the first time. "I used to work here summers. This is where they served the chow. I'm just planning to clean it up, knock down the cobwebs and polish up the wood. But nothing else. I'm envisioning long wooden tables and benches. Maybe a stage over there for bands in the evenings for dancing." He pointed to a spot in the corner and moved his finger to the other side of the room. "And a bar over there."

She nodded, liking his plan. "I can totally see that. Maybe some fun country-and-western neon signs."

"Yep," he said. "I like it. We could hang old rodeo memorabilia too."

"Absolutely." She couldn't believe how clearly she saw his vision, given that she'd never been to a cowboy camp or a dude ranch in her life. But somehow she could feel the Western vibe perfectly and supposed that her nearly five-month stay in Nugget had given her the required esthetic.

He walked her back to an industrial kitchen. It lacked the charm of the Lumber Baron's newly remodeled one, but it looked like it could efficiently accommodate a sizable crowd. Lots of stainless steel and bulky appliances.

"There are six outbuildings, including a couple of dormitories," Lucky said. "I was thinking the dormitories would make good bunkhouses. One of the buildings I'm converting into my digs and an office." He'd told her that he'd been getting by in a single-wide trailer.

Sam walked out onto the porch and scanned the lushly forested property. In the distance she could hear the Feather River and smell the warm spring air. She looked for Lucky, who'd hung back, presumably giving her space to get the lay of the land.

When she went back inside he asked, "What do you think?" His voice echoed through the empty hall.

"I think it's extraordinary." She could visualize the room filled with people, a live band and line dancing.

"Let me hear your ideas." Lucky was definitely a man of action.

"All right. Should we talk in here? Or would you rather go into town and get drinks?"

"I'm always in favor of drinks." Lucky looked around the lodge and at Samantha's white blouse. "And it's a little dusty here. So I vote for the Ponderosa. My treat."

"I'll follow you in the car." Griff had put on her new tire. Just in time too, because her chauffeur, Nate, had gone to San Francisco for a few days. He'd been gone barely a day and already she missed his overbearingness.

Unfortunately, she got the sinking feeling that he couldn't get away from her fast enough.

They got a booth in the far corner of the Ponderosa. Lucky called it the cowboy seat, because he could see the whole room in case of trouble.

"You expecting trouble, Lucky?" she teased.

"Not if I can help it." He really was a charming man. And handsome. "But I can handle it."

She bet he could. For the life of her she didn't know why Nate didn't like him. A server came and took their drink orders. Sam also asked for a bowl of pretzel mix.

As soon as the waitress left, Lucky said, "Let's get to it. I'm dying to hear your ideas."

"So this is the thing," she started. "The hospitality industry in Nugget is bad in winter. The Lumber Baron drops on average seventy percent in revenue during the cold months. And it will be worse for you, given that the cowboy camp is built around outdoor activities. What I suggest is that we work together to organize packages—special joint events that will bring tourists or even locals during the snowiest time of the year."

"I'm with you so far," Lucky said. "But what about summer?"

"Summer is the easy season. That's why I'm saving it for last. For winter, I've come up with a few ideas. I want you to be open-minded about this because I know you see the cowboy camp as a manlier alternative to the dude ranch. But I've been looking at dude ranches in Jackson Hole and other cold places to see what they do in winter and this is what I've come up with . . ."

She'd already lost him. Instead of listening to her plan, he was staring across the dining room at a perky little blonde. "Uh, hello." Sam waved her hand in his face. "Earth to Lucky."

He pulled his eyes away from the woman. "I'm sorry," he said, and then went right back to watching the woman.

Granted, she was pretty in that cheerleader kind of way, with big dimples and puppy- dog eyes, but please . . .

"Sorry, sorry," he said, clearly picking up on her annoyance. "We used to know each other."

"Do you want to go say hi?" Their drinks had just arrived and Sam took a big gulp of her margarita. "Go ahead."

"No, that's okay. The last time we saw each other didn't end well."

"How long ago was that?" Sam asked.

"A decade."

"What happened?"

"Uh, let's just say it was a misunderstanding." And Sam knew that was his polite way of telling her he didn't want to talk about it anymore. He turned back to her, all eyes now. "So about the winter months and us doing a joint operation, you were saying?"

"I was thinking that we . . ."

For the next half hour, Lucky barely heard a word coming out of Sam's mouth.

Raylene looked good. Thinner than he remembered, but her breasts seemed larger. He wouldn't be surprised if she'd gotten a boob job in Denver. She'd always complained about how they were too small, how they weren't round enough, blah, blah, blah. Sometimes he didn't get women, because Raylene's breasts had been fine just the way they were—large enough to fit into his hands, not too big to spill over. What did they say: More than a mouthful is a waste.

He covertly watched her lift her French fries to her mouth and suck off the ketchup from the tips, the same way she ate them when she was seventeen. It used to drive him crazy. She hadn't noticed him or she was pretending not to. Didn't she know he was a world champion bull rider and that he'd broken more records than Silvano Alves?

He supposed she'd find out soon enough. The gossip pipeline in Nugget worked overtime and his mama sure liked to sing Lucky's praises to anyone who listened.

He craned his neck, trying to get a gander at the other woman Raylene was with, but Lucky didn't recognize her. Possibly a friend from Denver. Hopefully not the one her husband had left her for. From what he'd heard, the breakup had been brutal. Raylene had gone as far as to push her unfaithful husband's SUV into the swimming pool. A brand-new Escalade. A little flashy for Lucky's choice of wheels, but it had probably set the guy back a wad of cash.

Raylene had always been what you would call vindictive. But he supposed under the circumstances, who could blame her?

The dude had cheated with her best friend, for Christ's sake.

Cheating was bad all the way around. But even for dirtbags, best friends were completely off limits. To add insult to injury, Raylene had allegedly caught the two of them together. The way he'd heard the story was that Raylene had come home from lunch to find Butch and the broad going at it in the shower.

While he looked over at Raylene's table again, Sam moved on to something about sleigh rides in the snow, hot cocoa and square dancing. The truth was, he hadn't been able to concentrate on a full sentence.

Sam leaned over the table to get his attention. "And strippers, we could hire strippers."

"Huh?" he said.

"You haven't been listening to a word I've said, have you?"

"No, ma'am."

She smiled at him in commiseration. Lucky thought she was a fine-looking woman. If she wasn't hooked up with Nate, he might've asked her out. It would be good to have someone to get his mind off Raylene.

"What do you say we adjourn this meeting until you can focus?" Sam said.

"I'm sorry, Sam."

"No need to apologize." She nudged her head at Raylene. "Clearly, it's not your fault."

He had to get his head on straight if he wanted to open by summer, which meant he didn't need any disruptions. "What do you say we do this tomorrow?"

"That would be good. I'd like to have something on paper by the time Nate gets back."

"How long you two been an item?" Lucky asked.

She looked surprised by the question. "We're not an item."

Now it was Lucky's turn to be surprised. "Could have fooled me. You two have combustible chemistry."

"No, we don't," she said, and cocked her head.

He decided it was best not to argue with the lady, but couldn't help smirking.

"Really? You think we have chemistry?"

"Yeah. So much so that I thought the two of you were hitched up. Does this mean you're available?"

Sam looked over at Raylene's table again. "What does it matter, since you're clearly not." She grinned at him like she was enjoying herself. "I've got to get going, Lucky. Want to come by the inn tomorrow about two? This time we'll meet in my office. No distractions."

"Sounds good. And again, my apologies. I'm usually more focused." Hell, no one made it to the eight-second bell as many times as Lucky had without being single-minded. But Raylene always had messed with his head.

Sam reached inside her purse, pulled out a wallet, and laid a couple of bills on the table.

"Hey," Lucky said. "What are you doing? I've got this." He stuffed the money back into her purse.

"Thanks, Lucky." She scooted out of the booth. "You planning to stick around?"

"Let me pay and I'll walk you out." Raylene would see him, but it was just a matter of time before she knew he was back in town anyway. The way the rumor mill worked in Nugget, he'd be surprised if she didn't know already. At least when she saw him now, he'd be leaving the restaurant with a beautiful redhead on his arm.

He flagged the waitress over and gave her his credit card. Sam and he were getting ready to leave when two young towheaded boys approached their table.

"Are you Lucky Rodriguez?" the older one asked.

"Yes, sir."

"Can I get your autograph?"

"Sure," Lucky said. "You got something for me to write it on?"

The boy patted his pockets, looking for anything he could come up with, while the other one ran back to his table, returning a few moments later with a couple of scraps of paper his mama had obviously fished out of her handbag.

"Will this work?" The kid was missing his front tooth and had a lisp. Lucky got a kick out of the boy.

"I don't see why not." He took the scraps of paper and borrowed a pen from Sam. "What're your names?" They told him and he wrote a quick acknowledgment to each one, ending with his John Hancock. "There you go."

They thanked him and ran off, reading their autographs.

"You get that a lot?" Sam asked.

"Yep." He wasn't boasting. Professional bull riders didn't get the same recognition as other athletes, but he had enough high-profile endorsements to get his face out there. He was especially popular in rural America.

"Does it bother you, having people invade your privacy like that?"

It wasn't like they were going through his trash. Most of the time it was kids and die-hard adult fans. Sometimes buckle bunnies who wanted more than an autograph. "Not really. Everyone is usually polite about it. Truth be told, I kind of like it."

Sam's lips quirked up. "That's sweet."

"Don't let it get around." He chuckled. "It could hurt my badass reputation."

"Your secret is safe with me."

Lucky put his hand at the small of Sam's back as they left the Ponderosa together. He couldn't tell whether Raylene had caught sight of them.

When they got outside, Sam said, "She saw."

He shrugged, like he couldn't care less, but Sam was on to him. They walked to Sam's car, waved goodbye, and Lucky got in his truck. He didn't feel like going home to the tin can he temporarily called his house. The stove top in the single-wide was busted and Lucky craved a home-cooked meal, so he headed to the place where the food was always good.

His mom's house smelled like fresh tortillas and lemon Pledge. For most of her adult life Cecilia Rodriguez had kept house at the Rock and River Ranch. Now she only kept her own. And it was always immaculate.

"Mijo." She kissed him "You hungry?"

"Starved," he said, and she ushered him into the kitchen, a big open space with all the latest appliances and gadgets. Lucky's mother enjoyed cooking and feeding people and he'd wanted her to have the best.

"How's the cowboy camp coming along?" She smiled up at him. At forty-eight, his mother was still a beautiful woman. Coal-black hair that fell to her shoulders and dark eyes that always seemed to dance with joy, even though her life hadn't always been joyous.

"It's coming. I just got out of a meeting with the event planner for the Lumber Baron. We're trying to do some cross promotion and work out a few packages that would include both our facilities."

"The runaway bride?"

He shook his head. "Samantha Dunsbury, a nice-looking redhead from Connecticut."

"That's her. You don't know her story?" She looked scandalized, then proceeded to tell him the whole sordid tale. "Everyone in Nugget calls her the runaway bride. You know, like that Julia Roberts movie."

"Don't you like her?" Most of the time Cecilia Rodriguez was a good judge of character. Unfortunately, not so much with Lucky's dad, who'd bailed the minute his son was born.

"I don't know her, *mijo*. But if you like her, I'm sure she's a very nice person. You want posole?" She dished him up a large bowl of the hominy-and-pork stew from the pot on the stove and warmed a few tortillas in the oven.

He dug in. He'd missed her cooking out on the road. Although Mexican food had become popular across the United States, most of it sucked. Hard-shell tacos and flavorless black beans. Yuck. "This is good."

"I have brownies for dessert." He didn't know how his mother stayed so slender cooking the way she did.

"I saw Raylene at the Ponderosa."

"Oh?" Cecilia scowled, having never made her disapproval of Raylene a secret.

"Ah, come on, Mom. Cut her some slack. You yourself said you felt sorry for her."

"I've known her since she was a little girl. So of course I feel bad about what happened to her. But, Lucky, that girl is no good for you. Stay away, *mijo*."

He couldn't really argue. Raylene had nearly cost Cecilia her job, not to mention ruining Lucky.

"Tell me about this Samantha Dunsbury. Does she seem as rich as everyone says?"

"Not really," Lucky said. "She dresses pretty slick, but she seems down-to-earth. Sam denies it, but I get the impression she and Nate Breyer, the owner of the Lumber Baron, have something going on. You know him?"

Cecilia shook her head. "Only the sister, Maddy. She's married to Rhys Shepard. Remember him?" Lucky nodded. "Both of them, sweethearts. Rhys's father died last summer. He had two kids from another marriage. One of them is grown, but the younger one, a boy, Rhys is raising now. Such a good man."

Lucky had gotten pretty well caught up since he'd gotten back. Except for the bit about Sam, nothing his mom said was new. But he let her talk, because like everyone else in Nugget, she liked to gossip. Nothing ever ugly, though. Cecilia Rodriguez didn't have a mean bone in her body.

"Hey, Ma, Clay McCreedy invited me to his wedding. You going?"

"Of course. You want to go together?"

"Sure." But Lucky had to wonder why after all these years his mother didn't have a man. Granted, Nugget didn't exactly have a lot of eligible bachelors his mother's age, but someone from one of her church organizations should've set her up. "You think Raylene got invited?"

"Probably," Cecilia said, and didn't sound happy about it. "The McCreedys have always been friendly with the Rossers. There's a couple of lovely new girls in town. Remember little Darla, Owen's daughter? She's running the barbershop now. And her best friend, Harlee Roberts, owns the *Nugget Tribune*. Darla is dating Wyatt Lambert and Harlee is engaged, but I bet they know some nice single women your age."

It wasn't like Lucky was hard up for women, but he knew his mother wanted to steer him away from Raylene. "Mom, you've got nothing to worry about."

But after having seen Raylene at the Ponderosa, he wasn't so sure that was true.

Chapter 12

Nate had only been back at the Lumber Baron ten minutes before Sam rushed into his office. He'd pulled in sometime before three after making the long drive from San Francisco, had barely taken off his jacket and gotten his computer booted up, to find her lurking in his doorway, looking as put together as usual. Today she had on a tight skirt and some kind of wraparound top that tied at the side. Her hair curled around her face in that choppy style Darla had given her and she wore red lipstick.

He looked her up and down. "The president coming to town?"

"We have a hot prospect to fill the chef's job."

"Why are you whispering?"

"Because he's waiting in the lobby and I wanted to warn you first."

"Warn me about what?" Nate kicked his feet up on the desk.

"He has tattoos covering his entire arms. Crazy, intricate designs that are a little scary, but kind of arty too."

"But can he cook?"

"We're not sure yet, but he dropped off a résumé yesterday. Emily knows some of the restaurants and she says they're good."

"Where's he from?" Nate asked.

"Charleston, originally. LA more recently."

Nate didn't like the sound of that. People coming up from big cities often got this romantic notion of living and working in a small town, until they did it for a few months and got bored out of their skulls. "How old would you say he is?" Employers weren't allowed to ask.

Sam lifted her palms in the air. "Late twenties, early thirties?"

Young was even worse. Not a lot of entertainment options unless you went to Reno. "I'll talk to him," Nate said. But he wasn't too hopeful.

"Nate, we need someone sooner rather than later. Emily is only filling in on the condition that we find someone permanently. Soon."

"All right, I'll talk to him." Hadn't he already said that? Pushy thing.

"Should we do it in the conference room?"

"Nah. We'll do it in here. But bring me his résumé, so I look like I know what I'm talking about."

She dashed off and returned with a neatly typed page. He quickly scanned the contents. The guy did seem to have a fair amount of cooking chops. Then again, people were known to lie on résumés. The test would be seeing what he could do in the kitchen. "Bring him in," Nate said.

"Yes, Your Royal Highness." Sam curtsied.

Yeah, he'd missed her mouth.

Sam came back with the guy, and sure enough he had serious ink. Sleeves going up both arms. Nate stood up and shook his hand.

According to his résumé, the man was Brady Benson, and he looked a little saddle worn. Nate offered him a seat and took his own. Sam sat on the couch.

"You live around here?" Nate asked.

"Nope. Just passing through."

"The job would require that you live here, or at least pretty close by." Nate wanted to ensure that this chef would stick for a while.

"That's what I figured," Brady said. "I'm down with that."

"You have a family?"

"Just me," the man of few words said.

Hell, Nate didn't care if the guy was a mute if he could cook and showed up on time. "If we were to hire you, when could you start?"

"Now."

Nate caught Sam's eye as if to say *What's with this guy?*

"Brady, why don't you tell us about yourself?" Sam said.

"Not much to tell." Brady looked from Sam to Nate. "I cook. And I really need a job."

Unfazed, Sam continued. "What would you say your style of cooking is?"

"New American."

"I'll be right back," Sam said, and quickly left the room. Nate wondered where the hell she'd disappeared to.

"What brought you through Nugget?" Nate liked stability in his employees, but it didn't seem like Brady had roots, not if he could settle here on a dime.

"Like I said, I was just passing through."

Sam rushed back in the room with a folder. "These have been our menus for the past two weeks. What would you do differently?"

Brady took the folder and slowly sorted through the menus. "These look pretty good, but instead of the croissants with olallieberry jam, I'd do biscuits and gravy with house-made sausage. Heartier and what people expect at a country inn. In fall, when berries go out of season, I'd replace the coulis-drizzled Belgian waffles with toasted-pecan pain perdu and apple compote.

"I've seen a lot of cattle ranches up here, so I'd probably do a chicken-fried steak using regional beef," he continued, surprising Nate with his sudden verbosity. "And I'd definitely make huevos rancheros one day a week using farm-fresh eggs and a nice *queso fresco*. For the afternoon wine and cheese, I'd stick with the local cheeses—I like to go local whenever possible—but I would add in some house-cured meats. I do killer *salumi*, and since you have the beef, a nice *bresaola* would be good. You have a cellar?"

"We have a crawl space that you can stand up in. I wouldn't exactly call it food safe, though," Nate said. Brady might be a mystery, but he had good ideas. So far, Nate had liked everything, he just didn't want it to cost him an arm and a leg.

"I can work with it," Brady said.

"Would you be willing to do a test run of a few of your dishes for Emily, our temporary chef?" Sam asked.

"Sure. Is she here now?"

"She left after breakfast, but I could try to get her back." Sam looked at Nate, who nodded in agreement, and slipped out to call Emily.

"I'll be honest with you, Brady. I like your ideas, but I'm worried there's not much to hold you here. It's a small town. Not a lot for a young single person."

"I'll make do," he said.

Sam came back. "She'll be here in ten. Why don't I take you into the kitchen and you can familiarize yourself with the equipment and help yourself to whatever ingredients we have."

Nate would give it to Sam. For someone who'd never worked a day in her life, she certainly had a knack for taking charge. It must've been all the charity events she'd planned. Part of the reason Maddy had been impressed with Sam in the first place was that she'd chaired so many big fund-raisers. Who knew Miss Junior League would come in so handy?

He let Sam get Brady situated in the kitchen and returned a few phone calls. He'd only left Tracy a few hours ago and already she was hounding him about the opera gala. Supposedly, the event organizer was turning out to be a real pain in the ass.

"The woman is certifiable," Tracy screeched into the phone. "She wants us to get Thomas Keller to cater the affair. I tried to explain to her that the Theodore does its own in-house catering, but she won't have it."

Nate didn't want to lose the event. It could be an annual feather in his cap. In the past, the ball had been held in San Francisco City Hall. But there had been a lot of political noise that the elite event—tickets cost thousands of dollars a head—being held in a public building was pissing off the 99 percent.

"Can we get Keller?" he asked.

"Uh, when pigs fly out of my ass. The man has two bicoastal Michelin three-star restaurants to run. Kind of busy."

"You want me to talk to her?" Nate offered.

"What can you say that I haven't, unless you have a direct pipeline to Alain Ducasse. That's her second chef choice. He doesn't even have a restaurant in the Bay Area. Seriously, the woman makes me want to kill myself."

"Well, don't do it on Breyer Hotel property. It's bad publicity, not to mention the mess."

"I'll be sure to keep that in mind," Tracy said.

"Trace, work this out, please. There's a bonus in it for you."

"When this is over, Nate, I want an all-expense-paid vacation in Hawaii."

"I'll see what I can do."

"Wanna come with me? Nothing but sun and fun."

"Not happening, Trace. Make nice with the lady, okay?" Sam

walked in, and the idea of going to Hawaii with her seemed much more appealing than Tracy. He started to visualize Sam in a bikini and stopped himself. "Hey, I've got to go. Have good news for me when I call you tomorrow."

Nate hung up and Sam said, "Brady's doing prep. I'll call you when he has something for you to try."

"Sounds good."

A half hour later, Sam motioned for him to follow her into the kitchen, where delicious smells made his mouth water. Both Brady and Emily wore chef whites and stood over a large frittata and some kind of potato dish.

"Sour cream coffee cake is still in the oven," Emily said. "But dig in while it's hot."

Nate didn't need to be asked twice. He hadn't had lunch and was starved. Emily handed him a fork and he dug into the egg dish first. "Jesus Christ, this is good."

"Not Jesus, just me," Brady said, and Nate was surprised to find that the reticent chef had a sense of humor.

Nate made eye contact with Emily and she gave him an affirmative nod. The message clear: Brady Benson could cook. Nate tried the potatoes, which were equally good, and decided to hang out in the kitchen until the coffee cake was done.

Brady seemed to loosen up. Maybe he felt more comfortable around a stove.

"You have any prospects on a place to live?" Nate asked.

"Does that mean I have the job?"

"We'll have to discuss salary first. I'll need to talk to a few of your references. You know the drill. But if everything checks out, the job is yours." It's not like Nate had a lot of trained cooks banging on his door.

The oven timer buzzed and Brady pulled the cake out. "Sounds good. Any of you know a cheap place I can rent?"

"I might," Nate said. "Let me make a few calls."

First, Nate wanted to talk money. As soon as Brady got a load of the pay, there was a good chance he'd turn the job down. But just one bite of the coffee cake, and Nate knew he had to strike a deal.

When Sam got home from work, her answering machine was lit up like Times Square. Two calls, which was peculiar, because no one used the landline. She dug her cell out of her purse only to find it dead. That explained that.

She plugged it into her docking station to charge and pressed the button on the answering machine.

"Oh. My. God." Wendy sounded positively apoplectic. "You would not believe what that turd, Royce Whitley, has done. Call me."

The next call was from her father. For the last couple of days they'd played phone tag—Sam intentionally calling him at hours when she knew he wouldn't pick up. She just didn't have the fortitude to fight with him.

"Samantha, I really wish you would stop ducking my calls." While he droned on about her being the worst daughter since Lizzie Borden, she changed out of her work clothes into something loose and comfortable. "I've been trying to let you know that Royce has gotten engaged and has let it leak that it was he who broke it off with you. Some rubbish about him being in love with Carolyn Bradley. That's who he's engaged to, by the way. Please have the decency to call me back."

Sam erased both messages. Carolyn Bradley? The woman was a year older than Sam, skinny as a toothpick and dull as C-SPAN. Sam should've been outraged, or at the very least insulted, that Royce was so desperate for an acceptable wife that he would choose anyone with the right last name. Instead, she felt nothing. Frankly, she couldn't be bothered, not even for her father's sake. That's what he got for being superficial. And Royce, well, he'd proven to be a complete phony.

In the time she'd lived in Nugget, last names and people's financial worth had ceased to matter. No one here cared about her bank account or the fact that she was a Dunsbury. If anything it seemed to be a liability, especially where Nate was concerned.

She peeked outside her window to see if he was home yet. Watching his house had become her latest preoccupation. But before leaving the inn for the day, he'd told her that he was heading over to Sophie and Mariah's house to see Lilly. He was devoted to that baby, and she wondered if it was difficult for him not having a more permanent place in the child's life. If not for Lilly, Nate never would have struck her as daddy material. He'd told her himself that he was a confirmed bachelor.

And today she was pretty sure she'd caught him flirting with Tracy on the phone. No question the woman wanted him in the worst way. Sam could tell from their first meeting. Tracy had practically drooled over him, shoving her breasts in his face every chance she got. Sam had gotten the distinct impression that Nate wasn't interested. But maybe while he was in San Francisco, Tracy had worked him over with those boobs of hers.

She certainly was attractive enough. Clearly, Nate thought she was the best event planner on the face of the earth. Sam, not so much. Good old Tracy had nearly blown the Landon Lowery deal. It had been Sam who'd saved it using some of the basic tricks she'd learned planning charity events. Getting people to cough up megabucks year after year for the same event took a certain degree of ingenuity. Every event had to have a gimmick, whether it was a big-name entertainer or a fantastic prize that wasn't otherwise available for any price. Like dinner with the *Times* restaurant critic, or winemaking with Helen Turley, or being Lady Gaga's roadie for the day. In order to snag these plums, you had to know people. So Sam had made it her business to know everyone, just like she'd been doing in Nugget.

As a result she'd managed to raise millions for organizations like the Make-a-Wish Foundation, Wounded Warrior Project, and United Way. Event planning for a hotel wasn't that different. If anything, it was easier.

Sam took a quick glance out the window again. Still no sign of Nate. If he knew how often she checked for him, he'd slap her with a restraining order. But she liked knowing he was there. Not because she was afraid of being alone. Griffin lived just a short distance away and there were others scattered across the development. It was just that Nate . . . Oh hell, she didn't know why. She just liked him. Like really liked him. Stupid, since he'd made it perfectly clear that he wasn't interested.

She checked one more time for his car or a light, and when she didn't see either, she called her father. It was ten o'clock his time. A bit late, but not late enough that he wouldn't still be up.

She waited while the phone rang, dreading the conversation. It was always the same old, same old, "Sam, come home." He answered in a gruff voice.

"Hi, Daddy. Did I catch you at a bad time?"

"Did you get my message?" was all he said.

"About Royce? Yes."

"The jackass." Her father grunted. "All right, Sam, you've won. Now stop this ridiculous charade and come home."

Right on cue, Sam thought. The man was nothing if not predictable. "Daddy, I don't think you understand. I've made a life for myself here. I'm happy."

"Working at a small inn in the middle of nowhere? You've got to be kidding me. Samantha, if I knew you wanted to work in the hospitality industry, I could've set you up in New York. The Waldorf, the Four Seasons, whatever you wanted."

"That's the thing, Daddy, it wasn't until I came here that I figured out what I wanted to do. I suppose all those years planning events on my charity committees were good for something."

The other end of the phone went silent.

"Are you still there?" Sam asked.

"I'm here. Well, at least come home and show your face until this absurdness with Royce blows over. Let people see you're unfazed by it."

"I am unfazed by it, Daddy. I don't need to let people see that, because it's the truth. Besides, I can't leave now. We're coming up on the thick of our tourism season."

"For God's sake, Sam, stop this. Your place is here, not in some town I've never heard of. Don't you want to spend a couple of weeks in the summerhouse? Or should I go back to selling it?"

"If you want me to go back to suing you." She still had that ace up her sleeve, even if her legal grounds were flimsy. The whole point of it was to make a scene, because George Dunsbury hated scenes.

"Enough, Sam. You know as well as I do that you don't have a case. But you know a lawsuit would grab headlines and embarrass me. It's extortion, plain and simple."

"Just like you selling the summerhouse. You know the house means the world to me. Yet you're willing to hold it over my head to get your way."

"When did you become so stubborn, Sam? You're my only child, and I want you home."

"Come visit me, Daddy. It's beautiful here. You could play golf and go fishing." And meet the town's crazies, like Owen. "There's a world champion bull rider who's opening a dude ranch nearby. We're planning to combine our facilities for various guest packages and I would love to show you the place. And the inn, Daddy. It's a fantastic

Victorian, built more than one hundred fifty years ago by a lumber baron for his bride. Between the gold rush and the Donner Party, the place is drenched in history."

All she got on the other end of the phone was a long sigh.

"Let me know when you plan to come home, Samantha," he said, and clicked off.

Well, that went well. He had some nerve calling her stubborn. The man could write the book on being obstinate. Next, she tried Wendy and left a message. Maybe her friend was out on a hot date. At least someone was.

Sam went into the great room, planning to watch some television, got a glass of water in the kitchen, and glanced out the window over the sink. Finally, signs of life at Nate's house. A few lights illuminated his interior. She must've missed the sound of his garage door opening and closing while she was on the phone.

After flipping through the channels and finding nothing on TV, Sam decided to read. But her book didn't hold her interest, so she put it down and leafed through Emily's wedding binder, checking on her to-do list. Except there wasn't much to do. She'd done it all.

Too early to go to sleep, she was bored senseless. Peering out the window again, she wondered what Nate was doing. She wandered into her bedroom and examined her outfit in the full-length mirror. A pair of lightweight cashmere lounge pants and a hoodie she'd gotten at Barneys. If she put her bra back on, she'd be acceptable for company. In the bathroom, Sam brushed her hair and freshened up her makeup. Nothing too overt. Just a little more mascara and a touch of lip gloss.

On her way out of the house she slipped on a pair of flats, grabbed a bottle of merlot, and walked over to Nate's house. Nowadays, it didn't get dark until well after eight. Maybe they could sit on Nate's back deck and watch the sun set.

She rang the bell and he came to the door in a pair of faded jeans with rips in the knees and a T-shirt that stretched across his wide chest and emphasized his flat stomach. Nate in a suit was perfection. But Nate in Levi's was a work of art.

"Hey," he said. "What brings you by?"

She held up the bottle of wine. "I thought we could hang out on your deck and drink this."

He pointedly stared at her deck, a twin of his own. "What's wrong with yours?"

"You want to come over to mine? We can do that."

"Sam, I thought we talked about this. It's not a good idea. I'm your boss and you're clearly obsessed with me." He grinned at her wolfishly. The man pretended to be full of himself, but Sam knew he wasn't. For some reason she felt completely comfortable with the sarcastic fool.

"Don't flatter yourself, Nate. You're not that great, but I'm desperate for company."

"Why?" He seemed concerned.

She lifted her shoulders. "Just frustrated."

"Oh?" He arched a brow.

"Not like that, you jerk. I had an argument with my father."

He swung his arm wide to usher her inside. His house, the same model as hers, was empty. No furniture, no pictures, no rugs, no nothing. Who lived like that? Nate led the way to the back deck, which had a beautiful view of the golf course and the surrounding mountains. But, like the rest of the house, it was bare, not even a folding chair. She sat on the edge of the deck and dangled her legs off the side.

"I'll be right back." He returned with two juice glasses and a corkscrew. "Sorry, this is all I have."

"You need to do some shopping. Get some furniture."

"Yeah, I'll get around to it eventually. I'm a little short on time these days."

"You could go online," she said. "Most stores will deliver right to your door, you know?"

"If you care so much, why don't you do it for me?" He grabbed a wallet out of his back pocket and shoved a credit card at her, grinning like he'd gotten the better of her.

"I'll do it." She snatched the card out of his hand. "When I'm done with the place, you won't recognize it."

"That's what I'm afraid of." He tried to grab the Visa back, but she wouldn't let him.

"What's your budget?"

"You seriously want to do it? Because if you do, I'll actually make an exception to the overtime rule. Be sure to keep track of your hours. Don't do anything on your own time."

She'd volunteered to do it as a friend, not as his employee. But that was Nate—all business. "Okay."

"You won't make it look like a girl's house, will you? I had a girlfriend once who put frilly pillows everywhere. It took two hours to make the bed."

She tucked the card into the pouch of her hoodie. "No frilly pillows." Sam pretended to make a note. "How about I get your approval before making any purchases. That work?"

"Yep," he said. "If you're sure you want to do it."

"It'll be fun. I like spending other people's money."

"I bet you do." He shook his head. "What's going on with your old man?"

"He's like a broken record. He's still harping on me to come home and take my rightful place as his only child. You're lucky you have siblings." And normal parents.

"You thinking of going back?" He watched her closely.

"No, Nate. Why are you so sure I'll bolt? I like it here."

"But for how long?" he muttered, then addressed her directly. "What did you tell him?"

"That he should come visit, see the place, see the inn. He practically hung up on me."

He gave her a commiserating look. "Maybe he'll come around."

Sam sincerely doubted it, but nodded her head anyway. Nate opened the wine and filled both of their juice glasses.

"Royce got engaged," she blurted. "I think that's what set Daddy off."

"Your ex? The guy you ran out on?"

"The one and only." She flashed him a saccharine smile. "Apparently Royce is telling everyone that he left me for his new fiancée."

"And that's not true, right, because you left him?" He said it like he almost wished Royce's version was the real one.

The reason she dumped Royce was no one's business, least of all Nate's. He didn't need to know her mortification.

"Right," she said. "I don't think Royce knew this woman as anything more than an acquaintance while we were together."

"Hey, he has a right to try to save face. You ever think you might've crushed the guy, like completely ruined him?"

She laughed and found him glaring at her as if she were the coldest of bitches. "You don't know anything about it, Nate."

"More than you think," he said.

Whatever that meant. Sam didn't want to get into it with him. As far as she was concerned, Royce was ancient history and the horrible things he'd said about her never needed to be repeated. "What do you think of Brady?"

Nate raised his shoulders. "We're desperate and he can cook. Do I think he'll last? Hell no."

"Why? It's a great job in a beautiful place. And he himself said he needs work."

"Sam, did you ever stop to think why someone who seems as competent in a kitchen as he does suddenly needs work? And who just wanders through Nugget?"

"I did," she said.

"My point exactly."

She nudged him. "What turned you into such a cynic? Perhaps he's looking for a fresh start."

"From what, is the question. If I were a betting man, I'd say he's running from something."

"You think it's bad, like he's wanted by the law?"

"I doubt it's anything that serious, but you can bet I'll have Rhys run a background check on him. Let's keep our fingers crossed that he's not an ax murderer, because we need him and I'm still dreaming about that coffee cake."

"It was good, wasn't it? Once he loosened up, he seemed sort of nice. Emily liked him. She didn't even seem fazed by his tattoos— said a lot of young chefs these days have them. Do you really know a place he can live? I don't get the sense he has a lot of money. He drives a beat-up van, which I'm pretty sure he's living in. While he waited for you to return from San Francisco to do the interview, he camped in the state park."

"Rhys owns a duplex on Donner Road," Nate said. "That's where he and Maddy used to live before they bought their current house. If Brady checks out, Rhys might rent to him. I think at least one side of the duplex is vacant. The price shouldn't be too steep and I might be willing to float him an advance if he seems solid."

"That's nice of you, Nate."

"No, it's good business."

She knew it was more than that. Despite his jaded-guy act, Sam could see that Nate was a good person. Look what he'd done for Sophie and Mariah.

"How's Lilly?" she asked, and watched his face brighten.

Sam had never seen a man get so mushy over a baby. Sometimes she'd watch him in the Ponderosa cuddling Lilly, and get shivers. A big, handsome man holding a little bitty baby was nothing short of hot.

"She's good," he said. "Growing fast."

"You mind if I ask you a personal question?"

"I won't know until you ask it," he said, and topped off their juice glasses.

"How does that work with the three of you? I mean as far as parenting."

"Sophie and Mariah are Lilly's parents," he said. "I'm her biological father, but they're raising her."

"Is it difficult . . . you know, giving that up?"

"That was always the plan," he said, which didn't really answer Sam's question. "They're great parents. Why, you have a problem with it?"

"No, of course not," she said. "I think it's wonderful what you did." Everyone in town did, which sort of surprised her, given her upbringing in conservative Greenwich. "I just figure that it could've gotten complicated. Do you ever want children of your own?"

He gave a nonchalant shrug. "Someday, I suppose. How about you? Were you and Royce planning to have a horde of rug rats?"

"We never talked about it." Unless she counted the night of the rehearsal dinner. "Don't you think couples should talk about something as important as children?"

"I don't know. Maybe he thought, why bother, since you were planning to give him the old heave-ho anyway."

She shook her head in irritation. Nate sure did seem to have a problem with her and Royce's breakup. You'd think it was him she'd left at the altar. "How many children do you want to have?"

"Two always seemed like a good round number. My parents had three. That would work too. How 'bout you?"

She smiled. "Two. Ideally a boy and a girl. But I'd be ecstatic no matter what."

He looked at her. Really looked.

"What?" she asked.

"Nothing. So why do you think you and Royce never discussed babies?"

It was a good question. She and Nate weren't even seeing each other and they'd discussed the topic more than she and Royce ever had. In hindsight, maybe she'd known all along that she and Royce were never meant to be.

"I don't think our relationship ever reached that kind of maturity," she said, wanting to shelve the topic. "What about you and Lilly? Are you planning to tell her you're her biological father?"

"It's not like we could keep it a secret in this town. Sophie and Mariah plan to tell her when she's old enough to understand."

"And what if you have children? How will that work?"

"It's complicated, Sam. Not stuff we've really worked out yet."

Her face heated. "I'm sorry. I'm usually not this prying. I've just seen you with Lilly . . . and . . . I can see that it's complex."

"Yep." He held up the bottle of wine. "Want a refill?"

"Sure. The first things I'm buying you are real wine glasses."

"A few plates would be good too. And a coffeemaker, while you're at it." He flashed her a cheeky grin.

"Are you staying in Nugget for a while?" She tried to make it sound like a casual question, but the days went by slower when Nate was in San Francisco.

"I've got to go back in a few days and put out some fires. You ready for the bridal expo?"

She nodded, excited about seeing the Belvedere. "Will I be able to visit any of the other Breyer properties while I'm in San Francisco?"

"I'll try to make that happen for you," he said, and she interpreted it as he would find someone else to give her the tour.

"I heard you talking to Tracy today," she slipped in. "Anything going on?"

He shook his head. "Nothing more than the usual craziness."

"Are you and Tracy . . . a thing?" She couldn't help asking. Besides it not being her business, why should she care? Other than the kiss, of course.

"Why? You jealous?"

"No . . . don't be silly. Of course not."

Brows up, he said, "I don't fool around with employees."

Ha, Sam laughed to herself. Not unless he was kissing the breath out of them. "But if she weren't your employee—?"

"Not my type."

"What is your type?"

"Physically, you. But everything else about you is wrong."

She flinched. "That was an awfully mean thing to say."

"I bet Royce doesn't think so."

She got to her feet, but before she could walk out on him, he pulled her into an embrace, crushed her against his chest and kissed her until she actually felt the world turn on its axis. Ravenous, his mouth moved over hers, plundering. He tasted like wine and man and she could feel his heat and hardness pressing against her.

"I don't want to do this," he whispered against her mouth.

"Then stop." He made her so crazy with desire she could barely find her equilibrium.

"Can't." It came out like a harsh croak.

"I'll make it easy for you." Summoning all her willpower—and her dignity—she pushed away from him. "Good night, Nate."

Chapter 13

Nate lay in bed, watching the morning sunlight stream through his blinds, trying to stave off a headache, while wishing that the previous night had merely been a bad dream.

What the hell had he been thinking, sticking his tongue down Samantha's throat, especially after he'd sworn off her following the first kiss? He clearly liked living on the edge. The woman would accuse him of sexual harassment and have his company if he wasn't careful—or worse, his heart.

There were a million females more suitable for him than Princess Samantha. Women who weren't dilettantes on a mission to find themselves at everyone else's expense. Women who didn't run away from their wealthy, powerful fathers just to be rebellious. And most of all, women who could commit—not sneak away at dawn's early light.

He got out of bed, hoping a hot shower would help him come up with a plan for damage control.

Nate needed to apologize to Sam in a big way. But instead of finding her at the inn, Dink Caruthers, Nugget's mayor, was waiting for him at the front desk.

"Your Honor," Nate greeted facetiously. There was nothing honorable about wearing a polyester Western suit. Or having a name like Dink, for that matter.

"Nate." The mayor tipped his head. "You got a few minutes?"

Not really, but he couldn't very well tell the mayor that. "Sure. Let's sit in my office."

"The Addisons are concerned that you're running a restaurant without the proper permits." Dink got comfortable in one of Nate's chairs.

"The Addisons clearly have a drug problem. I'm thinking black tar heroin."

"That's some strong allegations, boy."

Nate rolled his eyes. "Dink, do you see us running a restaurant? We're a bed and breakfast. Shockingly enough, we serve our guests breakfast."

"Now don't go getting all hot under the collar. They asked me to look into it and that's what I'm doing. They said you just hired a fancy chef down from Los Angeles, some reality TV star on that *Top Chef* show."

"Reality TV star?" If he was talking about Brady, the guy lived in a freaking van. "We hired a chef to replace the one we had. The one who cooked breakfasts for our guests, because I'll repeat: We're a bed and breakfast. No big conspiracy, Dink."

"All right, all right. But if you're running some kind of restaurant on the side, you know I'll have to shut you down, right?"

Nate blew out a breath. "Are you checking on their pool permits? How do you know they're not turning the Beary Quaint into Marine World? Hell, that damned dump is already the equivalent of Country Bear Jamboree. Do they have a permit for a theme park?"

Dink got to his feet. "All right, boy, you've made your point. We miss that sister of yours. When is she coming back?"

Not soon enough to suit Nate. "A couple of months," he said.

"How's that nice redhead working out?"

After last night, the jury was out on that one. "Great." Especially when she was climbing him like a tree for more kisses.

Before Dink could ask any more of his annoying questions, Rhys filled Nate's doorway.

"Hey there, Mr. Mayor," Rhys said, turning on his bullshit Texas charm. "How y'all doing?"

"Real fine, Chief. But maybe you ought to tell your brother-in-law here to take a chill pill." With that, Dink sauntered out of the inn.

"A chill pill?" Rhys cocked a brow. "What was that about?"

"The Addisons are complaining that we're running an underground restaurant."

Rhys chuckled. "See what Maddy has to put up with when you're not around? I've got some good news for you, though. The chef checks out. Nothing negative I could find."

"What's this rumor about him being on that *Top Chef* show? That's what the Addisons told Dink."

"It didn't come up in any of the searches I ran," Rhys said. "Does it matter?"

Nate hitched his shoulders. "It might drum up a little publicity for the inn."

"Then why don't you just ask him? Hey, Maddy and I want to give Clay and Emily a weekend getaway for their wedding gift. They're not taking a honeymoon until winter, when the kids are back in school. Maddy suggested the Theodore."

"You want me to hook you up?" Nate asked.

"Yep. We want all the bells and whistles. Will a thousand cover it?"

Rhys had to be kidding. "Consider it taken care of."

"Maddy said you'd say that. Look, it wouldn't be much of a gift if we didn't pay for it."

"Whatever happened to 'it's the thought that counts'?" Nate asked. "Buy 'em dinner and a show. That'll set you back. In the meantime, I'll reserve a suite for them in your name and have a complimentary VIP basket sent up. The works."

"Aw, that's great. Thanks, Nate."

"Not a problem."

"You bringing anyone to the wedding?" Rhys asked.

"I hadn't really thought about it. Probably not."

"What about the redhead?"

Nate pinned his brother-in-law with a glare. "Maddy put you up to this, didn't she? Tell her I'm perfectly capable of finding my own dates."

Rhys's top lip quirked. Other than that he wasn't giving anything away. "I heard she's done a hell of a job helping Emily put that reception together. Clay's invited near half the county."

"She's good at planning parties," Nate said. "She's had a lot of practice."

"She's also good-looking. Anything there?" Rhys arched his brows in question.

"Don't you have a town to keep safe?"

One thing about his brother-in-law, he could take a hint. He got up. "I guess that's my cue to leave. See you around."

"Thanks for checking out Brady."

"When does he start?"

"As soon as he can find a living situation. Which reminds me, you still have a vacancy in the duplex?"

"Both sides are vacant," Rhys said. "He can have his choice. Rent's six hundred a month with a twelve hundred dollar deposit. If that's a problem, I'm sure we can swing something."

"Great. I'll let him know."

After Rhys left, Nate could no longer put off the inevitable and called Tracy.

She picked up on the third ring and said, "It's about time."

"Nice to talk to you too. How's it going on the gala?"

"That's why I've been trying to call you," Tracy said, and Nate checked his cell, which he'd inadvertently turned to silent. Four messages. "Nut Ball, queen of the bitches, has now decided that she will accept the Theodore's chef as long as he does Thomas Keller's menu, which our chef says is plagiarism. Richard said, and I quote, *'I'd rather drain my own veins before I cook someone else's dishes.'* These people are driving me crazy, Nate."

"All right, I'll talk to Richard. We'll work something out. Stay calm. You ready for the bridal expo next weekend?"

"Oh God, you're not making me do that again, are you? Send Lisa or Randall."

"Tracy, you're head of event planning for Breyer Hotels—a vice president in the company. Why would I send anyone other than you?"

"Because my time is too valuable to be selling stupid wedding packages, especially when I can be snagging the big fish, like tech conferences and corporate events."

Yeah, because you did so well with Landon Lowery. "Wedding packages are our bread and butter, Tracy. So this is nonnegotiable. See you in a few days." He hung up.

One temperamental female down, another to go. Nate headed to Sam's office and knocked on the door.

"Come in," she called, and he went inside and shut the door behind him. "What do you think of these wine glasses?" She turned her computer monitor toward him so he could get a view of the stemware.

"They're fine," he said. "What are they for?"

"Your house." She flipped to another picture of goblets. "Or we could go with these."

"Sam . . . Sam. Look at me, Sam." She finally pulled her head away from the computer. "I'm sorry. I screwed up last night. *Again.* You think we could—"

"Forget it?" she said, cutting him off.

That wasn't what he was going to say, but—

"Okay, let's forget it," she continued. "In fact, let's pretend it never happened and move on. No more after-work visits. No neighborly chats on the deck. From now on, we'll keep everything strictly professional. So if that's all, I'm really busy."

"Fine," he said, duly chastised, and started to walk out the door.

"Which glasses did you want?"

"Uh, the first ones looked good. But whatever you think."

"Fine," she said as she clicked away on her computer.

"Sam?"

"What?"

"Uh, thanks for doing that." He pointed to the wineglass website, then left with his tail between his legs.

The next couple of days passed in telephone back-and-forths between him and Richard and Tracy, highlighting all the reasons why he needed to be in San Francisco and not Nugget. The truth was the Lumber Baron was in good hands. Sam, who rarely talked to him anymore, had conquered the place. Loved by the guests, more organized than anyone he knew and a multitasker by nature, she had no problem running the Lumber Baron in his absence.

What she had was a problem with him. He suspected that she hadn't taken well to his comment about her being his physical type but that he didn't like anything else about her. It was akin to saying, *I'd like to do you as long as you leave after I'm finished, because you bug the crap out of me.* And then, to make matters worse, he'd grabbed her ass and given her a tonsillectomy with his tongue.

Nate would never win awards for being the most sensitive man, but even he knew that he'd done irreparable harm to their relationship, such as it was. It was for the best, he kept telling himself. They'd been getting too friendly, reminding him all too well of how it had been with Kayla in the beginning. Back when she'd hung on his every word and then abruptly lost interest the night before four hundred of their best friends and family were due to attend their wedding. He certainly didn't need a repeat performance of that disaster.

He and Kayla had met at a Harvard mixer. Out of a roomful of brash MBAs, all tussling to appear smarter and more aggressive than the next, she'd chosen him to spill her drink on. Later, she confessed to doing it on purpose.

But that night, her cheeks pinked prettily and she apologized profusely, whipping off her Hermès scarf and patting him dry.

"It's okay," he assured her, taking her in from head to toe.

Her blond hair had been swept back in a sleek ponytail, showing off high cheekbones, a prominent nose, a slightly too-wide mouth and pale blue eyes that danced when she talked. She wasn't textbook beautiful, but she had that extra, undefinable something that turned heads. And his was spinning.

Two hours later he took her home, took off her clothes, and took her to bed. And when they woke up the next morning, he didn't want her to leave. Ever. And that had never happened to him before.

"What is it about you?" he teased.

Naked, she propped herself up on the bed and said, "I'm your It Girl."

He didn't even know what that meant, but he liked the sound of it, so from then on he called her his It Girl. That first month they were stuck like glue, attending parties at her society friends' homes, visiting Cambridge and Boston museums, and eating takeout on the floor of his apartment.

The next month she took him home to meet her parents. He had known that Kayla was a Cumberland, but not until they visited the estate did he fully understand what being part of one of America's most moneyed families entailed. First off, her family home was entrenched in history, from the portraits on the walls to the antique patina on the furniture. Second, there seemed to be an endless supply of relatives who lived there. Some, apparently, had never left the estate.

And as nice and down-to-earth as her parents seemed, they'd run a background check on him. They knew that his parents owned and operated hotels, his grandparents were Wisconsin dairy farmers, where he'd gone to high school (Kayla didn't even know that), and his GPA as an undergrad.

"You're one of those smart fuckers," her father announced. No one seemed shocked that Milton Cumberland, one of the richest men on earth, cursed like a truck driver.

At one point, sometime between dessert and cognac, Milton took him aside and said, "You seem good for our girl."

By the time they left, Nate felt like he'd passed the test. "I think that went well," he told Kayla.

"It went fabulous, darling," she said in a voice she reserved for self-deprecation. Kayla liked mocking her wealthy culture. It made her feel one with the people.

In their second month together, Kayla dropped out of Harvard law. She came to Nate's apartment after taking a torts exam and announced that she'd had an epiphany.

"The world is full of lawyers, people who make sense of civilization by twisting and manipulating the facts to serve their own ends. It's disgusting."

He wrapped her in his arms and kissed her on the forehead. "You blew the test, didn't you?"

"I most certainly did not." She pulled away. "If you must know, I aced it. Of course I won't get my grade for another week or two, but I knew every answer. The test was tedious, a lot of memorization of useless facts. I'm done with law school, Nate. I've decided that if I want to make a difference in the future of this great world, I have to study the past."

A few weeks later, she enrolled in archaeology classes in Harvard's Department of Anthropology. If Nate had been on his game and not crazy in love, he might've seen her impulsiveness as a red flag. Instead, he saw her newly found obsession with human bones and fossils charming. She was so different from him. He chose a course and stuck to it, no deviations, no last-minute lightning bolts, no newfound passions that would highjack his old ones. From childhood, Nate wanted to own and operate hotels. Even when the goal seemed unattainable, like during the 2008 recession, when obtaining bank loans and private venture capital seemed as likely as winning the lottery, Nate kept his nose to the grindstone.

So Kayla's spontaneity was infectious. She dragged him to exhibits, lectures, and even a local dig where construction workers had stumbled upon a Native American burial site. For weeks, she immersed herself in the study of human history.

And then, just like an earthquake when there are no warning

signs, her interest in archaeology caved in and crumbled like an ancient civilization.

"It's so incremental," she grumbled. "It takes years, decades, and even centuries to analyze a culture. I need to feel like I'm accomplishing something now, like I'm making a marked difference in someone's life."

She decided that the best way to immediately save the world was to feed it, and a few weeks later registered at Le Cordon Bleu College of Culinary Arts in Boston. The cooking school was close to Harvard and Nate told himself that this was a good thing. She was now entering his world—the hospitality industry—and together there wasn't anything they couldn't accomplish.

When he told his parents the news, they seemed less than enthused. "She sure does change her mind a lot," Nate's father said.

Maddy tried to be more optimistic. "It sounds like she has ADD, but hey, she's finding herself. That's good, right?"

A couple of months later, Nate thought Kayla's career indecision was over. He'd never seen her more happy. The woman was born to cook. Often she showed off her new culinary skills by whipping up gourmet meals and complicated pastries. As a graduate student, he'd never eaten so well and his belly was starting to show it.

"Hey, Kay, they teach you how to make anything healthy at that cooking school?" he said as he dressed one morning for class. "I'm getting fat."

"You are not," she argued, pushing him down on the bed and unbuttoning his shirt to have a look for herself. "And even if you were, I'd love you forever."

"Yeah? Maybe we should get married then." And there, without a ring, on the unmade bed with her sprawled on top of him, he proposed.

"Let's do it now, Nate, and surprise everyone."

"Don't you want a wedding, baby?"

"Weddings are so bougie."

He didn't think they were. Weddings were traditional and he liked traditional. But later, he would always wonder what would have happened if they'd just run off and done it.

"That would make my mother, and I suspect yours, unhappy," he told her, undoing the zipper on her jeans. "We don't have to do a long engagement, but we should plan something."

"Whatever you want, Nate. Because I love you that much . . . and this much," she said, stripping him bare and rocking his world.

They decided on spring, which was only two months away. Kayla vacillated between having a large wedding and a small one. Eventually, they settled on holding it at the Cumberland estate and inviting four hundred guests. And for a woman who originally didn't want a wedding, Kayla went to town. She delved into color schemes, menus, and seating charts with the same manic fervor as she did all her new projects.

At night, when they lay in bed, they talked about their future. Going to San Francisco, where Nate had a job waiting as soon as he finished school and Kayla had unlimited culinary opportunities. They talked about kids and where they should live and how they would grow beautifully old together.

Everything was perfect. No signals that Kayla was unhappy or having second thoughts.

After the rehearsal dinner, an intimate party with just immediate family and a few close friends, Nate dropped his parents and sisters off at their hotel. Superstitious, Kayla went back to the Cumberland compound, afraid that being together on the eve of their wedding would bring them bad luck.

At ten o'clock, while Nate packed a suitcase for the honeymoon, his phone rang. It was Milton Cumberland.

"I think you should come over," he told Nate.

"Is everything all right?" Clearly it wasn't, unless old Milt wanted to get his drink on early and wanted company, which wasn't totally uncharacteristic for him.

"Kayla's got a case of the jitters. Neither her mother nor I can talk her down. We thought you should come."

Nate bit back a sigh. "I'll be right there."

It took him eleven minutes to get to Back Bay, where Kayla had locked herself in her room. "Kay"—he knocked on the door—"let's talk it out, honey."

Still wearing her rehearsal dress, she let him in. "I can't, Nate. I've made up my mind. To go through with this wedding would be a farce."

"Slow down, Kayla, and tell me what's wrong."

"I should never have said yes to this." She held her arms wide, and he wasn't sure if she meant yes to having the wedding on the estate, to sleeping in her own room, or to marriage in general. That was the thing about Kayla; her internal dialog moved at warp speed and it was impossible for the rest of the world to keep up.

"Yes to what? Us getting married?"

She nodded and started to cry. "Being a wife . . . it's just so archaic. Tyrannical, actually."

He handed her a tissue so she could blow her nose and tried to stay calm. This was Kayla, after all. These little fits of whimsy had been what attracted him to her in the first place. "Kayla, honey, I don't know what you're talking about. Yesterday you were crazy about the idea of being my wife. When have I ever been tyrannical?"

"Not you, per se, but the institution of marriage. It's all bullshit, Nate." She wiped her nose on the sleeve of her dress.

"We don't have to be like everyone else, Kay. We'll have a different marriage. A completely non-tyrannical marriage." This talk about tyranny was completely crazy, but right now he'd say anything to calm her down and get her back on track.

"No." She shook her head. "Don't buy into it, Nate."

He gently clasped her shoulders. "What are you saying, Kayla? You want to call off the wedding?"

She took off her engagement ring and put it in Nate's palm. "It's for the best, Nate, before we start hating each other."

"Start hating each other?" Where the hell had that come from? "Up until a few hours ago you told me I was the love of your life."

"I've had time to think about it and I believe it was an illusion. I wanted to love you, so I convinced myself. But it was never real, Nate." She got off the bed and opened the door. "My parents will take care of notifying everyone. But I think you should leave now."

Nate was a proud man. Never in his life had he begged for anything, but he got down on the floor and groveled. He pleaded and said they could buck the institution of marriage and continue to live together, even though he wanted it all. He made a lot of promises that no self-respecting person makes. Anything to keep her from leaving him. But she was done, just like she'd been done with being a lawyer and an archaeologist.

After he left the Cumberlands he went to the hotel and told his family.

"The woman is obviously mentally ill," his mother said. "Who does something like this?"

But Nate knew the truth. Kayla's craziness was an act—an affectation that she thought made her seem more interesting. When in fact, she was nothing but a spoiled, mercurial rich girl who used people and hobbies to keep her entertained until she found something more amusing.

Samantha Dunsbury might come off saner than Kayla, but the two of them were cut from the same cloth. If you didn't believe him, just ask Royce Whitley.

Chapter 14

"No, I think they should go here," Sam told the furniture delivery guys who had put Nate's new couches in the wrong spot.

She wanted the seating to take advantage of the view, the fireplace, and the flat-screen TV. No easy feat, given the configuration of the room. The furniture had arrived in record time and luckily Nate had given her his key before he'd left for San Francisco.

Good riddance to the creep.

She'd only gone through with decorating his house because she'd said she would. Sam kept her word. And wouldn't he be surprised when he got home? The place was shaping up nicely. After approving her first few purchases, he'd given her permission to do the rest without him. Apparently, he trusted her taste, even though he didn't like anything else about her. Oh, except for her body. He'd made it perfectly clear he liked that just fine.

"That's much better," she told the men, who now had the two couches in the proper location. "I think the recliners should go here." They went back out to the truck to get them.

Sam had been dead set against the recliners. In general she found them tacky. But Nate had insisted. In fact, the chairs and big screen had been his only requirements. That, and the dictate that there be no throw pillows and no "over-the-top art."

In a spare bedroom she'd found boxes of books and arranged them on bookcases she'd purchased from Colin. She'd also gotten the coffee table and dining room set from him. Colin's pieces were works of amazing craftsmanship and she figured Nate must like the furniture because he had one of Colin's beds.

In less than a week, she'd managed to stock his kitchen with dishes—antique ironstone knockoffs she'd found at Nugget Farm

Supply—glassware, flatware, cookware, a coffeemaker and toaster she'd ordered from Williams-Sonoma. She was still waiting for the bar stools to come.

According to UPS tracking, the rugs and lamps were due in tomorrow. By the time Nate got back, his house would be a home. And she planned to charge him an arm and a leg in overtime for her hard work. She'd donate the money to charity.

In the meantime, she had a few more errands to make for Emily's wedding and a meeting later that afternoon with Lucky. Then tomorrow she was off to San Francisco for the bridal expo. Saturday night, after the expo, she planned to have dinner with an old friend from Greenwich at a restaurant that Emily had recommended near Fisherman's Wharf.

Andy had sworn up and down that he could be trusted to hold down the Lumber Baron while she and Nate were away. Sam got the sense that he was looking forward to having the inn to himself. Nate wasn't too thrilled about it, but Maddy had offered to check up on the place a few times during the weekend.

Once the delivery guys returned with both recliners, set them in place and removed the plastic wrap, Sam nearly texted Nate a picture of the room, it looked so good. Nah, she decided, let him see it in person with the rugs and lamps and all the other finishing touches. Maddy had volunteered to be here for the delivery tomorrow and Sam had drawn a diagram of where everything should go.

She eyed the room one more time and just for the hell of it tried one of the recliners, leaning all the way back to view the flat-screen. Comfortable, she had to admit, and had a hard time making herself get up.

On her way out, she stopped in Nate's bedroom. Earlier she'd replaced the ratty quilt with new bedding she'd also gotten at Farm Supply. Who knew the feed store was like Macy's? Seriously, it had a little bit of everything. The owners' daughter did the buying and although the home décor and clothing had a decidedly Western flavor, the woman had marvelous taste.

She carried the old quilt to the laundry room and couldn't help but notice that it smelled like Nate. Woodsy and citrusy and soapy, like Irish Spring. Nate was an ass, but he did smell good. And look good. And feel good . . . especially when he was excited.

Get your head out of the gutter.

She shoved the blanket into his laundry basket and left the house before she could have any more naughty thoughts about its owner.

The next morning, she made it to the Reno airport with just enough time to grab a muffin and coffee before her flight boarded. She was surprised to find that Nate had booked her in business class, even though it was such a short flight. Everything else—pamphlets highlighting their services, a portfolio of past events and a poster-board display of the inn—she'd sent with Nate in his car.

When she got to San Francisco, a driver waited for her, holding a big sign with her name on it.

"Slight change of plans, Ms. Dunsbury," he said as he loaded her carry-on into the trunk of the Town Car. "Mr. Breyer has you at the Theodore instead of the Belvedere. It's just a few blocks away, so you can walk or catch a cab for the bridal expo tomorrow morning. But he thought you would like the accommodations better."

"That sounds lovely." She'd searched all of Nate's hotels on the Internet and knew that the Theodore was his flagship as well as corporate headquarters.

Sam stared out the window as the driver zipped onto the freeway. She'd been to San Francisco many times and loved it. Tonight, after she got settled in, Sam planned to walk around Union Square and maybe do a little shopping. Boy, had she missed Barneys and Saks and the designer stores that dotted Manhattan and Greenwich Avenue.

"Sorry about the traffic, Ms. Dunsbury," the driver called back to her. "Friday, everyone's going into the city."

"No worries. I'm enjoying the ride."

Twenty minutes later, they inched up Powell Street as hordes of people vied for an open cable car. Most of the trolleys were packed so full that riders hung off the sides three deep.

"That looks dangerous," Sam commented to the driver.

"Nah. But you stay away from those Muni buses. Those drivers are either drunk or crazy. Every day there's another accident."

Sam made a mental note not to take any buses. She wanted to leave in one piece. When he finally pulled up in front the Theodore, she couldn't believe how big and centrally located the hotel was. It was just a few blocks away from the St. Francis, where Sam usually stayed. Pictures on the website didn't do the hotel justice.

A bellhop took her luggage and when she went to give the driver a tip, he said, "It's been taken care of, Ms. Dunsbury. You enjoy your stay, now."

She followed the bellhop into the lobby, an enormous space with marble pillars, high ceilings, and the most gorgeous moldings Sam had ever seen. The architecture was breathtaking. Sam had stayed in some of the finest hotels in the world, but the Theodore matched any of them in opulence.

For some reason, she'd thought Nate ran boutique hotels. Elegant but small, and less luxurious than places like the Four Seasons and the Ritz Carlton. The Theodore proved her wrong. She went up to the check-in desk, a long, graciously designed marble counter, where at least ten clerks tended to guests.

"Hello. Samantha Dunsbury. I'm checking in."

"Welcome, Ms. Dunsbury. Mr. Breyer has you on the thirty-second floor." The clerk smiled and handed Sam an envelope with a card key. "Enjoy your stay."

The bellhop took her up on an elevator and she noticed that the thirty-second was the top floor. When the doors slid open, Sam was greeted with a panoramic view of the city. She could see the Golden Gate Bridge, the Bay Bridge and a bridge to the south, which she didn't know.

"Is that Alcatraz?" She pointed to an island not far from the Golden Gate.

"Yes, ma'am." The bellhop turned slightly and motioned at the row of windows. "That's Oakland."

"Wow. You can see everything up here."

"You got the best room in the hotel," he said. "Mr. Breyer's penthouse is just down the hall."

She wondered if Nate put all the Breyer event planners working the expo up on the thirty-second floor of the Theodore. If so, mighty generous. The bellhop, Paul, according to his name tag, opened the door to a perfectly appointed three-room suite. Very posh. And the views every bit as breathtaking as the ones in the hallway. She couldn't believe Nate would give a room like this to the help. Sure, she was a Dunsbury. But in California she was simply Nate's employee.

"I hope it's to your satisfaction, Ms. Dunsbury," Paul said, and stowed her luggage in the walk-in closet.

"Are you kidding? It would be to the Queen of England's satisfaction."

"Actually, she liked it very much."

Sam did a double take. "Queen Elizabeth stayed here? In this room?"

"Yes, ma'am. It was in 1983. I was here, but it was before Mr. Breyer's time. The Theodore's a legend. It was one of Hollywood's favorite hotels. Samuel Taylor brought Audrey Hepburn here to persuade her to play the lead in *Sabrina*. At least that's how the story goes. Now that was even before my time." He laughed and tapped the wall. "The Reagans used to stay next door."

"Really?" She had no idea. Not once had Nate talked about what a storied hotel this was. "Paul, are Mr. Breyer's other hotels like this?"

"In my humble opinion the Theodore is the best, but the Belvedere also has a lot of history. Before the old owners let it go to pot and the big names came to town, the Belvedere was one of the city's crown jewels. Like the Theodore, Mr. Breyer renovated the place from top to bottom and brought it back to represent what this city used to be." Paul harrumphed. "Not like that InterContinental glass monstrosity on Howard. His other hotels are smaller, have fewer services, but are real swank."

"Thank you so much for sharing the history of this beautiful hotel," Sam said. "I wasn't aware that it was so famous."

"You're welcome, Ms. Dunsbury." As he went to leave, Sam handed him a tip. "It's all been taken care of, Ms. Dunsbury."

Alone, Sam took the time to really look around the suite. A big basket wrapped in cellophane sat in the middle of the coffee table. She pulled out the card. "Compliments of the Theodore," it said. "We hope you enjoy your stay." Sam took off the plastic. Inside was a bottle of Napa Valley cabernet sauvignon, Ghirardelli chocolates, Cowgirl Creamery cheese, Columbus salami, crackers, and fresh fruit. Nice how they included only local delicacies. She put the cheese in the mini fridge, once again wondering if all Nate's employees got this kind of treatment.

She unpacked her suitcase and removed the outfits she planned to wear from her suiter and carefully hung them in the closet, hoping they'd be wrinkle-free by tomorrow. Halfway to the bathroom to organize her toiletries, the phone rang. She dropped her cosmetics bag on the bed and picked up, fearing it was Andy with an emergency. "Hello."

"Hey. How was the flight?"

She smiled. "It was great. And so is this room. My God, Nate, this place is amazing."

"You hungry?"

She looked at her watch. It was already lunchtime. "I could eat." She wondered if he would have food sent up to her room.

"I've got a couple of meetings, so we'll have to go to one of the restaurants here. You okay with that?" He planned to have lunch with her. She hadn't expected that.

"Of course. Give me ten minutes."

The second he clicked off, she started pulling off her clothes. Damn! She hadn't packed a going-to-lunch-with-my-hot-boss outfit, just comfy travel clothes. She rifled through her offerings and decided on the dress she'd planned to wear to dinner with her friend Saturday night. It was a black-and-white Kate Spade. Very fitted. So she quickly shimmied into a one-piece Spanx number before pulling the dress over her head and grabbing the shoes to match.

By the time he knocked on her door, she'd had just enough time to run a comb through her hair and touch up her makeup.

"Hi," she said. "Let me grab my purse."

He stepped into the room and she saw him do a visual sweep of the suite. Cute. Obviously, he wanted to make sure that his staff had put everything in order. Then he did a visual sweep of her, giving no hint to whether he liked what he saw.

As they walked out he took her arm. "I got us a table at Mitch Mica."

Sam recognized the name of the high-profile chef and had seen the entrance to his restaurant in the lobby. "Do you eat there a lot?"

"Usually I grab a hot dog off the cart on Powell," he said, and she checked to see if he was kidding. He wasn't.

"Why don't we just do that?" she said.

"The health department shut them down for listeria," he said in that droll way of his.

This time she was sure he was kidding, but who could tell with Nate? He steered her onto the elevator.

"This hotel is spectacular, Nate. The architecture, the views, my room . . . Queen Elizabeth stayed there, for goodness' sake. I can't believe you never talk about it."

"I can't believe you're actually talking to me." He looked at her to gauge her reaction. "Does this mean you're no longer giving me the silent treatment?"

She sidestepped. "You're my boss. I don't really have a choice."

He smirked. "You have more choices than anyone I know, Samantha."

"You're one to talk. Look at this place, it's worth a fortune."

"This place is owned by hundreds of investors. I just have an infinitesimal piece of it."

"But you have nine more."

"Again"—he led her out of the elevator—"lots of investors. The only place I truly own is the Lumber Baron. And even that I share with Maddy."

"Isn't that the way most large hotels are owned?" she asked.

"Many. But some, like the ones owned by my ex-brother-in-law's family, are a sole proprietorship."

Sam knew he meant the Wellmonts. She'd heard through the powerful Nugget grapevine that Maddy had been married to Dave Wellmont, who'd been a "cheating son-of-a-bitch." A direct quote from Donna Thurston.

With his hand at the small of her back, he guided her into the restaurant.

"Mr. Breyer, we have your table ready." The hostess escorted them to a private spot in the back corner of the restaurant. "Chef Mica would like to send a few items out before you order. Either of you have any allergies or diet restrictions?"

Nate looked at Sam, who smiled. "I eat everything but shellfish."

"Thanks, Lucy." Nate spread his napkin over his lap and used the opportunity to discreetly glance at his watch.

"Do you have to go soon?" she asked, trying to reconcile this powerful, ultracommanding Nate with the down-to-earth Nate from the Lumber Baron. Even his suit was different. More formal, more expensive, and definitely more authoritative. Just looking at him made her knees weak.

"I'm good. But I have something this evening, so I'm afraid I won't be able to take you to dinner."

"Nate, I wasn't even expecting lunch. Do you give all your employees the red-carpet treatment—fancy suites, gift baskets, meals at Mitch Mica's?"

"Just the ones who are pissed off at me."

"I'm over it," she said, waving her hand in the air. But the truth was, he'd hurt her feelings. She glanced around the beautiful restaurant. "So this is all to make up for the fact that you like my face and body, but everything else about me you can't stand?"

"That's not what I said." He leaned over the table. "What I don't like is how much I like you."

She gulped. "Then this is to impress me?"

"I suspect it takes a lot more than this to impress Samantha Dunsbury," he said. "What're your plans for the rest of the day?"

The sommelier brought them a bottle of wine. "Chef thought this would be a nice accompaniment to some of the things he's sending out."

"Thanks, Raj." Nate swirled his glass, sniffed, tasted, and nodded his head. Raj proceeded to fill both their glasses and quietly disappeared.

"You know about wine?" she asked.

"Not a thing." Nate smiled. "Don't tell Raj, but I would've preferred beer. What're your plans?"

"I thought I'd check out the expo space at the Belvedere. You know, get a lay of the land. Then I wanted to walk around Union Square and do a little shopping."

"You need a driver?"

"Isn't it just a couple of blocks?"

"Three. The concierge will give you directions and hook you up with the folks over at the Belvedere. Your promotional stuff is already there. All the good shops in Union Square deliver to the hotel, so don't worry about having to carry your packages back."

She beamed at him. "Contrary to your opinion of me, I'm impressed, Nate." Maybe it was the restaurant lighting, but she could've sworn Mr. Cynical blushed. "Tell me, how did you ever get your hands on this hotel? Paul the bellhop, who by the way deserves a raise for promoting this place so well, said you renovated the Theodore from top to bottom."

Nate took a sip of wine and nodded. "It had been one of San Francisco's most famous hotels, but the last owners let it go to hell. By the time I got it, the Theodore needed millions of dollars of restoration—a hard sell to investors, especially given that in the last decade San Francisco has gotten a lot of the big luxury chains. Names that travelers know and value. But we were able to put together a long-term strategy that would put this place on top again. It would've been a shame to see it die. The hotel has a legacy."

"It's like what you did with the Lumber Baron."

"Yeah," he said, grinning. "Just on a much grander scale."

"You're a very good businessman, aren't you?" She supposed Royce must've been, too. But he didn't save architectural treasures.

"I just work hard. How about Saturday, after the expo, I show you some of the other Breyer properties?"

Her face fell. "I have plans Saturday evening that I can't get out of. Is there another time we could squeeze it in? I'm dying to see them."

"I'll see what I can do. What's up Saturday?"

"I'm seeing an old friend from Greenwich. He lives here now." She would've invited Nate to come along, but it seemed awkward.

"Sounds nice," Nate said, but Sam got the distinct impression that he was disappointed. "So about tomorrow, Tracy will show you the ropes. They'll be a couple of other Breyer event planners there as well. Lean on them as much as you need to. So how do you know this guy from Greenwich?"

"We grew up together, though he's a few years older. His sister, my best friend and I all went to Vassar together."

"I didn't know you went to Vassar." Nate genuinely looked surprised. "What did you major in, or did you skip around departments?"

Skip around? "Art history." It just so happened that she graduated with honors.

"Did you want to work in a museum or own a gallery?" he asked, leaning across the table.

Before she could answer, the server came with an amuse-bouche for the table—shot glasses of cold soup.

"This is delicious," she said, sipping. "As far as art history, my family owns a large collection that we lend out to museums and public spaces around the world. It's important to us to keep adding to that collection so that we can continue to share. Although I was raised to appreciate art, I wanted to be educated well enough to carry on the family legacy."

The server returned with four different appetizers, each one looking better than the last.

"You always get this kind of service?" she whispered. "All this food and I won't have any room left to order an entrée."

"Try to force it down. I don't want to offend the guy. He's on the temperamental side and having his restaurant here brings in a lot of traffic." He served her some calamari and took some for himself. "You giving up the art now that you're in the hospitality business?"

"Give it up? Why would I do that? It's part of my family history. I help administer the George T. Dunsbury Trust, which puts aside millions every year for new art acquisitions. Not just for my family's collections, but for museums like MoMA and the Met."

"How's that working out from Nugget?" She detected a hint of sarcasm in his voice. But that was Nate. Acerbic and cynical. At least he wasn't a con artist, like Royce.

"Quite well, thank you. I Skype with the board at least once a week." She wanted to stick out her tongue at him, but at the moment she had food in her mouth. What in tarnation ever gave him the impression that just because she'd moved to Nugget she would shirk her responsibilities?

The waiter was headed their way and quietly Nate said, "Let's order something. I don't want to eat his freebies and run."

She looked at her menu for something light. "I'll have the Caesar salad," she told the server.

Nate got the grilled Alaskan halibut. "How's things back in Nugget?"

"Good. Lucky's excited about my winter ideas." Nate rolled his eyes. "What? I've been working like a dog on that project."

He reached across the table and put his hand on hers. Electricity arced through her like she'd been touched by a lightning bolt. She credited the jolt to the fact that he had sexy hands. Large and strong with a smattering of dark hair that extended past his wrists.

"Sam, not you," he said. "You've come up with some great ideas."

"You still don't like Lucky? I thought he was starting to grow on you."

"I don't know where you got that idea. You ever notice that he stares at your chest the whole time he's talking to you?"

"He does not."

"Look, I'm a guy. I know about this stuff. He thinks he's being sly, but he's full-on checking out your . . ."

She could tell from how hot her face felt that she was turning red. "Since you're so concerned about employee-boss propriety . . . uh, conversation . . . slightly inappropriate, don't you think?"

"Nope." Nate took another sip of his wine. "As your boss, I'm supposed to protect you from untoward sexual advances."

"Nate, do you know how ridiculous that sounds?"

"Because I kissed you? Twice."

"No. Because I wouldn't let anyone harass me. As you've pointed out many, many times, I don't need this job. Therefore, I would have no qualms reporting any improper behavior from you or Lucky or anyone else."

"Good." He smiled. "So you don't think I harassed you, right?"

"No. But I do think you were insensitive. You don't have the first clue about Royce and me. And if you did, I don't think you would be so quick to condemn me for breaking it off with him."

Nate bent closer to her. "What did he do?"

"That's private," she said. "Now be a good boss and quit asking personal questions."

Their lunch came and they ate in silence until Nate finally said, "I'm sorry I was insensitive." Sam thought he sounded like a chastised little boy. For such a know-it-all, he could be quite adorable.

"Let's please stop talking about this, okay?" In an attempt to change the subject, she asked, "Where are the Breyer Hotel offices?"

"They're on this floor. There's a hallway behind the staircase that leads to our corporate headquarters. I won't have time to give you a tour after lunch, but I can have my assistant show you around."

"I would like that," she said.

After Nate paid the bill they went their separate ways—Nate to his meetings, Sam to get that tour and then off to see the Belvedere.

Sam woke up early the next morning. Went for a workout in the hotel gym, showered, and grabbed a latte at the coffee bar in the lobby before walking to the expo. On her way up Powell to Sutter Street, she wished she'd worn something warmer than her linen shift dress and cropped jacket. June in San Francisco was freezing.

The Belvedere, understated compared to the Theodore, was charming and elegant. The entire basement, a series of conference rooms, housed the bridal expo. Breyer Hotels had set up a large booth to exhibit its various venues. Yesterday, Sam had hung her display and arranged the Lumber Baron pamphlets. She noticed that Tracy was just now getting around to organizing the literature and pictures of the Theodore. As head of corporate event planning, Tracy was not only representing Breyer's flagship hotel but Nate had made it clear that all his other event planners were to defer to her.

"Samantha, I think you should move the Lumber Baron display to the other side of the booth. It looks weird to put it here with the San Francisco properties." In other words, Tracy was relegating her to Siberia.

Sam could have kicked up a fuss. Tracy didn't have a chance against her. Compared to the vipers Sam ran with—Muffy Vandertilten immediately came to mind—Tracy was amateur night. But it wasn't worth the trouble. Like her best friend, Wendy, always said, "Do you want to fight? Or do you want to win?"

So she moved the display.

"Hi, I'm Lisa. You must be Samantha." Lisa had a Southern accent, big green eyes, and a perfect blond bob. "I love your outfit."

"Thank you." Sam looked down at her dress, wondering if she'd overdressed. But Lisa was wearing a suit. "Which Breyer hotel are you with?"

"I'm with the Belvedere." Lisa held her heart. "I'm so glad to have the job. A few months ago, my boyfriend and I came out from Atlanta, where I worked events at the Hilton. For two months I couldn't get anything. I mean the phone—dead. And then miraculously the position at the Belvedere came up. Saved my life. So you work at the Lumber Baron?"

"Yes," Sam said. "It's small, but very sweet."

"Are you kidding? It's Nate's baby. The man dotes on the place. And isn't he just dreamy?"

Sam smiled. "Very handsome."

"Oh my God, he's the best boss ever. Let me tell you, I've had a hard time making the adjustment here. Everyone in Atlanta was so nice. In San Francisco, people are demanding, even mean. Oops"— she covered her mouth—"you're not offended, are you?"

Sam laughed. "I'm from Connecticut."

"Oh." Lisa looked at her like Connecticut wasn't much better than San Francisco. "Anyway, Nate has been so patient and so sweet."

Really? Sam must've gotten his evil twin as a boss. Or maybe he just liked Southern belles from Atlanta better.

By now, expo attendees started approaching the booth and both women moved up to the front to address questions.

"To be continued," Lisa said in a singsongy voice.

There were a lot more people attending this expo than the Sacramento one, which Sam supposed she should've expected. Two hours in and she felt parched from talking so much, which surprised her. She hadn't realized there would be so much interest in a venue four hours outside of the city, but it appeared that country weddings were even more in vogue than she'd originally thought.

All anyone seemed to want to know is if the Lumber Baron had a barn. Barns apparently were the new ballrooms. She couldn't wait to talk to Lucky about this. Here was another way they could combine their two operations. Although she didn't know how Mr. Bull Rider would feel about turning his cowboy camp into a wedding mill.

"You want to get a cup of coffee?" Lisa asked.

"Yes. Oh God, yes."

But before they could break away, a young woman approached Sam. "Hi, I'm getting married next summer and I'm interested in the Theodore. It's where my grandparents got married."

"That's lovely. Let me find someone who can help you," Sam said, and glanced around the booth for Tracy. No sign of her. Sam turned to Lisa. "You know where Tracy is?" When Lisa shook her head, Sam told the young woman, "Our resident Theodore expert seems to have stepped away for a few minutes."

"You mean the woman with brown hair?" Other than Randall, who worked at one of the other properties, Tracy was the only brunette in their group.

"She sort of blew me off, told me to call on Monday. But I came all the way from Walnut Creek."

"I'm sorry," Sam said. "Unfortunately, my hotel is the Lumber Baron Inn, but let me see what I can find here." She thumbed through the Theodore literature and found folders filled with descriptions of the party rooms available, menus and prices. "Aha. This should help." Why Tracy hadn't given her one of the packets was a mystery.

The woman sifted through the information. "This definitely helps, but I was hoping to set up an appointment so I could bring my fiancé and mother for a consultation. I know it's a year away, but it's a June wedding and I know how popular those are. It would be great to get a date on the books."

"Absolutely," Sam said. "Are you planning to walk around the expo for a while? I could call you as soon as Tracy gets back and she can set up an appointment."

"Couldn't I just deal with you?"

"I wish, but my hotel is four hours away from here. She's really your best person."

The woman reluctantly agreed and gave Sam her cell number. By the time Sam and Lisa broke away for coffee, Tracy still hadn't returned.

"I don't know what to do about that poor woman," Sam told Lisa.

"I would've helped, but I'm barely up to speed on the Belvedere. Plus, Tracy can be territorial and I don't want get on her bad side."

"But Nate likes you," Sam said.

"Uh, Nate likes Tracy more. According to the scuttlebutt, they're practically engaged. The woman has him wrapped around her little finger."

Sam's heart stopped. Nate had told her that there was nothing going on between him and Tracy. But then again men were liars. Just look at Royce. Whatever. It wasn't like she and Nate had a thing. He'd all but told her that they weren't going anywhere.

What I don't like is how much I like you.

As they headed to the elevator in search of caffeine, Lisa nudged her in the ribs. "Look over there."

Tracy had one hip cocked against the counter of the Simpson Hotel Group's booth, her head tilted back, laughing. A tall, arresting, gray-haired man was laughing too.

"I'm glad she's hard at work," Lisa said.

From the looks of their little tête-à-tête, Tracy was working all right. She was working the gray-haired man.

Chapter 15

By the time Nate got to Nugget Monday night he was wiped. He'd worked through the weekend, trying to catch up. He hadn't even had time to pop in on the expo, not that he normally would've, but he wanted to check on Sam. Make sure she knew the ropes.

Yeah, keep telling yourself that.

Okay, he'd desperately wanted to see and impress her. *Why* was the million dollar question, since he'd never felt the need to wow a woman before. Especially one who worked for him.

When he pulled into his garage, he didn't even bother to get his briefcase from the back of the car. He just wanted to get inside and collapse.

He walked into the mudroom, flicked on the light, and blinked. Whoa! He was in the wrong house. There was a bench where he usually piled random crap, a coat-tree that hadn't been there before, and cool-looking locker cages where someone had organized his sports equipment. He wandered the rooms, noting that this house had furniture. Nice furniture. Nate tested one of the recliners, tilting it back as far it would go. Comfortable.

The walls had pictures hanging on them—a gallery of all the people he cared about and lots of Lilly. Sam must've gotten the photographs from Maddy, because there were ones of his parents and his sister Claire and her family. A Colin farm table anchored the dining room with a big basket of fruit on it and matching chairs. There was a coffeemaker in the kitchen. Cupboards full of dishes and glasses. Even pots and pans. He found more of Colin's furniture—a few rockers and a swing—on the deck.

Damn! In the time he'd been gone, Sam had worked miracles. He never thought in a million years she'd come through like this, figuring she'd buy a few big-ticket items and get bored. But the house was done. Really done. Rugs, lamps, flat-screen TV, the whole nine yards.

Inside his bedroom he found new bedding and another flat-screen. The woman was a genius. He flicked it on to see if he even got cable. And hallelujah, he did. Apparently it was one of those smart TVs that worked off the Wi-Fi, like he had at the Theodore. Nice.

He tugged off his shirt, kicked off his shoes, pulled off his belt, and played with the remote control, cruising through the channels. On his way to the shower, he dropped his jeans and shorts and found a hamper in his closet, which hadn't been there before. He used to just use a canvas shopping bag for his dirty clothes. In the bathroom sat a stack of neatly folded towels and a brand-new mat, that looked thicker than anything he'd ever seen.

After his shower, he stepped into a pair of shorts, lay flat on his back in the bed, and propped the second pillow behind his head to check out his view of the TV from this angle. It was fantastic. He put the sound on mute, picked up his phone, and started to call Sam. Then he caught the time on his bedside alarm clock. Damn, it was ten o'clock. He called her anyway.

After the sixth ring she picked up. "Hello."

He couldn't tell if she'd been asleep. But her voice sounded good. Husky and sexy. "The place is insane," he said.

"Good insane or bad insane?"

"Are you kidding? Great insane. I love it."

"Good," she said, and giggled a little wickedly. "Because it cost you a fortune. Wait until you see my overtime bill."

"I don't care," he said. "It was worth it. I mean it, Samantha, the place is off the hook. You outdid yourself. How did the expo go?"

"Good. I got a ton of interest in the Lumber Baron. It appears that country weddings are all the rage. All we need is a barn."

"Huh?" he said. Honestly, he didn't really care about the expo. He just liked listening to her—too much, from the way the lower half of his body was responding.

"I'll tell you all about it tomorrow."

He thought about asking her to come over, looked down at his shorts and exercised a great deal of willpower by not. "How'd your dinner go with the friend from Connecticut?" *Ah, why'd I have to go asking that?*

"It was nice. The restaurant Emily recommended was fabulous."

"Sorry I wasn't able to show you around more. But Randall took you on a tour of the other properties, right?"

"Yes. He's a sweetheart and so is Lisa. The three of us went to dinner Sunday, before I caught my plane home."

"That's great," Nate said. He liked his employees to get along; it made for good team camaraderie. "Tracy didn't go?"

He heard Sam hesitate. "Uh, no, she had other plans."

Nate knew Tracy held herself above the other event planners and liked to be the queen bee. He tolerated it because she was incredibly good at her job. Although lately her incessant whining had begun to irritate him.

"I'll see you tomorrow, right?" she asked, and he could hear her stifling a yawn.

"Yep," he said, reluctant to hang up. Couldn't they just have phone sex? "And, Sam, thanks for the house. Seriously, you went above and beyond."

Nate found Sam in her office the next morning. So Andy hadn't burned the place down in their absence.

"What are you doing here so early?" he asked her.

"Working on a spreadsheet," she said, distracted. The woman had forced him to go to bed with a raging hard-on; the least she could do is look up from her computer when he talked to her. "I hate this Excel thing."

"Want help?"

"No. I'll figure it out."

"Why are you making a spreadsheet?"

She chewed on her bottom lip, lost in concentration.

"Earth to Samantha, I'm talking to you."

"I'll show you when I finish," she said, and proceeded to ignore him.

He dumped his crud in his office and headed to the kitchen. Starved, Nate hadn't felt like eating alone at the Ponderosa. Later, he'd go over to Sophie and Mariah's house to see Lilly. Instead of Emily, he found Brady at the stove, a bandana wrapped around his head, wearing baggy chef pants and an apron.

"I thought you didn't start until next week?"

"I don't," Brady said, pushing cookie sheets into the oven. "But Emily had wedding stuff to do."

"You taking the duplex on Donner Road?"

"Yeah. I think it'll work out real good. Thanks for hooking me up."

"No problem. You okay on the deposit?"

"I've got it covered."

"Hey, is there any truth to the rumor that you were on *Top Chef*?"

Brady laughed. "No truth at all. Where'd you hear that?"

"People in town." Nate shook his head. "Get used to it. They make shit up for the pure joy of it."

"You sound disappointed."

"Nah, but it could've stirred up a little chatter for the Lumber Baron on Twitter and Facebook."

"Yeah, I wanted to talk to you about that," Brady said. "I'd appreciate it if you didn't publicize my name or put up any pictures of me in cyberspace. I know it sounds weird, but it's a personal thing."

"You're not wanted by the law, the IRS, or an ex-wife wanting child support? Because if so, that becomes a personal thing for me and my business."

"Nothing like that," Brady said. "Hell, I let your police chief run a credit check on me for the apartment. You would've found out real quick if I had something to hide. It's just . . . I'm pretty private."

"All right," Nate said. It's not like the guy was Gordon Ramsay and his name would drum up all kinds of business. "Just keep making that coffee cake and we'll do fine. Speaking of, what's on the menu this morning? I haven't had breakfast yet."

Brady poured Nate a cup of coffee and fixed him a crepe filled with some sort of hash deal. The thing melted in his mouth and Nate truly hoped Brady wasn't a serial killer, because damn the man could cook.

"What's in the oven?"

"Mini lobster potpies for this afternoon," Brady said. "Hang on, they're coming out in a few seconds."

Nate waited, sipping the rest of his coffee and scraping his plate.

Sam rushed in. "Here you are."

"What's up?" Today she had on pants. He liked it better when she wore skirts or dresses. Sam had killer legs. But the frilly sleeveless top wasn't bad. It showed off her arms and her cute freckles.

"I'm ready to show you my spreadsheet."

"Well, you'll have to wait until the lobster potpies come out."

She sat at the island with him and Brady brought her a cup of coffee.

"Thanks," she said, and smiled at the cook way too brightly for Nate's taste. "How's it going so far?"

"It's all good," Brady said, removing the sheets from the oven and putting them on cooling racks. "The kitchen's got a good vibe. Perfect layout."

That had been Maddy's doing. Nate's sister couldn't cook to save her life, but after they'd gutted the decrepit kitchen, she'd redesigned it. Nate craned his neck to check out the pies. They looked and smelled fantastic.

Brady saw him ogling them. "Give 'em a couple of minutes to cool."

"You going to Emily and Clay's wedding?" Sam asked Nate.

"Yeah. What do you think I should get them? Maddy and Rhys are giving them a weekend getaway package at the Theodore. They've both been married before, aren't registered, and seem to have everything."

"What about a great bottle of wine?" Sam suggested.

"Something from Châteauneuf-du-Pape," Brady interjected, surprising Nate. The chef seemed to be coming out of his shell.

"That sounds good." Nate had a corporate wine buyer who could get him something special. "What are you getting them?" he asked Sam.

"I made a donation to the National Center for Missing and Exploited Children in their name." Years ago, Emily's daughter had been kidnapped from her backyard in the Bay Area and was still missing. It was so tragic that even the folks in Nugget didn't gossip about it.

"That was nice." Nate would give it to Sam. She was not only classy, but incredibly considerate. "So what's this spreadsheet?"

"I noticed a trend emerging at the expo," she said. "Maybe it's an old trend and new to me. But I think if we play our cards right we could take advantage of it."

"Yeah? What's the trend?"

"People want country weddings. They want barns. They want horses. They want bluegrass bands."

"It's true," Brady said. "I catered like twenty of them last summer. Where I come from in South Carolina that's just the way people get married. But in LA they go nuts for this kind of stuff."

"So what do you want me to do, build a barn and buy some horses?"

"No. But Lucky's place is perfect. He has an industrial kitchen, even bigger than this one. A giant lodge that could accommodate at least three hundred people. And plenty of barns and horses."

"How does that help us?"

"We partner with him. But to a guy like Lucky Rodriguez this might be a hard sell."

"Uh, ya think? The guy won't even call his venture a dude ranch, afraid it'll make him sound like a wuss," Nate said.

"Hey, money talks." Brady held his hand up and rubbed his fingers together. Nate was really starting to like the guy.

"Perhaps we just rent the venue from him for weddings," Sam said. "That way he doesn't have any part in it. But one thing I found at the expo is that these brides not only want a country wedding, they want a full weekend of activities. How great would it be to team up with Lucky and put on amateur rodeos that the guests could either participate in or just watch? Barn dances and trail rides. The possibilities are endless."

Her enthusiasm gave Nate flashbacks of Kayla. Right now she was gung ho, but how long until she petered out on the idea, leaving him to make good on all the country weekend weddings she booked? He didn't have the time.

"I'll think about it, Sam."

Her disappointment was palpable, and he was tempted to give in just to see her revved up again. Because watching Sam run high made him hot. Her cheeks flushed, her eyes dancing with possibilities, her body vibrating with excitement. The woman had a great business head on her. Nate would give her that. But being a success meant seeing an idea through to the bitter end.

"It's got major possibilities, Sam. It really does. I just don't like relying on other people outside my organization." Or inside for that matter, especially when he didn't know how soon until Sam would run. More and more that was starting to matter for more than work reasons. And Nate didn't like it.

"Lucky is big on this partnership, Nate. He wants more than anything to be a success. I don't see how it could hurt us."

"I said I'll think about it." He got up without having any lobster potpie. Somehow he'd lost his appetite.

On his way out, he heard Brady say, "It's a great idea, Sam. Nate'll come around. You'll see."

Great. He had the whole staff ganging up on him. Back in his office, he found a message from Tracy to call her. He didn't want to deal with her now, so he phoned Maddy.

"You up for taking a look at that place on Gold Mountain?"

"Thank God. I need to get out of this house and have some adult conversation. Give me thirty minutes. I can bring Emma, right?"

"Of course. We're just checking it out. You haven't told anyone, Maddy?"

"Nope. Well, just Rhys."

"Maddy, if this gets out, it leaves us no negotiating power."

She laughed as if he was being ridiculous. "He's my husband, Nate."

At least Rhys was the least likely person to blab. In a town of gossipers, Nate's brother-in-law knew how to keep other people's secrets. Nate suspected Rhys knew where all the bodies were buried in town, but to keep the peace he never said a word.

"Hurry up and meet me at the inn," Nate said. "I'll drive."

"It's easier for me. I've got the car seat for Emma."

"She can use Lilly's. It's already in the Jag."

Maddy showed up an hour later. "Sorry. Do you know how long it takes to get out of the house with a baby in tow?"

They loaded Emma and her twenty-pound diaper bag into the car and hit the road. Gold Mountain was a fifteen-minute ride on Highway 89. The place was a thriving community of cabins built around a lake that the same families rented summer after summer. The owner, a man in his nineties, had recently died and his children wanted to sell. The property required too much upkeep and they didn't have the money or inclination to bring it back to its former glory.

Nate had both. What he liked most about Gold Mountain was that it was fifteen minutes from Glory Junction, a small, quaint tourist town that catered to one of the most popular ski areas in Northern California. The place reeked of money.

When they got there, Nate could see just how badly the old man had let Gold Mountain go. As they wandered through, pretending to be guests, he noted that the cabins, badly weathered, and the pool, a concrete eyesore, needed updating in the worst way. The rec room had ancient Ping-Pong and foosball tables and the children's playground was full of rusted swing sets and monkey bars. The resort— Nate used the word loosely—reminded him of a 1950s trailer park.

Nevertheless, the place was packed and it was only June. People lounged at the pool and canoed and kayaked on the lake—the only part of Gold Mountain that remained pristine.

"Wow, this place needs work," Maddy muttered. "It'll take a good chunk of change to make it shiny again. Why do you think all these people still come?"

"Because they're getting the same rates they got in 1975," he said, having looked at Gold Mountain's profit and loss statements.

"That'll be a problem. As soon as we raise the rates to pay for improvements, we'll lose all these regulars." Maddy motioned at a group playing volleyball.

"Maybe not. There's a chance they'll be happy for the upgrades. If we winterize the cabins and run a shuttle service from here to the ski slopes, we could keep this place open during the cold months." Right now, Gold Mountain only ran from April to October.

Maddy gave him a lingering glance. "This doesn't look at all like your cup of tea, Nate. Way too *Kumbaya, let's sit around the campfire* for your taste."

"My taste is to make money, and Gold Mountain could be a gold mine." He took off for the lodge.

"Where are you going?" Maddy followed, bouncing Emma in her pack to keep up.

"I want to see if there's a barn on the property."

"A barn? What for?"

"Sam says barn weddings are huge right now."

Maddy looked at him like he'd grown a horn out of his head. "So?"

"We could do events." Nate followed an overgrown bike trail that wound around the perimeter of the property. "Doesn't look like they have one. But we could build a barn."

"Stop," Maddy said, out of breath. "The place has a big old lodge. Why would we build a barn?"

"I told you, Sam seems to think it'll attract events. She wants to use Lucky Rodriguez's place. I don't know how good I am with that."

"But you're *good* with Sam?" She waggled her eyebrows.

"No. In fact, I'm sure she'll quit any day now. It doesn't mean I can't steal her ideas." They wandered back to the car. So far, Emma had held up like a trooper, but knowing what Nate did about babies, it wouldn't last too much longer.

"Nate, did you do something to her that'll make her want to quit?" Maddy huffed.

"Now why would you say that? I'm the ideal boss." Yeah, when he wasn't sticking his tongue down Sam's throat.

"Then why are you so sure that she'll leave?"

He gave Maddy a long look, then opened the car door, took Emma from her, and buckled her into Lilly's car seat.

"Oh. My. God." Maddy held her hands up and lifted her face to the sky. "Kayla! That's what this thing is with you about Sam. You're comparing her to Kayla. Nate, Kayla was a complete and utter whack job. Do not compare the two."

"How do you know they're not similar? They have the same exact backgrounds."

"Because they're not. Sam is responsible. She's committed. She's . . . she's so not Kayla. From the first minute Claire and I met Kayla, we knew she'd been beaten by the crazy stick. The only reason we didn't jump for joy the night she dumped you is because you were so completely in love with her. The last thing we wanted to do was hurt you more. But, big brother, you dodged a Teflon-coated bullet. That woman would've made your life a living hell. My guess is that she's either living on an Israeli kibbutz or owns a sex-toy boutique on Newbury Street."

"Last I heard she was an interior decorator," Nate said.

"Well, how many minutes ago was that? Because by now she's probably working for the Department of Defense or trying her hand at macrame."

Nate had to laugh at that one. Maddy got in the passenger seat and shut the door while Nate started the engine.

"Did Mom and Dad hate her too?" he asked.

"Hate is a very strong word, Nate. But yes. They did."

For no reason at all, he wondered what they would think of Sam.

"Sam is nothing like her," Maddy said, as if reading his mind, because sisters could do that.

"Oh yeah, then why do you think she left her fiancé flat?"

"Owen says he was beating her," Maddy said, suppressing a laugh.

Nate highly doubted that. The woman would've kicked his ass. God knew she challenged Nate at every turn.

"If you're interested in her, why don't you just ask her?" Maddy said. "And while you're at it, you should do something nice for her, given all the work she put into your house. Your place is now gorgeous."

"What do you think of Gold Mountain?" He desperately wanted to change the subject.

"I think it has possibilities. Would we buy it on our own, or with investors?"

"That's why I'm interested in it. I think we could swing it on our own."

"I still have the money from my divorce settlement. Rhys won't have anything to do with it. *'I don't want to see any of that goddamned money coming through our household. I support our family.'*" She mimicked him in a deep Texas drawl. "The guy is such a Neanderthal."

"But you love him, right?"

"More than anything in the world, except Emma." She turned to the backseat. "Right, girl? We love your daddy."

He was happy for his sister. After her ex, she deserved the best.

"I want to get a few estimates on what it would take to spiff the place up before we make an offer," Nate said.

"That sounds smart. We'd need a full staff to run it. Between Emma and the Lumber Baron, I'll have my hands full."

"Yep. I've thought about that. It won't be easy, but we'll find the right people." He certainly couldn't keep up this back-and-forth situation without killing himself.

They returned to the inn, where Maddy came in to meet Brady, but couldn't stay long because Emma was having a volcanic meltdown. Nate hid in his office, looking to avoid Sam. He knew she still wanted to show him her spreadsheet, which despite himself he found cute. Tracy had left three more messages. Nate decided he'd better call her back before she had a volcanic meltdown of her own.

"What's up?" he said over the phone.

"Um, only that I've tried to call you a million times."

Nate could do without Tracy's lip. "Well, you've got me now. So what's the emergency?"

"The emergency is that I quit."

"Tracy, stop with the theatrics. I'm not at your beck and call, so you quit?"

"No. I quit because I got a better offer."

"That's great," he lied. Nate intended to play hardball, because he didn't think for one minute she'd really leave. Not with what he paid her. "So you're giving me your two weeks?"

"Nope," she said. "That ship sailed an hour ago when you didn't return my calls. I'm outta here, Nate. Today. Right now."

Uh-oh! He'd certainly miscalculated that one. But he'd be damned before he begged the prima donna to stay. "Can I trust you not to steal the computers, or should I have Security escort you out?"

"Screw you, Nate!" She hung up before he could ask about the opera gala file.

The opera gala. How the hell was he supposed to pull that off now?

Chapter 16

"Not now," Nate told Sam as she shadowed him down the hallway.

"What's wrong?" The man had been gone most of the day and she wanted to show him her spreadsheet and prove to him that partnering with Lucky on the barn weddings would be sound business.

"Tracy just quit. Didn't even give me two weeks." He kept walking.

"As far as I can tell, she did you a favor," Sam called to his back.

He spun around and glared at her. "You think leaving me in the midst of planning a huge event is doing me a favor?"

"All I know is that she couldn't care less about that expo. For most of it she disappeared to flirt with some man from the Simpson Hotel Group. And when she was present, she was rude to people. She couldn't even be bothered to give out simple information."

Nate folded his arms over his chest. "And you waited until now to tell me this?"

"Everyone said she's your pet. The rumor's that you're engaged. I thought that you would think I was being catty."

"For Christ's sake, Sam, I told you there was nothing between Tracy and me."

Yeah, and there was nothing between Royce and half the women under thirty on the East Coast. *The dumb cow is nothing more than a for-show wife*, rang in her ears.

Nate turned and continued down the hall.

"Where are you going?" she called to him.

He stopped again. "To the men's room. Did you want to come?"

"I'll help you with whatever work she left you."

"Thanks, Sam, but I'll manage."

Whatever. She was just trying to be a team player. But if Nate didn't want her help, then he could fend for himself for all she cared.

She had last-minute touches to make on Emily's wedding anyway. In her office she grabbed her purse, then headed out, got in her car, and drove to McCreedy Ranch.

She found Clay and Emily on the expansive front lawn, looking at her diagram, pacing off the measurements of the tent.

"You sure we'll fit everything in, Red?" Only Royce had ever called her that before. On Clay's lips it sounded much more endearing. Sam got the sense that Clay wasn't the type to call someone by a nickname unless he liked her.

"It'll all fit," she assured him. "I mapped everything out."

"Even the porta-potties?" he wanted to know. They'd ordered deluxe ones in trailers, which could pass for fancy powder rooms.

"I have those down there." She pointed to an area adjacent to the front lawn that afforded a little more privacy.

But Clay still looked doubtful. So Sam walked them through it, describing where the big tent would go, as well as various food stations and the band's stage and dance floor. The actual ceremony would take place between two oak trees on the property. Emily had told Sam that Clay had planted one of the trees in honor of Emily's missing daughter.

The chairs would be delivered the night before the wedding and Sam would be on hand to make sure they were set up just right for the ceremony and reception.

"I don't know how I could've done this without you," Emily said. "Everything feels so organized."

"That's because it is," Sam said. "I don't want you to worry about a thing. It's your day and I want you to enjoy it."

"You'll make sure the florist does the centerpieces and the chair boughs correctly, right?"

"Absolutely. I have everything sketched out." Sam showed Emily and Clay her folder filled with diagrams, drawings, and sticky notes.

"I don't know what Nate's paying you, but you could make a fortune organizing these types of shindigs," Clay said, and Sam laughed. It was nice to be appreciated.

"This is my first wedding," she confided. "But have no fear. I've organized enough large-scale garden parties that I could do it in my sleep."

"You've got the touch, that's for sure," Clay said. "If it's all right, I think I'll leave you ladies to the rest of it. I've got cattle to feed."

Clay kissed Emily goodbye. It was just a peck, but there was so much sizzle between the two of them that Sam felt like a voyeur standing there. For a second, Sam's thoughts flashed to Nate's kiss, but she forced the memory out of her mind. The man was a schizoid. Half the time he was flirting with her, the other half he was pushing her away.

"Are you bringing a date?" Emily asked.

Now where would she find one of those in Nugget? "I'll be too busy."

"You should come with Nate. Maddy says he's not bringing anyone and he's so handsome."

"I see enough of him at work." Sam sighed.

"Well, there's that." Emily tilted her head in question. "I thought there might be a spark between you two."

Sam shook her head. "More like a hail of gunfire."

"So it's that way, huh?"

"It's not that bad," Sam admitted. "We have our good moments." If only Emily knew. "He lost an employee today, so he's being testy. I suppose we could at least sit together." It made sense, since they'd probably be the only single people at the wedding, and since Sam was in charge of the seating arrangements she'd also make sure to put Lucky Rodriguez at their table. That way Nate could get to know Lucky better.

Emily's lips tugged up in a sly smile. "I think it's a great idea that you two sit together."

"Don't get any ideas, Emily." Sam shook her head. "I better get going. Is there anything else you can think of that you need between now and the wedding?"

"I just need to pick up my boots. Other than that, I think I'm good. How did Brady do today?"

"Great. I have a good feeling about the guy. At first I thought he might be standoffish, but this morning he jumped right into the conversation. Seems like Nate likes him too."

"Good," Emily said. "I'd invite him to hang out with the Baker's Dozen, but we're all women. I don't know if it would be weird for him."

The Baker's Dozen was a local cooking club and Nugget's unofficial chuck wagon. Community potlucks, celebrations, funerals—you name it, they cooked for it. They also traded as much gossip as they did recipes when they met at the Lumber Baron kitchen for their monthly meetings.

Sam had sat in once or twice for that reason. That and the fact that they fed her.

"I get the feeling that if Brady felt weird about it, he would tell you. He seems pretty straightforward."

"Should I invite him to the wedding?" Emily asked. "I know he hardly knows me, and Clay not at all, but I feel like everyone in town has been invited and that we'd be excluding him."

"How about you just let him know that he's welcome and leave it up to him?"

"That sounds good," Emily said. "I'll say something to him about it tomorrow during the breakfast service at the Lumber Baron. He's meeting Rhys there to get the keys to the duplex."

"Great. Then I'll see you tomorrow and we can go over any last-minute details you think of tonight."

"Thanks, Sam. I really don't know how I would've done this without you."

Sam gave Emily an air kiss on each cheek—a habit she couldn't seem to break, even in Nugget—and went home. She didn't see Nate's car, but he usually parked it in the garage. Promising herself that she wouldn't check every few minutes to see if he was home, she went into her house and scrounged through the pantry for something for dinner. Canned soup would have to suffice.

She made herself a bowl and ate in front of the TV. Midway through some reality show she couldn't get into, the phone rang. She picked up, half expecting it to be her father.

"Did you hear about Tracy?" It was Lisa, her new Breyer Hotel best friend. "She just walked out. Didn't even give Nate notice."

"Nate told me," Sam said. "What do you think happened?"

"Rumor is that he broke off the engagement and she was devastated."

Everything sounded so much more intense in a Southern accent, Sam thought. "Yeah, I don't think they were engaged, Lisa. According to Nate, they weren't even seeing each other." For some moronic reason she believed him.

"Do you think it has anything to do with that man she was slobbering all over from the Simpson Hotel Group? The one who looked as if he wanted to lick whipped cream off her boobs."

Sam couldn't help herself and laughed. "I don't know. I'm sort of out of the loop here in Nugget."

"Well, it's all anyone here is talking about," Lisa said. "Supposedly, Nate had Security escort her out of the Theodore."

Ouch. That seemed rather harsh. Sam supposed it might be the appropriate move for someone who had been fired and might act out vengefully. But Tracy had quit. Why make a scene in front of all your other employees? It would make Nate look weak. But maybe Lisa was wrong.

"He didn't say anything to me about calling Security," Sam said. "Only that she quit without giving notice."

"Are you planning to go for the job?"

Sam hadn't even considered the idea. But given Nate's reaction to her helping him pick up some of Tracy's work, she didn't think the position was on the table. At least not for her. "I hadn't thought of it," she told Lisa. "Are you?"

"I'm too new." Lisa was only slightly newer than Sam. And the Belvedere was much larger than the Lumber Baron. "You were so good at the bridal expo and you're so refined that I bet you can talk your way into the job if you want. Plus you'd be a much nicer boss than Tracy."

"I've never been a boss in my life," Sam said, leaving out the part that this was her first job, period. "What about Randall? He's been with the company a long time."

"I don't think he wants the responsibility. The job requires a lot of OT. As sweet as your little inn is, don't you want to come to the city? I would think it's lonely there being a single woman."

Sam loved the Lumber Baron, but being the event planner for the entire Breyer operation . . . It seemed like a dream job. She shook her head. When the heck had she become so ambitious? "Don't you think Nate will bring someone in from the outside?"

"Maybe, but why not start lobbying for the position?" Lisa said. "You don't know until you try. He likes you, right?"

Sam was pretty sure he liked kissing her. But as far as the job, she had no idea. Half the time he treated her like she was the world's biggest flake. "Mm-hmm," was all she said.

"Then throw your hat into the ring," Lisa insisted.

"I don't know, Lisa. I like it here and I have a lot of plans for the

Lumber Baron." Which she couldn't even get Nate to sign off on. "Are you sure you don't want to go for it?"

"Positive," she said. "Call me tomorrow and tell me what you decide."

Sam said she would, knowing full well that no matter what she decided, Nate wouldn't give her the job. He'd made it clear that he thought she was a dabbler, and he'd want someone he considered "serious." And experienced. Someone like Tracy.

"Well, look how well that worked out for you," she muttered to herself while taking her soup bowl to the sink.

Unable to help herself, she peeked outside the window, looking for signs of life at Nate's house. All his blinds were closed, so she couldn't tell whether he was home. And she had no plans to ever go over there again. Not after the last time, when he told her that he was attracted to her physically.

But everything else about you is wrong.

In his lame way, he'd tried to make up for it by giving her the royal treatment at the Theodore. But the hurtful words still stung. They reminded her too much of Royce's.

The next morning Sam arrived at the Lumber Baron to find Emily and Brady in the kitchen. For a guy who wasn't supposed to start until next week, he'd become a permanent fixture at the inn.

"Good morning," she greeted. "Coffee ready?"

Brady poured her a mug. "Will you bring one to Nate?"

"He's here already?" Typically he went over to the Ponderosa first.

"Yep," Emily said. "And he's not a happy camper. Apparently, that employee you told me about yesterday left everything in a shambles."

"Uh-oh." Sam grabbed the other mug and started to carry it to Nate's office.

"Hold on a sec," Brady said, and handed her a plate with a slice of coffee cake. "You better bring him this too."

Sam managed to juggle both cups of coffee and the cake and used her foot to knock on Nate's door. "I come bearing gifts."

He opened up and took one of the mugs from her. "Thanks."

She put the plate on his desk and took a seat, uninvited. "Heard Tracy left you in a pickle."

"That's an understatement. All her files on upcoming events are a joke—no status updates, no nothing. I don't know what she's been do-ing the past few months, but I'd like to wring her goddamned neck."

"Did you really have Security throw her out of the building?"

"No, of course not. Only an idiot would do that."

"That's the rumor," she said.

He cocked his eyebrows. "Since when are you in the pipeline? I threatened to have her escorted out. It was a joke. But she probably told some of the employees I really did it."

"Why did she leave in such a huff?" Sam asked.

"I don't know, I can only speculate."

"Speculate away."

"She didn't want to do the bridal expo—thought it was beneath her. She was having problems with the organizer of the city's annual opera gala. I'll grant you the woman is high maintenance, but that's Tracy's frigging job. Nabbing this event is huge for the Theodore—lots of San Francisco's movers and shakers attend this thing. To make matters worse, Tracy was fighting with the Theodore's chef about the gala's menu." Nate let out a sigh. "And I guess I wasn't fanning her ego enough."

"In other words, you weren't paying enough personal attention to her?"

He threw his arms up. "I told you before, Sam, there was nothing going on between us."

"But she would've liked there to have been?"

Nate just shrugged. "I can't tell you what went through the woman's head. All I know is that I'm screwed."

"Are you planning to hire a new corporate event planner?"

"Yeah. Eventually. First I have to figure out where we're at on the opera gala and all the other events she was in the midst of planning."

"What about me?" Sam blurted.

"For the position?" He gaped at her. "You're kidding me, right?"

God, could he be any more condescending? She didn't know if she really wanted the job. She certainly didn't want to give up the Lumber Baron. But the more Nate said no, the more she wanted to push for it. "Let me prove myself by cleaning up the mess Tracy left."

"You already bored with the Lumber Baron?" He took a bite of the coffee cake and watched her reaction.

"No. In fact I would combine both jobs. Fiscally, for you it would be a win-win."

"The Theodore alone is a full-time job, Sam."

"Not if I had a partner." Sam thought she and Lisa could do it together.

"So basically I would still be paying two salaries. And that would help me fiscally, how?"

"You just don't want to give me a chance."

"Sam, this is the first job you've ever had and you've only been here six months. Why don't we wait to see if you make it to your one-year anniversary before I give you a promotion? And for the record, being head event planner for all of Breyer Hotels would be one hell of a promotion."

Deep down inside she knew he was right. But he just seemed to have so little faith in her and she didn't know why. Everyone else thought she was doing such a good job.

"You're the boss," she said, and started to get up to leave, feeling deflated.

"Hey," he said. "Let me ask you something."

"What?" Maybe he'd changed his mind about letting her at least help him sort out the shoddy records Tracy had left behind. She'd love to sink her teeth into that gala. In New York she'd been on both the opera and symphony fund-raiser committees.

"You think it would be okay if I brought a date to Emily and Clay's wedding, even though I originally told them I'd be coming solo?"

"It would be incredibly rude," she said, knowing full well that Emily and Clay wouldn't mind, since they'd invited the entire county. "I can't believe you're a leader in the hospitality industry if you have to ask a stupid question like that."

Sam walked out and it wasn't until she was halfway down the hall-way that she heard him laughing. He'd been testing her. The creep.

Chapter 17

There were no hysterics or bridezilla moments on Emily and Clay's big day, just a cow that had somehow managed to break loose and trample everything in its path in its exuberance to make a feast of the flower garlands that had been strung along the rows of shiny white chairs.

Clay's sons, Justin and Cody, quickly rounded up the bovine. Now all they had to do was damage control. Sam persuaded the florist to bring more flowers and she and the boys spent the morning reconstructing the boughs.

"It's a good thing Emily didn't see what happened," Cody, Clay's youngest, said. "She would've gotten Dad's shotgun and killed that cow dead."

Perhaps tomorrow Sam would find humor in a cow running amok through her event. She could safely say that in all the outdoor events she'd planned in Greenwich, there had never been a livestock incident. But there was a first time for everything.

"How does this look?" Justin held up one of the garlands.

It certainly wasn't as professional as the florist's, but she'd had another event to rush off to, so their improvisation would have to do. "It looks fantastic, Justin. Who knew you had such a talent with flowers?"

The boy turned red. "Hopefully no one will notice the difference," he said, eyeing the ones still intact that the cow hadn't gotten to.

"They won't," she said. "The guests will be too focused on the handsome groomsmen." She winked at Justin. "You guys should get back to the house and get dressed. I'll handle the rest of this."

After making the remaining repairs to the boughs, she checked on the caterers to make sure they were setting up in their allotted spots. Lo and behold, Brady had shown up and was directing the bartenders.

"Figured you could use a little help," he said. "Plus, Emily's a good egg and if I butter her up enough, maybe she'll give me her recipe for those sweet rolls she makes."

Sam was just happy to see him. Brady knew a lot about catering and that's where her expertise was the weakest. "I'm thrilled you're here." She handed him one of her diagrams. "This is the setup for the food. You want to take charge of that?"

"I'm on it," he said, and herded a group of cooks to a row of barbecues and smokers.

She headed to the reception tent. At her direction, the tables had all been set beautifully. The floral tablecloths made the whole tent pop, and the topiary centerpieces were whimsical and fresh.

Donna found Sam talking to the leader of the string quartet while the rest of the musicians warmed up for the reception. Clay had hired a country-western band. They were unloading their equipment.

"Emily wants you to see her dress," Donna said, and then whispered, "That's code for champagne time."

They walked together into the house, where Emily had turned the main floor guest room into a bridal suite. Pam, the local yoga instructor, Maddy, and Harlee sat on the bed, sipping bubbly while Darla put the finishing touches on Emily's hair.

"You look amazing," Sam said, taking in the bride from head to toe. Because it was both Emily and Clay's second marriage, she'd forgone the traditional train and veil. "Seriously, you're the most beautiful bride I've ever seen."

"Check out the boots." Emily stuck her feet out. "They're something, aren't they?"

"Oh my God, they're fantastic."

"That Tawny knows what she's doing," Donna said, and handed Sam a glass of champagne. "Drink up, girl."

Sam took a quick sip. "I've gotta get back out there and make sure the trains are running on time. You look like you've got everything handled in here."

"Sam, will you do me a favor?" Emily asked. "Will you check on Clay and the boys? They'll probably need help with their boutonnieres."

"Absolutely." Before Sam left, she gave Emily a peck on the cheek and could've sworn that the bride misted up. "You okay?"

Sam knew that, more than anything, Emily wished her daughter could be here.

"I'm about as good as it gets," Emily said, beaming so bright that the room lit up like sunshine.

"I'll go check on the men. See you out there."

Sam climbed the stairs to the master bedroom and knocked on the door. "You guys decent?"

"Come on in," Clay hollered.

He and the boys were dressed in dark suits with string ties. All three wore cowboy boots with the McCreedy Ranch brand.

"Who did your boutonnieres for you? Emily thought you'd need help."

Clay pointed at Rhys, who sat sprawled in a chair and said, "I'm good for something."

"How's it going out there, Red?" Clay peeked out the window at the lawn below.

"We're good to go. So far, no glitches whatsoever." She looked over at Justin and Cody and put her finger over her lips.

"Emily okay?" he asked.

"She couldn't be better."

"Donna getting her tanked?" Clay's lips quirked up.

"They're just having a little pre-wedding champagne. Can I get you fellows something?"

"We're good," Clay said, and looked at his watch. "Should we come down now?"

"Sure. The guests should be arriving soon. I'm planning to do a last walkthrough, so I'll see you in a few."

"Hey, Red, you've done a great job." He pulled her in for a hug. "Thank you for making this easy for Emily."

"I loved every minute of it," she said, then dashed down the stairs and quickly conferred with Brady, who had the food and beverages under control.

Sam checked off the remainder of her to-do list as she circled the lawn. Then she took a second to lean against a tree to readjust her sling-backs. Next time she'd be sure to wear more comfortable shoes. These were killing her, though she had to admit that they made her legs look good. Long and lean.

The valets had already started transporting guests in horse-drawn carriages from the parking area.

Originally, Emily had argued that the carriages were a little kitschy for her taste, but ultimately they decided that the horse-drawn carts beat using vans or small tour buses. She saw Nate alight from one of the carriages in a suit and a pair of Oakley sunglasses that made him look like a movie star. Hugh Jackman. She pretended not to notice him and went back to looking busy.

The quartet started playing while the guests mingled. Servers passed lemonade in mason jars and the bar opened for those who wanted something harder. Clay's idea. Sam noticed Nate bellying up to get himself a drink. She also saw a striking older woman on the arm of Lucky Rodriguez. The woman had more of an olive complexion than Lucky, but Sam definitely saw a family resemblance.

Lucky came up alongside her and introduced the lady as his mother, Cecilia. The next thing she knew, Nate had inserted himself into their small group and handed her a glass of lemonade.

"I would've brought you wine, but I wasn't sure if you are drinking or not," he said, like he was her date.

Okay. "Thank you," she said, and introduced Nate to Lucky's mom.

"Lucky said you're the wedding planner." Cecilia took Sam's hand. "This is so beautiful, like something out of a fairy tale."

"It's really great, Sam." Lucky scanned the crowd as if he was looking for someone in particular. Perhaps the perky blonde from the Ponderosa the other day.

"Thanks so much. But most of it is Emily's doing," she said, looking over at the minister, who gave the signal. "I have to get everyone seated now."

She moved through the crowd, telling people that it was time to take their places. By the time the quartet started playing the introduction to the "Wedding March," she couldn't find an empty chair. That's when she saw Nate flagging her over.

"I saved one for you," he said.

"Thanks. I thought I'd have to stand over at the bar. How do the garlands look?"

He looked at the floral boughs hanging from the chairs. "Nice . . . I guess. Why?"

"We had an unfortunate incident this morning with a stray cow."

Nate chuckled. "Seriously?"

"Not funny. The boys and I fixed them up the best that we could."

As Clay, Justin, and Cody moved to stand between the two oak trees next to the minister, a hush descended over the crowd. Then the guests rose as Emily walked down the aisle. Sam could've sworn she heard a collective sigh.

"Nice boots," Nate whispered in Sam's ear.

The ceremony was one of the most moving Sam had ever seen. Clay and Emily had written their own vows and Sam had to wipe away a few tears. Rhys and Maddy were called up to witness the signing of the marriage license, which Sam had never seen before and thought was a beautiful touch.

After the recessional, the group made their way to the reception tent while the photographer took a few portraits of the newlyweds and the boys. Emily's mother too. Sam tried to beat the crowd to the tent to make sure everything looked perfect.

"Where's the fire?" Nate called to her as he caught up.

"I have work to do." What did he think, she could stand around all day, keeping him company?

She smoothed a couple of the tablecloths and rejiggered the placement of a few centerpieces. Brady stood behind the scenes directing the wait staff serving hors d'oeuvres to the guests who had started trickling in.

"Thank you." She squeezed Brady's arm. "Did you at least get to see some of the ceremony?"

"I caught most of it." He grabbed one of the servers on his way out to the crowd, pulled a towel from his back pocket, and cleaned a smudge from one of the trays.

Nate stole a shrimp from the platter and popped it into his mouth. "Quality control," he told Brady and Sam. "Damn, these are good."

"You know Emily. She's got great food connections," Sam said. He pointed to a table toward the back of the tent and told Brady, "You're sitting with us." He nodded and hurried off to check on the duck skewers.

"So I'm at your table?" Nate asked.

"That's where Emily put you," she lied. "If you don't like it, you could probably cram in next to Maddy and Rhys. Or Sophie and Mariah." Sam knew that both couples shared a sitter for Emma and Lilly.

"I'm more than happy with the arrangement." He grinned at her.

"You're a strange man." Just the other day he'd wanted to bring a date, now he acted as if she was his date.

She walked around the tent, Nate on her heels, making sure there wasn't anything she'd forgotten. Lots of guests approached her to tell her how beautiful the wedding was.

Grace from the Nugget Farm Supply gushed, "This is magnificent, Sam. The linens, the little lollipop trees on the tables, the whole setting is just . . . wow. You have quite a touch, dear."

"You're so sweet to say so, Grace."

Owen bumped into her with a couple of cocktails in his hands. "This is one hell of a hoedown. Heard you've been working day and night on it. Well, you done good, missy."

Nate snagged a small plate, filled it with appetizers, and handed it to her. "Eat."

Until that moment she hadn't realized how hungry she was. They wandered over to their table and Sam sat to quickly stuff her face before she had to attend to anything that came up. The band started playing as the newlyweds entered the tent to thunderous applause.

"They look so happy," she told Nate, who'd also gotten her a glass of wine.

"Yep. That a new dress you've got on?"

It was a flirty little Alexander McQueen. "I got it in San Francisco when I was there for the bridal expo."

"I like it."

"Thanks." Sam could feel her cheeks heat, not so much from the compliment but from the way Nate looked at her, like he thought she was beautiful. "I should probably make sure everything is running on time for dinner."

"You want me to come with you?"

"Mingle and enjoy yourself. I'll be back in a few."

It turned out that Brady had everything under control. "I hope you don't mind, but I changed the service. The servers are going to French everything."

Sam laughed because it sounded slightly pornographic, but she knew full well that he meant the waitstaff would serve the meal from platters instead of family style. It was a little formal for the event, but the guests would probably appreciate the convenience.

"I thought it could be messy for the guests to serve themselves. And the waitstaff seems pretty experienced."

"Very classy," Sam said. Brady was a godsend. "We can send them around repeatedly for seconds and thirds, right?"

"That's exactly what I'm thinking. I know Emily wanted it to be a feast."

"Excellent," Sam said. "Then I'll just go back to my table. You'll come out soon so you can eat, won't you?"

"Yeah," he said, but she got the impression that he liked hanging out behind the scenes, where the action was. And clearly the man knew what he was doing.

When she turned around she bumped into Nate. "I thought you were mingling."

"Just wanted to see what was going on back here. For someone who never worked in the hospitality industry, you know a lot about service."

"Nate, I've been hosting functions my whole adult life, not to mention attending a fair number. It's second nature."

"For the record," he said, perching his shades at the tip of his nose, "I think Frenching is good."

"What's with you today?" She shook her head and headed back to their table. "You're back to flirting with me again. Is it because Tracy's gone?"

He tugged her arm to bring her to a stop. "Get this straight, Sam. I never flirted with Tracy."

"So are you not flirting with me either?" She pulled away and found her chair. The rest of the guests at their table were either off chatting, dancing, or getting drinks at the bar.

Nate sat next to her. "I've been up front about being attracted to you. And I suppose I'm less professional with you because we live next door to each other and hang in the same social circle." He waved his hands at the crowd. "After all, this is Nugget with a population of fifteen people our age. Would you like me to stop?"

She didn't say anything, because, well, she liked the flirting. Hell, who was she kidding? She liked him. That didn't mean she trusted him.

Maddy and Rhys came over. "This is the best wedding I've ever been to," Maddy said. "Seriously, Sam, everything is breathtaking. The carriage rides, the mason jar lemonades, this"—Maddy swept her hand in the air—"it's so perfect that I can't get over it."

"Hey," Rhys said. "Our wedding was perfect."

"Of course it was." Maddy kissed her husband. "Because I was marrying you, but you know as well as I do that we did it on the fly, shotgun style as a result of Emma."

"Ah, that's bullshit. I wanted to marry you the first day I met you." Rhys nuzzled Maddy's neck.

"Why don't you guys go get a room and leave the rest of us alone," Nate said.

Platters of tri-tip, mashed potatoes, and grilled vegetables started coming from the kitchen and Maddy and Rhys went in search of their own table.

Donna came by, balancing a few drinks in her hands, and told Sam, "You outdid yourself, girl. The open bar—phenomenal." She tottered off to meet up with the rest of the Baker's Dozen and their husbands.

"She's a lush," Nate said into Sam's ear.

"She is not."

The Rodriguezes sat across from them, and once again Sam noted how lovely Cecilia Rodriguez was and how sweet it was that Lucky had escorted her to the wedding. Jake Stryker, a detective with the Nugget Police Department, was also at their table and seemed quite taken with Cecilia. He showed her pictures of his daughters on his phone while Lucky scanned the crowd.

"Is your friend here?" Sam asked Lucky knowingly.

"That obvious, huh?"

"Just a little," Sam said. "Is she here?"

He bobbed his head in the direction of the bandstand. "Over there."

"You planning to go over and say hi?" Sam asked. Nate was listening in on their conversation but trying to pretend that he wasn't.

"Nope," Lucky said. "She can come over here if she wants to get reacquainted."

"Ah." Sam lifted her brows. "So you'll just make yourself crazy tracking her every move?"

"Yep." Lucky took off his hat and finger combed his hair. "That's about the extent of it. If I haven't told you already, this is one exceptional party. We gonna do some of these over at my place?"

"As a matter of fact"—Sam looked at Nate—"just the other day we were talking about the possibilities, weren't we, Nate?"

He let out a sigh and touched her leg under the table. She wasn't sure if he was using the opportunity to feel her up or telling her to shut up. "Yep. We'll set up a meeting next week."

She locked eyes with him as if to say *Really?* And he nodded his head. The table got quiet as everyone dug into their food—some of the most succulent beef Sam had ever tasted. Then again it was raised right here on McCreedy Ranch.

Harlee came over. She'd been taking pictures of the event for the *Nugget Tribune*, while Colin sat at a table with Darla and Wyatt, looking uncomfortable. Sam knew that Colin had trouble dealing with large crowds. She hadn't been made privy to all the details, but knew that he was getting medical help.

Harlee scooted her butt onto Sam's chair. "Are you going to make my wedding as good as this one?"

"Of course," Sam said.

"This wedding could be on national television, that's how good it is," Harlee said. "I love the party favors." They were mini honeypots filled with McCreedy honey. "Can we do something like that for me?"

"I have an idea for that," Sam said. "But we'll need Colin's help. I want him to do little personalized boxes that we can put candy or chocolates in."

"I love it," Harlee said. "Oh, Clay's about to make his toast. I've got to shoot it." She dashed off, clutching her smartphone.

"You really did do a great job," Nate said close to her ear.

He was clearly working her for something, she just didn't know what.

After the toast and dinner, Lucky asked her to dance. She caught Nate scowling as Lucky spun her around the dance floor. When Lucky brought her back to the table, Nate took her out again and pulled her so close she could feel his body heat.

"Nate, what's your game?"

"I don't know what you're talking about."

She put enough distance between them to squint up at him. "You want my help fixing the mess Tracy left you, don't you?"

"Among other things." He smirked.

"What other things?"

"Things we can only do if you quit, and since I need you to save the gala right now, you can't quit."

"Why didn't you just ask me, instead of acting so smarmy? '*I like your dress. You really did do a great job on the wedding. I'm so at-tracted to you, Sam. I think I want to marry you,'"* she mimicked in a high-pitched voice.

"I don't remotely sound anything like that," he said. "Look, it's not easy eating crow. I shouldn't have rejected your help in the first place and now I'm desperate. But I meant every word I said, Sam. I do like your dress, the wedding is amazing, and I am attracted to you. I never said I wanted to marry you. I don't know where the hell that came from."

"Why should I help you if you won't give me the vice presi-dent job?"

"Because it would go a long way toward proving you deserve it. Come on, Sam, be fair. People work years to get promoted to an ex-ecutive position in a big hotel company. You've been working for less than a year."

"What about partnering with Lucky for the barn weddings?"

"You heard me before. I said I would set up a meeting to discuss it next week. See, I can be flexible."

"Just because you want something."

"Sam, it's an all-expense-paid trip to San Francisco. I'll put you up at the Theodore in the same suite you had before. Wine and dine you. It's not like I'm asking you to stick needles in your eyes."

"I just think the way you went about it was manipulative," she said, trying to keep her voice down so no one would hear. "You could've just said, *'Sam, I'm in trouble and need your help.'* I would've gladly helped you."

"Sam, I'm in trouble and need your help."

After the wedding, Nate spent the evening with Lilly, the only fe-male on the planet who still seemed to like him. All right, he should've been up front with Sam. Hell, he shouldn't have turned away her help in the first place, since she might be the only person who could save him from the mess Tracy had left him in.

But the accolades had been real, not just an attempt to sweeten her up.

Despite his doubts about Sam's staying power . . . at Breyer Hotels . . . in Nugget . . . she was pretty terrific. Beautiful. Smart. Defiant as hell. A fantastic hostess. And always appropriate. Her clothes perfect for every occasion, her manners impeccable, and without ever missing a beat, she always knew the right thing to say. He supposed it was part of her moneyed upbringing. But beyond that, she treated people kindly, was self-deprecating, and worked her ass off. The woman also had an instinct for business, which Nate found especially hot.

He was starting to think that Royce had been the problem, not Sam. She'd certainly implied that her fiancé wasn't exactly a prince. Nate got the sense that maybe Royce had cheated. If that was the case, good for her for dumping him.

Unfortunately, Nate was also on her shit list, though she'd agreed to help him get the gala on track. He might have lost the event due to Tracy's negligence, but the organizer seemed more than pleased to have Sam on board. Actually, the old biddy had been ecstatic.

His biggest challenge would be keeping his hands off Sam while they worked so closely together. There had been a few times during the wedding where he'd come close to pulling her away from the festivities so he could work on getting that dress off her.

But he was a man of restraint and no good could come of them sleeping together. Not while she was his employee and not when they lived next door to each other, leaving him nowhere to hide when the affair ended. Because with him, they always did.

Chapter 18

"It seems ridiculous to fly when I can just ride to San Francisco with you," Sam told Nate after their meeting with Lucky.

The meeting had gone far better than Sam had expected. Surprisingly, Lucky was all for the barn weddings and Nate had agreed to a partnership on the condition that the Lumber Baron ran the show and got the bulk of the proceeds. In return, Nate would pay for the refurbishment of an old barn on Lucky's property, including adding heat and electricity and bringing the building up to fire code.

"I may leave a day early," Nate said. "Plus you have a meeting with Landon Lowery."

"It's a phone meeting. I can do that on the road and leave when you leave." She didn't know why he was being so obstinate. By the time she got parking at the airport, went through security and dealt with any delays, it would be more time efficient to drive, which he was doing anyway.

"Trust me, it's better this way."

"Whatever." She lifted her arms in the air. "Are you happy with the deal we made with Lucky?"

"I suppose. Just don't leave me in the lurch by going back to Connecticut after you've booked a bunch of weddings. This is your baby, so don't screw me up on it."

Like your pet, Tracy, she wanted to say. "If you're so concerned, you should give me the vice president job."

"Come on, Sam, we've been over this."

"Fine," she said. "I'll see you at the Theodore."

After work, she called her father, who'd left a couple of messages that he hadn't been feeling well. But when she tried to pin him down on his symptoms, he admitted that he just wanted her to come home.

"I looked up that town you're living in," he said. "The place doesn't even have a movie theater. What do you do all day?"

"I work, Daddy. Today we cut a big deal and the whole concept was my idea." Of course she left out that the concept was throwing special events in a barn.

"I looked up Breyer Hotels too," he huffed.

"And?" She was curious what he'd found.

"I could get you a job at a hotel company twice that size. Something like the Hilton Worldwide or Marriot International. They at least own hotels here in New York or Greenwich."

"But I like my job, Daddy."

"I would just hate to think that you're staying there, in the middle of nowhere, to punish me for Royce," he said. "I was wrong about that, Sam. I should've stood by you when you were having second thoughts."

"I'm not punishing you, Daddy. I sincerely like it here. Besides, I'm vying for a new position."

"What's that?" he asked, and Sam described the VP position for Breyer Hotels.

She told him about Tracy, the gala, the Theodore, and how Nate was relying on her to mend the damage. For the first time she felt like George was actually listening. They didn't resolve the fact that he wanted her to come home and she wanted to stay, but at least they were talking.

By the time Sam got to San Francisco, she was up to speed on the gala and where negotiations had collapsed between Tracy and the organizer, Fifi Reinhardt. And she had to admit that Fifi sounded like a handful. The Reinhardts were wealthy West Coast philanthropists who had made their money in real estate. They weren't on the same social rung as the Dunsburys, so Sam had never met the Reinhardts personally. Still, she knew their ilk well.

She had some ideas on how to smooth Fifi's ruffled feathers, but it would take some compromise. From Sam's experience, people like Fifi didn't like to compromise.

True to Nate's word, he'd put her in the same suite she'd had before. This time, instead of the basket, a large gift box tied in a big bow sat on the coffee table. Much to her delight it was filled with adorable items from the Theodore gift shop: a hoodie with the hotel's logo, a San Francisco Giants baseball cap, a blingy nightshirt depicting the Golden Gate Bridge, a pair of furry slippers, a plush Theodore spa robe, and an industrial-sized container of aspirin with a note from Nate that read, "You'll need this."

Cute.

She called the front desk and asked that Nate be paged, as per his instructions, and ten minutes later he rang her room. "Thanks for the gifts," she said.

"You make this happen and I'll give you the gift shop."

"I'll do my best," she said.

"I thought we could work through dinner in my suite. We could get room service or have one of the hotel restaurants send up food."

"Sounds good."

They agreed to meet in an hour, giving her time to unpack and freshen up. She dressed in a skirt and blouse, not sure how professional she should be or whether others would be attending the meeting. But when she got to Nate's suite just down the hall, he was in jeans and a T-shirt.

"My assistant was supposed to be here, but she had an emergency at home," he said.

"I hope everything's okay."

"Her refrigerator went out and her husband is out of town. Maybe we should take this downstairs to one of the meeting rooms?"

"Why?" she asked, taking stock of the suite, which was as nice as hers but not particularly homey. "It's just the two of us."

"Precisely." He homed in on her skirt and blouse and then higher to her lips, where his eyes seemed to linger.

She cocked a brow. "Afraid for your virtue?"

"Nope. I'm afraid for yours, so stay on that side of the couch."

"You want me to get some tape and put a line down the middle?"

He laughed. "Food's on its way, smart mouth."

She sat down and tugged down her skirt, which had hiked up. When she looked up, he was staring at her legs, but quickly turned his head. Luckily, the awkward moment was interrupted by a knock on the door and someone announcing room service.

"I didn't know what you wanted, so I got a little bit of everything," Nate said while the attendant rolled in a table covered in dishes.

"I can see that," Sam said, and watched Nate tip the guy before he left.

She lifted a few of the silver domes and checked out the offerings. Everything looked delicious, including Nate, who'd dragged a couple of chairs to the table. He'd evidently taken a shower before she'd gotten there, because his hair was still damp and curled at the back of his neck. His shirt, stretched across finely honed muscles, made her mouth water. And he smelled so good, like a combination of citrusy aftershave and soap, that she wanted to nuzzle against his neck.

Instead, she pointed at the plates and asked, "Which is yours?"

"Whatever you don't want."

"There's enough here for us to have some of everything." She took it upon herself to serve them both plates of salmon, steak, wild rice, fried artichokes, and French fries. "We'll have the rest for breakfast." After the words left her mouth, she realized how they must've sounded and felt herself turn red.

Nate raised his brows. She couldn't tell whether he was amused or thought she was being overly suggestive.

Between bites and back to business, Nate asked, "So what's your game plan with Fifi?"

"The truth: I'm planning to kiss her derrière and give her what she wants." Sam cut into her steak, which had been prepared just the way she liked it. Medium rare.

"There's no way in hell we're getting Thomas Keller. And as much as I want this event, I don't want to go into the hole putting it on."

"I know that," Sam said. "Have a little faith, Nate."

"Have a little faith." Nate raised his face to the ceiling as if he was talking to the heavens. "Wait until you meet our chef, Richard, and tell me that. He's as high-maintenance as Fifi. If finding a good executive chef weren't so difficult, I would've fired his ass months ago."

"It'll be fine, Nate. I'm good with these kinds of people."

"I know." He stood up and paced the room.

"Do you like living here?" she asked.

"Yeah. What's not to like?"

She got to her feet and joined him at the window. "You've got great views, but it seems . . . impersonal."

"That's what my Nugget house is for. I like the pictures you put on the walls, by the way. Especially the ones of Lilly."

"I wasn't sure," she said. "I felt like I might've been overstepping, so I'm glad you like them."

He went back to the couch. "I have to be careful about not intruding on their family too much, but the pictures are okay . . . I think."

"I guess there's no protocol on these things. You just have to play it by ear."

"Nope," he said. "There's no guidebook to being the biological father of another couple's child when said couple also happen to be your best friends."

"You seem to be handling it rather well. It's a very beautiful thing you did for Sophie and Mariah, Nate." When he had his own babies, he'd be a good father.

She grabbed the folder she'd brought with her and moved to the loveseat across from him. "I was able to get ahold of the American Society of Hematology and figure out where Tracy left off with their conference. Same with the Gleasons' anniversary party. We're pretty much up to speed on everything now."

"Except for the opera party." He was back to gazing at her lips.

"Mm-hmm." She tried to focus, but kept thinking about his kisses, about how good they felt. If she closed her eyes she could taste him. "You sure you don't want to attend the meeting with Fifi and me tomorrow?"

"Yep. You're the one she wants to meet."

That seemed odd to Sam, since Nate was top dog. But she enjoyed a spark of pride at his sudden trust in her. Or maybe the spark was lust, because she couldn't help but wonder what he'd look like with his shirt off. Ripped, for sure. And a good bet, given the nice masculine smattering of hair on his forearms, that there would be a trail running down his chest. She felt hot just thinking about it.

Nate tilted his head sideways and tried to get her attention. "What are you doing?"

Uh-oh, she must've been staring. Hopefully she didn't have drool on her chin. "Nothing. Just thinking about the meeting."

"Is that all you're thinking about?" The side of his mouth quirked up.

"Of course." She tried to act like she couldn't imagine what else he could be talking about.

"Liar." This time he gave her a full-blown grin, and she noticed the five o'clock shadow on his face.

He must've forgone shaving when he'd showered. She briefly fantasized about how his bristle would feel rubbing over her entire body before reining herself in.

Nate got up to get a drink of water and stood behind the counter in his tiny kitchenette. "Maybe we ought to table this for tomorrow morning."

"Why? I wanted to go over some ideas with you about my presentation for Fifi."

"You know why. You've been sitting there for the last ten minutes, distracted. And I passed distracted a long time ago." His eyes moved down to his southern region and he smiled. "That's why I'm standing back here."

"Fine." She stood up and got her purse. "If you can't control yourself, I'll leave."

"I think that's an excellent idea. You won't mind if I don't walk you out, will you?"

"You're pathetic, Nate."

"Not pathetic, just a man."

She didn't know what possessed her, but she went right up to him, pressed tightly against his body and kissed him. "Is this a problem for you, boss?"

He held his arms up in the air. "Not touching you back."

She snugged up against his hardness, taking the time to watch his expression turn tortured. "How's this?"

"Good. Stay there as long as you like. But I'm still not touching you back."

"How about now?" She undid his belt.

"All good." But his voice sounded strained.

She pulled his jeans down and stroked him over his shorts. His eyes shut and she could feel him shudder. "Still good?"

"Never better," he said on a moan. "But still not touching you."

She pushed away from him and unbuttoned her blouse until it hung open, revealing her lacy demi-cup bra. His eyes heated as they wandered over her breasts and Sam could've sworn that he licked his lips.

"Shit!" Nate leaned his head back into a cabinet and squeezed his eyes closed. "I give up." He hitched up his pants, grabbed her around the waist, tossed her over his shoulder in a fireman's hold and carried her into his bedroom, where he dropped her in the middle of his Cal-king bed. "You up for this? Because if you're not, I suggest you go, now. Fast."

She stared up at him, a little smile playing on her lips. "I'm good."

"Honey, I'm planning to make you a whole lot better than good." He came down on top of her and kissed her until she thought she'd die from the pleasure of it.

She rubbed against him, wanting to twine her legs around his waist so he could nestle himself inside the part of her that ached for him, but her skirt was too tight. The damn thing needed to come off, but she didn't want to stop kissing him to make that happen.

Nate, on the other hand, was a multitasker, because he managed to get her blouse off and her bra unhooked without ever leaving her mouth.

"Mmm," he hummed as he fondled her breasts and rubbed her nipples with his thumb. "These are good." He lifted up to examine them. "They're big."

Sam reached for the blanket.

"What? You're suddenly shy?"

"No," she said, and squirmed to get under the covers.

"Hey." He pressed down on the top of the quilt so she couldn't pull them over her. "Don't. I like looking at you. You're beautiful."

"You don't have to say that."

"I don't have to, but it's the truth. Come on, you've got to know how stunning you are. It's not just me, everybody thinks so."

"Not everybody. But thank you."

He kissed her again, letting his hands wander reverently over her breasts and belly. "So pretty," Nate whispered. "Let's get this off too."

She lifted her butt up so that Nate could unzip the back of her skirt and tug it down her legs. He tossed it across the room and all she could think was thank goodness she'd worn her good underwear. Lace boy-shorts.

"What about you?" she asked.

Nate pulled his T-shirt over his head and Sam sucked in a breath at the sheer perfection of him. He was everything she'd thought he would be and more. Broad shoulders, solid chest, and a set of abs that made her mouth go dry. Whorls of dark hair sprinkled his chest, forming a strip down his stomach that disappeared underneath the waistband of his pants.

She pulled on his jeans until he finally arched up and shucked them off. "Happy now?"

"Mm-hmm." She kissed his neck and his chin and his lips while he played with the lace of her bottoms, dipping his hand underneath the elastic band to feel her wetness. "Oh God."

He scraped the lobe of her ear with his teeth. "You feel good, Sam. So ready for me."

She slipped her hand inside his shorts and wrapped her fingers around his thickness. He was long and unbelievably hard.

He put his hand over hers to hold it still. "Keep that up and I'll embarrass myself."

"I want you, Nate."

"I've wanted you since the first day I saw you."

She pushed up on both elbows. "You hated me on sight."

"That doesn't mean I didn't want you." Nate pushed her back down and rolled on top of her, putting his weight on both hands as he rubbed against her. "These have to go." He pulled her panties down and used his foot to kick them away, then yanked off his own, wedging himself between her legs.

She moaned with pleasure, pumping and rubbing until she thought she'd go mad.

From a drawer next to the bed, he grabbed a couple of foil packets and put them on top of the nightstand, then kissed his way down the length of her body, licking her bellybutton, the insides of her thighs, delving into the place that quivered for him.

"Nate," she whimpered.

"Hmm?"

"Please."

"Please what?"

She tried to roll on top of him, but he held her down and said, "Let me enjoy you. We've got all night."

Nothing had ever felt this good. Not even those wonderful starlit nights at the summerhouse, when she'd been impossibly young and in love. Nate continued to lave her in kisses and explore her body with his hands and mouth until she thought she would explode. And finally, finding it impossible to wait any longer, she did.

"Good?" Nate moved over her as he tore the wrapper off a condom and rolled it down the length of him.

"God, yes." She pulled him closer, wanting him inside of her. But when he entered her, she jolted; his size a little overwhelming at first.

"You okay?" He stopped, giving her time to grow accustomed to him, then slowly moving inside of her, making her feel like liquid fire ready to combust.

"Mmm," she whimpered. "More."

He gave her so much more that by the time they fell asleep it was dawn. And when she opened her eyes it was bright outside and he was gone. Just a note on his empty pillow.

*I had an early meeting and didn't
want to wake you. Break a leg with Fifi.
Thanks
Nate*

That was the extent of the note. No "Last night was great," or "Sam, you were the best sex I've ever had," or "Be mine forever." Not even so much as "Hey, let's have dinner later." Just "Thanks." And was that thanks for transcendent sex, or thanks for meeting with Fifi? Sam had no idea, but chided herself for being such a girl about it.

They had sex. Sex that she had initiated. They'd been dancing around it for months now and had finally nipped it in the bud. No big deal.

"So why are you anguishing over a perfectly innocuous note?" she asked herself aloud, shoved on her clothes, and made sure the coast was clear before making a run down the hall for her room.

It would all be fine, she told herself. They'd make a joke of it. *Ha, ha, can you believe we actually did that?*

But as Sam stepped into the shower, she decided that sleeping with Nate was possibly the stupidest thing she'd ever done.

Because now she liked him—like really, really liked him. And the best he had to offer was to tell her to break a leg.

Chapter 19

Nate couldn't care less about San Francisco's occupancy rates. Well, actually he did care about it, because it could make or break his business. He just didn't care about it at this very moment. Not when he'd had to leave a warm and willing woman in his bed to listen to someone from the city's travel board drone on about tourism and what it meant to the city.

Sam. Wow.

He was still trying to wrap his head around the fact that they'd done it. If he wanted to level with himself, they'd been working up to last night for some time. Flirting. Kissing. Throwing barbs at each other like school kids with a crush.

In bed, she'd been something else. She may have started out as the aggressor, but she'd ultimately let him run the show. Call him a caveman, but he liked taking the lead, making her feel so good that she lost her mind, because it made him lose his.

The whole night had been like that. Total sweet insanity. And if he thought she looked hot in clothes, she was a supermodel out of them. Weird how she had gotten insecure about her body, which did it for him like no other woman's body did. It made him wonder why. But then again, women could be strange about being naked.

After the meeting, Nate caught a Lyft taxi back to the hotel. He thought about popping in on Sam's conference with Fifi, but decided that he'd leave her to it. When he got to Breyer's corporate offices, his assistant, Lorna, waylaid him at the door.

"I've been trying to reach you all morning," she said.

Nate pulled his phone out of his pocket and found a blank screen.

"Sorry, I thought I had it on vibrate. What's going on?"

"Your sister is desperate to get ahold of you."

Lilly flashed in his head, then Emma. But it could just as easily be Rhys. He was the cop, after all. He brushed past Lorna into his office, grabbed the landline and hit automatic dial.

The phone rang only once before Maddy picked up. "It's about time."

"Is everyone okay?"

He must've sounded panicked because Maddy said, "I didn't mean to scare you, Nate. It's Gold Mountain. You told me to keep quiet about it, so I didn't know if I could tell Lorna. Someone's made an offer."

He took a deep breath, relieved. He could handle losing Gold Mountain, but his family . . . "How do you know?"

"The buyers asked Pat Donnelly to do an inspection and give them an estimate on fixing some of the cabins. Pat took Colin with him, Colin mentioned it to Harlee, and Harlee told me."

That was Nugget for you. Everyone knew everybody's business. "Is it a done deal or is there time for us to swoop in?"

"I don't think it's a done deal yet," Maddy said. "Apparently, Pat's bid was high and these folks are strapped for cash. It sounds like they're working with a bank. But if we came in with cash . . . I just hate feeling pressured to rush in."

"That's business, Maddy. Do we know who these folks are?"

"Harlee didn't know and I didn't want to seem overly interested."

Smart thinking, given that Harlee, nosy reporter, had good instincts when it came to sniffing out a story. Gold Mountain changing hands was just the kind of news people in Plumas County went for, since not a lot happened there. "I think we should make a cash offer, but lowball it. Even if they don't accept it, it'll stall a possible sale with this other party until we decide how high we want to go."

"All right. But you better get here quick."

"I can be there in five hours." He was allowing for traffic across the Bay Bridge and through Sacramento. "In the meantime, why don't you contact their broker and tell them we'd like to set up a meeting to present an offer. I'll have our lawyer draw up something and fax it to the Lumber Baron."

"Okay," she said. "Wow. I can't believe we're doing this."

"Sometimes you've gotta just go for it." Yeah, that had obviously been his motto last night.

Nate hung up, called his lawyer, and got on the road as fast as he could. Somewhere near Auburn, Maddy telephoned to say they had their meeting. He'd have just enough time to get home, change, and pick up his sister.

On the Bluetooth, he tried Sam a few times to see how it had gone with Fifi, but failed to reach her. By now their meeting should've been long over. He was anxious to hear how the two women had gotten along. Had he known how impressed Fifi would be with Sam's last name, he would've had her handle the account from the get-go.

They could talk tomorrow when she got home. A little distance right now would do them good because he couldn't stop thinking about her. It was more than just last night. More than her being his physical type, in and out of bed. She . . . well . . . she just got him. His house was a perfect example. Everything she'd done in there exhibited what was important to him. The pictures, the books and the warm, welcoming feeling he got when he walked in the door. She even understood about Lilly.

He'd just passed Sierraville when the phone rang. He pressed the Bluetooth button on his dash, hoping it was Sam.

"The papers have been faxed," Nate's lawyer said.

"Thanks, Josh. As soon as I know more we'll be in touch."

Thirty minutes later he pulled into his driveway only to find Samantha on his front porch. She hustled down the steps as he got out of the car.

"They told me you had an emergency at home, so I caught the first flight to Reno," she said. "I just got back and came here immediately. Is everyone—"

"Everyone is fine. It's just a business situation, Sam."

"Thank God." She visibly relaxed, then her expression turned worried again. "Is it the Lumber Baron?"

"No," Nate assured her. "I'm sorry. I should've told Lorna. It's a property Maddy and I are interested in buying, but we've been keeping it on the down-low. Look, we're supposed to present an offer and I still have to change and pick up my sister. I want to hear about your meeting with Fifi. Can we do it when I get back?"

"Of course," she said, and seemed a little disconcerted. Then again, she'd just hopped a sixty-minute flight from SFO and driven fifty minutes from Reno because she thought something terrible had happened to him. "I'm just glad everything's okay here. I guess I overreacted."

"I should have left you a note." He felt bad that he'd put her through the worry. For a piece of property, no less.

She gave him a weak smile. "We'll talk tomorrow. I'm exhausted."

He watched her walk away, wondering if he should go after her and ask what was wrong with talking tonight. But he still had to go to the Lumber Baron and pick up the paperwork, his phone pinged with text messages, and the clock was ticking.

That night, Nate returned home the proud owner of Gold Mountain. At least he would be as long as they got a passing property inspection on the derelict cabin colony. He still couldn't believe that the old man's kids had agreed to the price. But according to the broker, they barely spoke to one another after one of the brothers had roped the entire family into a bad investment. Some sort of pyramid scheme that forced one of the siblings into bankruptcy and another into losing her home. They were just happy to have a short escrow and the cash.

Instead of pulling his car into the garage, he left it in the driveway and considered wandering over to Sam's place. But her house was pitch-dark. If he didn't know better, he'd think she wasn't home. Nate looked at his watch. A little after eleven. After they'd cut their deal, he'd gone over to Maddy and Rhys's house to celebrate.

He made it as far as Sam's porch before turning around. Tomorrow would be soon enough to talk about the gala. Halfway back to his house, he hung a U-turn and rang the bell on her door. A few minutes later he heard movement, a light flickered on, and he saw one blue eye through the peephole. He smiled back at her and she opened the door in boxer shorts, a tank top, and a bad case of bed head.

"Were you asleep?" he asked with all the innocence he could muster, then let himself in and made his way into her kitchen. "Can I have a drink?"

She padded after him and got the bottle of brandy and two snifters down from the cabinet.

"I was thinking more in terms of coffee, but that'll work."

Sam looked at him like he was nuts. "It's nearly midnight."

"Yep. And I just bought a run-down, piece-of-shit cabin park."

"That's the property you made an offer on?"

"It's called Gold Mountain and it's about fifteen minutes from here and fifteen minutes from Glory Junction."

"That cute little ski town?"

"That's the one," he said, and watched her hop on one of the center-island stools. She wasn't wearing a bra.

"What's your plan for it?"

"Fix it up. It's one of those places that for generations the same families have been coming back to, year after year. But the infrastructure has gone to hell and none of the cabins are winterized, cutting the season short. I'd like to upgrade them and run a bus back and forth from Gold Mountain to the ski resorts in the winter."

"Sounds smart," she said.

"Yeah, I'm a smart guy." That's why he was contemplating doing something incredibly stupid, like taking her to bed again. But she was so damn pretty . . . the outline of her breasts in that tank top was arousing the hell out of him. Even though he no longer wanted to talk shop, he forced himself to ask, "How did it go with Fifi?" After all, that's why he'd come. To discuss business.

Keep telling yourself that.

"It went well," she said, stretching one pale, bare leg down the length of the stool. Her toenails, he noticed, were fire-engine red. Sexy. "For some reason, we hit it off."

"Not overly demanding?" Nate asked, and sipped his brandy.

"Oh, she's demanding. You should hear some of the crazy ideas she's come up with. She thinks she'll get Sting to perform. Hey, her problem, not ours. Our bone of contention is the food. She hates Richard. And frankly I can't blame her. The guy thinks he's Jöel Robuchon."

Nate laughed. God, she was hot. He loved the way she talked about business, like she'd been working in the hospitality industry for years. "I can't fire Richard."

"I know." She chewed on her bottom lip and Nate knew he wasn't going to like her plan. "I'm thinking of bringing in Brady." Sam put up her hand to stop him from interrupting. "Before you say no, hear me out."

He didn't want to hear her out. He wanted to carry her into the bedroom and get his hands and mouth on her. "Okay."

"Brady impressed me at Emily's wedding. He wasn't even getting paid and he jumped right in. And the man knows his stuff. He's also nice, not a diva like Richard. So we put him in charge of catering for the gala and let him use Richard's staff."

"Richard won't like us using his people," Nate said.

"Who pays them? Richard or Breyer Hotels?"

"Jeez, listen to you. I've created a monster." Nate scrubbed his hands through his hair. "You think Fifi will go for Brady? The woman wanted Thomas Keller, for God's sake."

"We'll tell Brady to turn on his Southern charm. No woman can resist it."

"What? You think Brady's charming? Brady's not charming."

"Of course he is," Sam said, and let out a little yawn.

"But I'm more charming, right?" He spun her stool sideways so that he could stand between her legs.

"If you say so." She flashed him a teasing smile and reached up to kiss him. It was dark outside, but her lips felt like sunshine, warming him all the way to his toes.

"Wanna go to bed?" He slid his hands under her tank top, inching up until he fondled her breasts. His brain was screaming *You idiot*, but the rest of him promised this would be the last time. Just tonight.

Right.

"With you or Brady?" she said.

"Not funny. You wanna just do it here?" He was partially kidding.

But when she didn't say no, he boosted her up on the counter and untied the drawstring on her shorts. She wrapped her legs around his waist and reached for his belt. He tongued her beautiful breasts through the thin fabric of her top.

"What are we doing, Nate?"

"Having fun," he said low in his throat because while she brushed her hand against his fly he was finding it difficult to breathe.

She undid the buttons on his shirt, running her fingers through the hair on his chest. He shrugged the shirt off, tugged off her tank, and she wiggled out of her shorts until they dropped on the floor. They kissed and touched and rubbed on each other until he couldn't wait anymore. He grabbed a condom from his wallet and dropped his pants.

"Is that all?" she asked, spreading her gorgeous thighs to let him in.

"All what?" He'd lost track of the conversation about two intense kisses ago.

"Just having fun?" she said as he pulled her to the edge of the granite, slid inside her and pumped so hard and fast he thought he'd lose his mind. "Because I think I may be falling in love with you."

And that's when Nate climaxed.

He didn't say anything when they were done, just pulled up his pants and lifted Sam off the counter. She stood there naked and sated and sure that she'd turned fifty shades of red. How could she have blurted such a thing? Hopefully he would think her declaration a mere spontaneous utterance. A lot of people said weird things in the throes of passion. Everyone knew it didn't mean anything. Maybe she was just a floozy who told every man she slept with that she loved him.

"I better get going," he finally said, and she scrambled for her tank top and shorts, throwing them on like a teenager who'd just been caught having sex with the boy next door.

"Okay." It came out like a croak. "See you tomorrow."

"Yeah, see you tomorrow." Maybe it was her imagination, but he seemed to run for the door.

As he was halfway across the lawn, she called, "Congratulations on Gold Mountain. I mean . . . you know . . . way to go." *And way to stand there like a freak show*, she chided herself.

"Thanks." He gave her a mechanical wave goodbye and disappeared inside his house.

Sam locked up and made a beeline for her shower, wanting to wash her mouth out with soap for her stupid, stupid confession. But after twenty minutes under the hot spray, she felt worse than mortified, she felt heartbroken. Nate only liked her for fun, and she liked him for everything.

For all his skepticism about her abilities, no man had ever made her feel more confident or beautiful or clever than Nate had. He was the only man who had ever made her see her full potential. And the only man who didn't care that she was a Dunsbury. In fact, she knew that he held it against her.

He was breathtakingly handsome and smart and funny . . . and cynical . . . and sarcastic . . . and imperfect . . . and perfect for her. Except he didn't think she was perfect for him.

She went to sleep, refusing to cry. And when her alarm went off, she seriously considered staying under the covers and calling in sick.

Coward. Pretty soon, Landon Lowery and his clan would be coming to town, and she had lots to do. So she dragged her butt out of bed, got ready for work, and drove in.

As soon as she got in the door of the inn, she smelled coffee and bacon and wandered into the kitchen.

"Hey," Brady said. "Grab a seat and I'll feed you."

"I'm not that hungry." But she sat down anyway.

He gave her a commiserating glance and shoved a plate under her nose. "Go ahead, have some bacon. Everything's better with pig."

She'd never heard that one before and despite herself, smiled. And nibbled. Brady slid a steaming cup of coffee her way.

"The meeting with Miss Priss didn't go so well, I take it?"

"With Fifi? It actually went better than expected."

"Oh yeah." He glanced at her again but didn't say anything.

"I need to talk to you about it because I want you to be in charge of catering the event instead of asshole Richard. Where's Nate?"

"He was in at the crack of dawn and said he had to go somewhere." Brady went back to his prep work.

It probably had something to do with Gold Mountain. Or maybe he was trying to avoid her. She planned to act like her idiotic confession had never happened. "Would you be up for doing the event? We'd pay you extra, of course, and put you up at the Theodore, where you would use the kitchen and staff."

"Sure. It would be a kick. But who'll cook here?"

"The event isn't until September, so maybe we can rope Emily into covering for you. It would only be a weekend and whatever advance prep time you'd need. But I'm not going to lie to you; Fifi's a ballbuster."

"I've worked with my share of ballbusters." The corner of his mouth tugged up. "I can handle her."

"That's what I told Nate." She finished her breakfast and locked herself inside her office.

Landon wanted an itinerary for the week of his family reunion. She finalized the plans and emailed them to him. Then Sam wrote a thank-you note to Fifi, dropped it in the mail, and returned a few calls. And at noon she strolled over to the Ponderosa to get lunch. Harlee and Darla sat in one of the back booths and waved her over.

"You guys don't care if I join you?"

"Don't be ridiculous," Harlee said, and pushed a plate of fries toward Sam. "If I keep eating those, I won't fit into my wedding gown."

"You getting excited?" Sam asked, although the last thing she wanted to talk about was weddings and couples in love.

"I am." Harlee hugged herself. "I can't believe it's happening so fast. Even Colin is getting into it. He's already finished half of the little boxes. They're the sweetest party favors you've ever seen. He's buying a laser etching machine so he can put each guest's name on their box."

"So adorable, right?" Darla said. Today she had lime-green streaks in her hair and had done her nails to match.

"They sound wonderful." Sam ordered a salad and iced tea from the server and tried to change the subject. "Any good gossip?"

"I'm hearing rumors that Nate and Maddy are in the process of buying Gold Mountain." Harlee nudged Sam's shoulder. "What do you know? I'm trying to get a story on the website today."

"No comment, I'm afraid."

"You're no fun."

Apparently that's all Nate thought she was. Fun. "I would just like to keep my job, Harlee."

"You know you just indirectly confirmed it, right?"

Sam pretended to lock her lips and throw away the key. "What else do you have?"

"Apparently some chick named Raylene Rosser is back in town," Harlee said. "Darla knows her."

"I don't *know her* know her, I just know of her," Darla said. "She's from the Rock and River Ranch. Married some rich guy from Denver, who cheated on her with her best friend. All pretty unremarkable, except that there was some big scandal with her and Lucky Rodriguez when she was a senior in high school. Afterward, Lucky left town. Weird that they both came back at the same time, isn't it?"

"What kind of scandal?" Sam suspected that Raylene was the blonde from the Ponderosa—the same woman Lucky had been scoping out at the wedding.

"I don't know," Darla said. "All I know is that Lucky's mom was a housekeeper at the Rock and River and Lucky used to wrangle there on weekends. I don't think Cecilia likes the Rossers much."

From the little Sam had talked to Cecilia at Emily's wedding, she thought the woman was lovely. Sam had never met the Rossers.

Sophie brought Sam's salad and grabbed a seat at their table.

"Who's taking care of Lilly today?" Darla asked.

"She's upstairs with Mariah. We're trying to get the apartment ready to rent."

"You have any prospects?" Harlee asked. Sam had seen the apartment and it was not at all what she would've expected for a flat above a bowling alley. It had lots of open space, great views, gleaming hardwood floors, and oodles of old-world charm.

"I think Tater wants it," Sophie said. "He's been living in a rental cabin out in the boondocks and would like to be closer to town now that his parents are getting older."

Tater had always been a mystery to Sam. With his grizzled face he could be thirty or sixty. It's not like she could tell from his voice, because the man barely spoke. But Nate liked him. Sometimes she'd see him standing near the kitchen window conversing with the Ponderosa cook. That was the thing about Nate. As sophisticated and Harvard and big-time hotelier as he was, he fit in around here. He played basketball with the guys at the police station, got his hair cut at the barbershop, and hung out sometimes with Griffin at the Gas and Go.

"That would be perfect," Harlee said. "Then he could just roll out of bed to get to work."

"Exactly." Sophie laughed and turned to Sam. "Have you seen Nate? I went over to the inn a little while ago, but he wasn't there."

"No. Brady said he had an errand to do." Sam speared a tomato in her salad and popped it into her mouth, wondering if Nate would tell Sophie that they'd slept together. He and Sophie were best friends, after all.

"Speaking of Brady, how's that going?" Darla asked. "I want to get my hands on his hair. The guy is so hot."

Harlee nudged her best friend. "Hey, you have Wyatt."

"It doesn't mean I can't admire a good-looking man. Uh . . . it's sort of my job as a stylist."

Harlee rolled her eyes. "What's his story? It's like he materialized out of nowhere."

Just like Sam. She'd only been here six months, but already felt like part of the town. She had wonderful friends, a great house, and an even better job. Here, no one cared that her family's money was older than California. And here is where she met Nate. And lost him.

"He seems to be fitting in well," Sam said. "I don't know what brought him here, but he came at a perfect time." Maybe, like Sam, he'd been running from his past, looking for his future.

Sam finished her lunch and went back to the inn, feeling even more melancholy than she had before. Talking about Harlee's wedding hadn't helped, not that Sam wanted to get married. Not after her last catastrophe.

"Hey." Andy, who stood behind the front desk, wearing his usual morose attitude, nudged his chin at her. "You got a delivery."

"What is it?"

"It's inside your office." He rubbed his fingers together. "Big bucks."

Apparently he planned to keep her in suspense during the four steps to her office. Andy. She shook her head and went to see what it was. Dozens of red roses sat in a vase on her desk. At a glance, she'd say three or four dozen. They had to be from George. Her father must've finally figured out that you get more bees with roses than by selling off your daughter's prized summerhouse.

She took the time to inhale the flowers' sweet aroma, then picked up the phone and dialed.

"Thank you for the roses, Daddy."

"You're welcome," George said. "But I didn't send you roses. If you'll come home, though, I'll buy you an entire flower shop. How did your meeting go?"

The question surprised her, since he'd never taken her job seriously. For Sam, his interest was even better than flowers.

"It went great," she said. "Thanks for asking. I think you would like this Fifi Reinhardt. She's incredibly bullheaded."

"What's that supposed to mean?" he said, but Sam could hear the smile in his voice. "The Reinhardts. Real estate, right?"

"Yes. You know them?"

"Nope, don't believe we've ever met. So who sent you flowers?"

Good question, since Sam had thought it was George. "I don't know. Come to think of it, maybe it was Fifi." It was something someone like her would do.

"Hmm. You get any further along with that VP job?"

"No. Nate doesn't think I have enough experience."

"Then what are you waiting for? Come home."

Maybe visiting Connecticut for a week was a good idea. She could hide from Nate until she got over her embarrassment and come back in time for Landon Lowery's family reunion. "I don't know, Daddy. I'll have to see if I've accrued any vacation time."

George let out a loud harrumph. "If you haven't, quit."

She shook her head. Her father might be making strides, but he still didn't get it. "I'll let you know."

"You do that. And, Samantha?"

"Yes?"

"I miss you."

"I miss you too, Daddy." Suddenly she missed him so much her chest ached.

After hanging up the phone, Sam searched the bouquet for that ubiquitous white envelope, which she grabbed out of the holder, opened, and read the card.

I'm pretty sure I love you too, which will probably screw up everything.
Nate

She read it fifteen times and even cried a little bit.

Chapter 20

Sam headed down the hall to Nate's office as if she were walking on air. Happiness flooded every fiber of her body. And her heart did cartwheels at the possibilities of what their life could be together.

He loved her. And God, did she love him—the man who'd been her nemesis since moving to Nugget. She could hardly believe it. But didn't they say that love came when you least expected it? And Sam could safely say that she'd never dreamt of finding Nate Breyer.

Not here. Not now.

The door to his office was shut. The poor man was hiding, clearly wanting to give her time to digest his message. And she supposed the flowers were his way of apologizing for running out on her after he'd made love to her on the kitchen counter, of all places.

She went to knock but heard him talking on the phone, so she cracked the door an inch. He sat with his back to her, looking out the window, caught up in his conversation.

"I'm glad you liked her, Fifi, and I'm glad we'll be doing business together . . . Yeah, she definitely has good ideas . . . No, I don't think she can get you Sting. We're leaving that feat up to you. But Samantha definitely knows what she's doing."

Sam got a lump in her throat. That was high praise from Nate and it made her a little emotional. She'd obviously come a long way in his eyes. *And he loved her.*

"Well, she's definitely got that going for her," Nate continued. "Being a Dunsbury certainly has its privileges—and connections." There was a long pause. "No question her name will add gravitas to your event. Are you kidding? Why do you think I put her on the job?" He laughed, and as if suddenly sensing he wasn't alone, turned his chair, catching a glimpse of Sam in the doorway. "Hey, Fifi, I have to go."

"I didn't hear you come in," he said to Sam by way of a greeting. "What's wrong? Didn't you get my note . . . the flowers?"

"Is that why you gave me Fifi's event, because I'm a Dunsbury?" Sam said, stunned.

"It impressed her, so why not?"

"Why not?" She jerked her head back and blinked back tears. "Because you were using me . . . my name . . . my connections." Just like Royce had. She heard his mocking voice in her head: *The dumb cow is nothing more than a for-show wife.*

"You gave me the assignment because my social status impressed Fifi, not because of my abilities. I'm just a token," she said, and spun on her heels, running out of the inn.

She needed to get out of there, to be alone where she could cry and no one would see her shame. So Sam got in her car and drove away, just like she'd done in New York. After Royce. This time, however, she only made it as far as the Nevada County line before turning back to Nugget. Back to her house in the woods, where she could spend the rest of the afternoon under the covers, like she should've done in the first place.

But when she got home, Nate was sitting on her front porch. She thought about pulling away, but was nearly out of gas and didn't feel like running into anyone she knew at the Gas and Go. On her way out of the car, her heel caught on the hem of her pants and she had to grab for the door to keep from falling on her face. Graceful.

She marched up the stairs, where he'd made himself comfortable in her Colin rocker with his feet propped up on the railing.

Nate stood up. "Please tell me what I did wrong."

"If you don't know, we have nothing to talk about." She pressed the code into her keypad and started to go inside when he held the door closed.

"I get it," he said. "I tell you that I'm falling for you, so you drum up some ridiculous offense to give you an excuse to run. Just like you did with 'what's-his-face."

She pointedly glared at his hand, flicked it away, went inside her house, and slammed the door in his face.

He pounded on it. "Come on, Sam, talk to me."

"Please go," she called through the door. She watched through her window as he paced the porch, then finally got in his car and drove away.

The man had used her pedigree to get business for his hotel. He'd traded on her name. All along, she'd thought that Nate had assigned her the job because of her capabilities and competence. Because she had the grit to clean up Tracy's mess. She thought he believed in her. But he'd dangled her in front of Fifi Reinhardt like a shiny party favor.

Here's a Dunsbury. She'll impress your rich friends and bring in big donors.

No wonder Jacqueline Kennedy Onassis had chosen publishing as her vocation. She'd got to lock herself in a room to read book proposals all day, instead of exposing herself to the vultures. How could Nate do this to her? How could he tell her that he loved her? It was like déjà vu.

The dumb cow is nothing more than a for-show wife.

Apparently she was nothing more than a for-show event planner, too.

"Sam in yet?" Nate asked when he arrived at work the next morning. He'd passed her office on his way to the kitchen for a cup of coffee, but her door was closed. After a good night's sleep, he figured he could talk some sense into her.

"She called in sick," Brady said, and handed Nate a plate of coffee cake. Nate loved Brady's coffee cake, but today he had no appetite.

Sick. Great!

"I think there's something going around." Brady gave him a pointed glance and passed the cream.

Yeah, she had the avian flu and was getting ready to fly right out of Nugget—and his life. Nate knew it. As soon as things had started getting hot and heavy between them, she'd concocted the ludicrous drama about him using her to get Fifi's business. A: He wanted Fifi's business, but he didn't need it bad enough to put Sam in a bad position. B: He would never intentionally hurt Sam—he loved the woman, for God's sake. C: It was bullshit. Fifi was impressed with the fact that Samantha was a Dunsbury. So what? Who better to help plan a fund-raiser for the opera than a big-time philanthropist for the arts? Someone who knew exactly what high-society guests would expect from a function like this. Even Randall, who'd been with him since the beginning, didn't have her background for this kind of event.

But that's not why he'd given her the project. He'd given it to her because the damn party was scheduled for September and she was the most competent person on his event staff to pull it off. After he saw what she'd done at Emily's wedding, he was 100 percent sold. Hell, he'd been prepared to make her the vice president of event planning for Breyer Hotels in a few more months.

Clearly, however, she was pulling a Kayla and was just looking for an excuse to pull the plug. On him and the Lumber Baron. The sad part was that he'd known better but he'd still fallen for her, convincing himself that it would be different this time. That she was the real deal. Well, forget her. He didn't need this. He didn't need her.

"If anyone wants me, I'll be across the street getting a haircut," Nate told Brady, then stomped across the square to Owen's barbershop.

It was Darla's day off, but Owen agreed to give Nate a trim. "Heard some high-tech mogul's coming into town to stay at your inn."

"Yeah, where did you hear that?"

"I've got my sources. Who is it? That Apple fellow, Steve Jobs?" Owen snapped a cape around Nate's neck.

"You're kidding me, right? Steve Jobs died three years ago. His death made international news."

"I must've missed it," Owen said. "Well, whoever it is, it can't beat Della James."

The country music star had come to Nugget last summer for a photo shoot for her cookbook—the one Emily had ghostwritten for her. People here were still talking about her temper tantrums, which were legendry in the music industry.

"Not too short," Nate told Owen, who could get a little overzealous with the scissors.

"You're not going to spill the beans?"

"Nothing to spill," Nate said. Even if he told Owen that their mystery guest was Landon Lowery, the barber wouldn't know the famous game-maker from Adam.

"You want me to clean up your neck?" Owen didn't bother to wait for an answer, just got out the clippers. "How about Clay and Emily's wedding? Folks here will be talking about that one for a long time. Your girl Sam did one hell of a job."

Used to be his girl. For about ten seconds. "It was a nice wedding."

Owen let out a low whistle. "How much you think that bar tab was? I saw folks double-fisting drinks."

"I have no idea. You almost done?"

"Now hold your horses, boy. You want this done right, don't you?"

Nate didn't really care. He'd only come because he wanted to get out of the Lumber Baron, away from Sam, who wasn't even there. Home, sick, his ass. But maybe he should cruise by her house just to make sure. God, he was an idiot.

"Griffin got himself another tow truck," Owen said. The man talked in non sequiturs. "Waste of money, if you ask me. He'd be better off investing in a snow plow. But I suppose if the roads are clear, there won't be as many vehicles getting stuck, which would put his tow business under."

"I'm sure it's a huge conspiracy." Nate didn't know why he was taking out his foul mood on Owen. Most of the time he sort of enjoyed the guy.

"So I hear you and Lucky Rodriguez are in cahoots." Owen made it sound like they were planning bank heists.

"We're working together on a couple of joint packages." No need to get into details. Now that Sam was leaving, who knew what would come of their barn-wedding plans.

"Interesting how he came home at the same time as Raylene, isn't it?"

"Who's Raylene?" Nate asked, only mildly interested.

"Little gal from the Rock and River Ranch. Used to be the toast of Nugget. Head cheerleader, homecoming queen, Plumas County Rodeo Queen. She married some rich fellow up in Denver. Word is that he cheated on her with her best friend and she drove his Escalade into the swimming pool."

"Nice."

"Years ago, there was a scandal at the Rock and River, something involving Lucky. Some people say he shot a ranch hand for molesting Raylene." Nate suspected that was a crock, but folks here loved their drama. "Whatever it was," Owen continued, "Lucky blew out of town the next day. Only came back to visit his mama. Until now, of course, when he comes moseying back to Nugget at the same time as Raylene."

"He bought property here, Owen. He's doing tons of work at the old Roland camp. It's not exactly like he just *moseyed* into town. Escrow, construction, that kind of stuff requires planning."

"An awful big coincidence if you ask me."

Whatever. Nate didn't know why he got caught up in town gossip. Half of it was wrong and the other half was nobody's business. "He's probably here to dig up the ranch hand's corpse before Raylene goes to the authorities. You and the rest of the Nugget Mafia ought to stake out the place. There might be a reward."

Owen muttered something about Nate being a smart aleck and used a fat brush to wipe the hairs from his neck. He took off the cape. "You're done."

On Nate's way back to the Lumber Baron he bumped into Rhys in front of the police station. "How's it going?" Nate said, and looked at his watch as if he was in a big hurry. He wasn't in the mood for chewing the fat with his brother-in-law. He was actually hoping that Sam had gotten over whatever ailment she supposedly had and had come to work.

"All's quiet on the Western front," Rhys said.

"Good to hear," Nate said, and started for the inn.

"Hey, come into my office for a few minutes." Rhys held the door to the police station open, motioning for Nate to follow him in.

"Uh . . . I've got a thing back at the Lumber Baron," Nate said.

"You can spare a few minutes for family." When Rhys put it that way, there wasn't much Nate could do but go inside.

"Hi, Connie," Nate said to the police dispatcher whose desk sat right near the door.

She pointed at her headset to let him know that someone was talking to her and, without missing a beat, got up and poured him a cup of coffee.

"Thanks," he whispered, to which she nodded her head.

He went into Rhys's office and took a chair. "What's up?"

"Nothing. Just thought we should have some quality time together." Rhys flashed him a smart-ass smile.

Nate shook his head. "Why? You dying?"

Rhys sailed a dart across the room and hit a bull's-eye on the board. "Other than buying real estate with my wife, we haven't seen too much of you lately."

"I've been busy."

"With a certain redhead?" Rhys cocked his brows.

"No. She's no longer talking to me."

"Why? You put gum in her hair? Why don't you two just sleep with each other and get it over with?" Rhys nudged his head at Nate. "What's this deal I hear about you and Lucky Rodriguez putting on barn weddings at his place?"

"Nothing set in stone," Nate said, because he didn't know where the deal stood without Sam. "Why? You've got a problem with it?"

"Not at all. I told you, I like the guy. It just seems like you're taking on a lot, especially with Gold Mountain. Maddy says your chief event planner left."

"Yeah. I may have to restructure things."

"The chef working out okay?" Rhys kicked his boots up on the desk.

"Brady?" He was about the only employee working out right now. "So far, so good."

Connie knocked and popped her head into Rhys's office. "We've got a 2-11 on Freedom Ranch Road. A chicken coop."

"Oh, for Christ's sake. It's Leonard stealing eggs again."

"You want me to send Wyatt?" Connie asked.

"Nah, I'll take it." Rhys grabbed his keys off a hook behind his desk.

Nate smirked. "Glad we could have this talk."

"I'll catch you later."

Nate followed his brother-in-law outside and watched him jog to a police SUV and peel off with his lights flashing. Apparently egg theft was a big emergency in Nugget. He walked back across the square to the inn and wandered down the hall to his office. Still no sign of Sam. But his flowers were still on her desk.

That night the lights were out in her house. Four or five times he started over there and pulled himself back. He wasn't going to beg like he'd done with Kayla. That had crushed his pride, but getting rejected by Sam . . . would crush his soul.

He couldn't eat, he couldn't sleep, and when dawn finally broke he got in his car and drove to San Francisco.

Worse came to worst, he'd call Maddy to fill in for Sam at the Lumber Baron. But he needed to get away, bury himself in work, and try to forget her. When he got to Sacramento, he stopped for coffee and made the dreaded call. Andy answered on about the seventh ring.

"Did Sam show up?" Nate asked, not bothering with a greeting.

"Yeah. You want to talk to her?"

Nate paused. "No. Tell her I'm in San Francisco the rest of the week." If she wanted to talk, she could call him.

By the time he got to the Theodore there was a message from her waiting for him. Written in Lorna's signature scrawl, it sat on top of his keyboard. He read as much as Sam's name before stopping. It could wait. Bad news could always wait.

He took the elevator up to his suite, changed, and went to the gym. He ran six miles on the treadmill, until he dripped sweat. Then he rinsed off, jumped in the pool, and swam fifty laps. In the shower, he leaned his head against the cool tile, let the jet-spray sluice over him, hoping that the water would invigorate him to face whatever Sam had to throw at him. Instead, he felt the shower stall closing in on him. Like he was suffocating.

How had everything gotten so screwed up? Correction: How had he let himself get suckered in? Because he'd known from the get-go that anything between him and Sam was fated to fail. Only this time it felt different than with Kayla, like maybe he'd been the one to screw up. He just didn't get why telling Fifi that Sam was a Dunsbury was so terrible. Should he have lied to Fifi and told her Sam's last name was Smith? And if Sam's name had been Smith, he would've given her the project anyway.

He dressed, went out onto the street to buy a hotdog from the vending cart, took two bites and threw it away. When he got back to his office, he shoved the note under a paperweight and returned a few calls.

Nothing like avoidance.

Lisa had gotten engaged and wanted a long weekend to go home to Atlanta to celebrate with her and her fiancé's parents. Great. He was already short staffed. But he left her a message that she could take the time.

"Nate?" Lorna pushed through the door. "Sam's called three times. She needs an answer. Yes or no?"

"Tell her yes," he said, and deliberately turned from her in a subtle—okay, not so subtle—dismissal.

When she left, he pulled out the note, worried about what he'd just said yes to. *Yes, you can leave without two weeks' notice. Yes, you can go back to Connecticut. Yes, you can stomp my heart out.*

But all the note said was that Sam wanted to know if she and Brady had permission to fly to San Francisco to meet with Fifi. He read it again just to make sure he hadn't missed any secret meaning, and picked up the phone.

"Lorna, when did Sam say she was coming?"

"She didn't."

"Uh, okay." He hung up and dialed Sam. "When are you coming?"

"Saturday," she said, her voice terse. "Right after the breakfast service."

"I won't be here. I have to go back to Nugget. We have a meeting with the contractor for Gold Mountain."

"I know," she said. "That's why I planned it."

"Why are you doing this, Sam?"

"Because it's my job," she said.

And it hit him like a Mack truck. Sam wasn't anything like Kayla. She was responsible and reliable. If she said she would do something, she did it. Like the work on his house, helping to plan Emily's wedding, overseeing her family's trust for the arts. Even resuming being Fifi Reinhardt's event planner when Sam thought she was being used. Because she kept her commitments.

"Look, I didn't think it was a big deal for Fifi to know that you're a Dunsbury. It's who you are, right?" Why was she making such a federal case out of it?

"I'm a lot of things, Nate." Pissed was obviously one of them. "The one thing I'm not is for show. I have to go."

"Come on, Sam. Don't do this."

"Do what? Stand up for myself? Stop people from taking advantage of me? Refuse to be someone's for-show wife?"

"Sam, honey, I have no idea what you're talking about." He'd never asked Sam to be his wife. Though two days ago, being married to Sam was something that might've appealed to him . . . before she'd become so thin-skinned and difficult. "What's this really about?"

"What it's about is preserving my dignity. Do you know why Royce wanted to marry me?" She sounded hysterical now and he wished they were doing this in person. "For my name, Nate. The night before our wedding he told his entire wedding party that I was nothing more than a for-show wife and after the wedding we could live in separate houses for all he cared. He didn't even want to live with me. So I'm sure you can you see why I can't be with someone who would trade on my name."

Nate stiffened. "He didn't say that?" No one would say that about beautiful, generous Samantha. She was just being dramatic.

"You're right, I made it all up, because I like degrading myself in front of the man I love . . . loved."

"So what are you saying, you don't love me anymore because I made one stupid mistake? Don't compare me to Royce. This isn't the same thing, Sam."

"Maybe not, but you have to admit, you weren't going to give me Fifi's event until I suddenly became real handy for you. Until suddenly my being a Dunsbury became an asset."

"Sam, that's bullshit. That's not at all what happened. You're blowing this whole thing out of proportion. You're just looking for an excuse to run and take the easy way out, instead of trying to make this work. And I'm telling you, you run and I won't take you back. I've been down this road before and I'm not going down it again.

"On second thought, let's just forget it," he said. "I'm your boss, it was wrong for me to get involved with you in the first place. I told you a romantic relationship would screw everything up. From here on out, we just work together—nothing more."

He hung up before she could respond . . . before she could pulverize what was left of his heart.

Chapter 21

A week had passed and Sam had seen little of Nate. They were like two ships passing in the night, except Sam's ship had lost three pounds. Ordinarily, she would've been thrilled.

Brady tried to feed her. For a tattooed alpha male with bulging biceps, he was quite motherly. "Go ahead, give it a try," he told her over chicken and waffles.

"So people in the South actually mix the syrup with the fried chicken?" It seemed disgusting to Sam, who poked at the dish with her fork.

"Not just in the South. This is hipster food, woman."

She pulled a face and poked some more.

"If you don't mind me saying, he seems as miserable as you do," Brady said.

"Who?" For the sake of being professional, she tried to play dumb.

"Ah, give me a break. You think I'm blind?"

Sam leaned her head back and let out a breath. "That obvious, huh?"

"Uh, yeah. You both walk around all day looking like you're trying not to cry."

"Nate looks like he's going to cry?"

"Nah, he looks like he wants to hit someone. For a guy that's the same thing." He wiped down the counter and nudged her plate. "You're not going to eat this, are you?"

"No offense. I'm sure it's delicious, but I just can't seem to get anything down."

"That bad, huh?" He took her plate and ate the chicken and waffle himself.

"I didn't even feel this bad when I found out my fiancé had been cheating on me our entire engagement."

"Ouch. That the guy you left at the altar?"

She supposed she shouldn't be surprised, but asked anyway. "How'd you know about that?"

He managed to appear sheepish. "The folks in this town have diarrhea of the mouth."

"Yeah, they do. Do they know about Nate and me?"

"No, I don't think so. Hey, what happens in the Lumber Baron, stays in the Lumber Baron." They both laughed. "Not my business, but can't you work it out? You seem like a good couple."

"Why do you say that?" She was curious since they'd never actually been a couple.

"He acts like the sun rises and sets on you. And you act the same about him. I also like the way you two work together. You want something, he tells you he'll think about it and then he gives in. It's nice."

"Do you know who I am?" she asked, deciding to tell him the whole story, because she could use a sounding board. Then she realized how that must've sounded—*Do you know who I am?*—and cringed a little.

"Like I said, Sam, the town has diarrhea of the mouth. Everyone knows who you are. At first I thought you'd be stuck-up, or self-entitled like that Paris Hilton chick, but you're cool." He grinned and it made her feel good. Well, at least better than she'd been feeling.

Sam told Brady about Royce and why she had left him. She told him about the telephone conversation she'd overheard between Nate and Fifi Reinhardt—at least Nate's side of it. And she told him how much it felt like history repeating itself.

Brady listened quietly, shook his head and said, "Not the same. Nate was trying to sell you, not use you. There's a difference. Clearly he believes that your unique position makes you more suitable to plan a big opera fund-raiser than most anyone else. He should've figured it out from the beginning, but I get the sense that he didn't know whether you'd stick around. I can't say I blame him, Sam. I mean this is freakin' Nugget and you're Samantha Dunsbury."

"You're here. You could be cooking at a four-star restaurant somewhere in New York, San Francisco, anywhere."

"Extenuating circumstances." He looked down at his plate. "Besides, I'm a good ol' boy. This town is twice the size of the one I grew up in. I think you should talk to him."

The truth was, Nate seemed done with her. He barely looked her in the eye when they passed each other in the hallway. Every night she stared out her window into his, hoping, praying, that he would just come over and talk. But he never ventured past his side of the split-rail fence.

"I will," she told Brady, because it was better than saying *Nate won't give me the time of day*. It was funny how quickly Nate had given up on them, when he'd always accused her of being the one with the short attention span.

Andy rushed into the kitchen. "There's an old dude in the lobby looking for you."

Why couldn't Andy be like a normal receptionist and get a name? Sam hopped off her stool and followed him back to the front of the inn. It was two days early for Landon Lowery's people to show up, so she couldn't imagine who'd come calling without an appointment.

She craned her neck around the corner to get a better look. "Daddy?"

It was him all right, looking the worse for wear, his hair disheveled and his Nantucket Reds torn in the left knee. And was that straw sticking out of his Gucci loafers? Lucky stood next to him, holding his cowboy hat.

When George didn't immediately answer, Lucky said, "I found him on the side of the road trying to change his tire."

"Daddy, are you okay?" She'd never seen him this way . . . looking a little shell-shocked.

"This godforsaken place is where you live? This"—he gazed around the lobby of the inn—"is what you left home for?"

"Shush, Daddy. You're being rude."

Andy gawked. Brady had ventured out of the kitchen to see what the commotion was about. Lucky clutched the brim of his cowboy hat tighter. And Nate, who'd obviously heard the entire outburst, came out of his office. He took one look at the situation, moved into the fray, and stuck out his hand.

"Welcome, Mr. Dunsbury. We've heard a lot of great things about you." He turned to Lucky. "Where did Mr. Dunsbury get his flat? I'll have Griffin tow in his car."

"Over on Highway 70, near Beckwourth, right before the twenty-four-mile marker. Let me get his luggage out of the back of my truck."

"He has a sheep back there," George said, and wrinkled his nose.

"That's Bernice," Lucky said on his way out. He returned a few minutes later with enough Louis Vuitton luggage for a trip around the world.

Nate lined the suitcases neatly against the wall as Sam stood there, paralyzed. Mortified would actually be a better description.

"Andy, call Griffin," Nate said. "Would you like something to drink, Mr. Dunsbury?"

"I'd like a scotch, three aspirin, and a one-way ticket out of this hellhole."

That's when Sam burst into tears. "Why are you being so awful?"

"Sam"—Nate pulled her aside—"the man had a flat tire, he's frustrated, maybe even a little embarrassed. Let it go."

Her father couldn't fix a flat tire and was taking it out on the whole world. Nate could've fixed it in five seconds, and was being so nice. A gentleman.

Nate walked back into the lobby and eyed George's torn red pants. "Would you like to change, sir?"

Sam wanted to know why he'd worn those pants, of all things? In Nugget, of all places.

"Yes," George muttered.

From behind the check-in desk, Nate grabbed a key to 212, one of the best rooms in the inn, and carried some of George's luggage up the stairs, directing Andy to bring the rest when he got off the phone with Griffin.

George trailed behind and told Nate, "Have my scotch sent up."

"Daddy!" Sam dried her face with the back of her hand as she followed him to the second floor. "He's the owner of this hotel. Don't talk to him like he's your servant."

Sam started to go into the room with her father, but Nate grabbed her by the arm. "Give him time to decompress." He reached for his wallet and handed Andy four twenties. "You call Griffin?"

"He's picking up the car and fixing the tire," Andy said, puffing out his chest like he was Nate's right-hand man. "He said he'll have it back in a couple of hours."

"Good job," Nate said. "Now go over to the Ponderosa and buy the best bottle of scotch they have. Tell them it's for me."

"Why are you doing this for him?" Sam asked. "We have wine. He can drink that."

"Let the guy have his goddamned scotch."

He started to walk away, and anger welled up in her. Nate had ignored her for a week and now he treated her father like he was the Sultan of Brunei. "You must be looking for an investor," she spat.

He glared at her over his shoulder. "Get over yourself, Sam. Believe it or not, not everyone on the planet gives a rat's ass that you're a Dunsbury, least of all me."

He left her standing there, feeling like the world's biggest bitch. She sat on the step and swiped at her eyes, wishing she had a tissue. Lucky had left and she hadn't even thanked him for rescuing her dad. The fact was, she was embarrassed for George and his high-handed behavior. These were good, hardworking people, and to call Nugget a hellhole . . . Well, it was unacceptable.

She had herself a good cry, got up, patted down her dress, and went back downstairs. Nate was right; George needed time to decompress before she dressed him down for being such an ass. Andy returned with a bottle of Bowmore and a scotch glass.

"Thank you, Andy. I'll take it." Sam took the bottle into the kitchen, poured some into the glass, found a tray, and carried it upstairs.

When her father opened the door he was in khakis and a polo shirt and his hair was damp. The room smelled like George, a good mixture of hot shower and cologne.

"Here's your scotch." She put the tray down on the coffee table and straightened.

"No hug for your old man?" George pulled her toward him and enveloped her in his big arms. "Let me have a look at you." He pulled away without letting go, so he could examine her from head to toe. "The place agrees with you."

"You mean this hellhole?"

He chuckled and drew his thumb down her face. "Why are you crying, Sam?"

"Because you were a complete ogre down there. You embarrassed me in front of my employer and my friends. Yet, I'm still so, so happy to see you." And for the second time that morning she burst into tears. Then she clung to her father like she was that ten-year-old girl who used to stand on his feet while he waltzed her around the terrace.

In return, he squeezed her tight as a boa constrictor.

"Why didn't you call, Daddy? I could've picked you up at the airport."

"I wanted to surprise you."

She wiggled free, sat on the loveseat, and patted the space next to her. "You rented a car and got a flat?"

He sighed. "Yes. Then that Lucky fellow came along. I'm pretty sure his sheep ate my luggage." George glanced around the room like he was seeing it for the first time. Pushing to his feet, he wandered over to the window and lifted the lace panel.

She joined him and pointed. "Those are the Sierra mountains." Even in July, the highest ones were still capped in white. "Down there is the square, Nugget's main business district. And that crowd of people over there are at the farmers' market. They hold two every week in summer."

He lifted a snowy brow. "It doesn't look like much."

She ignored him. "See over there." Sam pointed to the trestle bridge. "That's the Feather River."

"So that young man from earlier, he's Breyer?"

"Mm-hmm."

"Seems to have a good head on his shoulders."

Why, because he kissed your ass? "Yes. He's very successful," she said, and motioned toward the Ponderosa. "We'll eat there tonight. It's a restaurant, Western saloon, and bowling alley all in one. You'll get a kick out of it." Or maybe not. "The women who own it are originally from San Francisco."

"Good-looking fellow, that Breyer. Married?"

"No, Daddy, he's not. Don't you want your scotch?"

"I'll have it later. Where do you live?"

"It's just a few miles from here. We'll go after dinner. You'll stay in my guest room."

"You don't want me to stay here?" he asked, surprised.

"I got the distinct impression you didn't like it here. But, no, I want you to stay with me." She wanted to spend time with him, make him see how wonderful Nugget was.

"I'd enjoy that, Sam. But for the record, I never said I didn't like the inn."

"You want to see the rest of it?" She looked at her watch and pulled him by the arm. "If we hurry, there may be leftovers in the kitchen."

Sam showed him the downstairs, including all the common rooms and then the kitchen, where she found plenty of Brady's fried chicken in the refrigerator. She made them up two plates—unexpectedly, she had an appetite.

"You just help yourself?" George asked, scanning the walls of white cabinets and stainless-steel counters.

"Usually Brady, he's our chef, is here, but he's probably at the farmers' market getting ingredients for tomorrow. These people down the road who own a motor lodge keep accusing us of running a restaurant. Our permits are strictly for a B & B. They're putting in a pool shaped like a bear or something crazy like that, since they're called the Beary Quaint. Beary"—she spelled it—"Get it? So to retaliate, Nate told the mayor that they're putting in a water park." Sam laughed.

"Are you running a restaurant?"

"No. Of course not. Although if we were, we'd make a killing, 'cause Brady can cook." She took their lunches and a couple of lemonades to the veranda. It was probably eighty degrees out, but under the porch fans, it didn't feel so hot. "Sit, Daddy."

He made himself comfortable in one of Colin's rockers. "Nice chair."

"A local guy makes them. I'll take you over to his studio later so you can see his work. He and his fiancée are getting married at the inn next month. I'm planning the reception."

Together, they ate the fried chicken and potato salad Brady had made for the staff and watched people shop at what was left of the farmers' market. A few passersby, including Harlee and Darla, who were eating ice cream on the green, waved.

"You know them?" George asked.

"Everyone here knows everyone. But those two are my good friends. Harlee is the fiancée of the furniture builder I told you about. She owns the *Nugget Tribune*. And Darla and her father have the barbershop."

"Can a person make a living in this town?" George seemed to be enjoying his chicken, so Sam gave him a piece of hers.

"Yes. A lot of small business owners, ranchers, and railroad workers. A number of people commute to Reno, though."

George blinked. "That's an hour's drive."

"About fifty minutes when there's no snow."

"And this Breyer fellow, he owns another nine hotels in San Francisco?"

"Mm-hmm. The Theodore is his flagship and it's spectacular. And he just bought a bungalow colony fifteen minutes from here. It's next to a touristy town with lots of ski resorts."

"Why does he bother with this?" He waved his hand at the inn. "I mean, it's handsome enough, but it can't bring in that much revenue."

"I don't know whether it does or not," Sam said. "But he and his sister Maddy bought it when it was practically falling down, and restored it. Maddy lives here full-time—she's married to the police chief—and runs it, but is on maternity leave. They love the inn."

She told him about the Landon Lowery family reunion. He'd never heard of Lowery, but Sam explained that in the tech world he was a god. Later, after she'd gotten most of her work done, she took her father on a tour of the town, introduced him to some of the town's characters, including Owen and Donna, and bought a soft-serve at the Bun Boy. Tomorrow, when he'd had time to settle in, Sam wanted to show him McCreedy Ranch and Lucky's fledgling cowboy camp.

Griffin dropped George's rental car at the Lumber Baron and Andy gave Griff a lift back to the Gas and Go. George begrudgingly admitted that folks here were pretty accommodating.

"We all help one another out," Sam said. "It's nice."

That evening she treated George to a steak dinner and martinis at the Ponderosa, which he seemed to enjoy.

"Is it always this full?" he wanted to know, as pins crashed in the adjoining bowling alley.

"Yep. It's the only sit-down restaurant in town."

"They should charge more." George scanned the menu.

"Then it wouldn't be so crowded," Sam said. "This is a modest town, Daddy."

"I can see that."

After dinner George followed her back to her house in Sierra Heights.

"Interesting place," he said, standing on her back porch, taking in the big log homes. "You say that young man, Griffin, owns the development?"

"Until he can sell all the houses, he does. He bought it while it was in bankruptcy, as an investment. And I think he's having a hard time selling homes. They're expensive. But the place has beautiful amenities. I thought that tomorrow, while I'm at work, you could hang out at the pool."

"Sounds good." He looked longingly at the golf course. "Anyone use it?"

"Of course. It's open to the public and it's Griffin's bread and butter as far as Sierra Heights is concerned. There's a driving range if you want to hit balls tomorrow. I don't have any clubs, though."

"Don't worry about me. I'll be fine."

In the morning, George was still sleeping when Sam slipped out of the house. She left a note telling him how to find the pool and that she would call him later. If it weren't for the Lowery reunion she would've taken time off to spend with her dad, but Landon's family would start streaming in tomorrow and she wanted to make sure there were no glitches.

"How's it going with your dad?" Brady said when she strolled into the Lumber Baron kitchen to get a cup of coffee.

Sam wondered if the whole town was talking about George's rude entrance. "So far, so good."

"Parents can be a real pain in the ass, but you've got to love 'em." Brady grinned.

Yep, she thought, and her father in particular. She grabbed her coffee mug and hunkered down in her office, where she spent the day confirming each and every event planned for the Lowerys, including a bus that would shuttle them to and from the rodeo. Before leaving, Sam checked every vacant room to ensure that it was spotless. The occupied rooms would undergo thorough cleanings tomorrow at check-out time, when the entire inn would be turned over to Landon's family reunion.

On her way out she snuck a peek inside Nate's office. He'd been there earlier, but she'd seen neither hide nor hair of him all day, which seemed odd given their big event tomorrow. When she got home her dad's rental car sat in the same spot he'd left it the night before. Perhaps he'd walked to the pool.

"Daddy?" She walked around the house looking for him, only to find a note on the kitchen island.

I went golfing with Breyer. Afterward, your young man is taking me to see that new development he bought with his sister, but I'll be home in time for dinner.

Nate sat in his car outside Sophie and Mariah's house. He'd played nine holes of golf with Sam's old man, then taken him to see Gold Mountain, had dinner at Rhys and Maddy's, then driven here, where he camped, trying to get his head straight.

After ten minutes of working up the nerve, he finally got out of the Jag and knocked on their door.

"Nate," Mariah said. "Come on in."

"Hey, you." Sophie came out of the kitchen, a dishrag in her hand. "We just put Lilly down for the night. You want a glass of wine?"

"A glass of wine sounds good." He gazed around the room.

No matter how many times he saw it, the house never ceased to impress him. Not just the architecture, but there was love here. He could feel it oozing out of the walls, floating off the ceiling, and radiating up through the floors. Everywhere he looked he saw happy family.

"You okay, Nate?" Sophie held out a glass of wine and he followed her into the front room with Mariah.

"Yeah, but I wanted to talk to the two of you about something."

"Okay." Mariah patted the sofa next to her and Nate took a seat.

"It's about Lilly." He instantly saw the fear in both women's eyes.

"Oh God, Nate." Sophie moved closer to Mariah. A show of solidarity. "You promised."

"I know." He held up a hand. "I'm not going back on my word. That's not what this is about." Lilly was as much a part of them biologically as she was Nate. He just needed to know where he stood in their family, because he was so unsure. "What do we do when she's old enough to understand? I don't want her to think I turned my back on her."

"Of course not," Sophie said. "Why would she think that?"

"Because some day she'll want to know why her father isn't a bigger part of her life."

"But you are a big part of her life," Mariah said, and for emphasis added, "You gave her life."

"What's going on here, Nate?" Sophie asked. "Why would Lilly ever think that you're not a big part of her life? Unless you're planning not to be."

"That's the problem, Soph, I don't know how much I'm allowed to be involved. From the beginning you made it clear that you and Mariah would raise Lilly. So where do I fit in? How close am I allowed to get to Lilly without usurping you and Mariah as parents? What if I have my own kids? . . . I mean more kids . . . You see, I don't even know what I mean, because I don't know what the hell I'm supposed to be to Lilly. An anonymous sperm donor?"

"Of course not, Nate." Sophie sat on the floor in front of him and took his hands. "Have we made you feel that left out? You'll always be Lilly's biological father. Nothing will ever change that fact. And as soon as she's old enough to understand, we will explain it to her. It has always been the plan that she know exactly who you are, Nate. Is there something we should know? Are you expecting?"

"Don't make a joke out of this," Nate said.

"I'm not, nor would I ever make a joke out of this. I'm just trying to understand where this is suddenly coming from. I thought we had worked all this out in the beginning."

"I don't want Lilly to think that I gave her away," Nate blurted, and he could feel his eyes well with tears.

Mariah jerked her head back. "She won't ever think that, because you'll always be there for her. And when you have children, they'll be her half siblings, just like all the other blended families out there."

"You won't have a problem with that?" Nate asked.

"Of course not," both women said in unison.

"Nate, you've been a huge part of Lilly's life from the day she was born," Sophie said. "Haven't we made you feel welcome?"

They had. It had always been he who felt like he was walking on eggshells, trying so hard not to impose on their family. Not to overstep his bounds. "You have. I guess I just need my position defined. Am I allowed to hang pictures of her in my house, to talk about her like she's my daughter, to establish a college fund for her? Where am I supposed to draw the line? Because it's all pretty damned blurry to me right now, and the last thing I want to do is go back on my promise."

"Of course you're allowed," Mariah said. "You're Lilly's biological father. We're the parents raising her. In other words, we're the ones stuck being the heavies and you're the guy who gets to take her to Disneyland. And there is always room for another college fund. But seriously, Nate, you're in this with us. We want you to be an integral part of Lilly's life. Always."

He swallowed hard. "So you don't mind that I come around so much?"

"Never," Mariah said. "Look, I know in the beginning I was the one least in favor of you being Lilly's birth father, concerned that this could cause problems in our friendship. But Lilly loves you, Nate. We would never deprive our daughter of her father. Does that mean there won't be bumps along the road? Hell no. But we'll learn as we go. All that matters is that Lilly is loved."

Nate wasn't the best at expressing his feelings and hadn't wanted Sophie and Mariah to fear that he was reneging on their pact. But he felt like an enormous weight had been lifted just by finally talking about it.

Mariah was right. There was no playbook for their situation. They would make mistakes and at times Nate would feel left out—and probably a little lost. But their baby's wellbeing was most important.

And from where Nate sat, no child could be loved more than Lilly.

Chapter 22

When Nate arrived at the Lumber Baron the next morning, the place was in chaos. Andy was up on a ladder, hanging the Lowerys' family crest—who the hell had a family crest? Emily had volunteered to help Brady in the kitchen. Apparently as far as the food was concerned it was all hands on deck. Even Maddy had come in for a few hours to be part of the welcome wagon.

"Nice of you to show up," she told Nate, looking at her watch. "Nine o'clock, really? There's like a million things to do."

"You've been gone how long and already you're bossing me around? For your information, I had to put out fires in San Francisco."

"Nothing with Fifi Reinhardt?" Sam asked, lugging a small card table into the parlor, draping it with a lace cloth, and stacking it with itinerary packets.

"No, not Fifi," he said. "What do you want me to do?"

"Uh, could you tell Brady to start putting out the appetizers?" It was the most she'd said to him in a week except when they'd squabbled about George.

Just the sound of her voice caused a tightness in his chest.

"By the way, thanks for keeping my dad company yesterday. He said he had a lovely time."

"No problem," he said to her back. Okay, she was clearly done talking.

"What's he doing today?" Nate asked, just to force her back into a conversation.

"Hanging out at the pool. He may come over later, when things settle down." She brushed past him and for a second he was tempted to pull her into a corner and tell her that he'd made the wrong decision by breaking up with her. Breaking up? They hadn't even been a couple. Not really. They'd only fought like one since the day she'd gotten here.

Instead, Nate went to the kitchen to deliver Sam's message to Brady. Not necessary, since Brady had already started bringing out trays and arranging them on the antique sideboard. With Sam at the helm, Operation Lowery ran like a well-oiled machine. Nate snagged a cheese puff and went in search of his next task.

All around him the place buzzed with activity, everyone taking their directions from Sam.

"I think it should go more to the left," she told Andy, who had moved on to hanging a welcome banner in the lobby.

Maddy looked over at Nate and gave him a thumbs-up.

"Could one of you turn on the music, please?" Sam called.

Maddy went off to do Sam's bidding and a short time later classical music wafted softly from the sound system. Sam had moved on from the placement of the banner to fussing with a gigantic floral arrangement at the front desk. It reminded him of the types of arrangements they had at the Theodore. Elegant.

Nate crept up alongside her. "It looks great, Sam. You've done a great—"

"You're welcome," she finished, and gazed at her watch. "He should be here any time now."

When Landon Lowery finally made his entrance, Sam was there to greet him. He embraced her like an old friend. Nate supposed they'd spent a lot of time on the phone planning the reunion.

He got lost in watching her. She was so poised and adept at putting people at ease. And when she smiled it was like the sky shooting sun rays. Seeing her that way made his throat constrict and he had to leave the room. On his way out, he backed into George.

"She's pretty good at this, isn't she?" he said.

"Yep." Nate nodded.

"I probably shouldn't be here, but Sam talks so much about this place that I wanted to see her in action. You want me out of the way?"

"You're fine," Nate said. "There's food in the kitchen if you're hungry."

Out of left field, George said, "I want her to come home. She's all I've got and she's living clear on the other side of the country. I know she loves this job, and planning events, but she could do that at home. I could get her a job with any number of large hotel groups."

Nate thought it was rather bad form for George to tell his daughter's boss that he intended to steal her away. It also made Nate sick with worry that the old guy just might pull it off. What if Sam left and Nate never saw her again?

"I was wrong about Royce," George continued, almost as if he needed to confess to someone that Sam's ex-fiancé had been a prick. "But I'm right about this. In the long run she'll be happier at home." He gave Nate a pat on the arm. "You know, I think I will get myself something to eat."

Nate watched George walk to the kitchen. More guests had started to trickle in. Andy went up and down the stairs, carting luggage to various rooms. Maddy showed a young woman, probably one of Landon's siblings, something on a map. Emily poured wine for a group that had assembled in the dining room. Sam stood vigil at the door, greeting newcomers and directing the show.

Nate swept past a few recent Lowery arrivals and tugged Sam's arm. "I need to talk to you."

"Right now?" She gave him a look like *This better be life or death.* "Uh, sort of busy."

"Sam," Landon called. "These are my parents."

Sam left Nate and glided across the room as if her high heels were roller skates. "So wonderful to meet you," Nate heard her say and wanted to pull Landon Lowery by the back of his ridiculous hoodie and lock him in the bathroom.

"Hey." He grabbed Brady, who'd just come out of the kitchen with more appetizers. "We're having a meeting at three o'clock. I'm making a big announcement."

"Today?" Brady asked, and gave him the same WTF look that Sam had just given him. Jesus Christ, you'd think the Lowery family reunion was the most important event ever held at the Lumber Baron. And so what if it was?

"Yeah. Today. After the guests settle in."

"Okay," Brady said. "Emily too?"

Technically, she wasn't an employee, but what the hell. "Yes."

He found Maddy in the parlor, cleaning up a spill.

"There's a staff meeting at three o'clock. I'm making a big announcement."

"In the middle of the Lowery event? Are you freaking kidding me?"

"No. It's important."

"It can't wait until tomorrow morning when all the guests are still asleep?"

"What's the big deal? By three"—he gestured toward the dining room where most of the arrivals were milling—"they'll be largely handled."

"Whatever," Maddy said. "But Rhys is coming over so I can feed Emma."

"That's fine. He can hear the announcement too."

"What is it?" When Nate wouldn't answer, she said, "Oh for goodness' sake, just tell me. I'm your partner, jerk."

"Not on this."

At three o'clock everyone gathered in the kitchen. Sam found it rather odd that Nate would hold a meeting on the first day of the Lowery reunion, especially since he'd been so obsessive-compulsive about the event in the first place. Even Clay, who'd come to pick up Emily, and Rhys were invited to stay.

Luckily, the guests were either out and about, touring the square, or resting in their rooms. Some had traveled from as far away as the Midwest and were exhausted after their long flights.

Brady had put out refreshments for the meeting. Andy stood in the corner, texting on his cell phone, like he couldn't be bothered. Maddy was discreetly feeding Emma using one of those nursing covers. George perched on one of the bar stools like he'd been made an honorary staff member.

Nate came in and told everyone he was conferencing in the corporate office, including Lorna, Lisa, and Randall. Maddy looked over at Sam as if to say *I have no idea what this announcement is about.*

Clearly, whatever it was, it was very last-minute.

Nate fidgeted with the phone for a bit. It took a while before everyone from San Francisco joined the group, given that some of them hadn't yet seen Nate's email with the passcode to get on the call.

He cleared his throat and the room fell silent. "Thanks, everyone, for doing this on such short notice. There are a couple of things I wanted to talk about. For those of you who don't already know, Maddy and I are currently in escrow on a property not far from the Lumber Baron. It's an eighty-cabin resort called Gold Mountain that needs a complete redo and will become part of the Breyer Hotel family as soon as it's a done deal. Maddy and I have a few ideas, but we'll want to roll out a marketing plan as soon as possible."

Maddy nodded in agreement and Emma gurgled, eliciting a few laughs.

"For those of you on the phone, that was my niece." Nate propped one shoulder against the wall, very much at ease. "Any questions so far?"

"It's Randall, and I have one. We planning to book events at Gold Mountain?"

"Good question, Randall. Absolutely. It's a perfect setup for week-end weddings, family reunions, group ski trips, and anything else you can think of. The Lumber Baron is also doing a joint venture with a dude ranch up here that wants to attract corporations interested in team building, but doesn't have the luxury lodging that we do. So it'll be a reciprocal thing.

"In addition," Nate continued, "Sam has worked out a deal with the owner of the dude ranch to lease his barn for events too large for the Lumber Baron to handle. Apparently there's a good market for people who want to hold weddings and parties in a barn."

There were a few titters on the other end of the line and Nate grinned. Clay shrugged his shoulders like he didn't know what was so funny. Rhys wrestled Emma out of Maddy's arms and tried to burp her. George just sat there expectantly.

"I also wanted to discuss the position that Tracy left open. After much consideration, I've decided to make Samantha Dunsbury my new VP of corporate events."

The room erupted in applause while Sam gripped the countertop for support. Now she knew what the cliché "a deer caught in the headlights" felt like. The announcement caught her totally off guard. Nate, who stood across the room smiling at her, hadn't said one word about the promotion. Not one word. In fact, he'd made it more than clear that he had no intention of giving her the VP position. What happened to her not having enough experience? Or not being with the company long enough? It seemed to her that Nate had made a split-second decision based on her ability to greet guests at the door.

Before she could dwell on it any more, Brady did one of those two-finger whistles and Sam could hear Lisa and Randall cheering over the phone.

Nate calmed everyone down and said, "As far as event planning at the Lumber Baron, there will be some restructuring, which I'll get back to you on. But I think you all know how hard Sam works, how much she's done for the Lumber Baron, and how much innovation she'll bring to this company. And based on the warm welcome you've already given her, I take it that you agree."

More applause.

Maddy wrapped her in a hug. "Congratulations, Sam. Oh my God, I never saw that one coming . . . uh, not that you don't deserve it, but Nate just stole you from me. When are you moving to San Francisco?"

San Francisco? When Sam had asked for the position, she hadn't even considered where she would live if she got it. She supposed a part of her had hoped that she could do the job from Nugget. Perhaps a tad unrealistic. "Uh, I don't know yet. Nate and I haven't talked about it."

Understatement of the year.

"Way to go." Brady gave her a squeeze and winked. "You guys kiss and make up?"

"Well deserved," Emily said, moving in closer to give Sam a hug. "But we're sure going to miss you."

Clay and Rhys both wished her congratulations and Andy clapped her on the back. "Take me with you," he said. "Get me out of this hellhole."

She scanned the room for Nate, but he'd already gone.

Her father came up alongside her. "Well, how about that?" he said, and gave her a kiss on the cheek.

She couldn't tell whether he was happy for her or pretending to be. "Thanks. We'll talk about it later, okay, Daddy?"

On their way home that night Sam told George how the job announcement had come out of the blue. That in fact, when Sam had originally asked for the position, Nate had nixed it.

"Now you would know this better than I," Sam said, "but isn't it common practice to offer the job first, before announcing it like it's a fait accompli? I mean, we haven't talked about salary or whether I'll be headquartered in San Francisco. His sudden change of heart—it's weird, right?"

Her father gave a blasé shake of his head. "Perhaps something happened in the last twenty-four hours to change it."

"Like my performance on the Lowery event?"

"Could be," he said, but he sounded evasive. "You like this fellow, right?"

"What does that have to do with anything?"

"Sam, it's no good working for a person you don't like or don't respect."

She sighed. "I like him." Too much.

"You sure talk about him enough," George said. "Nate this. Nate that. You never talked about Royce that way."

She'd never once felt for Royce what she felt for Nate. "I don't think Royce and I were ever meant to be, Daddy. What do I do about this job? I feel like Nate and I should have discussed the requirements of the position first."

What she really worried about was working side by side with him every day, given that she was totally in love with the man and he no longer returned the sentiment, if he ever had. At least at the Lumber Baron she was on her own a good portion of the time. And when Maddy returned, Nate would go back to spending most of his time in San Francisco.

"I should've had an opportunity to sleep on it and make an informed decision," she continued. "Don't you think? Now, I just feel like it's being foisted on me." And again, the specter of her last name raised its head. Was that the real reason Nate had given her the position?

"Last time we talked on the phone, you said you wanted the job," George said. "It was all you could talk about. Make up your mind, my girl. But it sure wouldn't kill you to play hardball. Tell him that you're thinking of returning to the East Coast to be with your dear old dad."

She gazed over at him in the passenger seat. It was too dark in the car to make out his features. "You mean to negotiate a better salary? Benefits? That sort of thing?" God, she knew nothing about the business world. To her, the money didn't mean much, but watching Nate at the meeting today, cool, confident. and in command, made her wonder what his game was. Was he trying to torture her? Make her want him even more than she already did?

"That . . . and anything else you want." George said it kind of funny, and somehow she could sense him smiling.

* * *

The Lowery clan flooded the dining room the next morning for breakfast. Today they planned to take the gold-train tour, which would give Sam a few hours to breathe. Nate decided to show up at ten, which was two hours later than his usual time. For the life of her, she didn't know what was going on with him.

Yesterday, after making his big announcement, he'd disappeared. Just vanished.

"We need to talk," she told him as she hefted an egg soufflé to bring out to the dining room.

He put down his coffee mug, grabbed the soufflé from her and said, "No need. I saw your dad this morning. He told me you've decided to go back to Connecticut."

What? Sam had no idea what her meddling father was up to. But he was certainly up to something. "I'd like to talk with you about it."

"What's the point?" He left with the dish and didn't return for his coffee. Sam suspected that he'd locked himself in his office.

With a slew of chores still on her list to get the Lowerys off on their field trip, she didn't have time to deal with Nate. But as soon as the guests were gone she planned to have a long, in-depth conversation with him.

As Sam set up rows of brown-bag lunches on a table in the lobby for team Lowery to take on their train ride, she tried her father on the phone. No answer at her house, but he finally picked up on his cell.

"Daddy, what did you tell Nate?"

"What? It's a bad connection."

It sounded perfectly fine to Sam. "What are you up to, George Dunsbury the Fourth?"

"Can't hear you," came his muffled voice. "I'll try to call you when I get to a landline." He clicked off, and Sam wondered where he could be where there wasn't a landline.

She returned to Brady for the vegetarian lunches. On her way back to the lobby, she noticed that Nate's office door was open and he was gone. *Damn him.* In the dining room, she cleared the dirty dishes and brought them back to the kitchen.

"Brady, did Nate say where he was going?"

Nope." Brady went back to rolling his pie dough.

She returned calls in her office and organized her calendar. Before she knew it the Lowerys were back from their train ride. The entire group had a reservation for dinner at the Ponderosa. Sam just had to make sure that everyone knew where to go and what time to be there. A few of the guests wanted to go on a short bike ride before supper. Sam opened the shed and showed them where the bikes were stored and gave them directions to a nice flat trail along the Feather River. A few of the older guests wanted to relax in their rooms. Landon stopped by Sam's office to tell her how pleased he was with the reunion so far.

For a nerdy guy, he could be fairly charming. After Landon left to join the bike ride, Sam popped her head in Nate's office. He still wasn't back. After dinnertime, she'd given up on him altogether. Perhaps he'd gone to San Francisco.

With the Lowerys handled for the evening, she started to pack up to go home. She hadn't heard back from her dad and was starting to worry.

Then the Lumber Baron door opened and Nate came in.

"You okay?" Sam asked because he didn't look quite right. All that cockiness he usually carried around with him seemed to have dissipated.

"I didn't expect you to be here so late. I just came back to finish up some paperwork."

"Okay," she said, deciding that they could talk another day. He seemed tired and disjointed. Not at all like himself. "I'll let you get to it then."

He shoved his hands in his pocket and rocked back on his heels. "Good night."

"See you."

She was reaching for the door when he said, "Don't go back to Connecticut, Sam."

"We'll talk about it tomorrow." She stepped out into the July evening. The sun hadn't yet set and the Nugget sky burned a fiery red. Summer in the Sierra was the way the locals described their colorful twilight hours.

"I'm sorry I told Fifi Reinhardt who you are." He'd followed her outside. "I never intended to trade on your name, but when I mentioned you, she obviously recognized Dunsbury and got excited. Never in a million years did I think there was anything wrong with it, but I'll never do it again."

"I know," she said as she started for her car. "Thank you for apologizing. It means a lot."

"I love you, Sam."

She stopped dead in her tracks, her heart pounding like a herd of wild horses running through her chest.

"I love you so much I ache with it," he said. "And if you leave . . . You can't leave."

"I thought you wanted to go back to just being my boss?"

"I was an idiot, Sam. I was just being defensive because I was afraid of getting hurt." He came down the stairs and joined her in the parking lot. "I don't want to be your boss anymore."

"You don't?" she asked, confused. Just yesterday he'd offered her a vice president position in his company.

"I want us to be partners. Before you say no, hear me out, okay? I think we're perfect for each other. You soften my rough edges, mostly because you don't take my crap. And I trust your judgment one hundred percent. You want to build a barn at the Lumber Baron or on Gold Mountain, we'll build a barn. You want to fire Richard, we'll fire Richard and bring in Brady. Whatever you want to do."

"And my title will still be vice president?" Because this sounded like a much bigger job to Sam . . .

"Your title will be Mrs. Nathaniel Breyer and anything else you want tacked on to it."

She stared at him, stunned. "What are you saying?" And then she held her breath.

"I'm saying"—he reached into his shirt pocket for a little velvet box and dropped to one knee on the hot, sticky pavement—"you're everything I ever dreamed of and more, Samantha Dunsbury. Give me another chance and I'll spend my life making you happy. Marry me?"

She exhaled and saw stars, maybe from holding her breath so long. But Nate Breyer had just proposed.

"Yes," she whispered as he slipped the ring on her finger.

"I got it in Reno today. The best jewelry store I could find on short notice. If you don't like it, I could exchange it for something else. But when your dad said you were leaving, I panicked. I can't imagine this place without you . . . without you in my life."

"You can't?" She was dazzled by him. And she'd never seen a ring more beautiful, more sparkly or more perfect. She held it up to him. "I love it . . . not too big, not too small, just right. Because you know me, Nate. I love you . . . I love . . ." Oh God, she was rambling like a lunatic. But Nate, who had gotten to his feet, was too busy kissing her to notice.

"You won't change your mind, will you?" he said against her lips.

"Never."

"Promise? Because you've been known to—"

"I promise." She wouldn't let him say it.

"We'll have to talk to your dad." He stopped kissing her to look into her eyes. "He's counting on you going back with him to Connecticut."

"I wouldn't worry too much about him." She planted her lips back on his and felt him smiling against her mouth.

"You sure?" he whispered. "Because you kind of have a reputation, you know?"

"It depends," she teased. "Is your love for me for real or for show?"

"I'll let you decide." And when he kissed her into sheer oblivion there was no doubt left in her mind.

Epilogue

"You think she'll actually show up this time?" Owen whispered to Darla, who told him to keep his yap shut.

Nate overheard the entire exchange, even over the din of the string quartet and stragglers still looking for seats. Not for one minute did he think Sam would stand him up, but for insurance he'd put Maddy on the case. She wasn't to leave the bride's side, not even for a bathroom run.

And just to hedge his bets, Nate had asked for a short engagement—he didn't want to give the bride too much time to change her mind. A person couldn't be too careful. Fortunately for him, Sam didn't want to plan another extravagant wedding. She'd just finished Harlee and Colin's and did enough of them for her clients. So here they stood at the Lumber Baron, ready to tie the knot on one of those perfect Northern California September days when the sun shone and the temperature registered a balmy seventy-eight degrees. Afterward, the wedding party and one hundred of their closest friends and family would move to Lucky's barn for barbecue and dancing. The next day, they had flights to Nantucket for a week-long honeymoon at Sam's summerhouse.

Initially, George had balked at the informality of his only daughter's wedding, but Sam had persuaded him to go with the flow.

"Daddy, you're in Nugget now. Get over yourself."

Since becoming a part-time resident of the town, George had gotten much more laid-back, trading in his large collection of red pants and loafers for jeans and boots. Coincidentally enough, he'd bought a house in Sierra Heights the very day Nate and Sam had gotten engaged. George had said it was a good investment.

Nate, however, suspected that he'd been hoodwinked by the scheming old man, that Sam had never intended to move back to Connecticut, and that George had been playing matchmaker.

Thank goodness. Sam was the best thing that had ever happened to him.

And of course Lilly, who Sophie shoved into his arms. "We want a picture of you two on your wedding day," she said, snapping various shots with her smartphone.

"Get into the picture," Donna told Sophie and Mariah. "I'll get all four of you."

"I want one of Sam, Lilly, and me after the ceremony," Nate told them.

"We'll take it in front of the Lumber Baron," Mariah said. "It'll be beautiful."

Although Sam had enthusiastically agreed to take the top event-planning job, she'd persuaded Nate to let her make the Lumber Baron her main base of operation. Like him, she'd travel back and forth. But with Gold Mountain in the works, and plenty of barn weddings on the horizon at Lucky's cowboy camp, they needed their focus to be in Nugget for now. So they'd agreed to live in Nate's house and maybe buy a second place in San Francisco later.

The processional music started up, signaling that the ceremony was about to begin. Nate took his place under the arbor Colin had built. The minister stood stiffly at the lectern. Brady came out the back door, near the kitchen, and grabbed a chair at the end of the front row.

As the quartet launched into the "Wedding March," it seemed that the entire audience held its collective breath. Harlee had discreetly positioned herself to get the photo op if the bride decided to make a run for it. And Owen kept turning around to see where she was. Lucky, on the other hand, seemed to have more faith than the rest. He sat with his mom, scanning the crowd in front of him. Nate could only presume he was looking for Raylene Rosser, who if rumor had it right was seeing the champion bull rider.

As the music continued to play, the guests waited a beat before getting to their feet, still uncertain. Then Sam appeared in a white strapless gown and a long veil. Coming down the aisle on her father's arm, Sam took Nate's breath away. Like an angel, she smiled at him, her big blue eyes so beguiling and full of love that for a moment Nate was suspended in time and eternally grateful that of all the country inns in all the small towns in the world, Samantha Dunsbury, soon to be Breyer, had walked into his and decided to start over.

Please turn the page for an exciting sneak peek of
Stacy Finz's newest Nugget romance

GETTING LUCKY

coming in November 2015!

Chapter 1

"Come back here!" Lucky propped up on both elbows and watched Raylene shimmy into her denim skirt. "What's the rush?"

"I promised my parents I'd be back in time for dinner."

Lucky reached over and grabbed his watch off the nightstand. "It's still early."

"I have to shower and change," she said, pulling a miniscule tank top over her head.

"Shower here." *With me.*

Raylene scanned the singlewide trailer and Lucky could've sworn she grimaced. Granted, it wasn't fancy—a tin can, really, with a few pieces of shabby furniture Lucky had rummaged from some of the outbuildings on his property. But he got the bed new and the place was clean. And temporary. Pretty soon his construction crew would finish converting one of the bunkhouses into his office and private quarters.

"It's best if I get home before anyone sees me in this." Raylene looked down at the mini skirt that barely covered the dental floss she called underwear and pulled on her cowboy boots.

The slutty getup might've gotten him off with the buckle bunnies he typically consorted with but not Raylene. On her it didn't sit right with him. It made Raylene seem cheap.

"Don't you think it's time to take us public?" Lucky swung his legs over the side of the bed, found his Levi's on the floor and shoved them on, buttoning the fly.

"We've been over this, Lucky."

"Yeah, well I'm tired of all this sneaking around." He'd loved the woman since middle school, and was getting weary of the clandestine booty calls. Sometime soon he'd like to take her on an actual date.

"I don't want Butch to find out while we're still hashing out the settlement. Besides, there's my father and your mother to consider."

Neither would be happy that Lucky and Raylene were seeing each other. A lot of bad blood between the two families.

Raylene pushed Lucky back onto the bed and straddled his lap with her long tanned legs. "Try to be patient, baby. For me." She pouted prettily and then kissed him until he was snaking his hands under her top, reaching for the good stuff. "I've gotta go, Lucky."

"Ten more minutes," he moaned, hard as a rock.

"Uh-uh. Daddy'll be home soon."

"For Christ's sake, Raylene, you're twenty-eight years old. A grown woman."

"You know how he is."

Yeah, Lucky knew Raylene's old man. A prick and a bigot. "Then go now. Because in another minute I'll have you on your back."

She giggled, reminding Lucky of their teens when she used to flirt with him mercilessly. Of course then she'd been dating Zachary Baze, captain of the football team.

"When's the divorce final?" he asked as she wiggled off of him.

"I'm not sure. Butch is being difficult."

"What the hell does he have to be difficult about? He was screwing your best friend."

She put her finger over his mouth. "Shush. I don't want to talk about it."

"Well I don't like it, Raylene." He waggled his hands between the two of them. "Going around everyone's back. . . . It feels slimy."

"What do you want me to do, Lucky? Divorces take time. Colorado isn't California."

Lucky didn't know anything about the legalities of divorce in either state, but for the life of him he didn't know what the holdup was. Raylene and Butch had been separated for months now. "I want this to be good between us. . . . I want it to be right."

She bent down and kissed him again. "It is good between us, Lucky. And nothing has ever felt more right."

"Yeah?" He stood up and wrapped her in his arms. "God, I love you, Raylene."

"I love you, too. But if I don't get home . . ."

"Go then," he said, patting her bottom. "When can I see you again?"

"Mama and I are taking a shopping trip to San Francisco this weekend. As soon as I get back."

"Get some clothes that cover you, while you're there," he said, staring at her ass—the same bubble butt that had filled those itty-bitty uniforms she'd worn while cheering for Nugget High.

She bent over, letting her denim skirt ride up, giving him more than just a view of her behind.

He dove for her, but Raylene darted away, laughing. "They've got a name for girls like you."

"Oh yeah, what's that?" Raylene rucked up her tank top, making a big show of fondling the double "Ds" Butch had bought her. Apparently, the man hadn't thought his wife's natural breasts were big enough. Lucky had liked them just fine.

"I'm going now," Raylene said, giving him one last peep show of her nether regions before darting out the door of the singlewide.

A couple of ranch hands were sitting on the fence, taking a break. Lucky shot them a dirty look when they gaped at Raylene like she was a hooker.

"Call me when you get back, you hear?" he shouted to Raylene, who hopped up into her truck and peeled off.

The girl had gone a little wild, but Lucky chalked it up to Butch keeping her on a string. She just needed a good man to give her the proper love and respect she deserved.

Lucky's phone vibrated inside his back pocket. Fishing it out, he checked the display and answered when he saw it was his agent.

"Hey, Pete."

"How's the cowboy camp shaping up?"

"It's coming along. I'd hoped to have it up and running by now. But we've run into a few glitches. Nothing insurmountable, though." After ten years on the road living out of hotels, he'd purchased the property with plans to settle in his home town.

"That's good," Pete said. "Hey, I just wanted to give you a heads up. A reporter for *Sports Illustrated* is interested in doing a profile on you before the World Finals. I know you said you want to lay low for a while to recoup from that fall you took in Billings and to focus on your new business. But this sounds like a great opportunity, Lucky."

Lucky scratched his head. "Maybe I could give him an hour over the phone." Not too many pro bull riders made it into the pages of *Sports Illustrated*.

"That's the thing. He heard about your cowboy camp and how you're raising rodeo stock up there in the California Sierras, and wants to come up and spend some time with you. He seems to think this new enterprise of yours is a good hook for his story."

"First of all, it's the Sierra. Singular. It means mountain range in Spanish," Lucky said. People were always getting it wrong. "How long would he need? Because, Pete, it's September. I was supposed to open in summer. If I want to get this camp off the ground, I don't have a lot of time for schmoozing with a reporter."

"I know. But, hey, being featured in *Sports Illustrated* . . . you can't get better publicity than that."

True that. "Yeah. All right. When does he want to come?"

"I'll check with him and get back to you. Is there a place for him to stay or should I tell him to book a room in Reno?"

"We've got a five-star inn in downtown Nugget. The Lumber Baron. Besides, Reno is a good forty-five minute drive."

"Hang on, let me get a pen. I want to write that down. What's the hotel called again?"

"The Lumber Baron. Hold a sec and I'll get you a contact." He searched his phone and ticked off the bed-and-breakfast's phone number to Pete.

"Great. I'll let him know and talk to you soon." Pete ended the call.

Lucky needed the distraction of a reporter like he needed a hole in the head. Ordinarily, Lucky never shied away from the press, loving the attention. But he was way behind schedule. Once the snow came—which could be any day now—it would slow construction. The bunkhouses still needed to be winterized and as it turned out, the lodge, which he'd originally thought to be in good shape, needed all kinds of electrical work. Then there was the fact that most city folk didn't want to ride, rope or wrestle steers in the freezing cold. Lucky hoped to attract Silicon Valley executives interested in using the ranch for corporate team building.

At least in future winters he and the owners of the Lumber Baron planned to team up on various ventures. The inn's event planner, Samantha Dunsbury—now Breyer—wanted to rent out Lucky's cowboy camp for weddings and other functions where the guests could indulge in their warped vision of ranch life—hay rides and barn dances. It wasn't exactly the rough-and-tumble cowboy camp he'd envisioned, but it would help pay some of the overhead of the ranch. Right now it was paid for with Lucky's winnings from professional bull riding. But at twenty-nine, this would be his last year.

He wasn't getting those eighty-five and ninety-point rides like he used to. Not with the bulls getting tougher every year. Not when he had a couple of inches of height and thirty to forty pounds on the average bull rider. He'd never been built right for the sport, but he'd had youth and vigor on his side. Now there were younger and stronger contenders.

Lucky planned on the cowboy camp being his next chapter. That and raising prime rodeo stock. So far, though, bull riding, despite the broken bones and bruises, was still paying the bills. He gazed across the ranch, a defunct camp used by church organizations, clubs, and schools for retreats. The place was still in a shambles and nowhere close to welcoming guests.

But when he finally got the cowboy camp off the ground, a *Sports Illustrated* story would be good for business. Lucky couldn't buy better advertising than that.

On his way to the lodge, a massive stack-stone and timber-log building that would serve as the camp's combination mess hall and cantina, an early-model Jeep Cherokee crawled down his road. He didn't recognize it as belonging to one of his workers. Then again there were so many of them swarming the place who could keep their vehicles straight?

Lucky stood to the side of the singlewide, out of sight, shielding his eyes from the sun, as a woman climbed out of the driver's seat. She headed to the trailer door and knocked. He continued to watch her, debating whether to see what she wanted or to continue to the lodge. Occasionally, over-zealous fans—usually women—showed up on his doorstep uninvited. Crazy as it was, just being on ESPN was enough to bring all kinds out of the woodwork.

Today, he wasn't in the mood to send one of them packing. But the lady didn't strike him as a groupie. Her clothes were too conservative for one thing. A skirt that hit mid-calf and a nice blouse. It was her boots, though, that caught his attention. Even from yards away he could tell they were quality. Not gaudy, but definitely expensive. And a good chance, custom. Not what you would expect from someone driving a beater car.

His curiosity got the better of him and he made his presence known. "Can I help you?"

She jerked up, like he'd caught her off guard, then just stood there staring up at him.

Finally, he stuck out his hand. "Lucky Rodriguez. Were you looking for me?"

The woman shuffled her feet in the dirt and cleared her throat. "You don't remember me, do you?"

"No, ma'am. Should I?"

She didn't say anything, just let her eyes drop to those elegant boots of hers. "Donna Thurston said you lived here now."

He nodded. It wasn't a secret that he'd purchased the old Roland Camp and had moved back to Nugget, even if Donna was the biggest mouth in town.

"Could we go inside?" she asked.

Lucky hesitated, but the woman didn't look particularly threatening. Hell, soaking wet she couldn't weigh more than 120 pounds. There was something desperate about her though, like maybe she was looking for work. "Yeah, come on in."

The door to his bedroom was open and the bed showed signs of his and Raylene's recent love making. He motioned to a ratty plaid couch and the woman took a seat while he chose the chair across from her.

"How can I help you, Miss . . . ?

"Tawny."

Something about her rang a vague bell with him. But after a few seconds of searching his brain, Lucky couldn't place the name.

She stared down at her hands, which were locked together like a fist.

"Would you like a drink?" Lucky asked.

"Water would be nice."

He got up, hunted through his cupboards for a decent glass, filled it from the tap and brought it to her.

"Thanks." When she looked up he noticed that her eyes were green. They too sparked an elusive memory, but like the rest of her he couldn't quite pinpoint it.

She was pretty enough that if they'd crossed paths he would've remembered. The boots too. On closer inspection, Lucky thought they were some of the finest leather work he'd ever seen. Lots of hand tooled flowers and a monogram. As a world-champion bull rider, Lucky knew good boots when he saw them. And those must've cost a boat load. Strange, because she gave off the vibe that she was down on her luck. Sad. And tired.

"So what can I do for you, Miss Tawny?"

"Just Tawny," she said. "Tawny's my first name."

Didn't tawny mean orange or brown? The thought popped into his head that her name should've been Jade and again he got the distinct impression that he knew her from somewhere. He watched, waiting for her to state her business, then grew impatient when she just sat there.

"You looking for work, Tawny?"

She jerked her head in surprise. "No. Why would you think that?"

Clearly, he'd insulted her, though he didn't know why. Nothing embarrassing about needing work. Until Lucky had made it big riding the rodeo circuit, he would take any job that came his way to put food on the table. His mother's wages working at the Rock and River Ranch had never been enough.

"Unless you're looking for rodeo stock, I can't imagine what else I could do for you," he said.

"My daughter needs a stem cell transplant," she blurted. "I need your stem cells."

Lucky registered surprise. That was a new one.

As a high-profile athlete, he'd been asked for a good many things. Autographs, pictures, bull-riding lessons, and yes, even bodily fluids. But never once had anyone requested his cells. The woman was clearly a nut job. He rose from his chair, walked to the door and held it open for her.

He wanted to tell her to have Donna lose his address, but tried to remain as polite as possible. "I think you've got the wrong cowboy, ma'am."

She didn't budge. "I'll go to your mother then."

"My mother? What does she have to do with this?" Where the hell did this broad get off?

"Katie has acute myeloid leukemia," Tawny said, and her bottom lip trembled. "The chemotherapy didn't work. The radiation didn't work and the cancer is back. You're my only hope."

Lucky stood by the door, wondering if she was just trying to scam him for money. She certainly wouldn't be the first. But his earlier assessment that she was crazy seemed more on the mark.

"How's that?" he asked, unable to help himself.

"Your HLA antigens have the best chance of matching Katie's."

Oh, yeah, she was *loco* all right, and he'd just been beamed into an episode of Star Trek. "Katie's your daughter?"

"Yes." Tawny sniffled, and Lucky went into the bathroom and grabbed her a roll of toilet paper. It probably wasn't smart turning his back on her, but the woman was crying.

He shouldn't, but asked anyway. "How old is she?"

"Nine." Tawny locked eyes with him long and hard, like the kid's age should've meant something to him. It was slightly unnerving, because when she did that she looked saner than shit.

"And you think I might have these special. . . . What did you call them?"

"HLA antigens."

"Right," he said. "And that would be . . . uh . . . because I ride bulls for a living?"

"No." She stood up. "That would be because you're her father."

Chapter 2

"What the hell are you talking about?" Lucky said, but Tawny could see the wheels in his head turning and sudden recognition blazing in his eyes. "Thelma Wade? You're Thelma Wade. But you don't look like Thelma Wade."

That's because as far as Tawny was concerned Thelma Wade didn't exist. That girl had been puny, plain, painfully shy, and madly in love with Lucky Rodriguez, who'd clearly forgotten her existence as soon as he'd slept with her.

"For the sake of my business, I changed my name to Tawny."

"What's your business—shaking down wealthy bull riders?"

"I don't want your money. I want your stem cells."

"Fine, give me proof that the girl is mine and we'll work something out," Lucky said.

At least he realized it was a possibility. Maybe he hadn't forgotten Tawny altogether. She had to admit that she didn't remotely resemble the seventeen-year-old girl she'd been when Lucky had left Nugget.

Tawny grabbed her phone out of her handbag and cued up a picture of Katie to show him.

"Nope," Lucky blocked her. "This ain't my first time to this particular rodeo, Thelma . . . Tawny, or whatever you go by now. You know how many women have tried to jack me up like this? So I don't want to see any photographs. All I want is a paternity test. Have your lawyer talk to mine."

He went inside the kitchenette, pulled a pen out of a drawer, scribbled something on a piece of paper and handed it to her. "Here's his contact info. I'd appreciate if you go through him for now."

"Look, we don't have to tell anyone." She didn't have time to take offense at his insinuation that she was a liar and a grifter. Her daughter's life depended on him. "If you're a match, the entire procedure shouldn't take too long."

"So you're telling me that our one and only night together produced a baby and that you waited until I came back to Nugget—until the child is nine and has cancer—to tell me all this? It's hard to swallow."

Tawny blinked back tears. "If you'd bothered to take my calls, you would've known about Katie."

"What calls? I never got any calls from you."

"I left messages and I emailed the address on your website. You never got back to me."

"Thelma, my mother lives in the same goddamned town as you. Did it ever occur to you that I didn't get any of those messages and that she was a direct pipeline to me?" His voice trembled with anger and Tawny backed away from him, although he made a good case.

"Given the reasons why you fled Nugget, I figured it was best not to tell anyone, especially your mother," she said. She'd done it for him, because her stupid teenaged heart had convinced her that she was in love with the cowboy and she hadn't wanted to ruin his life.

"Do me a favor, Thelma, call my lawyer." And with that he ushered her out of his trailer.

Fine. Tawny would do just that. Hell, she'd even hire her own attorney if that's what it took to get Lucky on board. Anything for her daughter. Although she felt guilty for springing Katie and the leukemia on Lucky the way she had.

Perhaps she should've tried harder to reach Lucky nine years ago. But at the time she'd done what she thought best. Especially since Lucky had left town under a cloud and she knew if she told him about Katie he'd come home—even if it meant facing scandal. And possibly criminal charges. Because the old Lucky Rodriguez hadn't been a man to shirk his responsibilities. The only person Tawny had known who'd worked harder than she at taking care of her family had been Lucky. Growing up, she'd worshipped the boy who'd worked any odd job he could find to make ends meet.

But away from Nugget, he'd made something of himself. Lucky was the most famous person to ever come from their little ranching and railroad town.

So even when Katie got sick and Tawny was drowning in debt

from putting her business on hold during long stays at the Ronald McDonald House while Katie got treatment at Lucile Packard Children's Hospital at Stanford, she'd never asked Lucky for help.

But this was different. Lucky was the best and possibly the only chance Katie had to survive the cancer. Because chemotherapy and radiation had failed, Katie needed the cancer cells in her bone marrow replaced with healthy ones. Siblings were typically the best candidates for a transplant, but Katie didn't have any. Biological parents were second on the list, yet Tawny hadn't been a match. There weren't enough proteins on the surface of her cells that corresponded with Katie's.

If it turned out that Lucky didn't have enough matching proteins, the doctors would have to look at other relatives and even strangers, decreasing the chances for a successful transplant. That's why Lucky was so critical.

Tawny headed back to town and swung by the Nugget Market to pick up a pint of ice cream for Katie. The girl barely ate anymore. Ethel, who owned the grocery store with her husband, Stu, stood behind the cash register.

"How you doing, Tawny? How's that girl of yours?"

"Feeling better." Tawny gave a wan smile and paid for the French vanilla, Katie's favorite.

Ethel bagged the ice cream and said, "If there is anything you need, you let us know, you hear?"

"Thank you, Ethel."

The town had been good to her. First when her father had suffered from emphysema and she'd had to drop out of high school to take care of him. And later with Katie.

Tawny still remembered coming home from the hospital after giving birth and finding a giant gift basket of baby clothes and boxes of diapers on her doorstep. Later, she'd learned that Donna Thurston, owner of the Bun Boy drive-thru, had organized the gift.

With her father gone, it was just her and Katie now. At least the house where she grew up was paid for. It wasn't much, just a two-bedroom, one bath Craftsman in a modest part of town, but it was sufficient. And the old stand-alone garage in the back served as a perfect studio for her business. Before her father had died, as sick as he was, he'd managed to install a heating system in the space for Tawny so she could work well into the night, even in winter.

She pulled into her driveway alongside a truck she didn't recognize. Maybe the babysitter's boyfriend was home, visiting from the University of Nevada.

But when she walked into the house Tawny found Colin Burke on his back, under her kitchen sink. The furniture maker was also Nugget's resident handyman.

"Hey," he said, tightening something with a wrench. "Harlee mentioned that your garbage disposal wasn't working."

"Not for a long time," she said. "I kept meaning to call you, but money's been tight."

"Yeah, well this one's on the house. I fixed your tub, too. That leak must've cost you a fortune in water bills."

"Thank you, Colin. I'll pay you as soon as I can."

"No worries." He got up and collected his tools. "The Nugget *Tribune* is making my wife a fortune."

Tawny laughed. Harlee had recently taken over the struggling newspaper and had turned it around by going digital only. Although Tawny doubted that the website was making anything near a fortune. "I really appreciate it."

Katie came in. "Hi, Mommy."

"How you feeling, baby?" Out of habit, Tawny felt her head. Cool to the touch, thank God. "Could you put this ice cream in the freezer for me?"

Colin grabbed up his tool chest and headed for the door. "Next time you need a home repair, call me. Financially, things are good for Harlee and me. I like to pay it forward when I can."

Her throat clogged, so she just nodded. After Colin left, Tawny paid the babysitter and made alphabet soup for Katie. They ate together at the small table in the kitchen nook. The same place Tawny used to study for the GED to get her high school credential. Someday she'd like to go to college. But with Katie and trying to keep her business on track, school would have to wait.

After dinner Tawny got the scrap of paper with Lucky's lawyer's contact information out of her purse. She knew the 415 area code was San Francisco. It was too late to call now. First thing in the morning, she told herself. She didn't know the law regarding transplants and biological fathers, but she would move heaven and earth to get Lucky tested to see if he was a match. Then she would take it from there.

If worse came to worst she would appeal to Cecilia. The woman would likely be angry that Tawny had kept her granddaughter from her all these years. Still, she'd make Lucky do the right thing. Everyone in Nugget knew that Lucky doted on his mother and that Cecilia Rodriguez had raised him on her own. Just like Tawny had done with Katie.

She hoped it wouldn't come to that. The last thing Tawny wanted to do was make trouble and put her daughter in the middle of it. Tawny just wanted Katie's health back and to live her life in the same quiet obscurity she had for the last twenty-eight years.

Lucky didn't know what to believe. Thelma Wade's transplant story was so farfetched that it might actually be true. But a daughter . . . ? They'd only been together one time. It was the night after everything had gone sideways with Raylene at the Rock and River Ranch. Lucky had spent much of the evening getting drunk at the crappy little park near Thelma's house and wound up having sex with her behind the swing set in the wee hours of the morning. Afterward, he blew out of town, hoping that with him gone, the dust would settle between his mom and the Rossers. She needed her job. Badly.

The thing about Thelma is she never would've struck him as a gold-digging con artist. As a girl, she'd barely said boo to anyone in middle school. In fact, by the time high school rolled around, Thelma had disappeared. There was some rumor that she'd dropped out because of family problems.

The truth was no one noticed her even when she was in school, so no one had missed her when she was gone. That night in the park had been a mistake and he'd forgotten the whole incident until today. Until she'd shown up on his property.

Tawny? What the hell kind of name was that anyway? It sounded like something a stripper would call herself. She had said something about changing it for business. Maybe little Thelma Wade was an exotic dancer now. And a bloodsucking hustler.

As he pulled up in front of his mother's house, a Nugget police SUV backed out of her driveway and turned around in the cul-de-sac. He didn't bother to lock his truck, just jumped out and dashed for the back door.

Lucky burst inside to find his mother washing dishes in her stainless steel farm sink. "What's wrong?"

"Nothing, *mijo*. Why should anything be wrong?"

"I just saw a cop leave your house."

"That was Detective Stryker on his dinner break."

"He comes over here for dinner?"

"Sometimes." She looked at him. "Do you have a problem with that?"

"No." *Maybe.* Lucky wasn't sure how he felt about it.

His whole life Cecilia had been single. Except for his father, who'd taken off as soon as Lucky was born, he couldn't recall his mother ever dating. Weird, because at forty-eight she was still a beautiful woman. What was odder, though, was the fact that Jake Stryker was having dinner with his mother and it hadn't gotten back to Lucky. In Nugget, people's love lives, or lack thereof, may as well have been stripped across a billboard. People here liked to gossip. That's why he wanted to come clean about him and Raylene, since their relationship would leak out anyway. And the conjecture of why he'd left all those years ago would start all over again. Nothing he could do about that.

"Are you hungry?" Cecilia asked.

"I could eat." He smelled pot roast.

Sure enough, she ladled him a large portion of beef and potatoes from the pot on her stove. As long as Lucky could remember there had always been something good simmering in that pot.

"What are you doing?" Lucky watched her chop vegetables.

"Making you a salad to go with it. You need greens." She put a bowl in front of him with a bottle of dressing.

"Thanks, Ma. So, Jake Stryker, huh?" He was still digesting that piece of news.

"We're friends. Don't make more of it than it is. How's progress on the cowboy camp?"

Lucky let out a long sigh. "Slow, if you want to know the truth. I wanted to be up and running by June and here it is September. And now some writer from *Sports Illustrated* is coming up to interview me. It seems like every time I turn around there's a new distraction to keep me from my goal." Like today's craziness. "And in December I'll have to leave for Vegas."

"*Ay Dios mio*, you're getting too old to be banged around like that." He knew she was talking about the concussion he'd gotten in Billings. Between the concussion and the cracked ribs, he'd been slow to recover.

"It'll probably be my last world championship for the PBR. I'd like to go out a winner."

"You are a winner." She kissed him on the cheek. "You don't need another one of those buckles to prove anything."

"No, but another one would go a long way toward putting my cowboy camp on the map. Not to mention that the money would help pay the bills."

Cecilia's brows creased. "Are you having money troubles, *mijo*?"

He laughed. "Nope. Not even close, but you can never have too much green."

"I think you feel that way because you grew up poor. But if you ever need money, Lucky, I would sell the house."

Lucky did a visual lap of the grand kitchen. He'd bought her the rancher because her whole life she'd worked hard, taking other people's shit, to care for him. Now it was his turn to be taken care of. "Don't be crazy, Ma. I have enough for a lifetime." He pulled her in for a hug. "The pot roast is good."

"I'm glad you like it." She sat next to him at the big center island.

"Did you know that Thelma Wade changed her name to Tawny?" Lucky tried to sound casual.

"Of course. She did it when she opened her boot business."

"Boot business?"

"You don't know? She makes beautiful custom cowboy boots. A lot of celebrities wear them, even rodeo stars. I would've thought you knew."

Well that explained Tawny's fancy boots, the ones Lucky had so admired. But it didn't explain why she was driving a piece-of-crap Jeep from the 1990s. "I ran into her today and got the impression she wasn't doing too well." God, he hated lying to his mother.

"Her little girl is very sick. Leukemia."

Shit!

"She has a kid, huh? I hadn't heard she was married."

"She's not. I don't believe Katie's father is in the picture."

"You know the guy?"

"No. That's always been a bit of a mystery, but no one's business but Tawny's."

"You've met the little girl, though?" Lucky asked.

"Maybe once or twice. They spend a lot of time in the Bay Area for Katie's treatments. I didn't know you and Tawny were back in touch. Oh how she had a crush on you when you two were younger. Used to follow you around like a lamb. Such a nice girl and you barely gave her the time of day," Cecilia chided. Lucky knew the subtext, though. *You were too busy getting into trouble with Raylene Rosser.*

"We just happened to run in to each other. I barely recognized her, though." he said as calmly as he could, but was starting to panic. What if the kid really was his? "I've gotta get going, Ma."

"You just got here," Cecilia said, and took his empty plate to the sink.

"I know, but I thought I'd stop by McCreedy Ranch before it gets dark and check out some stock Clay wants to unload." Okay, he'd say a few Hail Marys.

"All right, *mijo*. Will I see you tomorrow?"

"Yeah," he said. "I'll be over."

On his way out he tried to remember where Tawny lived. It had been ten years, yet he found her tiny bungalow with little effort. He still knew the town like he did the back of a bull.

He parked across the street and sat behind the wheel, feeling edgy about going in. About seeing the little girl who might or might not be his. Nine goddamn years. Finally, he climbed Tawny's porch stairs and rang the bell. He could hear movement inside and a few seconds later a young girl opened the door.

"Hello." She looked up at him with big brown eyes. Eyes too large for her pale, gaunt face.

Lucky studied her. "You must be Katie."

"Mm-hmm. Who are you?"

"A friend of your mom's. She home?"

"Yes. Would you like to come in?"

Tawny needed to talk to the kid about inviting strangers into their home. "Sure."

He crossed the threshold and gazed around the front room. There was an unfinished puzzle on the coffee table and the TV was on. The furniture, a set of mismatched chairs and a couch, looked pretty lived in. Tawny came out of one of the side doors in sweats with her head wrapped in a towel.

"Hey." He bobbed his chin at her.

She quickly turned to Katie. "Go brush your teeth and get ready for bed, baby."

Clearly curious about him, the girl seemed reluctant to go. Tawny gave her a look—the kind Cecilia used to give Lucky when she meant business—and the kid scampered off.

"What are you doing here?"

"I can't tell if she looks like me."

"Shush." Tawny grabbed his arm and pulled him out of the house. "I don't want her to hear you."

"Why?"

She glared at him like he was a fool. "Why do you think?"

"Beats the hell out me. Unless you're lying."

She gave him another venomous glare. "Did you just come over here to tell me what a liar I am?"

Lucky blew out a breath. "I came over because I wanted to see Katie for myself. How long has she been sick?"

"She was diagnosed when she was five."

"It's bad, isn't it?" The girl looked so ashen that it broke his heart. No little kid should have to go through that.

Tawny nodded, and Lucky could tell that she was trying to keep it together. Even if it turned out that the woman was the world's biggest liar, Tawny was looking out for her daughter, like any good mother would do. His heart broke a little for her too.

"Why didn't you try to get a hold of me when she was diagnosed?" Lucky asked.

"I figured you weren't interested in returning my phone calls when I was pregnant, why would you suddenly call me back five years later?"

"Tawny, I never got your messages. If I'd known that I got you in trouble, I would've done the right thing."

"You didn't get me in trouble. You got me pregnant. And until now, I didn't need you."

"Did it ever occur to you that I deserved to know that I had a child, whether you needed me or not? Did it ever occur to you that Katie deserved her father? What have you told her?"

"Look, I don't have time to do this now. Katie's waiting for me."

He stabbed his finger at her. "You better make time to do this. You dropped a goddamn bomb on me today."

"Does that mean you're willing to help?"

He paced the porch. "That's the thing, Tawny, I would've helped whether she was my daughter or not. Because that's what people do.

But out of the blue you tell me I have a kid after all these years . . . that's she's sick and needs this cell transplant . . . It's . . . I'm just reeling a little here."

She swallowed hard. "I know. It's a lot to take in. But I don't want to do this with Katie here."

"Then I suggest you show up at my place tomorrow and explain. Merely leaving a couple of lousy messages for a guy who's supposedly the father of your child doesn't cut it, Tawny. You should've done more."

"I had my reasons," she said.

"Well I'd sure as hell like to hear them. Tomorrow."

She gave him a faint nod and slipped back inside.

Printed in the United States
by Baker & Taylor Publisher Services